HOW TO WAKE AN UNDEAD CITY

HAILEY EDWARDS

Edited by Sasha Knight
Proofread by Lillie's Literary Services
Cover by Gene Mollica
Tree of Life medallion drawn by Leah Farrow

HOW TO WAKE AN UNDEAD CITY

The Beginner's Guide to Necromancy, Book 6

Savannah has fallen to the vampires, and it's up to Grier to take out their leader, Gaspard Lacroix, and restore peace. Lacroix might be more powerful and immune to her magic, but she's got a plan. Too bad it's got holes big enough for a new threat to waltz through while the city is on her knees.

Now Grier must risk her very soul if she hopes to slay her enemies and prevent her world from going up in flames. But salvation comes at a steep price, and she's not the only one who will pay. The cost just might break her, and the man who owns her heart.

PROLOGUE

Dearest M,

I'm pregnant! I wrote you the second I received the news. I know how you feel about children. You don't have to fake excitement on my account. I'm thrilled enough for us both. G is beside himself. This child is a miracle, in so many ways. I hope to see you soon.

All my love,

E

Darling E,

Babies are messy, loud, and far too much work. Plus, they smell. Strongly. But you've always suffered from an excess of maternal instincts. I'm not surprised you find yourself with child. Goddess knows you've tried hard enough. Every time I visit, I wait on G to find his pants or for you to pull on a fresh outfit. The true miracle here is that you're not on your fourth or fifth offspring.

I'm the guest of honor at this year's symposium yet again. Honestly, they ought to rename the award after me and be done with it. They act like I'm the only scientific mind worth honoring when genius abounds. You'll visit once it's behind me.

Yours always,

M

Dear M,

G fought with his father again last night. I'm no better. I had another spat with one of the drones Mother has sent to try to lure me back home. What kind of family are we bringing this child into? What kind of parents can we ever hope to be if we can't reconcile with our own?

I'm unsurprised the Society wishes to honor your genius. Yet again. You're brilliant, my friend. Your mind is a wonder. I'm not shocked you can't see it, but we all do. Bask in your accolades. You've earned every kind word and every awed expression.

Best,

E

Dear E,

Your mother is a vapid twat. I'm sorry, but facts remain facts. The Society brings out the best and worst in us all. She embodies the ugliness of spirit that excessive wealth, mediocre talent, and a lifetime of privilege so often produces. Ignore her. Failing that, I will ignore her for you. Or pay someone to do it for us. Honestly, who has the time to nurture a decent grudge these days?

As for G, I don't know his people. You've kept me blissfully in the dark. But if you love him, which you obviously do, and if he loves you, which any fool would, then you two have as solid a foundation to build a family upon as anyone.

I do worry, given G's nature and your mother's sudden interest, just how special this child of yours might be.

Always,

M

M,

The mood on the estate has changed since I started to show, and I don't think we'll be staying much longer. G says I fret too much, but his heart is cast in solid gold. He always sees the best in people. He's willing to take a hit in order to give those he believes in a second or third chance to find the mark. But I'm not.

Perhaps my heart isn't as big, but I tend to believe the face people show me. Maybe my hormones are making me crazy, but I can't settle. It's more than wanting our own place, which I do. Or nesting, which I am. I'm not thrilled at the prospect of house-hunting while I'm waddling, but I fear we're no longer safe in his father's home, and I don't want to overstay our welcome.

I'm worried, M. For my daughter—did I tell you it's a girl?—and for my husband.

Tell me good news. Brighten my day however you can.

E

E,

I have more empty rooms than your mother has mirrors in her boudoir. You'll both stay with me until you find a suitable home. Pack your things, then make your excuses. I arrive in two days, and I won't take no for an answer. G should learn to accept that about me if he's going to remain a fixture in our lives.

M

How can I ever repay you, M? You're the best friend anyone has ever had. That's why you'll accept when I ask you to be my daughter's goddessmother. You're the only one, aside from G, I can trust with her best interests. I don't expect you to be happy about it, but I do expect you to say yes. For me.

Fine, fine. For you, I will accept. Though you're right. I'm not happy about taking on the obligation. I have no use for a daughter, goddess-given or otherwise, but then I had no use for a best friend until you claimed me as yours.

Your rooms are ready, and so am I. See you tomorrow.

ONE

The aged paper crinkled, but I forced my fingers to still before the last message crumpled in my fist. I set aside the stack of notes two best friends had exchanged when I was just a bulge on my mother's waistline and let the ache of revisiting their friendship wash over me in waves that lodged a knot in my throat and left Woolworth House in a tizzy over the spike in my emotions.

"Here." Linus patted the nearest wall, comforting the old girl, then crossed the bedroom that used to be his before my things started migrating down the hall. "Drink this."

"I didn't know Linus's Shake Shack delivered," I teased. "Do I tip the delivery boy or...?"

Leaning down, he brushed his lips over mine. "That will suffice."

How he always started his day looking so refreshed when I was the one who slept for eight hours never ceased to amaze me. The dark wash jeans molding to his butt I suspected had been tailor-made for him. The fitted navy button-down highlighted his lean musculature and brought out the blue in his eyes. The cuffs, as usual, were rolled up, exposing his corded forearms. But there was nary a loafer in sight. He wore sneakers that matched the exact shade of denim in his pants, a feat I would have claimed impossible.

He had gathered his dark-auburn hair at his nape with an elastic, and my fingers itched to set it free, to comb through the silky length. Those same fingers twitched with ardent longing to trace the smattering of freckles sprinkled across the bridge of his nose and cheeks, particularly the daisy beneath his left eye.

Fingers.

You just can't trust them.

Not around Linus anyway.

"Thanks." I sipped the breakfast smoothie, but not even the rich flavor of my favorite berries spiked with a shot of Vitamin L could soothe away this persistent hurt. "Maud knew." That was the lump I couldn't swallow, the most recent lie stuck in my craw. "All that time, she knew George Lacroix was my father, and she didn't tell me."

"Maud says in the letter she didn't know his people." He raised his hands to ward off my temper. "That could mean she didn't know his family name, or his clan name. She never called him George outright, but she must have known that much since your mother visited her." His arms fell to his sides. "It's hard to say without more letters, and this was the last one from that period. There's no other mention of a George or a G in any of their later correspondence."

"Their next exchange is from years later, long after I was born." I patted the mattress, and he sank beside me into a ray of sunlight. Unable to resist the rare treat of touching his sun-warmed hair, I toyed with the gilded tassel at his nape. "He would have been dead by then. That must be why his name doesn't come up again."

"I wish I had brought you answers instead of more questions, but I thought you would want to read them."

"How did they get back here?" I leaned my head on his shoulder, breathed in the familiar scents of fresh-cut mint rubbed between a thumb and finger and the tang of old pennies, and relaxed against him. "Maud made good on her threat. She picked up my parents and brought them here. Mom must have had her half of the letters on her. Maybe she forgot them when she left? Then Maud found them, filed them away with hers?"

How many times had Maud relived these old conversations? How often had she wondered if she might have altered her best friend's fate—*my* fate—by acting sooner or not at all?

Regret. Grief. Sorrow.

Holding on to these faded letters spoke of soul-searching that failed to reveal any new answers for Maud, or for me.

"Hey." Amelie bounded into the room. "Oh. Sorry." She hooked a thumb over her shoulder. "The door was open…"

The invitation into his space, into his arms, was pure Linus, and I wouldn't change how the gesture filled my heart from corner to corner with simple welcome, even if it meant others got drawn in too.

"We're just skimming old letters." I gestured toward the yellowed pile. "What's up?"

The clock read four o'clock, as in p.m., early—or late, depending on your perspective—for necromancers to be awake.

"Your escorts have arrived." She chewed on her ragged bottom lip. "Boaz is downstairs."

Ah. That explained it. She must have stayed up late or woke early to visit with her brother.

"Great," I said, proud when I didn't wince upon hearing his name.

Two days ago, Gaspard Lacroix, my paternal grandfather, marched on my city. That is to say, Savannah.

Gah.

Falling for the Potentate of Atlanta had turned me downright territorial.

Savannah was my home, my refuge, but she wasn't just mine. She belonged to all of us. And we wanted her back.

"There's not much time," Amelie prompted. "They're cutting it close. Two hours until dark."

Vampires emerged after the moon rose and began hunting the

streets for dinner. There were too few Elite as it was, and not many more sentinels. The reinforcements Linus had requested were slow to arrive, a steady trickle unable to staunch the wounds of a city under siege.

After sunset, every man and woman in uniform pounded the pavement to keep the casualties to a minimum. But the vampires had started targeting humans in other ways. Cutting power supplies, poisoning water sources, siphoning gasoline.

They were, quite literally, draining the city dry in every sense of the word.

If we lost the light, we lost our armed transportation until tomorrow, and Savannah couldn't afford many more lawless nights.

Already the Society's official cover story had been debunked. Humans might be willing to buy that a hurricane necessitated an emergency evacuation. After all, this was coastal Georgia. But while tornadoes popped out of thin air, hurricanes...not so much.

Only the barricade manned by sentinels was keeping the curious and the furious from their homes. Too bad that didn't help with the humans trapped in Savannah, who had been unable to evacuate thanks to poor health, lack of funds, or sheer stubbornness.

Daytime was safe enough, for the most part. Nights were getting bitter, and bloody.

Traditional means had gotten the Elite no closer to rousting Lacroix from city hall. He was simply too well fortified to be forced out like an annoying splinter wedged in the Society's heel. And, thanks to his ability to compel vampires to join his cause, the numbers were on his side.

The Lyceum itself remained secure, due to the Grande Dame's forethought prior to its evacuation, but that also meant we were cut off from using the tunnels running beneath the Lyceum to infiltrate the building from underneath.

All this meant it was time to pursue nontraditional means.

We needed more allies who were naturally immune to Lacroix's influence. In a word, we needed gwyllgi. Lucky us, we knew just where to find the largest pack in the southeast. Between Linus and me, we *would* convince their alpha to play ball, no matter how slim Lethe judged the odds of her mom joining our team.

And the odds got longer from there.

Our petition for an audience with Alpha Tisdale Kinase had been granted, under the condition we groveled in person, and that meant a return to the dreaded Atlanta. That was bad enough, but while Linus and I were asking to borrow sugar from our neighbors, I got the dubious honor of holding out my beggar's cup to my grandmother, Dame Severine Marchand, in the hopes she would fill it with an education on the goddess-touched condition. The CliffsNotes version anyway.

For Lacroix, an ancient, to wear a pendant for protection against my kind, I must be capable of bringing him down.

If Plan A failed, I was a solid Plan B.

"We're packed and ready." I pushed out a long breath then let Linus pull me to my feet. I turned to Amelie, whose eyes shone with a determined light, and let the worry come. "Are you sure you guys will be okay here alone?"

Woolly was packed to the gills with guests, and she was thrilled about it, but I still worried for them.

Neely had refused to budge, and that meant Cruz wasn't going anywhere either. Busy having the time of her life, Marit was doing her best to convince one of the gwyllgi with a passing resemblance to Hood that she was mate material. Amelie had no choice but to stay. Neither did Oscar, or Woolly. For the last two reasons, I was grateful I would be leaving my home in the capable hands of friends who were more family to me than my own blood.

"We've got shelf-stable food and candles if the generator goes." Amelie flashed a silver lighter on her palm to show they had that covered too. "We've got enough clean water to keep our throats wet *and* the toilets flushing thanks to the creek out back."

"The gwyllgi pack will be hard on your resources." But they were a goddess-send when it came to protecting what I was leaving behind, however short the trip. "Remind them to hunt before they hit the fridge. There's plenty of wildlife to keep their bellies full."

More than a dozen gwyllgi originally from the Atlanta pack, the same hotheads who'd come to Savannah demanding Lethe's head on a platter after I killed Ernst Weber and she killed his sister Tess, had sworn themselves into her service.

Predators in those numbers would put a strain on the local wildlife, but that only motivated me more.

"Does that go for Lethe too?" A hesitant smile accompanied the question. "Or does she get special privileges?"

The former bestie checking on the current bestie left me twitchy with awkwardness.

"Ah, no. I would never get between Lethe and food unless you're tired of having hands, arms..." I shrugged, "...a head."

"We'll secure resources once we're out of the city," Linus cut in, nudging me along. "We'll have them delivered to the barricade so the Elite can transport them to Woolly. She will act as a distribution hub for the Society. The Elite will hand-deliver food, clean water, and medical supplies to anyone in the city."

Using our linked hands, I tugged him into me and brushed a tender kiss across his lips.

Heat flushed his cheeks, sparkling in his eyes. "What was that for?"

"For being you." I kissed him again, slower. "For caring."

This was my mess, my family's mess, and I couldn't thank him enough for helping me clean up after them.

"As much as I love watching you guys make out," Amelie said, averting her gaze, "I hear your window of opportunity slamming shut."

With a quick nod, I whipped a modified pen out of my pocket and popped in a fresh cartridge that smelled of copper and herbs.

Before Linus could protest, I drew what we had nicknamed the impervious sigil on the side of his throat, right below his collar, in a tempting hollow I had learned turned his knees to jelly when I nipped him just hard enough to make him gasp.

I told myself it was his delicious reaction, not the thin pink scar, that caused me to fixate on that spot. The smell of his skin caused water to pool in my mouth, but the mark was a brutal reminder that I had almost lost him. That Odette, who I had loved as family, almost took him from me.

Angling away from him while I composed myself, I slid on a backpack stuffed with necromantic paraphernalia before he read the undercurrents of my upset and delayed us longer to soothe me.

Eager to start referring to this trip in the past tense, I was raring to go...and get back home.

Leaving Savannah and my friends vulnerable went against every protective instinct I possessed.

After a final check of its contents, he slung a messenger bag across his shoulders. We were traveling light on the first leg of our journey. All clothes and supplies would be purchased outside Savannah, a cringeworthy expense that left my palm too damp to hold the debit card I would soon be swiping.

Though the truce with Amelie might still be fragile, I couldn't stop myself from crossing to her and gathering her in a tight hug. "Be safe."

"You too." She squeezed me hard, tears in her voice. "I'll protect Woolly until you get back." Drawing away, she wiped her cheeks dry with the backs of her hands. "I won't let those fangy bastards touch one shingle on her roof. I promise."

Around us, the old house groaned, softening toward Amelie despite her best attempts at keeping her at arm's—floorboard's? —length.

That made two of us.

While the old girl was paying attention, I stepped into the corner and pitched my voice low. "Tell Oscar we'll be home soon." I patted the wall in front of me. "Make sure he doesn't get into any trouble."

Ghost boys and full sunlight don't mix. He and I had already exchanged our goodbyes, but even if he was more than three times my age, he was still a six-year-old boy at heart, and this trip preyed on his abandonment issues.

As he had pointed out multiple times, I could have brought him along in the dented brass button Linus had anchored his spirit to, but he would be safer here with Woolly than with me.

The old house rustled my pant leg with a warm gust from the floor registers, a promise she would do her best to direct Oscar's energy toward positive outlets.

"Don't do anything I wouldn't do," I told Eileen, who slept on her podium beneath a blanket treated to protect her from UV rays.

I hit the stairs behind Amelie and Linus, and we entered a living room that forced me to squint against the sun pouring through the open curtains.

Craning my neck, I spotted the Torreses in the kitchen preparing an early dinner that made my stomach rumble. Music poured from Neely's phone as he enacted his favorite moves from some celebrity dance show while Cruz looked on, amused. Several hours into their day, they had moved past the coffee I so desperately craved and onto sweet iced tea.

Having humans in the house was so weird. They were so *perky* before dark. It was unnatural. Even Keet dozed in his cage, uncovered since he had started attacking the sheet I used to cover him during the day the way a dog might shred its bedding. At least, from the growls, that's what I assumed was going on.

I really needed to chat with Lethe about how to behave around impressionable parakeets.

With a coquettish flutter of his lashes, Neely convinced his husband to give him a turn around the room. I didn't interrupt their moment to tell them goodbye. I left them attempting a tango that promised to send them both crashing to the floor if they didn't get their legs untangled. But then again, maybe that was the point.

Since Woolly still enforced her Boaz ban with relish, we had to meet him and his team on the front lawn.

The sun was so...*sunny*.

Ugh.

Already my skin felt hot, itchy with the promise of a burn, and I was nowhere near as pale as Linus.

Amelie stayed on the porch, honoring the spirit, if not the letter, of her house arrest, and waved to her brother from there. The casual goodbye told me they had already done their catching up before she fetched us.

"We need to get moving." Boaz kept his tone distant, his manner professional, and I was glad for it. "I borrowed six men to get you two out, but we need them elsewhere at dusk."

Unsure of my reception, given our last encounter, I stepped lightly. "Trouble downtown?"

"The looters are at it again," he said briskly. "Chaos breeds opportunity."

The conversation died a quick death after that, and I kicked dirt over its grave.

"Take one step, Grier Woolworth, and I'll rip out your throat. You know I will." Lethe strode from the tree line with her freshly trimmed and dyed-blue hair swinging, sharp green eyes narrowed, and a cheeseburger in each hand. "As soon as I finish this." She popped the remainder of one in her mouth and gulped without chewing before pocketing the second. "You were going to leave without saying goodbye? Are you serious? Do your donut promises mean nothing?"

"Do you remember the conversation we had about me telling my nocturnal friends goodbye last night?"

"Hello?" Palms up, she spun a tight circle. "The sun is up there, and I'm down here."

"You're not half as smart as I thought you were if you believed for one hot minute you were getting past her," Hood said conversationally as he trailed his mate with a sandwich bag full of her favorite cereal in hand that he shook to get her attention.

Eyes the tawny brown of crushed pecan shells looked on her with adoration. Hood dwarfed his mate, but Lethe's attitude put them at the same height. The sandy-blond dreads that once reached the small of his back now brushed his shoulders. She must have given him a trim while they were playing salon in the hall bathroom.

"I'll bring you a dozen maple bacon donuts, the cake ones, if you can forgive my oversight." I crossed to her, and our hug pressed her baby bump, which was getting larger every day, against my abdomen. "I'll make it a double if you spare me one."

"Hmph." Her breath smelled like pickles when she huffed in my face, but a calculating glint sparkled in her eyes. "I suppose I could forgive you if you also bring me one dozen cherry cordial cream filled donuts. From Clancy's." Her nose shot up in the air. "I will accept no substitutions."

Thirty-six donuts. In exchange for one. Yep. That was Lethe math for you.

"Remember." Hood clamped a big hand on my shoulder. "Don't let Tisdale intimidate you. She can smell fear. Don't make eye contact. She'll view it as a challenge. Don't lie to her. She'll rip out your tongue and beat you to death with it if you try."

Gulp.

"You'll be fine." Lethe pried Hood off me so he could deal her snacks. "Mom's not that bad."

Hood just stared at her.

"She hasn't killed *that* many..." Abandoning that line, she chose another. "Midas will have your back."

"I don't need a babysitter."

"Um, yeah," she mumbled around a mouthful of cereal Hood provided. "You do."

"You didn't really think we'd let you go alone," Hood asked, chuckling at my budding scowl.

"This isn't pack business," I said gently. "You don't have to draft Midas to shadow me."

"You're pack," she said sweetly. "That makes it our business."

Lethe held out her hand, and Hood dumped more cereal in her palm.

"She's a slow learner." He clicked his tongue. "That's what we get for adopting a necromancer."

"True." She crunched thoughtfully. "She is cute, though. And she pays in meat. I'd say we still came out ahead on the deal."

"We need to move this along." Boaz raised his voice over our conversation. "We're losing the light."

"Take care of you." I stole a marshmallow off Lethe's palm. "And baby." I crunched loudly while she snarled. "And Hood."

"The first rule of survival in any pack is you don't steal food from a pregnant gwyllgi," Hood chided me then topped her off. "She's not herself when she's hungry. She would feel terrible for ripping out your throat to reclaim what you stole. Eventually."

"Boaz is right." Linus rested his hand at the small of my back. "You two will have to continue this via text message."

Lethe fished out the exact shape and color marshmallow I had stolen then threw it hard enough to leave a dent where it bounced off my forehead. "Bye."

Lip curled, I did my best Lethe impersonation. "*Grr.*"

"Pups are so cute at this age." Hood reached over to ruffle my hair. "Keep working on the growl. You'll be scaring birds out of trees before you know it."

Annoyed, I snapped my teeth at him, but it only made him smile wider.

Applying gentle pressure, Linus guided me away from the Kinases before we started a food fight on the lawn that would end with Lethe trawling the grass for snacks later.

Boaz grunted what might have passed for thanks, then set out without another word.

Happy to pretend he and I shared no history, that this was strictly business, I followed him to a nondescript black SUV. If I studied his smooth gait, his easy strides, for longer than was polite, Linus didn't notice. He was too busy conducting his own visual examination.

Questions must be itching his brain over how Boaz had regenerated his leg from the knee down. The healing sigils I scribbled over him hadn't been recorded. There had been no time. For now, they were lost. Along with any answers about what I had done to Lethe and her unborn child.

"Step up," Linus said, drawing my attention to the open vehicle door. "Grier?"

"I'm good." Shaking off thoughts of Boaz, I took Linus's hand and let him help me onto the bench seat.

An SUV wasn't so different from a van. I could do this. Just a short trip to the barricade. Easy-peasy.

Slowly, drawing in breath through my nose and blowing it past my lips, I settled into the small space.

For once, I saw the use in window tinting as the dark interior cut out the harsh daylight. As my vision adjusted, I noticed the four Elite crammed onto a bench seat behind us. Ahead, a woman rode shotgun.

"Good to see you, Grier." She pinned on a hesitant smile. "Linus."

"Becky?"

"Don't tell me the facial prosthetics, ballcap, wig, and contacts have you fooled."

"The last time I saw you, you were marching with Lacroix." Her undercover work with the Elite had saved many lives, mine included, and she would accomplish more good before this was over. "I expected you to be tucked in city hall with him."

"I'm safe in my foxhole as far as he's concerned, waiting on sunset. He asked me to stay on the outside, to keep an eye on things. For once, I was happy to oblige. I pick up my orders from the Elite daily, and nightly I run interference with the vampires." She adjusted her cap. "That's why I'm not looking myself these days. We can't be too careful."

Frowning, I wondered, "When do you sleep?"

"I can get by on an hour here or there." She rolled up her sleeve to reveal a sigil tattooed on her forearm. "This keeps me alert. I'm sure there's a technical name, but we call them insomnia tattoos."

Wistfulness had me sighing after the design. The next twenty-four hours promised to be brutal.

"One of yours?" I asked Linus, who studied her arm with a tight mouth.

"The design is unfamiliar." His pinched expression made me chuckle. "It must belong to a competitor."

Unable to resist teasing him, I leaned in. "You have competitors?"

"Fiducial tattoos require, as the name suggests, a certain amount of trust. They're too individualized to be mass-produced, so their margin for profit is slim." He picked imaginary lint off his pants. "Everyone has an upper limit for stimuli, one you can't exceed without their body shutting down to preserve itself. With fiducial tattoos, you must learn your clients, their needs, and tailor the design to suit them. The time requirements alone made dismissing that area of study an easy decision."

"I had no choice." Becky shrugged, her spine rigid beneath his censure. "We do what the job requires."

"Wearing that, you'll drop dead on your feet. Without warning." Pulling back, Linus compressed his lips. "Depending on that design is more dangerous than any field assignment." Eyes hard on the spot where the inferior work had been done, he frowned. "I'll think on a solution, in thanks for what you did for Grier. But warn your colleagues, and don't bet your life on that ink's ability to keep you lucid."

"Thanks," she grumbled with reluctant appreciation. "I'll get the word out."

The illusion of a leisurely Sunday drive evaporated when we hit the main drag and all the shattered store windows came into view. Groceries had been dumped in the streets to rot, clean water in bottles and jugs dumped and tossed aside, electronics looted, and furniture destroyed in the whirlwind of depravity that swirled around the vampires each night.

As we passed Madison Square, I noticed the Sergeant William Jasper monument had been knocked off its base to make room for the vampire I had turned to stone while visiting Lacroix's former manor. As far as statements go, I wasn't sure what this one said unless they meant to paint their fallen as heroes.

"This has to stop," I murmured, exchanging a look with Linus. "We have to stop this."

"We will." Eyes gone black and depthless, it was the potentate who stared back at me when Linus closed his fingers over mine, black mist dancing across his knuckles. "We have a plan, and it will work."

Hearing his certainty bolstered my confidence, but I couldn't dismiss the dread brewing in my gut. Tisdale Kinase wouldn't be my harshest critic. No, that honor would go to Dame Marchand and her granddaughter, Eloise.

Eloise would never forgive me for the role I played in her twin sister's death, but Heloise had intended to present me to her grandmother on a silver platter. Taz was the only reason Heloise hadn't dished me up, but fear of Marchand retribution had forced her underground to escape the repercussions.

The sensation of being watched dragged my attention to the rearview mirror, where Boaz stared at me.

Quirking an eyebrow, I waited on him to tell me what was on his mind, but he switched his attention to the road while muscle bunched in his jaw as he chewed over whatever he had no intention of sharing.

"What's your ETA on supplies?" Becky shifted to her left, angling toward us. "How soon should we have transpo in place?"

"Expect the first convoy to arrive within six hours," Linus answered when I deferred to him. "Our first priority will be supplying the city in our absence. Our people must come first."

"Our?" Boaz tightened his hands on the wheel. "This isn't Atlanta." He ground his teeth. "This isn't your city."

"You're right." I tapped his shoulder until he flicked his gaze up to the rearview mirror. "It's ours, all of ours, and we'll do whatever it takes to keep Savannah safe. That includes accepting aid from a visiting potentate, who was born and raised here, to keep her on her feet until we can knock Lacroix off his."

"Think of Adelaide," Becky said with the rhythm of an oft-repeated phrase. "What would she say?"

"That I'm being an ass." He sighed through his parted lips. "But she always thinks I'm being an ass."

To keep from agreeing with his absent fiancée, I pasted my polite-interest face on. I had honed it to wear during particularly odious speeches given in Maud's honor, usually at award dinners, which made Linus chuckle as if he remembered the exact expression and its purpose from all those years ago.

"Goddess, is that Detective Russo?" I pressed my nose against the glass. "The Elite might want to shadow her. She believes there's something hinky about how Maud died. The city closing for a hurricane that wasn't is going to ping on her hinkdar. She's like a dog with a bone. She won't let go once she sinks her teeth in."

"We've been wiping the short-term memories of the human first responders and escorting them past the barricade," Becky informed us. "She must have slipped through the checkpoints." Pulling out her phone, she punched in a number. "I'll get her picked up before she ghosts again."

A rolling boom sounded in the distance, and I pressed my hand to the glass. "What was that?"

The noise reminded me of cannon fire during the reenactments held at Old Fort Jackson.

A second boom hit closer, and a plume of asphalt erupted on our right.

"Those bastards planted another minefield." Boaz gritted his teeth. "How did the sweepers miss this?"

"They didn't." Becky scowled out her window. "I checked this route at noon, and it was clear."

"Call it in." Boaz slammed his palms against the wheel. "They've got humans doing their dirty work. That means no routes are safe without inspection prior to use."

"You want to help the city?" One of the guys from the back leaned forward, swinging his head between Linus and me. "Drop some of your inheritance in these potholes, yeah? These bastards don't even have to dig. They just drop in a homemade boomer and kick pebbles over the top."

"I'll take that under advisement," I said dryly, but it got me thinking.

I hadn't considered what I might do to improve the city. I never had a reason to involve myself in its maintenance. Until now, when my family, and our feud, was wreaking havoc. Unless I stepped in, checkbook in hand, the city might not recover for years after another few days under siege.

A third boom rocked the vehicle, and I found Linus's hand with mine as a fourth and fifth ignited beneath us. With a scream of wrenching metal and shattering glass, I was flung against the window where my head cracked on the trim before blackness engulfed me.

Except unconsciousness didn't claim me, Linus did. His midnight cloak wrapped me tight as he cushioned us while the SUV rolled, setting off other mines and igniting a twisted pinball game that blasted us from one side of the road to the other.

When the creaking frame rocked to a stop on its side, I couldn't tell where we ended up until Linus dissipated enough to let me see through the gaping maws of former windows to the pockmarked road behind us.

"Roll call," Boaz growled from the front seat, the driver side of the vehicle resting flat against the pavement.

"I'm alive," Becky wheezed, head limp on her shoulder from where she hung in her seat belt. "I think."

"Ricco."

"Brown."

"Martinez."

"Jung."

Boaz twisted in his seat for visual confirmation that Linus and I were both still breathing. "The gang's all here."

"We have to move." Linus unfastened my seat belt, and I dropped into his arms. "Whoever set those might be watching to see who tripped them."

Smiling my thanks, I shifted my focus out the windshield. "What are the odds the vampires' humans knew to reseed this area in particular?"

"This was random." Becky hissed out a curse as she freed herself. "This trip wasn't cleared through official channels, if you catch my drift. No one except for the six of us knew it was happening, and the four guys in the back didn't know until fifteen minutes before we tagged them."

The four guys in question grunted as they cut themselves free of their seat belts, but their mouths were set in grim lines, and their eyes glinted with barely restrained violence and the need to give back as good as we had gotten. Flowing like water, they climbed out of the wreckage and moved into position to flank the vehicle while scouting the area.

The SUV groaned and rocked as Becky accepted a hand out from Jung then fell into position.

"The vampires tend to hit the main drags and the most logical alternate routes. All this means is they're doubling down, a nightshift and a dayshift. Twice the fun for us." Boaz hauled himself out the window and sat perched on the SUV's side. "Wait by the vehicle until we come for you."

His boots hit the ground, and he ordered his men to fan out, sweep the area.

Linus boosted me through my smashed window, careful of the teethlike glass shards, and I swung my leg over the side. I dropped to the asphalt, and he hit a second later. Following Boaz's orders, we crouched together with our backs to the undercarriage. Laughter hitched in my chest when the quick examination I conducted on him left us with our gazes clashing after he finished his own visual sweep over me.

"You're all right," he said softly, a reassurance for himself.

"You saved me." I rested my hand against his cheek, his cool skin contrasting the hot sun overhead. "Again."

"Even damsels such as myself manage a rescue once in a long while." A tiny smile played on his mouth. "You'll balance the scales soon enough. You always do." He tapped the side of his throat where his spent sigil was smudged beyond recognition. "I could argue you already have."

Much to his amusement, I located my pen and drew a fresh impervious sigil on him in a less-distracting spot before we took turns rooting through our supplies to see what had survived the impact.

"*Clear.*"

The word echoed six more times, from six different directions, before they converged on us.

"Looks like we're walking the last half mile," Boaz informed us as he gazed across the pitted asphalt. "Step where I step." A thin sheen of sweat coated his skin, but I didn't think the heat was to blame. "Unless I'm blown to bits." His smile was full of bravado, but I saw through the strain to the memories churning behind his eyes. "Then you go around me."

Unable to let it go when the past had sunk its teeth in him, I grasped his arm. "Are you okay?"

"This is the job." He pushed out an exhale. "I can do this." He reached down, rubbed the top of his left thigh, right where his prosthetic used to fit. "You can always grow me another one, right?"

"Um, don't count on it." I let him go. "The first time was a fluke."

"Figures." He hesitated, then offered me a thinner smile, but a genuine one. "Thanks. For...everything." He dropped a brotherly kiss on top of my head. "I'm the same man with or without the leg, but you saved my life, Squirt."

Tension strung my spine tight as a bowstring at the unexpected endearment, once so familiar, but I shrugged off my discomfort. This —a return to normal—would be a blessing. For all of us.

When Boaz turned to rally his troops, I caught Linus staring at him, but it wasn't a territorial thing. Curiosity had rekindled in those dark blue eyes, and I elbowed him in the side before Boaz noticed and took offense to the bug-under-the-microscope routine.

Heat blossomed in Linus's cheeks at being caught, and I couldn't resist the urge to kiss the pinkest spot.

A throat cleared behind us, and I turned to find Becky wearing a goofy expression. "Ready?"

"Linus?" I held out my hand for his, and he laced our fingers. "Let's do this."

Eyes going tight, Boaz took point, and I fell in line behind him. Linus followed me, and a guy flanked each of us, on both sides, with Becky bringing up the rear.

We had almost reached the barricade when rapid gunfire peppered the air.

"Take cover," Boaz yelled as the Elite shuffled Linus and me to relative safety behind an overturned semi that had met the same fate as our SUV.

Eyes on Linus, I bit the inside of my cheek until I tasted blood, but I didn't ask him not to go.

Midnight swirled around him, engulfed him, and his cowl covered the bright auburn of his hair. But instead of nudging me into the darkest shadows or the deepest recesses, he held out his hand, inviting me to join him.

If I hadn't already been hopelessly in love with him, I would have fallen then.

"One second." I palmed the pocketknife I had no intentions of returning to him and opened a wound across my hand. Dipping my fingers in the stinging cut, I painted protective sigils down my arms, waiting until a solid wall of air formed Kevlar-dense around me. "Okay. I'm ready."

The Elite exchanged concerned looks that slid toward Boaz, telegraphing their worry he would skin them alive if I got hurt. While I appreciated the sentiment, I was learning to take care of myself, and I never felt more bulletproof than when Linus stood beside me.

Together, we stepped out into the open. Within seconds, bullets pinged off my wards and his body.

Heart pounding in my ears, I blocked out the fear slicking my palms and broke into a sprint, aiming straight for the source of the attack.

Light glinted to my right, sun dancing along the edge of Linus's sickle-shaped blade.

The enemy wore black fatigues and dark face paint.

Two snipers.

Both human.

Neither stood a chance.

Linus took their heads with a clean arc of his scythe, and they rolled to a stop in a crater made by their own bombs.

With silence restored, Linus remained standing over the corpses, his shoulders bowed under his burden.

"They would have killed us, all of us, if they had gotten the chance." I rested a hand on his shoulder, and black mist licked up my wrist. "They almost did, thanks to that minefield."

"I hate when you see me like this."

"I'm glad you let me." I bent my forehead until it rested against his spine. "It means you're sharing all of yourself with me." I rubbed my cheek against the wispy fabric of his cloak. "No masks. Not between us."

When he turned, the mantle of potentate evaporated, and he searched my face for a long moment before nodding. Though it was habit for him to withdraw until he resettled into his skin, he didn't make it far. I shackled his wrist with my fingers and led him back to where the Elite huddled in wait for us to signal the all clear.

"We got out of bed for this?" Becky shot Boaz a scathing glance. "They can take care of themselves."

Sharing a look with Linus, whose fingers twined with mine, it felt good to finally say, "Yes. We can."

TWO

Thanks to Linus's advanced planning, a gleaming van so green it veered on black sat off the shoulder of the road where I-16 intersected I-95, the key fob resting in a cupholder. A ward protected the vehicle from theft, and it took him seconds to disarm it. He opened the front passenger door for me, handed me up, then lingered to see if I would prefer the backseat.

"I'm good." A seed of disappointment lodged in my gut that I wasn't past this yet, but I was trying.

"If that changes"—he leaned in and kissed my stubborn chin —"let me know, and I'll secure alternate transportation."

Onto my tricks, he retreated before I could loop my finger in his collar and tug him closer. He shut my door then trotted around the vehicle, which gave me a moment to inhale the scents of fresh leather and new car. As I settled into my seat, I forced myself to notice its spacious interior, and started to relax bit by bit. By the time Linus slid behind the wheel and his hand covered mine, the tension knotting my shoulders had eased.

Tisdale's requirement that we visit Atlanta had doubled the length of our trip. I wasn't thrilled with that math, not when our friends and family were still at Lacroix's mercy in Savannah. But, as Linus had pointed out, Atlanta was home to the busiest airport in the world. We could hop a flight from there to Raleigh and make up the lost time, easy as pie. It was also an ideal spot to acquire a new wardrobe, toiletries, and anything else we needed before making the final leg of our journey.

Fashion was armor, and we had to suit up before visiting Dame Marchand.

Eventually, the early hour conspired with my full belly, and I stifled a yawn.

"Rest." Linus made it an order. "I could navigate this trip in my sleep."

Safe in the knowledge he was as likely to drift off behind the wheel as Lethe was to pass on an extra rasher of bacon, I dropped into a dreamless sleep with my head propped against the glass.

"We're here."

The crick in my neck confirmed I had slept wrong for several hours to be this sore.

The dash clock read ten p.m. Ten hours until our meeting with Tisdale.

"I had forgotten Rodgers and Hammerstein's *Cinderella* had returned to the Fox Theatre," he mused, sounding content to sit in a traffic snarl near the venue.

I didn't have to look to know he was smiling out at his city. The gleaming skyscrapers, the frenzied traffic, the bustle of humans sprinting through crosswalks murmured welcome to him in the same way the sight of old growth oaks strung with Spanish moss said home to me.

Rubbing the sleep from my eyes, I blinked around us. "Where are we staying?"

Thanks to Meiko, his catty former familiar, the Faraday was no longer secure in his mind. I didn't have to ask to know he wouldn't risk using his loft there on this trip, gwyllgi on staff or no.

"We're keeping a low profile." A smile twitched in his cheek. "We'll be staying with friends."

"Oh?" A peek into his life was more than I could resist. "Anyone I know?"

As he snagged a coveted street parking spot, he peered out the windshield and up at a corner building. "Yes."

Twisting in my seat, I got an eyeful of a sprawling shop with flickering neon signs announcing *The Mad Tatter* and *We're All Inked Here*. "We're staying with Mary Alice?"

"We need to find out what's being said about the situation in Savannah." He touched my shoulder. "She'll be able to tell us how far our trouble has been broadcast, and if the rumors are perking the wrong ears. We don't want Savannah's stumble to turn into a Society-wide fall if other clans or factions get it in their heads this is the time to strike us while we're down."

Already he suspected the lethargic response to our SOS was the result of an impending coup against the Grande Dame. Mary Alice might be able to confirm his suspicions, giving him the scoop to pass along to his mother. Though in present circumstances, I'm not sure how much good a heads-up would do her.

"Let's hope it doesn't come to that." I let myself out and waited for him on the sidewalk while he locked the vehicle. "She lives above the shop?"

"She lives in the penthouse, but she converted the fifth floor into a guest suite for her kids and grandkids. We'll have the entire place to ourselves."

"That's handy." I was liking his plan better already. "Are we going through the shop or...?"

"No." He cast a wistful glance at the stations beyond the glass where artists worked on their human, and inhuman, canvases. "We'll take the side entrance." He guided me around the corner. "I need to be seen around town, and soon, but not now. I would prefer it if people assume I'm in Savannah, with you."

Unsure how potentates held on to their power, I had to ask, "Doesn't that put Atlanta at risk?"

"Yes." The corners of his eyes tightened. "But this is bigger than a single city. Lacroix attacked the Society's American seat of power. He attacked necromancers as a whole, and that's how we have to respond." He led me through an ornate glass door to a bank of elevators. "The city isn't without its protectors. The Atlanta pack will step in if I barter for their aid. Even if Tisdale won't extend her help to Savannah, she'll stand for Atlanta."

"Sounds like you've got it all planned out." I huffed out a laugh. "Why am I not surprised?"

"Because you know me," he said, and I heard his simple happiness in that.

The trip up was quick, and we didn't pass another soul on the way. The doors opened on a short hall I could tell had been remodeled to suit Mary Alice. The red-and-white plaster mushrooms rooted in the black-and-white-tiled carpet would have tipped me off even without the psychedelic background that ignited a migraine at the base of my skull.

"This is..." I left the sentence trailing while I searched for the right words. "Really...something."

"This is Mary Alice." He smiled a little smile as he scanned the homage to her Wonderland namesake. "Wait until you see the suite."

"There are plenty of nice hotels in town." I dragged my feet when he shackled my wrist and led me toward the door painted with a black-and-white vortex. On the way, he plucked a small white dot off the fattest mushroom, revealing an oversized key dangling from the end. "They have this thing called beige. It's actually quite soothing. I think we should give it a try."

Laughing under his breath, Linus fit the absurd key into a lock shaped vaguely like a puckered mouth, and then it was too late to escape.

"Doodlebug." Mary Alice glanced up from the ledger balanced

across her knees. "You're right on time." She hopped to her feet and set the book aside. "I wasn't sure if you would eat on your way in, so I ordered dinner for two and put it in the fridge. There's a new soul food restaurant a few blocks over. I got honey pecan fried chicken, bacon-infused collard greens, home-style mac and cheese, and the best cornbread muffins you've ever eaten."

Saliva pooled in my mouth, even though I hadn't brushed the strawberry seeds out of my teeth yet.

Genuine fondness softened his expression when she came in for a hug. "It's good to see you."

"Ditch the broad," she grumbled, "and you'd see a lot more of me."

"Hi, Mary Alice." The broad—well, me—gave a wave. "You have a lovely home."

Relieved to find that true, of the suite's interior, if not its hall, I began admiring our accommodations.

Shades of pale gray on the walls and floor calmed, and gleaming windows framed by gauzy curtains opened out onto the city. The furniture had been chosen for comfort over style, probably with her grandkids in mind, but the quality was there. The appliances, what I could see of them, were all top-notch too. She had spared no expense, and that she loved so hard made me even more grateful she had been there for Linus when he had no one else.

"Don't think I didn't see your eyes bugging out when the door opened." She released Linus and wrapped her wiry arms around me in an unexpected embrace. I wouldn't consider it a hug. It was more like a snake looking for the softest place to squeeze. "And don't think I don't know about your plans to steal Doodlebug away from me for good." She snapped her fingers at him. "Show me the ring."

Pride wreathing his face, he held out his left hand, adorned with a bread tie that had seen better days. The waxy paper was starting to degrade, leaving a thin strand of soft metal wrapping his finger.

"You've got to be kidding me." She rubbed her thumb over the twist. "I've seen better rings in gumball machines."

A spike of embarrassment left my nape stinging with reprimand, but it's not like I had intended to ask Linus for his hand that night. Eventually, yes. But his mother had lit a fire under me when she tried to marry him off to keep us apart.

"This is the part where it's polite to say it's the thought that counts, but you're both loaded. The first High Society windbag to spot this will laugh until she deflates. You might want to consider upgrading sooner rather than later." She patted my cheek, almost a slap. "Still, I can't fault your taste in men. I would have licked off his freckles if I were a few decades younger."

Linus made a strangled sound that forced me to twist a laugh into a cough.

"His freckles are my favorite," I confessed, the daisy-shaped cluster under his left eye in particular. "I hope you'll come to the wedding."

"Any wedding of yours is bound to be a catastrophe," she announced. "I hope you'll serve popcorn."

Painfully aware she was right, and what I had cost those closest to me, I gave the ceiling my full attention to prevent my eyes from overflowing.

"Grier is worth it." Linus crossed to me, sank his fingers in my hair, and held on tight. "She always puts others first and never asks for anything in return." Warmth suffused his features. "There's nothing I wouldn't do for her."

"That's because your blood is pooling in your lap." Mary Alice snorted a laugh. "You think I can't spot the resemblance between those doodles in your sketchbook and her? I'm old, but I'm not blind. The second I saw her with my own two eyes, I knew it was over. All I had to do was look at your face to tell you'd walk into traffic for her." She flicked me a glance. "I'm glad she's a goner too. Otherwise, we would be having a very different conversation. I wouldn't allow just anyone to marry my protégé, you understand?"

Grateful I didn't have to hear that talk given the course of this one, I asked, "We have your blessing?"

"I might as well give you my stamp of approval." She mimed the action. "You'd marry him anyway."

"I love him," I ventured. "If that helps."

"I can tell." She shook her head. "That night he dragged you through here, you couldn't take your eyes off him. He's got a nice ass if you like pancakes, but it wasn't butter you wanted to pat."

Unable to look her in the eye, I dropped my face into my hands. "I need to use the little girls' room."

"Sheesh." Mary Alice folded her arms across her chest. "You socialites are so fragile."

"The bathroom is the second door on the right." Linus released me with reluctance. "I'll walk Mary Alice out."

"Thanks for your hospitality," I murmured, happy to make my escape.

On the way, he began quizzing her on what chatter had reached Atlanta and beyond about Savannah's troubles, no doubt plotting ways to spin the news to our advantage.

Behind the closed bathroom door, I shut my eyes and counted to ten.

The knocks at my back came right on time.

"I died of embarrassment," I called. "Invitations to my funeral will be delivered shortly."

The soft laughter brushing against the other side of the door lured me out despite my stinging cheeks. I couldn't resist Linus when all the masks fell away, and I saw the man I was going to spend the rest of my very long life with.

"You look good for a recently deceased."

"Mary Alice doesn't like me." The whine in my voice annoyed me. I ought to be used to my outsider status by now. There was no point in trying to impress folks this late in the game. "She's not thrilled we're getting married." I tapped his finger. "*And* she made fun of your ring."

"You put that ring on my finger." He looked at it, really looked at it, like he worried it might have been his imagination when I could have told him he never would have pictured an engagement ring like that one. "Nothing else matters."

"You're right." A smile curled my lips. "You're mine. That's all that counts."

But I was going to buy him a decent ring the first chance I got, even if it meant knocking him out with a sigil to pry this one off his finger.

A familiar ringtone interrupted my plotting, and I waited for Linus to answer.

"Midas," he said for my benefit. "Lethe mentioned you would be joining us."

A knock rang through the suite, and I frowned toward the entry-way. "I'll get it."

No sooner had I opened the door than a muscular arm shot through the gap and made me gasp. I caught the thick wrist, twisting into a hold designed to take down larger opponents, before my brain registered the network of crosshatched scars. I slammed Midas face-first against the wall then yelped and jumped backward, tucking my hands under my armpits like they had minds of their own.

"What the heck?" I glowered at him. "I could have hurt you."

The spun-gold hair that had given him his name fell into vibrant aquamarine eyes that showed amusement mingled with pride, a defi-nite upgrade from the sorrow that crept into them when he thought no one was looking. "Just checking to see if you and Lethe do more than eat takeout and...well...eat takeout."

"We train." I anchored my hands at my hips. "She works me harder than you ever did."

"Mmm-hmm." Pocketing his phone, he invited himself in. "I came to tell you in person that I can't go to Raleigh with you."

"We'll be fine on our own," I assured him. "Lethe was being over-protective by asking you."

"Grier, I know what's happening in Savannah. I can't keep

secrets from my alpha, not ones that involve my sister. That means Mom knows too."

"I understand."

"I don't think you do." He raked a hand through his hair. "Until and unless Lethe returns to Atlanta, I'm the stand-in. With the true heir in Savannah, knee-deep in vampires, Mom won't let me leave. She's made it clear I'm to remain within the city limits, and I can't break her commands. It's not a matter of choosing her over you, I mean I physically can't disobey a direct order."

The Atlanta pack was a meld of fae gwyllgi and warg genes. Their Faerie origins were ancient history, meaning they had more warg DNA than fae, and their pack hierarchy borrowed heavily from that culture, but they definitely had their own unique quirks.

"We don't want to put you in an awkward position." I indicated a couch where he could sit. "Linus and I can go on alone. An escort to meet with your mom, however..."

"You can't afford to appear weak in front of Mom if you expect her to offer you aid," he said grimly. "If I escort you, it sends the message that you're prey in need of protection."

"Oh." I had to restrain myself from smacking my forehead. "I should have thought of that."

"Just because Mom doesn't recognize our bond doesn't make it any less tangible to me." He dropped onto the sofa with a grimace. "You're pack, Grier. I won't let you face this alone. Lethe and Hood would kill me if I wimped out and tried." Amusement surfaced when he glanced up at me. "That's why I brought an old friend."

"Your old friend or my old friend?" I eyed the door. "I didn't see anyone else in the hall."

Granted, the design punched you in the face each time you looked at it, so you had to wait for your double vision to clear before taking in any new details.

"See for yourself." He jerked his head toward the door. "Go on."

After squaring my shoulders, I approached the door and—almost took a boot to the face.

"Taz." Luckily, instinct took over, and I ducked before kissing her tread hello. "You're here."

"I got you into this mess." Her grin was just as crazed as I remembered. "I'm here to get you out of it."

"*I* got *you* into this mess," I corrected her, too afraid of what she might do to me if I risked hugging her. "The Marchands put a price on your head. You never would have crossed paths with them if not for me."

"Evil Twin attempted to murder me." A spark of anger flashed in her eyes. "I'm sorry Good Twin has her lace panties in a wad over it, but her sister deserved what she got and then some."

Setting aside my excitement to see her, I had to give it to her straight. "You're not going with us."

"Yes, I am."

"No, you're not. It's dangerous enough for Linus and me, but it would be a suicide mission for you."

"We're having her glamoured," Midas volunteered. "I have a distant relative who specializes in tailoring appearances. The disguise will hold until she releases it."

"Glamoured." A trick of the fae to alter a person, place, or thing's appearance. "I see."

Just how many *distant relatives* the Atlanta pack sheltered made me nervous. The only one I had met so far was Shane Doherty, and Lacroix killed him. One minute, an ancient power. The next, an empty shell. Society members in good standing weren't supposed to intermingle with fae, but thanks to the Marchands, Taz was a dead woman walking. She could afford to bend the rules.

"Take a good look." Taz framed her face with her hands. "This might be the last time you see this mug."

A ripple of shock fluttered through me. "You would keep the disguise?"

"I'm tired of hiding. It's not in my nature. This is a second chance at life. A new life. Free of baggage from the old one." Lower, she confessed, "I would be a fool not to take it. Without Midas brokering the deal, I could never afford it."

The sentiment mirrored Amelie's so clearly, I was forced to admit I might have judged my old friend harshly. Taz was a soldier. She had done her duty, and it cost her. Amelie had brought misfortune on herself, but who was I to judge who got handed a second chance? Who was I to deem one person worthy over another? The very nature of a second chance dictated it should go to someone, not necessarily worthier, but more determined not to repeat past mistakes.

"I'll cover the expense." It was the least I could do. "Whatever it costs, I'll pay."

"No," he said solemnly. "You won't." He stood before I could protest. "Fae have no use for cash. She won't charge Taz a sum. She'll ask for something only Taz can offer." A frown wilted his full lips. "I wish there was another way, but big magic requires big sacrifice."

"All right." I didn't like it, but I couldn't fight him on that point. I had no clue what fae bargains entailed. All I knew was I didn't know enough to make one. "I'll wish you luck then."

"I'll bring her back to you in one piece," he promised. "We better go." He caught Taz's eye, and she headed to the door where he hesitated. "I'm trusting you not to share this information with anyone. The pack is..." He flattened his lips. "Losing Shane hurt. We can't risk any of our kin. There aren't many of them left."

"I'm sorry for your loss." Inadequate, as always. No words held the power to soften death. "I didn't know him well, but he was a fascinating man, and a kind one."

Expression tight, Midas nodded then joined Taz in the hall and closed the door behind them.

"I don't like this." I cut Linus a look. "Not even a little."

"Taz will do what Taz wants to do." He crossed to me and rubbed my shoulders. "She's a stubborn woman. That's why you two understand each other so well."

"Hmph." I swatted his hands. "I'm not stubborn."

The barest edges of his lips curled. "Of course not."

"What's next on the agenda? A trip to the mall? The corner pharmacy?"

We had hours left to burn, and I was too pumped to sit around and wait for them to crawl past.

"Our wardrobe should be arriving tonight via courier, coordinating luggage as well." He absorbed my shock with amusement. "Neely handled the details. For both of us."

"I didn't realize he was already on the clock." I massaged my forehead. "This is too bizarre."

Human friends helping in necromancer business. The Grande Dame would have kittens when she found out that I had brought so many into my household, including one poached from her payroll.

"The best employees do their jobs without having been asked." He kissed my temple. "He's in his element."

"He does love to shop." And he had a great eye for fashion. "I don't want to see the receipts, though."

Initiating him into our world meant he was aware how deep my pockets reached these days. Neely had excellent, and therefore expensive, taste. Given cart blanche, I could only imagine the hurting he had put on my bank account, and I preferred to keep it there—in my imagination.

"His only complaint was not being able to accessorize you in person before you face the Marchands."

"What about toiletries?"

"Those should come in separate orders as well. He sent cosmetics he deemed foolproof as well as our preferred shampoos and such."

A frown gathered across my forehead. "I don't have a preferred shampoo."

"Apparently you do now."

"I was fine stealing yours."

"You're Dame Woolworth." His cool fingers skated across my cheek. "You need to look the part."

"I'm not a fan of masks."

"I know." His expression shuttered. "But, with the Society, they're necessary."

"As long as we don't wear them when we're together, I can deal." I tapped his chin until he looked at me. "The Society can see what it wants, as long as I get to see it all."

"No," he corrected me solemnly, "the Society can see what we choose to show them."

Understanding creeped in, a warm flutter in my chest. "They don't get to see us."

The tentative smile hanging on his mouth told me, ring or not, he wasn't convinced this was real. I worried that was why he didn't want to show our true faces to our peers. He might fear what I felt for him wouldn't stand up to their intense scrutiny. Rumors and speculation would chip away at him, at his confidence. Better to show them a united, if false, front so any cruel jabs would slide right off him.

Oh, Linus.

At this rate, I might have to commit to something as permanent as ink to show him how I felt. The proposal hadn't done the job if he still doubted me. *Us.* Though, as everyone and their momma was quick to point out, that might be the fault of the ring. It proved the decision had been a spur-of-the-moment reaction, not what it should have been—a carefully planned occasion.

Hmm. He wasn't the only one capable of making grand gestures. Maybe it was time I showed him his worth to me in a language he spoke fluently—currency. You can't buy love, but perhaps his upbringing required me to take an uncomfortable step into debt to show him, in all ways, he was mine. Forever.

"It sounds like Neely has everything handled." At this rate, I would owe him a bonus soon. "What's left for us to do?"

Our rendezvous with Tisdale was at eight the following morning, since gwyllgi tended to keep a diurnal rather than nocturnal schedule.

"I have a meeting with my team."

"Ah." I scanned the room, already searching for something to do until he or Taz returned. "I should have anticipated that."

"Would you like to come?" He ducked his head. "It can be tedious, but they would love to meet you."

"I can go?" Excitement thrummed through me, and not just to have something to do. "That's allowed?"

"I am the potentate, and you are my fiancée." He took my hand. "Allowances can, and will, be made."

THREE

On the circuitous drive to meet the mysterious team who helped keep Atlanta free of supernatural crime, I kept turning over Taz's reappearance in my head. "How did she end up with Midas?"

"The pack is hooked into an extensive network of gwyllgi across the country. They have the means to hide and protect individuals in the short term, and do, as part of their security work." Diverting his attention from the road for a second, he flicked me a glance. "I didn't know they were sheltering her, if that's what you're wondering."

"I was wondering," I admitted. "You're in a position to make those types of connections happen, so I would have understood if you made the arrangements."

"Boaz claimed responsibility for her safety. I'm guessing he clued in to the vastness of the gwyllgi network too and hoped that, as a favor to you, they would be willing to help for the right incentive." He peered through the windshield, his expression more relaxed than it had been in days. "The Society is so insular, they wouldn't have looked for her among the pack. They would have assumed she had gone underground alone or was holed up with other necromancers."

"Just how much interaction have you had with the Atlanta pack?"

"Not much. I met Hood, Lethe, and Midas through their work at the Faraday." He canted his head to one side. "I met their mother through the course of my duties. She made it clear I could report gwyllgi crimes, even detain them, but I wasn't to punish any of hers. She would do it herself, and I was welcome to watch."

Having witnessed a gwyllgi trial in my front yard, I would rather take my chances with the potentate.

"We're almost there." Linus passed me his phone. "Text this code to this number."

Thumbs at the ready, I waited as he rattled off both sets of digits. "Done and done."

The screen lit up seconds later with a string of numbers I read back to him.

Back and forth, we traded texts and lines of code with the person or persons on the other end.

"This is all very cloak-and-dagger." Not to mention it required a knack for memorization.

"We have to be careful." He pulled into a parking deck and placed his hand on my thigh. "Keep your eyes open."

The cool of his fingers raised chills up my leg. "Your meetings are dangerous?"

"We might have been followed. I'm careful, but I'm not perfect."

I fluttered my lashes to do Neely proud. "Says you."

A blush swirled over his cheeks, ripening them to apples, and I could have taken a bite.

How did he conceal this part of himself from the world? How did he partition his heart from his head?

There was so much he could teach me about how to blend in among our High Society peers, how to take my place in their ranks, but I resented his proficiency in social survival skills stemmed from his complex relationship with his mother.

Kids were down the line for us. Way down the line. Way, *way* down the line. But I couldn't help but hope that we could raise them with clear eyes and open faces. I wanted them to know love came without price tags. That it cost nothing. It was given freely, and we had endless amounts to gift.

Kids.

Kids?

Exhaling through my teeth, I reached for Woolly on instinct. Of course she wasn't there. Our connection was strong, but it wasn't two hundred and fifty miles strong. Still, I would be giving her an earful when I got home. I was starting to suspect she was beaming images of infants and toddlers direct to my brain during the day while I was sleeping.

Bypassing the grungy elevator, Linus guided me to the stairwell. We climbed two floors before I noticed the discreet numbers painted within circles on the walls. Five levels after that, we hit a shorter staircase than the others. There was no number at all, just a door marked *maintenance* with a keypad beside the handle. Linus approached it, punched in a code, and it swung open, admitting us into a sleek office space that must exist between floors.

"Welcome to Base Two," he said, ushering me across the threshold before locking us in.

"Good to see you, boss," a tinny female voice rang out from across the room.

"Good to see who's with you, boss." The masculine voice lowered to a purr. "Mmm. Me likey."

"I caught you humping a light post once," another woman countered. "You don't set a high bar."

"I can't tell if I'm supposed to be insulted," I muttered to Linus.

"I hope not." A tall man rounded the corner with a steaming mug cupped between his palms. His hair was the bright white of fallen snow, and his eyes were pure titanium. "Wilting violets don't last long around here." He stuck out his hand, warmed from the ceramic. "I'm Bishop."

The scent of copper hit my nose, but no shiver coasted down my spine. "You're a vampire?"

His smile revealed even, white teeth. Nary a fang in sight. "Can't a man enjoy a mug of hot O negative without being judged?"

"Grier has earned her reservations about vampires." Linus clasped hands with him. "She'll behave if you do."

"Are you dangerous then?" Interest sparkled in his eyes when he looked at me. "You must be, if you're with him."

"I'm a violet, remember?" I tried my best to look unassuming. "What harm could I possibly do?"

"My mistake," he murmured. "I never make the same one twice."

"Why should you?" I chuckled. "There are so many new experiences out there."

"Stop flirting with her, Bish," one of the women called. "Bring her over here. I wanna see."

"Come and meet the team." Linus cupped my elbow and walked me to a bank of monitors that belonged in a superhero flick mounted on a wall painted black. The layout reminded me, on a much grander scale, of the teleconferencing suites he had designed for the Society. This must have been his inspiration. Outlines of men and women filled the screens, but filters shadowed their features. He gestured to each one in turn. "Lisbeth, Reece, Anca, Milo, this is my fiancée, Grier Woolworth."

"You just love saying that, don't you?" Lisbeth chortled. "He only called you his fiancée like five times when he called control earlier."

"Five?" Milo scoffed. "I counted ten, and I wasn't half listening. I was watching those surveillance tapes." His jaw cracked on a yawn. "Riveting stuff."

"You were dozing off," Reece accused, his accent pure Good Ol' Boy.

"I was zoning in," Milo countered. "Big difference."

"It's a pleasure to meet you," Anca interrupted. "I can see your influence in Linus's work."

Surprised by the comment, I paid her closer attention. "You've seen his paintings?"

"Paintings? No. I haven't had that particular honor." She leaned forward in her chair. "Our lives intersect very little offscreen." An embarrassed chuckle escaped her. "But I must confess, a job brought me to the Mad Tatter once, some years ago, and I couldn't resist the temptation of touring his workstation. You're the little girl from the mural. I recognized you at once."

"Ah." Much to my shame, I realized I had been jealous to think he had shared such an intimate piece of our history with another woman. Silly to let it cramp my gut, but there you go. As much as Linus was still learning to trust us, I must be too. "I haven't decided yet if his memory is just that good, or if he borrowed a photo album from his aunt to get the small details so perfect."

"You knew each other as children?"

"Yes," Linus answered for me, saving me from admitting how I had ignored him when we were kids in favor of Boaz. "Grier was my muse from the start."

The ping of an incoming text had me searching for my cell. "Midas says their ETA is thirty minutes."

And then he would hand Taz off to us, and we would hope no one saw through her glamour.

"We better get this meeting started then." Bishop sank into a chair in front of the monitors. Until he woke them, I hadn't noticed other screens winking to life below the main displays. This was more than a teleconferencing suite, it was a first-class control room worthy of the name. "First order of business... There's a ghoul, maybe two, terrorizing Ben's Fried Chicken customers."

While Linus and the others decided on a plan of action, I stood against the far wall, marveling at the seamless way his team coordinated their efforts so that he wasn't spread thin across the city but sent only where there was a critical need. As I listened, I came to understand three of them weren't only techs but deputized to patrol the streets in black garb reminiscent of his tattered wraith's cloak.

The overall effect was of him being omnipresent. It was a brilliant strategy, and I wasn't the least bit surprised he had implemented it during his reign as potentate.

A flicker on my periphery alerted me to Cletus's presence, and I dared to hope. "Do you have news?"

Cletus had been dispatched to watch over Corbin, who Lacroix had detained in his clan home. So far, the reports had been more of the same. Nothing. The house had been warded against wraiths, which meant Cletus could no longer pop in and out to pass messages between Corbin and me.

Corbin, who came from vampire hunter stock, was continuing the family tradition of protecting humans in his own fangy way. He had volunteered to infiltrate Lacroix's organization to help us dismantle it, but he got caught relaying a sensitive message to us via Cletus that brought Lacroix's wrath down upon him.

Progeny or not, I owed him. His intel had saved lives. Dozens, if not hundreds, of them.

One way or another, we were getting him back.

Linus spared us a concerned glance, and Bishop frowned our way, but Cletus behaved himself and let me follow the safety procedures we had put in place before imparting his message.

Sitting on the poured concrete floor, I wedged my back into a corner then gave Linus, who acted as my spotter, a thumbs-up.

"Okay, Cletus." I braced my palms to either side of me. "I'm ready."

The wraith rushed me, dunking me in its cowl, and I spun out into a darkness so vast there was no beginning or end. And then Corbin was there, his mouth pressed against a two-inch high crack at the bottom of a window in what must be the room where Lacroix ordered him to be detained until Savannah was his.

From firsthand experience, I knew Lacroix opted for plush suites over actual cells with bars on the windows for his guests, but a cage was a cage was a cage in my opinion. All the gild in the world couldn't change that basic fact.

"I finally made enough noise about the heat that they cracked a window so I don't suffocate," he rasped. "There's no AC in the attic where they moved me after my last escape attempt, but they'll figure out what I'm up to soon enough."

The sawing breaths spoke of more than heat exhaustion. Corbin was hurt. Bad.

"This might be my last report unless I can trick them into giving me access to your wraith again." He wiped sweat from his brow. "From what I've overheard, there are about fifteen vampires in residence. They're all loyal to Lacroix, not compelled, which means they need to be dealt with." A pained laugh escaped him. "You can take out the trash after you pick me up, huh?"

Hearing he still trusted me after all this tightened my throat until swallowing hurt.

"I haven't eaten in a few days," he admitted. "I need to...sit down now."

Bruised eyes closing, he sank onto the floor to rest.

The image swirled, draining away, until the room came back into reluctant focus.

Linus knelt in front of me, waiting on an update as my vision cleared fully.

Cletus, waiting on a return message, hovered at my shoulder.

After relaying the information to Linus, I waved Cletus closer to record what I said next.

"Take care of yourself, Corbin. You've done enough. More than enough. Don't take more risks. We have your location. Cletus will remain on watch and check in regularly. You are not alone." I gave that time to sink in. "We're coming for you the second Lacroix is out of power, sooner if we can spare the manpower to extract you safely."

Nodding to Cletus that I was done, he stroked bony fingers down my cheek then vanished in a swirl of black mist.

"We need to get you back to our suite so you can rest." Linus straightened. "Can you stand?"

"Just give me a minute."

Wraith vision always left me disoriented afterward.

"Hold up." Reece tapped a few keys on his end that seized control of one of the lower monitors. "Before you go, look."

"Gwyllgi." Linus leaned in to examine individual faces. "These are all dominants in the Atlanta pack."

"They're swarming the city." Bishop flattened his lips into a thin line. "You know what isn't?"

Linus unfurled to his full height. "Submissives."

"What does this mean?" Slowly, I got to my feet. "The dominants are the protectors, like Lethe, right?"

"And the fighters," Milo added. "Usually we see submissives out and about too. They tend to run errands, like buying groceries and paying bills. Taking the pups to school, that sort of thing. Dominants tend to work alone, but we see them in pairs often enough. But in these numbers? Never. Not unless the alpha is on the move, and she rarely leaves the den."

"They're hiding their vulnerable and putting on a show of force," I said, grasping the situation. "Do they expect the fighting to spread this far?"

"This might all be a show for your benefit," Anca murmured. "You two have an upcoming meeting with the alpha. Perhaps she's employing intimidation tactics?"

"Tisdale is a good alpha," Linus said. "I don't see her dragging her people out of bed to patrol the streets without good reason."

"The Society was dealt a blow," Lisbeth countered, "and that weakens their position, including who they ordain to run their cities."

"Lethe's mom is planning a coup?" The bloody implications made my heart skip a beat. "Taking out Linus makes no sense. The Society won't leave Atlanta in gwyllgi hands. It's too valuable. She must realize that."

"Our relationship is stronger now than ever, thanks to your friendship with Lethe." Linus tapped his fingertips on his chin. "Because of that friendship, she's aware of what's happening in

Savannah. She may simply be taking precautions with their most vulnerable members in the event there's spillover."

Given his ties to Atlanta, and his relationship with me, that was entirely possible. "Want me to touch base with Midas?"

"He's loyal to his alpha." Linus dismissed the idea with regret. "He can't tell us anything without his mother's express permission. The only way to override her is to challenge her, and he won't do that. He doesn't want to take up the mantle."

Frowning, I studied the screen, wishing I saw answers there. "Lethe is her heir."

"Lethe followed you to Savannah, and she remained there. There's a reason she was challenged for her position as second in the pack."

"Pregnancy made her an easy target," I argued.

"It's more than that. They must believe she plans on establishing her own pack, in Savannah." Linus made it sound like a done deal when Lethe and Hood hadn't breathed a word of that possibility to me. "If that's the case, the sooner they dethrone her, the better for the stability of the pack."

"You did buy her a house to grow into," I reminded him. "If she wasn't considering a move before, she will once she realizes how close that puts her to my refrigerator."

"Plus, she's memorized your debit card number and security code." A tiny smile cut his mouth. "She could still have food delivered to Woolly, meet the driver at the gate, and walk it back to her place."

Able to picture it clearly, I sighed. "Remind me to have a new card issued when we get back home."

Home had been a slip of the tongue. He was already there. I was the fish out of water. But I had gotten so used to him in my home, in my life, I couldn't see him fitting elsewhere. A lifetime of memories of him and me at Woolworth House just cemented the absolute certainty he belonged there, with me. Always.

Since he couldn't very well deny his ties to Atlanta while in his city, with his team, I backed away to give him space to handle his business.

After the team wrapped up their meeting, we exchanged good-byes then exited the way we had come. To prevent our conversation from carrying, I kept my thoughts to myself until we were back in the van.

"You told me you kept your team anonymous," I began, "and you meant it."

Cranking the engine, he guided us out and onto the street. "The meeting didn't go how you imagined?"

"You could say that." I shoved him for teasing me. "Why was Bishop present?"

"He was given the same choice as the others. He prefers to coordinate our efforts." Linus let the silence drag for a moment. "He was in a bad place when I found him. Perhaps he feels since he was hand-picked there's no point in hiding his face from me?"

While it made sense, it was still risky. "What about the others?"

"He's our point of contact," Linus explained. "He travels the bases, knows each of us, and protects the team's identities."

Linus, as potentate, would be a talking point. There was no hiding him, no protecting him. And that went for me too. Our engagement would be announced in a lavish party as soon as Savannah had dusted herself off and gotten to her feet again. But it was nice to think these people could do good without painting a public bull's-eye on their backs.

The trip back to Mary Alice's building was short now that we could take a direct route. Facing down the garish hallway leading to our suite wasn't any easier the second time around. The bright colors were quick to remind me I had a slight headache, but the suite itself offered instant relief from the psychedelic assault.

"Um." I spotted Midas in the kitchen first. It was hard to miss him. But I wasn't as sure about the lean black man sharpening his knife while he sat on the couch. "Hello?"

"Mary Alice let us in," Midas explained. "I hope you don't mind."

"No," I said slowly. "Who's your friend?"

"Your face right now." End over end, the man tossed his knife, catching it without looking. "I wish I had a camera. Boaz would pay good money to see you speechless."

"*Taz?*" I gawked as she—*he*—rose. "You're—you're a *man*."

"Yep." Brown eyes dancing with mirth, he traced the waist of his pants. "Want to see—?"

"No. Goddess no." I covered my eyes with my hands. "You're worse than Boaz."

Until he offered, I hadn't realized glamour transformed a person to that degree. I assumed it was an illusion, but this meant a tangible illusion or a physical manifestation. Either way, I wasn't keen on finding out which, even if she—*he*—had offered.

"No need to be rude." He harrumphed. "Or a prude."

If passing on an illusory peen viewing got me labeled a prude, I could live with that. Happily.

"I'm going by Jake Clemmons from here on out," Taz said. "You can call me Clem."

The smug twist to his smile told me there was a story there, but I was afraid, after the peen, to ask.

"You mentioned staying in deep cover. You're good with doing that as a man?"

Afraid I might have offended her—*him*—with the question, I was ready to backtrack when he cracked a smile.

"I've always wondered how the other half lived," he admitted. "And it's not like I can't go back if I decide I miss being a woman." He made a show of hiking his junk. "I peed a minute ago. Standing up. No toilet paper required." His grin was infectious. "It changed my whole perspective on life."

Returning his maniacal grin, I stuck out my hand. "Nice to meet you, Clem."

Tempted as I was to ask if the sacrifice had been worth it, I could tell he thought so.

As we shook, he shot a wink over his shoulder. "What do you think, Lawson?"

Shock had prevented me from noticing when Linus joined us, but it was hard to miss him now.

"Remarkable." He walked a circle around Clem. "I've never seen glamour before and after."

"You've done it now," I teased. "He's going to take you up on the offer to see your, um, *perspective*."

A glint sparked in Linus's eyes, and I debated how I should feel about his eagerness to peek down another woman's pants, even if she was currently a man. I settled on amused. The man truly was curiosity personified.

"I got used to stripping with the women in my unit." Clem shoved his hands in his pockets. "Men, not so much."

Patting my fiancé's arm, who was hiding his disappointment well, I ventured, "I'm sure Linus would be just as happy if you answered a few questions."

Linus's eyebrows winged up, daring to hope again, and Clem rolled his eyes.

"Sure." He dipped his shoulders. "Why not?"

"I have to get back," Midas interrupted before the interrogation began. "Mom has a barbeque scheduled the day after tomorrow, and she expects me to take several eligible females from the pack on a hunt for the main course."

"Mothers do love matchmaking, don't they?" Unable to stop from meeting Linus's gaze, I winked at the man Maud and the Grande Dame had selected for me long before I chose him for myself. "Sometimes they even get it right."

"I understand my duties to the pack." Darkness wreathed Midas's face as he glanced down at his forearms, at the scars there. "I will fulfill them."

"Soon your mother will have her hands full of Lethe Jr.," I said, hope for him in my voice, "and you'll be off the hook."

"For a while." He smiled, and his grim mood lifted a fraction though it never fully went away.

"On the topic of your mom—"

"You'll have to ask her about the enforcer presence in the city." He crossed his wrists in front of him. "My hands are tied."

Smiling to let him know there were no hard feelings, I said, "Can't blame a girl for trying."

After Midas left, Clem took position out in the hall. I didn't envy him the eye-blistering job.

"We could heat up the takeout in the fridge." I cozied up to Linus. "Watch a movie. Make out on the couch."

With it close to midnight, I might even squeeze in a few more hours sleep before our early meeting.

"Mmm." His arms came around me. "That sounds..."

Clem shoved open the door. "Expecting a delivery?"

"Yes," Linus answered over my groan. "We are."

The first order had arrived by courier, the poor guy struck mute or blind or both by the hall décor. Seconds later, Neely set my cell buzzing, ready to live vicariously. Reluctantly, Linus and I set aside the dream of a quiet dinner and put on a fashion show via video chat for my friend and fashion consultant instead.

AFTER WE GOT the clothing folded and packed in our new suit-cases, the rest was easy. I didn't care about the underwear. No one but Linus would see it, and after a man saw you modeling granny panties, there was nowhere to go but up from there. The toiletries didn't matter either. Once I got home, I planned on resuming my theft of Linus's shampoo and body wash. Or maybe, though probably not, buying my own. The cosmetics came with detailed instructions from Neely, who forced me to make up my face while he watched and critiqued before signing off when Cruz came to collect him for bed.

With the luggage stuffed to capacity and our flight booked, we had nothing to do with the rest of our night but lounge around the suite and indulge in the meal Mary Alice had provided for us.

Or so I thought until a hard knock thwarted my stomach and hormones yet again.

Clem didn't wait on us to acknowledge him, just opened the door wearing a grim expression. "You've got company."

"Another delivery?" Visions of dollar signs twirled through my head. "Just how much did Neely order?"

"Trust me." Clem flexed his hand where it rested on the door. "He didn't order this."

The tight set of his jaw warned me I wouldn't like whoever or whatever waited for me in the hall.

"Show them in." I shrugged. "Might as well. They're already here."

"Suit yourself." Clem nudged the door wider. "I'll be right outside if you need me."

The thin hope Clem was wrong, that Neely was behind this late arrival, died a sudden death.

Hat literally in hand, an ornate walking stick tucked beneath an arm, Johan Marchand, my grandmother's current husband, invited himself in without so much as a hello. Legs dragging, he shuffled toward the couch with the gait of the thoroughly defeated.

Given how our last encounter ended, with him threatening to declare war on the Woolworth and Lawson families, I had to wonder at the symbolism. And how he knew where to find us in the first place. Heck, how he got here from Raleigh so fast. There was no way, unless he had already been in the city, waiting, and that led to a whole host of other questions.

Linus must be asking himself the same things. Black had crept into his eyes, a warning sign Johan better have the right answers.

But all I could think was *thank the goddess* Clem had passed inspection. Having a Marchand so close was dangerous on multiple levels, for all of us.

"Grier." Johan dipped his chin at Linus. "Scion Lawson."

"Johan." I applied the mask of Dame Woolworth with as much care as my earlier makeup tutorial, and it made me itch. "This is an unexpected surprise. Are you in Atlanta on business?"

"Yes." He focused on me then slid his gaze past my shoulder to Linus, who held his scythe loose at his side as he circled the room toward the door. "Of the family variety."

"How did you find us?" I spared him from interrogation at the edge of a blade by asking outright. "Who told you we were in the city?"

"I was given the address." He presented an envelope suffering a calligraphic overdose as proof. "I assumed you had given Severine a copy of your itinerary, that her secretary had addressed this and left it for me on her orders."

"Her secretary handed it to you?"

"Well, no." His watery eyes lifted to mine. "But I found it on my desk and recognized it at once."

Based on his puffy eyes and mottled cheeks, tonight must be the night for hand-delivering unpleasant news. There was nothing to do but brace for impact and hope we walked away from this encounter without being slapped with a declaration of intent to feud.

Over his head, I met Linus's gaze, and his expression mirrored the turmoil of my thoughts.

The Marchands had located us, located *me*, but how? And who had done the tracking? Eloise? Her mother? Even Johan was suspect.

Fingers itching for the letter, I demanded. "This is from Severine?"

"Yes, she…" He swallowed hard. "My wife…passed in her sleep yesterday."

Shocked, I didn't call him out on the obvious lie about his source, just watched him sink onto the couch without waiting to be offered a seat. The bit about Severine dying was easy enough to confirm, but he hadn't packed up and fled Raleigh the second her time of death was announced. Either she had been dead longer than he claimed, or he came by his information through means he was unwilling to disclose.

"There's nothing for you in Raleigh." He set his hat on the cushion beside him. "The girls' mother inherits the title of Dame Marchand, and Rhiannon is still in mourning. She refuses to leave her rooms, hasn't left them since Heloise passed. She sees no one and, in the wake of this latest tragedy, has closed the estate to visitors."

Plan B went up in smoke, and I plopped down beside him, at a loss for words.

"I won't pretend Severine didn't have ulterior motives for allowing your visit." He twisted the cane in his hands. "I also won't pretend she made me aware of her intentions. I was her companion, not her confidant. She had the girls for that."

While I doubted his claims of ignorance very much, I wasn't going to rake a grieving man over the coals. "I'm grateful you caught us before she stood us up at the front gate."

"Don't be too grateful." Fingers leaving dents in the paper, he extended the crisp envelope, its calligraphic address made ominous by the fact no one should have known where to find us. "Severine put this aside for you in case she passed before you reached out to the family. I never expected..." A tear rolled down his cheek. "Her will was so strong. She should have outlived us all."

There was nothing for me to say. I hadn't known her, and what I had known about her didn't make me sad to hear of her passing. I felt...nothing, and that was something all its own.

"I should go." He used the cane to stand. "I made arrangements to stay with an old friend while I'm in town. He'll be expecting me."

The way he walked, like life had lost all meaning for him, filled me with a hollow dread, like the message from my grandmother gained weight with each of his steps.

Clem saw Johan out, and that left me alone with Linus...and a sealed envelope that carried the faint scent of a perfume I couldn't name.

Linus made no move to join me. He just watched, hands in his pockets. "Will you read it?"

The fabriclike texture under my thumb convinced me of its provenance. "It can't be anything good."

"I'm inclined to agree."

"I could burn it." I twirled her final words for me between my fingers. "Then I would never have to know what she cared enough to burden me with that she made its revelation a condition after her passing."

Expression solemn, he nodded. "Do you want privacy to read it?"

I almost dropped the note in my surprise. "Are you that certain I will?"

"To leave it unread is to allow the dead to hold sway over the living."

Thinking of Maud, of Cletus, I had to contradict him. "They do anyway."

A shrug left me in doubt if I had won the point or if he had simply let it go. "I'll cancel our tickets."

"That's it?" I cocked my head at him. "You're really going to let Johan walk away without a fuss?"

Lifting his hand, he revealed his phone and a string of texts that grew as I watched the screen.

"I touched base with my team," he admitted. "They're verifying Johan's information—both Severine's time of death and the chain of custody on the letter you received. Perhaps if we can track down its origin, we'll discover who and how they located us so quickly." His lips thinned. "They'll stick to him while we're in the city, make sure this is the only surprise he has in store for you."

The man was a pawn, a willing one perhaps, but a pawn all the same, and his queen was dead.

"I'll place a few more calls," he said, interrupting my thoughts, "see what I can learn."

Aware he was giving me the privacy he thought I would need and a chance to decide if I was as ruled by curiosity as he, I hooked my pointer beneath the wax seal and ripped it open before I changed my mind.

You have proven yourself to be Evangeline's daughter in all ways.

There was no endearment, but I would have been a fool to expect one.

And like your mother, I expected great things from you, but you have disappointed at every turn.

A stone sank to the bottom of my stomach, but I had come this far. I might as well press on.

You are a convicted criminal who murdered the woman responsible for your upbringing. You fraternize with Low Society rabble. You live as a human, with a human job and human friends. You disgust me. You are the worst possible outcome of the gamble your mother took on your father, and I have no one to blame but myself for not dragging Evangeline home where she belonged and locking her in her room until your birth. At least then I could have salvaged you. But no. She robbed me of my chosen heir and produced, just to spite me, a goddess-touched necromancer. With you under my tutelage, I might have gone on to claim the Society's highest honor—the position of Grande Dame. Instead, you threw those aspirations in my face when you got involved with Clarice Lawson's son and heir.

At that point, I had to laugh. It was that or cry, and I wasn't going to give her the satisfaction, even in death.

As if that wasn't enough, you twisted the blade in my back. You wounded me, Grier, when you allowed Heloise to be murdered on your grounds. She was your kin, and you watched her die. Her blood is on your hands, the same hands that would have one day reached out to me for guidance now that you have embraced your powers in a gauche public display no doubt engineered to curry favor with that wretched upstart Clarice Lawson.

Anyone in a position to call Clarice Lawson an upstart was on the far side of a necromantic lifespan. The far, *far* side.

To ensure you never claim your birthright, that you are forced to blunder through your awakening to the detriment of all those around you, I have entrusted every scrap of knowledge, every artifact, every tome in the vast Marchand collection, to a third party who will not be swayed by your fortune, title, or wiles.

The paper fluttered from my limp fingers, and I had to catch it again to finish reading.

As no light will ever pierce the black veil you've shrouded this family in, neither will enlightenment lift the blanket of ignorance swaddling you in darkness.

That was it.

That was all.

The spiteful old bat had known I would need guidance, and she had taken pains to snap the olive branch before I could extend it.

"You might as well come back in," I called. "I'm done."

Linus rejoined me, pocketing his phone. "As bad as you feared?"

"Worse." Unable to read them aloud, I passed her final wishes for me to him. "I can't believe she hated me so much."

As he read, he drifted closer. By the time he finished, he sat next to me, the note pinched between two fingers like touching it offended him.

"This has nothing to do with you." He set the paper on the coffee table and wiped his hand on his pants. "I hope you can see this is the resolution of the feud she started with Evangeline. Severine lost her chance to get in the last word before her daughter died, so she vented her anger on her granddaughter instead. It was petty and mean-spirited. You gave her no cause to be so cruel."

The fate that befell Heloise gave her license to hate me. How freeing it must have been to be absolved of any pesky qualms about how she ought to feel about her other granddaughter.

"Do you think she wanted to tell me to my face?"

The promise of me getting my comeuppance would explain why she deigned to extend the invitation.

"After your display at the ball, she wouldn't have had to think hard to come up with a reason for your sudden interest in mending fences. Yet she still offered us a weekend pass to visit her at the

Marchand family home. She had her reasons, and we'll never know them."

"I can't believe I wasted money on all this crap to impress her when she planned on kicking me in the teeth when I arrived."

"Grier." His lips hooked to one side. "You're a wealthy woman."

"Live on ramen and ketchup packets for a few months, and then we'll talk." I sighed when his smile grew more lopsided. "I forget you don't eat. You really could live on ketchup packets for weeks on end."

"You make yourself forget that quirk in my biology because fasting is anathema to you."

"Do you know the best thing about having money?" I didn't wait for him to answer. "I never have to go hungry. I can buy all the food I want, any time I want. I don't have to count pennies, I don't have to cross my fingers and pray when I swipe my debit card. I see it, I want it, I buy it, and I eat it."

"I've never had to make do, but I am sorry for the months you scraped by on minimum wage."

"There we'll have to disagree." I traced his elegant knuckles. "After Atramentous, I was grateful to have those problems. They taught me respect for things I had always taken for granted."

The muscles in his hand flexed, his fingers curling into a fist, but I soothed them each smooth again.

"Our schedule just got cleared." Eager to wipe Atramentous from our thoughts, I leaned closer. "Looks like we'll be heading home after our meeting with Tisdale, but we have a few hours to ourselves."

The pulse at his throat quickened. "You have something in mind?"

Hand on his thigh, I walked my fingers higher. "I was thinking—"

The windows I had admired upon our arrival exploded in a glittering rain of glass.

Blood ran hot down my cheek, and I dipped my finger in the trickle. I reinforced Linus's sigil before painting one on my arm. That's all the time I had before spotlights swept through the room, blinding us.

A familiar shiver danced up my spine as four vampires dressed in black from head to toe swung through the opening armed with crossbows.

"You've got to be kidding me." I really, *really* hated Atlanta. "Please tell me they're filming a new *Mission: Impossible* movie and hit the wrong floor."

"No proof, no payday," the shortest one barked, zeroing in on me. "Take her head."

"My head?" Sinking into a ready stance, I shot a frown toward Linus, but his expression was covered by the thick folds of his black cowl. Around him, his tattered wraith's cloak fluttered, and when he lifted his hand, the lights caught the wicked curve of his scythe. "My freaking *head?*"

Decapitation was next level compared to simply shooting me in the head with an arrow.

The vampire really should have kept his directives to himself. Shouting his orders gave Linus permission to dispatch him without a shred of guilt. And that went double for me. I didn't want to hurt anyone, but I had strong objections to getting beheaded.

The door burst open behind us, and Clem moved into position, covering my exposed left side.

"I lost the damn bet," he grumped. "Seven whole hours before someone tried to kidnap, murder, or otherwise manhandle your person. That's all I needed to win. Seven is supposed to be a lucky number."

"Next time, I'll have my kidnappers/murderers/manhandlers touch base with you first."

"I would appreciate that," he said, too primly to pass for a guy.

The second vampire identified Clem as the bigger threat—which stung my pride—and got a boot heel to his hairline for his trouble. Clem's aim wasn't as good as usual, but his legs were longer, his reach greater. I wasn't too worried, though. Already he was compensating for his wider frame and larger mass by stomping the attacker into the carpet.

The third vampire had gone straight for Linus, and he no longer had his head.

The fourth darted furtive glances between his boss and Linus and me, his chest pumping like he'd run a marathon. Panic. He was scared of Linus. And who wouldn't be terrified after watching him manifest and behead a team member?

Seizing the opportunity, I charged him. Once he realized what I meant to do, he flung his crossbow onto the carpet and threw up his hands like he was warding off the plague.

The force of my ward smashing into the loyalty-torn vampire flung him against the far wall where he cracked his skull and slid to the floor in a heap.

"Three down." Clem rubbed his hands together. "One to go. Who wants the honors?"

The pool of darkness that was Linus eased forward, and blood dripped in his wake.

"Fuck it," their not-so-fearless leader snarled. "No reward is worth this."

He leapt out the smashed window, his harness catching him, and rappelled out of sight.

"I got this." Clem walked over, palmed a hefty pocket knife, and cut the rope. "Wait for it."

The dull thud of a body hitting pavement wasn't music to my ears, but it was a relief. The threat had been dealt with, we were all still alive, and we had one vampire left to question.

Face to the night, Linus murmured, "This shouldn't be your life."

"This path brought me to you." I reached beneath his cowl, dipping my hands in icy midnight to rest my palms on his cool cheeks. "I can walk it, as long as you're beside me."

Light fractured around him, illuminating his face. "You shouldn't have to—"

Bringing him down to me, I silenced him with a kiss.

"Ah." Clem sidestepped us. "I see you've learned how to win arguments."

"Shhh." I released Linus to slant him a look. "It only works if they don't realize they're being handled."

"Oh, we realize." Linus brushed his lips over mine. "We just don't care."

Snorting out a laugh, I shoved him away. "What do we do with our new friend?"

The moment's amusement lost, his features hardened into the potentate's. "We bring him with us."

"Where?" I glanced around the ruined suite. "The Faraday?"

"No, we can't risk the exposure. Too many people know me there."

And some would be happy to spread the gossip about the potentate bringing his fiancée home, meaning Savannah's tender underbelly, already vulnerable, would be even more exposed to circling predators.

"Mary Alice is not going to be happy about this." I sighed at the night sky that loomed so much closer, brighter as we moved toward dawn. "I didn't think this type of glass could be broken. It's tempered, right? There's some kind of laminating process between panes? They must have..." I crunched over the debris, kicking it aside in search of clues. "But that's not possible."

"You were thinking they must have cased this building prior to our arrival." Linus watched a moment before crouching near me and examining a blackened clay shard. "They used charms that self-terminate." He lifted it, and it glittered. "They embedded crushed tempered glass as foci. They likely planned this attack based on the Faraday, or under the assumption we would stay in a hotel in downtown. Any window made of the same material would work as a trigger for the charm to detonate on cue."

"How is it we're so popular tonight?" We might as well have hung up flashing neon lights to match the parlor downstairs. "A visit from Johan and one from the vampire assassins. That can't be a coincidence."

I only told a select few about coming to Atlanta, and they were all staying under Woolly's roof except for Boaz. He had expanded that to include his partner and their backup, but they had no details. I hadn't known where we were staying to tell any of them, and whoever was behind this had us pegged down to the address.

Linus's team knew our whereabouts, I was certain, but he trusted them with his life on a daily basis when he was on the job and had for years. They could have taken him out at any time, so it didn't jive for me that they would choose now to switch teams.

As much as I wanted to check Mary Alice off our suspect list, I had to remember—for the both of us—that she was an information broker. She was the one who had originally told me about the price on my head. While she might be fond of Linus, she had proven earlier she was no fan of mine.

For the right price, a quick call to her could have given the Marchands our location.

That would explain Johan showing up on our doorstep. And who knows? Maybe she ran two-for-one specials? Maybe she double-dipped, sold the information to two or more parties. The vampire assassins might have gotten tipped only *after* Johan left if Mary Alice was a big believer in customer service.

The utter stupidity of staying above the hub of underground intel gatherers struck me hours too late to do anything about it. We should have been safe here, but I was learning safety was an illusion.

The question, no matter how uncomfortable, had to be asked, "Are you sure Mary Alice...?"

"Mary Alice is neutral." Quick, hard, certain was his answer. "The moment she picks a side, she becomes obsolete. People won't trust the information she sells not to be slanted toward her beliefs. She can't have her own agenda, or no one will trust her to further theirs."

It was clear he wanted to believe the best of her, so I didn't point out she had helped us. A few times. Or that Linus wasn't her only friend. She might be helping others along too. To our detriment.

Unbidden, Odette's once-beloved face rose to the forefront of my mind, weathered from the sun and wrinkled by time and a life I had thought well-lived. Recalling her forced me to remember my own battle to believe the worst in someone I had trusted for so long. For his sake, I hoped his friend proved truer than mine.

"We've got to be missing something…" I glanced around, my gaze landing on a discarded hanger sticking out of the trashcan. The dots connected in a flash, and I felt stupid for not considering it sooner. "Neely."

Following my line of sight, he asked, "You think Neely is responsible?"

"Yes." I yanked the hanger out of the can like it was proof. "No. Not directly." I started pacing. "He ordered our clothes. He charged them to my account. Anyone with the means to monitor those types of transactions would have known I was planning on being in the city, and that you were coming with me. They would know where to find us since the packages had the address of Mary Alice's building."

"You're right." His brow slanted downward. "There are only so many places in the city who tailor clothes to the High Society aesthetic. I pointed them out when Neely asked me for recommendations." It was easy to see he was beating himself up for being predictable. "A bribe could buy that easily. There are Low Society necromancers and other factions within the city who sell that type of information to interested parties."

Interested parties, like Mary Alice. Ugh. I hated that her name kept popping into my head. Just because my nearest and dearest continued to betray me didn't mean he shared the same curse. His taste in friends might prove better than mine. I followed my heart, for all the good it did me, while he used his head and let relationships grow from there.

"Neely placed two big orders, both online. That gives us two stores, and goddess only knows how many employees. Someone took the order, someone filled the order, and someone delivered the order." Thinking back, I made room for a third factor. "A courier service walked the orders up, but was it the same company both times? I can't remember."

"Yes." Linus shifted on his seat. "I recommended them as well. They're discreet and always on time."

Picking at the loose thread, I asked, "Who would know you use them?"

"Anyone who has business dealings with me as Scion Lawson. As the potentate, I hand-deliver what needs passing on, or I entrust the task to a member of my team."

"That leaves us with too many variables. We can't shorten our suspect list and still get home on time."

"I'm not staying behind." His blue-black stare dared me to suggest otherwise.

"Are you going to call Mary Alice?" I gestured to the wreckage. "She might appreciate the heads-up."

Proving our thoughts often traveled the same paths, he shook his head. "This happened right under her nose. Even if Clem hadn't splattered a vampire on the sidewalk outside her shop, she would have heard from one of her sources."

"There is that." Rorschach vampires did tend to send a rather specific message. "I'll send a floral arrangement."

Though Maud had never taught me which flower meant *sorry vampires blew out the side of your building.*

"Flowers are a nice touch. Let my team handle the rest." He gestured toward the monitors. "They'll touch base with us as they hunt down new leads or if they make progress on what we give them."

"Okay." I gusted out a long breath, grateful to be one step closer to home. "That works."

Not a perfect solution, but I would take an iffy one at this point and smile about it.

FOUR

Running short on time, we packed the van in a rush, including a man-shaped duffle with a rust-colored stain spreading across the bottom. After we strapped in, Linus placed a call to the cleaners. Though the job paid well, it was ugly work mopping up supernatural messes before human cops could get involved.

"I need you to send a text for me," Linus said, handing over his phone as he pulled into traffic.

One text turned out to be five as he arranged for a second rendezvous with his team through me.

This time, we met at Base Four instead of Base Two, which made me wonder how many of them he had secreted across the city.

With a hostage in tow, Clem providing an extra set of hands came in, well, handy.

Bishop wasn't thrilled we had acquired a third wheel, though his eyes glinted at the word *interrogation*, making me more curious than ever about what manner of supernatural creature he might be. But it was rude to ask, so I bided my time until I could bribe Linus for the details.

Deja vu spun my head as we entered Base Four and discovered it resembled Base Two right down to the squeaky castor on Bishop's worn desk chair. Had we not gained access from a different parking deck, on a different floor, on a different street, I would have assumed this was the same place. But that was crazy talk.

Right?

While I tucked our suitcases out of the way, Linus held the door for Clem, who carried our hostage, still in the duffle taken from the suite's closet, in a fireman's carry. How the duffle got there, or if there were more, I chose not to ask. Let alone how Linus knew where to find it. There are some questions best left unanswered.

"Let's get your friend down to the cell." Bishop opened a slim door that illuminated even narrower steps. "I have a one hundred percent success rate when it comes to extracting information." He winked at me. "I'll have your answers before dinner."

While I had no love for assassins, I was extremely tired of them. I wanted answers I could trust, and I wanted them fast. Lucky for our unconscious friend, there was an easier way to get them than letting Bishop have his fun.

Striving for diplomacy, I winked back at him. "Let me go first?"

"Are you sure?" Bishop rubbed his jaw. "Interrogations get ugly fast."

"I spent five years in Atramentous." Ice encased my heart at the memory. "Nothing is uglier than that."

Regret mingled with respect on his face. "Have at him."

With a tight nod to banish the ghosts of that dank, wet cell, I trailed Clem down two flights of stairs to a narrow room with a single cot, a toilet, and a sink. Linus and Bishop came down to watch the show, but it was a tight fit. Clem dumped his load on the mattress then looked to me for orders.

The pocket knife felt as warm as the blood I was about to spill when I palmed it, flicked open the blade, and cut deep. Liquid pooled in my cupped hand, and I used it as ink for the sigils I drew on the man's forehead.

No sooner had I completed the design than he gasped awake, eyes wild as they spun around the room.

Clem took the opportunity to cuff the prisoner's hands behind his back, then he attached a chain to the convenient anchor mounted on the wall for just that purpose.

"You're going to answer some questions for me." Despite his frantic struggles, I managed to line up the same truth sigils I had once used on Linus across both his cheeks. "There." Sitting back to admire my handiwork, I flushed at the pride on Linus's face. "Let's begin."

"I won't tell you anything."

Green.

Green meant he was telling the truth.

Guess I was going to have to be more persuasive.

Eyes closed, I sorted through the genetic memory passed down to me through generations of goddess-touched necromancers until I discovered a sigil that coerced the truth rather than verified it. With the design in the forefront of my mind, I opened my eyes and applied those across his forehead.

The change in his demeanor was instant. The fight drained out of him, and he slumped forward, relaxed.

I started him off easy. "Who do you work for?"

"I follow the money."

Green.

"Who paid you?"

He shook his head, tipped sideways. "No names."

Green.

With Clem's help, I propped him upright again. "That's all you've got?"

"They wanted proof." He blinked at me, eyes gone hazy. "Your head or your heart."

Green.

Linus drifted to my side, silent as a wraith. "How did you know where to find Grier?"

"Got the address an hour before via text."

Green.

Getting nowhere fast, I demanded, "Did they tell you why?"

"Questions cost time," he intoned with the cadence of a familiar mantra. "Time is money."

Green.

Frustrated, Bishop kicked the wall. "Can you kill the laser show, please?"

"Sure." We had verified his answers were true. There was no reason to keep testing them if it put Bishop more on edge. "There." I swiped the vampire's cheeks clean. "Happy?"

"Not as happy as I would be if I hadn't agreed to let you go first," he grumbled. "You're taking the fun out of it."

Clem huffed behind him. "As much as I hate to agree, he's right."

"Grier's methods are more effective." Linus smiled, just a tiny bit. "You can always try your hand with him after."

He passed judgment without a flicker of doubt, and I envied him that. Things hadn't been so black-and-white to me since finding myself on the other end of a life sentence.

"I can't think of anything else to ask," I admitted. "He doesn't know who hired him, what they wanted with me, or how they knew where to find me. Taking him was a waste of our time."

Bishop wet his lips. "Not a total waste."

Thinking my curiosity was about to be sated, I waited for him to elaborate, but he was busy staring down the prisoner like the man was prey who would bolt if given the opportunity.

"Don't kill him." Linus drew me toward the stairs. "Yet."

Linus and I left the vampire sitting in his cell, sedated by the sigil that had yet to wear off.

Color me surprised when both Clem and Bishop followed us back into the control room.

"We need to discuss our findings with the others," Linus explained at my confusion.

Or the lack thereof. We hadn't learned anything from him. All we had done was condemn him to a slower death than his fellows. Unless...

Waiting until we were all upstairs, I rapped on the door we had just shut. "Is this soundproof?"

Linus brushed his fingertips over the knob, checking that it was secure. "Yes."

"What if we plant a tracker on him, let Bishop rough him up a bit, then let him go and see what happens?"

"It's not the worst plan I've ever heard." Bishop cracked his knuckles. "His comrades will sweep him for bugs before they let him anywhere near their headquarters, but that doesn't mean I can't try my luck." He cut Linus a look. "Escaping from the potentate's clutches is rare enough to raise eyebrows." He shrugged. "At least with your head still attached."

"I was thinking a sigil." I rubbed reddish-brown flakes off my palm. "I could draw them on in a few places no one would think to look."

Linus, who wasn't the jealous kind, turned eyes gone black on me. "Where did you have in mind?"

Biting the inside of my cheek, I kept from smiling. "Maybe it's best you don't know."

I could tell he wanted to press the issue almost as much as he wanted to support my plan.

With a sharp inhale, he drained the darkness from his vision. "I'm sure you're right."

The skin on my palm had healed, but I could always pick the scab. "When should we get started?"

"Bishop." Linus took the out he had been given. "Escort Grier to the cell?"

Once I got down to it, the process was about as much fun as I expected, but at least it didn't take long.

Thankfully, with the vampire still zoned out, all the cleanup required afterward was a good handwashing.

"Between your sigils and my trackers," Bishop said, walking up the stairs behind me, "we make a good recon team."

"Any hope for a shower while we wait?" The clothes I had on were stained with blood and unpleasantness. "This isn't the first impression I wanted to make on the alpha."

We were closing in on six a.m. Two hours until our meeting. Two hours until Tisdale decided our fate.

"Bishop," Linus said as he woke the monitors, "show Grier to the bathroom, please."

While Linus presided over an on-screen meeting with the rest of the team, Bishop guided me to a large room stacked with enough bunk beds to sleep a dozen people. There was one en suite bathroom, but it was full-size, and it had two enclosed toilet stalls.

Clem shouldered in behind us, taking in the facilities with a sharp eye.

"Why bother with amenities when you're never all in one place at one time?"

"We break up domestic disputes and all sorts of ugly on the streets. Victims need safe places to stay, even when the shelters are full. We can partition the command center off, containing our guests in the residence area. That gives them access to the bunkroom, the bathroom, the kitchen, and the dining room. There's a lockbox we can activate as well for remote entry. That way, we don't see them, and they don't see us."

"Clever." It was just the sort of thing Linus would dream up, well, think up since he didn't sleep often.

"Linus built his own world within his city, back when he had nothing else." Bishop kept his voice pitched low. "Now he has you, and you're bigger than the world he imagined for himself."

"I don't know how we're going to manage," I admitted. "I can't abandon Savannah. It's my home, my whole life is there, but I would never ask him to leave all this."

Without understanding how potentates were elected, or selected, I wasn't sure he could set aside his mantle, even if he wanted to.

"You'll figure it out." He cocked his head, hearing something I had missed. "They're asking for me."

"I'll get cleaned up and be right out."

After Bishop left, Clem followed me into the bathroom, and we stood there for an awkward moment, jostling for space, before I caved. "Um, I don't think there's room for two?"

"You wouldn't be saying that if I had red hair and freckles."

I hid my blush by digging through the bags of supplies Neely had arranged for our doomed trip to see my grandmother and selected clothing fit for groveling. The tone ought to be fitting for the alpha, considering both women were leaders.

"Give me a minute." He shuffled me out the door and shut it behind him.

"All you had to do was ask if you needed to go." Worried he might decide to demonstrate his newfound aim, I elected to check and recheck my outfit choice. The toilet didn't flush, and no water came on, but Clem opened the door looking mighty pleased with himself. "What did I miss?"

"A camera and two tiny speakers." He opened his hand to reveal the small devices and the fine tangle of cords that had powered them. "I figured they would want to keep tabs on the occupants in a place like this."

"Thanks." A shiver blasted down my spine. "Bishop did say people let themselves in. I can see why they would want to protect their investment, even at the cost of their guests' privacy."

"People do all kinds of things in restrooms because they believe it's the one place no one is watching."

"Bishop won't be happy you broke his toys."

"What about Linus?" He closed his hand over the knot of electronics. "What will he be?"

"Not happy he didn't remember to warn me." I traded places with him. "Since this is Bishop's domain, Linus might not have known."

"It's possible," he allowed. "There are no trapdoors for you to fall through or secret passages that could swallow you whole. Even you should be able to manage getting clean without being kidnapped and/or murdered."

When he turned, I stuck my tongue out at his back. Too bad he caught my reflection in the mirror.

Fiddlesticks.

By the time I finished scrubbing myself clean, wrapped up in a surprisingly plush towel, and got my hair dried, a heated argument had broken out in the bunkroom. Tired of the bickering, I shoved open the door. "What's going on in here?"

"Bishop and Clem have a difference of opinion," Linus informed me, a cord dangling from his hand.

The towel earned a raised eyebrow and a more thorough examination that set off butterflies in my tummy.

"Your friend here could have asked me about the cameras, and I would have told him I already shut them down as a courtesy to you." Bishop made certain to look anywhere but at me. "He didn't have to rip the equipment out of the walls."

"I didn't rip anything." Clem swung the camera in a lazy circle by a single black wire. "I clipped each one, nice and tidy. You can reinstall them in ten minutes a pop if you'd stop crying and do the job."

The growl that revved up Bishop's throat was animalistic, and it sparked interest in Clem's eyes.

"You're not brawling in here," I warned before he threw the first kick. "Apologize to Bishop, Clem. Better yet, help him with the reinstallation. Maybe you can offer tips on better hiding places."

Linus shut his eyes, and it took me a second to grasp what I had said wrong.

"I didn't mean to imply you didn't place them well." I winced under Bishop's withering stare. "I just meant..."

"Go on." Clem waited. "Tell him what you really meant."

"You're not helping," I snarled between clenched teeth.

"I'm here to protect your ass, not kiss it."

"Out." I pointed at the door. "I need to get dressed, and you two need to cool off."

Not bothering to wait until they cleared the doorway, Clem and Bishop resumed their argument while Linus continued his referee duties.

Ten minutes later, I emerged in a navy pantsuit that matched the color of Linus's eyes. The cream blouse was thin to compensate for the trim jacket. I expected to sweat buckets, but Neely had proven his taste reigned supreme when I didn't so much as dew.

The matching jewelry I told myself was paste. They had to be. Otherwise the sapphire and diamond combo were going to cause tears to well and ruin the eye makeup I had applied with a light hand since I couldn't remember what went where and how much to use.

Linus, who had been watching the dominant gwyllgi on screen over Bishop's shoulder, glanced up when I walked into the control room, and the look in his eyes as he swept them down my body made me hot in ways I couldn't blame on the fabric.

"You clean up nice, Woolworth." Clem wolf-whistled at me. "What do you bet that fashion designer friend of yours packed a matching tie for Linus?"

"He's not a fashion designer." *Yet.* Give him time, money, and free rein, he might well become one. "But that does sound like a Neely thing to do." I caught Linus on his way to the bunkroom. "You don't have to put it on."

Either Linus had excellent natural taste, or he learned how to dress well as a protective measure during his formative years. Adhering to his mother's exacting standards while living under her roof had turned out a son whose polished appearance gave the impression that he must be a clotheshorse but, as evidenced by his acceptance of my often holey and ill-fitting wardrobe, was fashion blind outside of the rules hammered into him for himself.

Button-down shirts were casual for him, but ties were rare. I didn't want him to feel he had to change to please me, and I didn't just mean his outfit.

A shrug rolled through his shoulders. "I don't mind."

"He's actually going for that matchy-matchy crap," Clem marveled. "A guy like him...what he can do...who he is...and he gets his jollies matching his fiancée like you're teens about to head out to prom."

Eyes narrowed, I dared him to make an issue of it with Linus. "He knows the value of a good presentation."

While that was true, it wasn't the whole truth. The fact was, Linus enjoyed being included. It had been such a rare occasion in his life up until now, he leapt at the chance to belong. And when it came to an outward sign of belonging to me, he was a sucker for symbolism.

As I thought it, I groaned inwardly. I had just outlined my failures in the proposal department yet again.

Bishop flicked a glance toward the door leading down to the cell. "I'd better go plant the vamp before he wakes."

The vamp implied Bishop wasn't one, but dang it. I had manners. I would not ask him outright.

"I'll help," Clem volunteered, not sounding suspicious. At all.

After they left, I waited on Linus, who had decided to shower while he was at it by the sound of things, in the control room. "Anybody home?"

Three out of the four monitors showed movement, but there was no sound.

When no one answered, I claimed Bishop's chair, pulled out my phone, and texted Lethe.

Change of plans.

>>*I heard. Midas called earlier. Wimp. He could fight Mom, he just won't. He's such a momma's boy.*

Not that. Johan Marchand paid us a visit. Severine is dead, and so is that lead.

>> *Sorry to hear that. Not about her, but about the lead.*

You have a heart of gold.

>>*It's only gold plate. I had to up my game if I wanted to hang out with Dame FancyPants.*

That's not my name, and no one has ever called me that.

>>*To your face.*

I'm the least fancy pants dame in the history of the Society.

>>*You're fancy by association. Linus is a walking billboard for the Society. He ups your street cred.*

How are things in Savannah?

>>*Not great.*

We'll figure out something.

>>*The Society would cry about it, but we could burn the vamps out of their nest.*

An image of the Lyceum shrouded in smoke popped into my head, and I cringed. I had no love for city hall's secret subbasement. Nothing good had ever come of me going there—except for my proposal to Linus in its elevator. But I could respect its history, its value, and its symbolism.

The Lyceum was a bastion for necromantic arts, and its loss would cripple how other supernatural factions viewed us. Worse, it would prove Clarice Lawson couldn't hold on to the power she had so recently been granted. There would be a coup, likely more than one, and it would get bloody before it was done.

Savannah had bled enough for my grandfather. I wasn't about to let him rip open her very heart.

I'll touch base before we head home.

>>*Bring food.*

I already owe you donuts...

>>*That's dessert. I want something that bleeds.*

Fine. I'll see what I can do. It's going to be hard enough smuggling what I've got across the barricade.

The sentinels, who had been switched to rations served at their chow hall, would smell the fresh donuts and descend on us like locusts. Factor in fresh burgers or steaks, and we would have a riot on our hands. I had already decided to buy extra glazed to hand out, but meat got expensive fast when you multiplied it by those numbers.

Maybe Linus had a point. I was a wealthy woman, and those men and women were serving their community. They deserved what little reward I could give them.

Linus is calling me. Gotta go.

>>Liar.

>>MOO.

With that text handled, I shot Amelie an update to let her know to expect us back early so she could tell Woolly, who would inform Oscar.

Despite our trip sucking royally so far, Linus had arranged for the first shipment of nonperishable food items to be delivered to Woolly ahead of schedule. According to Amelie, she expected to have the first deliveries prepped and ready to go once the bottled water arrived.

After that, I checked in with Neely, who had volunteered for packing duty and was dragging Cruz along.

Marit had also pitched her hat in the ring and was supervising while the gwyllgi unloaded the truck. The pictures of taut biceps she forwarded, I ignored. The abs got deleted. When the pictures started following happy trails, I cut off my phone.

Still, a warm glow ignited in my chest when I thought of my friends working together for a cause that impacted us all, human and necromancer alike. The uninitiated citizens of Savannah might be aware they were barreling toward a crisis, but they had no clue what it was or who had orchestrated it. I was lucky enough to have friends unafraid of opening their eyes to the reality of our worlds, how they intersected and often collided.

"We're at your disposal as well, you know."

Jolted by the intrusion into my thoughts, I glanced around. "Are you talking to me?"

"Whatever we can do to help," Anca reiterated, "we're happy to do so. For Linus. He's such a dear man, and he's given so much to us all."

About to do the polite thing and wave off her offer, I hesitated to first consider. "Can you track books?"

"I assume you mean rare and expensive tomes, not quarter finds at the bargain bin."

"Rare, yes. Expensive..." The blood drained from my cheeks, leaving me cold. "The information they contain is priceless, but I don't think they were sold. I believe they were donated."

The note from Severine hadn't given me much to go on, but I had a gut feeling she hadn't accepted cash for the transaction. No, she had been paid in spite. Buckets of it.

"That muddies things. Unless provenance is a concern, which is more often the case with a purchase and not a donation, there is little paperwork to form a trail to follow." She hummed low in her throat. "Do you have the seller's information?"

Without making a conscious decision to do so, I sought out Linus for support he was too distant to offer.

I had to make this call alone. He wouldn't have brought me here if he didn't trust these people, so I would show a little faith too. "Severine Marchand."

"Oh, dear." Anca brought her fingers to her lips. "Your grandmother. I can guess what she gifted, but gods. The possibilities. A woman in her position, in possession of that particular information..."

"You've brought the term goddess-touched back in vogue," Milo chimed in, his monitor flickering. "You and your kind were a well-kept secret until the ball. Now those who didn't know are learning all they can, and those who had forgotten are remembering what you can do. There have been few goddess-touched necromancers named in what remains of our history on the subject. You'll be the first in modern times, and having your face out there... It's going to be tough. People will want you to perform miracles for them, and some won't stop with paying for a one-time service. They'll want to own you exclusively. They'll want all rights to your designs, your services, your everything."

"I'm beginning to see why Maud kept her secrets," I admitted, and it was a bitter confession.

As much as I wanted to continue railing against her memory,

discovering Cletus's true identity had burst my self-righteous bubble. I was so much in need of Maud's forgiveness for trapping her in a wraith's existence it was hard working up the mad to call in my own markers. She had done what she thought was best for me. I could see that now.

While her efforts had stunted my growth as a necromancer, they had also allowed me to live a normal life. Well, as normal as any High Society darling's life ever was when their adoptive mother was Maud Woolworth. The fact was, if she hadn't been murdered, and if I hadn't been blamed, I might have lived my entire life certain I was a no-talent hack. I would have kept to my wards, my small magics, and let my pedigree go to waste.

A Marchand raised by a Woolworth. The Society had expected great things to come of that combination, just as my grandmother's letter claimed. Two prominent names, two powerful bloodlines. I should have been a rising star instead of a falling one.

"Secrets?" Linus eased into the room. "Whose secrets are we sharing?"

"Maud's." A twin pang of loss moved through me as his features tightened before he schooled them back into neutral lines. "I was saying I understand her better now."

"Hindsight." Joining me, he rested a cool hand on my shoulder and curled a strand of hair around his long finger. "It's like spending months painting a mural, focused on the individual details and small sections of your canvas. You spend all that time pursuing one goal: completion. You develop tunnel vision where you see only what's in front of you. And when your last brushstroke is done and you step back for the final time, you get your first complete look at what all those hours and days bought you."

"*But,*" I pointed out, "you can touch up a mural. You can correct imperfections. The past is what it is. There's no changing it. We can step back and take it all in, soak in the details we missed at the time or didn't assign enough importance, but that's all we can do. Reflect and regret."

"Perhaps I should have compared it to a timed quiz. Once the pencils are down, it's done. All that singular focus on each individual question evaporates, and you're left sweating the results of the whole."

"Let's stick with the mural analogy." A pained groan rose in me. "Your quizzes are brutal."

"You quizzed her?" Milo chortled. "That's hardcore." His shoulders bounced. "Let me guess. Anatomy?"

"Make it stop." I turned my face into Linus. "Please."

Amusement laced his tone. "Aside from our curriculum—"

"—which did not include anatomy lessons," I grumbled against his side.

"—what were you discussing before I interrupted?"

Uncomfortable with asking a favor of a stranger, despite my earlier resolve, I wriggled in my chair. "Anca offered to help locate Severine's missing collection."

Aware of what the admission cost me, he squeezed my shoulder for support. "She's a talented researcher. If anyone can uncover its location, it's Anca."

Milo cleared his throat then attempted to mimic Linus. "That Milo chap is a right golden egg too."

"A right golden egg?" Linus shifted his weight toward the monitors. "I don't talk like that."

"You're going too heavy on the Brit," Anca agreed. "Linus doesn't use British lingo, assuming that's what accent you were butchering."

"The sun's coming up," Bishop spoke over them, and I started at his voice. "Time for me to crash."

Curious if biology or scheduling was the reason, I glanced back at him. "You're bleeding."

"You told us to get square." Clem entered behind him, also bloodied. "Now we're good."

Suddenly, their decision to work together to deliver the vampire assassin to his home made a lot more sense.

"Make no apologies," multiple voices chorused to Bishop from the screens.

"Survive," he answered, then exited through the door we entered with a wave over his shoulder.

Hearing Maud's credo adopted and adapted by them...

I ducked my head and brushed away tears, grateful Linus had ensured her words lived on outside of us.

"I should be going too." Anca covered a delicate yawn. "You'll be gone by the time I come back online, but I'll stay in touch and update you on my progress."

Stifling my own yawn, ready to get this show on the road, I smiled. "I'd appreciate that."

"Thanks for offering to help," Milo parroted my voice. "Your big, strong man brain is such an asset to the team."

"You got the *asset* part right," Anca countered, her screen going dark before he got in a parting shot.

"I get no respect," Milo pouted in his own voice. "None."

"Thank you, Milo," I said obligingly, "for offering to help."

"You didn't mention my big, strong man brain, but it's still more credit than these losers give me." With a final sniff, he blacked his screen.

"They like you." Linus took my hands and drew me to my feet. "I knew they would."

"They're loyal to *you*." I cozied against him when he wrapped his arm around my shoulders. "Anything they're feeling for me is spillover from that. They want to help me, because it helps you." I rose on my tiptoes and pressed a kiss to the underside of his jaw. "They see you too, Linus. They know you're a good man, and they trust you to lead them."

The sigh he pushed out wasn't agreement, but at least it wasn't argument either. Maybe he was starting to come around to the idea he was more than he ever imagined himself to be, and that it had nothing to do with his money, his name, or his titles. He was a remarkable man because of his heart, his mind, and the simple kind-ness and thoughtfulness that came so easily to him.

How the Grande Dame managed to raise him boggled the mind. Then again, he had more or less raised himself, with help from her staff. Not that he would admit it, but that fit too. He had made himself what he was, and what he was, I found extraordinary.

Clem, never a fan of PDA, grunted, "How do I track pulp-for-face?"

The failed vampire assassin had been released back into the wild with trackers in his clothes and on his person. Bishop had taken care to plant one or two for him to find so he would begin to relax, thinking he was in the clear. As expected, he located and smashed the obvious devices. However, he missed one. As long as it kept going, I wouldn't have to resort to bleeding for answers.

"He isn't moving." Linus pulled up an aerial map of the city with a red dot blinking over an apartment building that had seen better days. "Either he hasn't been contacted with a new assignment, or he's afraid to get caught out in the open." The tracking sigil would have terminated if, well, *he* had been terminated. "He knows it won't look good for him walking out of here alive. He won't even be able to tell them where *here* is, which means he has no bargaining chip to earn his way back into their good graces."

"I'll keep an eye on him," Clem offered, settling in. "Might as well be productive."

The pack hadn't extended an invitation to cover three, so we weren't risking a plus one.

Leaving Clem to amuse himself in the control room, Linus and I got in the van he expertly guided into the early traffic already promising a miserable morning commute.

Smoothing my thumb over my phone's screen, I wondered, "How long do we have?"

"Between twenty minutes and three hours," he said, smiling, "depending on construction, the number of wrecks, lane and ramp closures, and general congestion."

How the prospect of sitting in bumper-to-bumper traffic made his eyes dance was beyond me.

Ignoring his obvious love for this city, a skill I was perfecting the longer he stayed in Savannah with me, I dialed up a guaranteed distraction, hoping she might offer us insight into the pack's militarization tactics now that my tactical-minded other half was present for consulting.

"I don't like this," Lethe growled in my ear from the comfort of my couch in Woolworth House after I explained the situation. "I talked to Mom yesterday, and she didn't breathe a word about this. When the pack goes on the offensive, it's protocol to alert all members, even those not in residence. Especially the freaking beta. She slipped this past me on purpose, which means she wanted to get the drop on you. I can't advise you if I don't know what the hell is going on."

"Do you think Linus is in any danger?"

A snort escaped her. "Not with you by his side."

The flare of pride at being considered formidable by a predator of her caliber gave me a case of the warm and fuzzies. "I protect what's mine."

"Pups." She sniffled. "They grow up so fast."

"I'm not actually a puppy." Though I wasn't sure how long gwyllgi lived, or how old Lethe and Hood were for that matter. With fae in their lineage, they could be old. Seriously old. "I'm a grown woman."

"How were you not born gwyllgi?" As usual, she totally ignored me. "You've got the killer instinct and the stomach for it."

The abundance of compliments made me wonder if pregnancy hormones weren't to blame for her effusive, by Lethe standards, praise. But I wasn't stupid enough to even hint I might suspect as much.

Since the clock was ticking, I asked, "Can I talk to your other half?"

"Sure." Without putting down the receiver, she yelled, "*Hood.* Grier wants to talk to you."

A few seconds later, ears ringing, I overheard his hello kiss to his mate then he answered, "Hey."

"We might have a problem." Briefly, I outlined the issues. "I told Lethe, but she seems..."

"Like she's caught a case of the weepy-gooeys?"

"I'm not sure I've ever heard it called that, but sure. She's sniffling and very mushy."

"It's probably the H word neither of us are dumb enough to use. Otherwise, she seems fine."

A peculiar note in his tone had me asking, "What aren't you telling me?"

"She attempted to knit the baby a pair of booties."

"Aww. That's sweet."

"She got mad at the yarn, muttered something about it defying her, and hurled it across the room. It kind of...hit the birdcage."

"Oh goddess." I pressed a hand over my heart. "Is Keet okay?"

He might be undead, but he still had feelings.

"Lethe has been watching old Disney movies with him so he doesn't get lonely. The yarn was this off-white shade, and I guess he decided to reenact that scene with the two dogs and the spaghetti?"

I dropped my head into my hands. "And?"

"He bit off a long string and offered it to Lethe. Except, she didn't take it. She opened the cage and made a grab for him. It scared him so bad, he dropped the string and flew past her. But he saw the ball of yarn on the floor and snagged the loose end."

"Go on." I sighed. "Tell me the rest."

"He flew around the chandelier a few times and now it looks like drunk teens TP'd the whole thing. And while he was up there, out of reach, he might have eaten several inches of yarn. We lured him down with lunch meat, but he's been pooping string ever since. We didn't know if we should just let it kind of hang there or cut it—"

"*Dowhateveryouthinkisbest,*" I blurted in a rush to avoid hearing more details. "I trust your judgment."

A tiny roar belted out in the background, and Hood cleared his throat. "They're watching *The Lion King*."

"Tell Lethe to keep an eye on him. He might decide Scar is cooler than Simba, and then we'll all be in trouble."

"Your bird farted." He paused. "Can they do that?"

"Just how much yarn did he eat?"

"He's a warthog," Lethe yelled in the background. "Tapumba? Pumon? I can't remember."

"Gassy warthogs are better than homicidal lions," I decided. "But I'm really going now. We can't afford to be late."

Pressing the end button, I drew in a breath and nearly jumped out of my skin when Linus touched my shoulder.

Searching my face, he must have read my exhaustion, which was only partially to blame on lack of sleep. "Did Lethe offer any insight?"

"Not so much. But she did let Keet eat an undetermined amount of yarn, and she's apparently taught him to fart like a cartoon warthog. Those two things do not mix well, and I worry about the state of the house when we return. Woolly may need to be decontaminated after this."

"The appeal of the needles I could understand," he said, his eyebrows winging higher, "but yarn? Lethe attempted to knit?"

"We need to introduce her to Etsy," I decided. "Let her buy what she wants from qualified crafters able to do the job with minimum casualties."

"Just make sure you set her up an account first. Don't give her access to yours."

Unable to resist, I leaned over and planted a smacking kiss on his forehead, right where his frown lines gathered. "I like you."

"I first suspected when you asked me to spend the rest of my life with you."

Backing away, I shook my head. "That was your first clue?"

"That was the first time it felt..." he said softly, "...*real*."

Staring at the simple metal strand circling his finger, I felt ashamed all over again for not doing better by him. The man had bought a building for me, had taken steps to give me back some of what I had lost by urging me to start my own ghost tour company, and I had given him...a bread tie. "Linus?"

There was a slight hesitation I hoped to one day erase. "Yes?"

"You're not getting rid of me."

The earnestness of his expression when he glanced over at me tore at my heart. "I hope not."

"Hope has nothing to do with it. I proposed, you accepted. You're stuck with me. For life."

"Mine." The wonder of it flavored his tone. "For life."

"Yep." I brought his hand to my mouth and kissed his ring finger. "All mine. For-basically-ever."

FIVE

The den of the Atlanta gwyllgi pack was and wasn't what I expected. Lethe and Hood were happy to shift and sleep out in the woods in Savannah. That seeded the expectation they were used to roughing it. Though I'm not sure you could call it that when their primal souls were most at peace in the outdoors. And, being from the city, they were taking full advantage of having acreage to run and hunt at their leisure.

But the Atlanta pack paid homage to both sides of their dual natures. A modern glass and metal sculpture some might call a house rose from a lawn that would have made this address the pride and joy of any homeowners' association. Its ruthless uniformity must have required gardeners to get down on their hands and knees to measure the individual blades. Beyond the house, an overgrown meadow sprawled, its wild carpet leading into a forest thick with trees and heavy with undergrowth.

For the first time, I understood why Atlanta was sometimes called a city in the forest.

Given the dress code, I assumed Linus meant for us to conduct our business inside the sculpture, and he did park at the side of the house. But after he got the van door for me, we took a flagstone path cutting through the tame front property to brave the encroaching wilderness.

Unnerved by the sensation of so many unseen eyes on me, I struck up a conversation. "Do you often conduct business out here?"

"Tisdale prefers to meet downtown. Gwyllgi aren't tolerant of outsiders in their personal space. I've only been invited to join her at the den once, the day after I assumed the position of potentate."

"A power play." Invite him out, show him the house that meant they had money and taste, the land that indulged their primal needs, and the somewhat isolated location that meant no one was getting through her sentries to offer help without her permission. "I assume it went well?"

"As well as can be expected, given the present circumstances." The mask of Scion Lawson blanketed his features, and he looked at me through eyes gone distant. "Prepare yourself."

Taking my cue from him, I donned my Dame Woolworth persona with more ease than I would like to admit. After working the ghost tour circuit, I had gotten entirely too comfortable with showing customers the face they wanted to see, even when they were shouting about refunds or the lack of ghosts.

The trek to our rendezvous point lent our procession the air of marching into battle, and I regretted the only weapon I had on me was the pocket knife I was never without. But power ran in my veins, and I was never defenseless as long as I had means to call it forth.

Eventually, a small seating area came into view. Pavers laid out a design a dozen feet in either direction of the slender woman swinging from an egg chair suspended from a gnarled limb over her head. I would have recognized her as Lethe's mother, even without expecting to see her. Only a smattering of lines and freckles distinguished them from one another. That and the silver hair spilling around her shoulders. She wore a sleeveless top cut to fit her narrow build and capris I had no doubt had been tailored to her petite frame as well. Her feet were bare and dirty, but her nails matched her outfit. The only piece of jewelry she wore was a battered locket strung from a chain thick enough to be a collar.

"Ah." She rose in a languid stretch of muscle designed to draw the eye, and it worked. I saw at once she was fit, trim, and in fighting shape. The color of her hair might date her, but age was only a number. This woman was in her prime. "You must be Grier." Her gaze slid past my shoulder. "Linus, always a pleasure."

"It's good to see you, Tisdale. Thank you for welcoming us to your home." Tone light, he smiled his Scion Lawson smile. Polite. Empty. Bored. "The grounds are even lovelier than I recalled from my last visit."

"We have five students enrolled in Auburn University's College of Agriculture. Thanks to their education, we have a farm, gardens, and a landscaping business." Pride widened her smile. "The teens even started a lawn care service to earn money during the summer months."

Appearing mildly interested, he nonetheless made a sound of approval. "You're diversifying."

"We're only carnivores half our lives. The rest of the time, we enjoy our fried green tomatoes like every other Southerner." She indicated a stone bench for us to sit on while she reclaimed her much comfier chair. "But you're not here to talk about our adventures in agriculture. You want to ask me for a favor." Her assessing gaze swept over me. "And I wanted an opportunity to meet the woman my heir is so enamored with that she refused a summons home to remain by her side. I'm curious what about you inspires her loyalty when she has never given it to anyone else."

Unhappy to find myself the center of her attention, I held firm and resisted the urge to fidget.

"I didn't request for Lethe to remain in Savannah. I would never presume, given her status as your heir. But her mate insists he owes me a debt of honor, and I accepted their offer rather than insult the pack."

A snarl churned up her throat, and her upper lip quivered with annoyance that dumped adrenaline in my veins.

"This isn't you." She pushed off the pavers with her toes to keep up the rocking motion. "Lethe wouldn't align herself with a High Society mannequin. There's more to you than glossy manners and a vacant smile, there must be. My daughter is a dominant, and she would only respect the same. Not this simpering façade of the Society ideal."

Determined to be civil in the face of insult, I bit the inside of my cheek.

"Be yourself with me, as you are with her, and I'll return the favor." Tisdale forced eye contact. "Keep up the charade, and you'll have to hope you can see through mine as easily as I saw through yours."

Checking my intentions with Linus would give the appearance that he held sway over me, and a woman like Tisdale, an alpha, wouldn't respect that. Holding her stare, I peeled off the mask and breathed a sigh of relief. And then I told her the truth.

"Your daughter is my friend because I feed her as much as she wants, whenever she wants." Basically, a lot and often was the magic combination. "She's memorized my debit card number and security code, so she mostly feeds herself and charges it to me. Sometimes she remembers to thank me. Sometimes I just find greasy receipts on the kitchen table as a heads-up so I won't faint if I check my bank balance."

Laughter rumbling through her chest, she smiled. "Now that sounds like my little girl."

"I didn't ask her to stay in Savannah, but I'm grateful she did. We need her. *I* need her."

Expression unreadable, she pressed, "And my son-in-law?"

"Hood treats Lethe like a princess, and me like family. He's one of the best men I know."

"And the baby?" Leaning forward, she planted both feet on the ground. "Do you think I don't know what you did?"

Unused to being frank about my gifts, I kept my mouth shut and let her tell me what she thought she knew.

"You saved my granddaughter's life." A liquid sheen covered her eyes. "You saved my daughter's life too."

"I made a mess of things." Hit fast-forward on gestation in my fumbling attempt to save them both. "But I would do it again. In a heartbeat."

A dominance fight could last until submission or death. It was left to the combatants to decide.

Ernst Weber, the gwyllgi who challenged Lethe for second in the pack, lost the fight after submitting, and then committed suicide by going for her gently swollen belly afterward. A move that had cost him his life, at my hands.

I healed Lethe, and through her, saved the baby, giving the unborn child a boost in the process. Much like Boaz and his regenerated leg, we had no clue what long-term effects to expect, but it mattered more to all of us that there would be a long term to worry about in the first place.

"I understand Hood made you pack because of the debt he feels is owed to you," she said, "and that Lethe and Midas agreed to this unorthodox arrangement."

Squaring my shoulders, I sat up straighter. "I am a member of the Kinase pack, yes."

"A member of the Savannah Kinase pack at any rate," she murmured. "Midas?"

Her golden child loped into the seating area from the forest with a reassuring smile for me.

She patted his arm when he came to stand beside her chair. "You claim this woman as pack?"

"I do."

"No, you don't." Steel entered her voice. "Rebuke her. Sever her ties to the Atlanta pack, here and now. Her allies belong in Savannah, with her, not in Atlanta, with me."

A tremor worked through his jaw, the damning words threatening to spill, but he held them in.

"Enough." I leapt to my feet. "I'll sever ties with the Atlanta pack if you want, but you leave him alone." I couldn't stop from glancing at his arms, those crosshatch scars that would never fade, from his skin or his memory. "I won't let you inflict more pain on him, not on my account."

"You won't *let* me?" A surprised laugh escaped her. "I suppose you'll have the potentate take my head?"

"Grier fights her own battles," Linus told her, sliding into his darker persona. "She's a powerful necromancer in her own right. She doesn't need me to shield her." He placed a hand over his left pectoral, where I had drawn his sigil for the day. "In fact, she is often mine."

"I require absolute loyalty from my heir, however temporary the designation may be in your case," Tisdale growled at Midas. "You can't serve two packs or live in two cities. You must choose."

Sweat beaded on Midas's forehead, but he held firm. Eyes on mine, he shook off her order. "No."

Tisdale stood slowly, unfurling to her full height, and circled in front of him. "No?"

"Grier is pack, and pack bonds don't break. You taught me that. Atlanta is my home, but if Savannah needs me, if Grier needs me, I will go." A crimson sheen veiled his eyes. "And then I'll come back, with or without your permission, and take my place within *our* pack."

Expecting an explosion of teeth and claws, I rocked forward onto the balls of my feet, ready to intervene if she drew first blood and didn't stop there. But rather than snarl and snap, Tisdale threw her arms around his shoulders.

"My sweet, sweet boy." She drew back, grinning wide. "I knew you had it in you."

Leaning in to Linus, I whispered, "What did I miss?"

"The passing of a mantle, it appears." Intrigue pried up the edges of his mask, a testament to the rarity of the event, let alone the fact it had been witnessed by outsiders. "Midas disobeyed a direct order from his alpha while holding her stare. That makes him the new heir. Lethe will have to fight him for second in the pack when, or if, she returns."

When Tisdale turned back to us, Midas closed his eyes, his expression more desolate than usual.

Awe might have been the appropriate response, but I couldn't stand how his shoulders bowed under the full weight of his choice.

"You used me." The words shot out before I could call them back, and I wouldn't have even if a do-over were possible. "You brought me here to provoke Midas." A pitiful excuse for a snarl rattled in the back of my throat. "You forced this on him."

"You cost me one heir," Tisdale said, shrugging. "And now you've provided me with another. I would say this makes us even."

Rage vibrated through me until I shook with the itch to open a vein and paint terrible retribution on my skin. But that would make me the same as Lacroix, and I refused to follow in his footsteps.

"Even," I repeated, awed by her gall. Midas had sacrificed his autonomy, for me and for Lethe, while she looked like the cat who ate the canary. Since she valued frankness, I laid it on her. "What about Savannah?"

With Midas keeping her in the loop, she knew exactly why we had come here.

And now we knew why she had agreed to this meeting and demanded it take place in person.

"I'm not sending more of my people to Savannah." She attempted to soften the blow by rearranging her features from smug to smug-lite. "You've got my daughter, my son-in-law, and over a dozen gwyllgi who defected to join her, including some of my best fighters." She toyed with the locket around her neck. "That's all I can spare."

Unable to control my temper, I snapped, "You've spared plenty to roam the streets of Atlanta."

"The reason there's a stronger enforcer presence in the city is I have more cause than ever to see our current potentate retain his position. Our pack has enjoyed several years of peace with other supernatural factions thanks to his careful handling. I would like that to continue. And, with Midas as my heir and you under his protection, there's not a single objection anyone can raise."

Tremors set my fingers twitching in the outline of sigils with purposes I didn't know or want to know. I made a fist to keep from giving them life. "This meeting is over."

"Grier..." Midas took a step toward me. "I didn't know this was why she brought you here."

"I'm an old pro at being manipulated by a parent." Maud had been a master of the art. "I won't hold this against you." I cut my eyes toward his mother. "Don't wield my friendship as a blade to cut him again, or you'll find out there are few actions in service to a friend that I regret."

Make no apologies for surviving.

I wasn't about to start now.

"Your fiancée just threatened me." Tisdale arched a brow at Linus. "That's hardly diplomatic of her."

"You baited this trap," he said coolly. "I can't help if you didn't snatch your hand back fast enough." Taking my elbow, he tipped his chin at Midas. "Congratulations, or condolences. I'm never sure which is the appropriate response in these situations."

The skin around Midas's eyes crinkled in the promise of a smile that never made it to his lips. "Thanks."

I noticed he didn't claim victory or defeat, but I could see what this interlude had cost him.

His freedom.

While he might have forgiven me for the role I played, I wasn't so sure Lethe would be as understanding when I had just cost her the position of second in the Atlanta pack, a title she had killed to maintain.

Fiddlesticks.

There might not be enough donuts in the world to make up for this.

SIX

After leaving the gwyllgi pack home, me with my tail tucked between my legs, we secured more supplies and directed the distributors to offload them at Woolworth House.

Finally, *finally*, it was time to return home. As soon as we picked up Clem, who had been using Bishop's setup to watch cartoons, from Base Four.

Ignoring the bowl of cereal that made my stomach growl, I searched the blank tracking screen. "Vampire watch got boring?"

"There's no longer a vampire to watch unless your sigil turned this one flame retardant. He took a long walk right into the sun. I'm guessing his assassin buddies finally got around to cleaning house."

And if they were busy erasing leads, they would make sure there was nothing to find in his apartment, even if we made a pit stop on our way home to search it.

"There goes that lead." The more we caught, the faster they slipped through our fingers. "Great." Pushing what had been a long shot out of my mind, I focused on my friend and what was best for him. "Are you sure you want to go back to Savannah?"

"It can't be more dangerous than Raleigh," he pointed out. "I should be safer there." He turned off the monitor then walked his dishes into the kitchen. "Maybe Boaz can help me get a commission with the sentinels again, as Clem."

As loathe as I was to ask for favors, I would make an exception for him. The Grande Dame drove tough bargains, but she might be his best chance for reinstatement if Boaz struck out. "Let me know what he says."

While Mr. Hacohen was drawing up contracts for my household, I could draft Clem as personal security if the sentinels wouldn't take him back on agreeable terms.

Gratitude on his face, Clem let a shrug roll through his shoulders. "I'll do that."

"I'll grab our bags." Linus started for the bunkroom then turned to Clem. "Give me a hand?"

"Sure."

Once they left, I claimed Bishop's seat. "Anybody home?"

"For a few minutes," a disembodied voice replied. "I pulled dayshift this week, so I have to get jumping."

I tallied her position to come up with a name. "Lisbeth, right?"

"Yep." Keys clacked in the background without missing a beat. "What can I do you for?"

Checking to make sure the guys were gone, I explained what I needed in exact detail. "So, can you help me?"

"Oh, you came to the right girl. I got you." A printer came alive nearby and spit out two sheets filled with names, phone numbers, and various other information. "These guys—and girl—are the best in the city."

"Thanks." I snatched the papers, folded them tight, then shoved them in my pocket. "Can I ask for another favor?"

"I won't tell him." Her arm raised in a vague gesture. "My lips are zipped."

"I have to go." I backed away from the monitors. "Thanks again."

"See you around, Grier."

The screen went dark before I could wave, and then Linus was there.

"I thought I heard voices." He examined the empty screens. "Were you checking in with Lethe?"

"Just chatting with Lisbeth." Eager to make my escape before I compounded my white lie, I nudged him and Clem out the exit and into the parking garage.

Clem climbed in the back of the van, and I sat beside Linus, knee bouncing in my eagerness to get going.

With Atlanta nearly in the rearview mirror, Linus aimed us toward the legendary Clancy's Bakery.

Much to my shame, I was too sleepy to steal a single donut from the orders I had promised Lethe.

Not that it stopped me from holding them on my lap and inhaling like a diver finally come to the surface.

Once the orders I placed for the sentinels filled the cargo hold and most of the backseat, Linus aimed us toward home, sweet home. Just the knowledge I would see Woolly and everyone else again in a few hours soothed me enough I fell asleep with my cheek pressed to the cool glass and Linus's equally cool hand on my thigh.

THE UNIVERSE MUST HAVE FELT it owed us an apology for the last twenty-four hours. The trip back to Savannah passed quickly and without incident, the parts I was conscious for anyway. We hit the barricade, handed out donuts to everyone on duty, and left more for those who would come on next.

With that bit of gratitude doled out, we climbed into the SUV waiting to carry us to Woolworth House.

Our new clothes, toiletries, and even the van, all safe behind a ward, would be retrieved later.

With the three of us settled, the driver-side door opened, and Boaz swung himself in behind the wheel.

"Have a nice trip?" He met my eyes in the rearview mirror. "Any trouble in Atlanta?"

"There's *always* trouble in Atlanta."

Boaz grunted agreement. "Who's your friend?"

"Oh, yes. My, uh, friend." I patted Clem on the shoulder. "Say hello to Jake Clemmons."

Boaz whipped his head toward us. "Taz?"

Eyes rounding, I jerked in my seat. "How did you...?"

"Jake Clemmons was the birthname of one of the most famous black cowboys, well, ever. The Hollywood version anyway. I caught one of his movies on the classics channel Amelie was addicted to as a kid and got hooked on westerns. We watched them in the barracks during our downtime."

Ah. That explained Clem's earlier smugness. Other sentinels would be in on the joke, and Taz would be able to reconnect with her close friends through Clem.

"Where's Becky?" I hadn't noticed her in line for free donuts. "I didn't see her."

"Lacroix drafted her for a special mission." His hands tightened on the wheel. "She left last night."

Linus set aside his distaste for Boaz long enough to ask, "Anything we should worry about?"

The muscles in the back of Boaz's neck bunched and flexed, but he didn't voice whatever thoughts had twisted his expression into mulish lines. "No, but we'll update you if that changes."

Eager to take the focus off Linus, I blurted, "What about the rest of your guys?"

"They're tailing us." He pulled onto the road. "Our last trip taught us a valuable lesson about putting all our eggs in one basket. Granted, splitting up isn't half as effective when the two most valuable targets refuse to be separated, but at least this way we'll have transpo if this ride gets blown sky-high."

"You can't blame us when you didn't ask in the first place."

A derisive snort blasted out of him. "Which one of you would have volunteered to ride with me?"

Habit almost tricked me into claiming the honor, but I was still mad enough at Boaz to not want to be alone with him anytime soon. He would want to talk, and I didn't want to hear him out. I wanted to put our history behind me and do what I did best. Pretend everything was fine.

"Savannah was standing long before us, and she'll be here long after we're gone," Boaz said a few minutes later, as we passed the blacked-out hulls of stores emptied by looters. His wistful tone made me wonder if he meant to put voice to thought when he asked, "Do you ever think about leaving?"

"No."

Woolly was here. My friends were here. And even if Linus's future was in Atlanta...mine wasn't.

His city might not be alive in the same sense as Woolly, but Atlanta pitched a hissy each time I visited, it seemed. Nothing good ever came from my trips there. If I didn't know better, I would swear she was trying to get rid of me. But that was crazy talk. Right?

We arrived at Woolworth House before my paranoia could fully blossom, and she zinged a welcome into my head that felt like my skull was a bell and her exuberance the clapper.

Twilight had fallen during our drive, a twinkling curtain that made it possible to see the lightning bugs flash against a starry backdrop.

Clusters of my diurnal friends, almost done for the day, worked alongside my nocturnal ones, who were just getting their night started.

Tables had been set up, and most were stacked with boxes of food and supplies. Together, they loaded trucks and crosschecked lists. The three groups functioned as a single unit, and I wasn't sure how much was the result of Lethe and Hood's leadership versus the banding together of a community to support its own during a time of crisis, but I was moved to tears all the same.

From here, I could see Amelie seated on the porch, as close to the action as she could get without leaving the house. A clipboard filled her lap, and she called out questions to nearby volunteers before marking down their answers on a form.

Wasting no time, Boaz headed straight for her to say his goodbyes before reporting in.

With any luck, Woolly would be in a good enough mood to allow them a hug. As long as Amelie remained on the bottom step, and he didn't get closer than the length of her arms.

"Clem," I said, resting my hand on his shoulder, "before you report to the sentinels, I have a mission for you."

After I explained the Corbin situation to him, his face lit up with glee. "I'm on it."

"Don't kill more vampires than you have to," I reminded him. "Corbin believes they're all there willingly, but we can't verify that without more information."

"I won't kill more than necessary," he promised, which was not the same thing at all.

About to point that out, I groaned when he yanked open the door and took off at a run for the trees.

Linus, though clearly amused, was smart enough not to comment on my shaky leadership skills.

Summoning Cletus required a concentrated effort with my attention so divided, but I finally managed.

The wraith drifted, expectant. The fabric of his tattered cloak rustled on an unseen breeze.

"Tell Corbin we're coming for him if you can." I touched the wraith's bony hand. "If you can't reach him, keep an eye out for Clem. Help him break Corbin out, then get back to Woolworth House, all of you, whatever it takes."

A low moan confirmed he was on board, and he dissipated to resume his watch over my progeny.

Loaded down with sugary bribes, I stepped onto the lawn and into the chaos.

"*Grier.*"

A ball of excited ghost boy smacked into my knees, and I staggered back. "Oomph."

"You're back." Oscar climbed up to settle on my hip. "Early."

Unable to resist those black eyes shining up at me with such joy, I juggled my boxes and gave him a quick hug as discreetly as possible. "Yep." Releasing him, I let him hover on his own. "Remember, you have to keep a low profile around this crowd."

Boaz in particular would sniff out Oscar if we weren't more careful. With everything else going on, Oscar ought to be safer than ever, but I didn't want to take any chances when it came to the Elite. The dybbuk incident might have blown over, but he was unique thanks to my blood. Much like Cletus, I had to keep their differences a secret in order to protect them.

Sentient wraiths might never catch on, but restoring ghosts to their former selves?

The psychic and medium trade raked in millions of dollars annually, and that was only the Society's take. Humans dabbled too. Most of them were con artists, but a few with diluted supernatural blood in their heritage were legit. And that didn't take into account the other factions with divination powers.

But there was a vast difference between hiring someone to talk to your great aunt so-and-so's ghost and having her chat you up in the kitchen, having her *remember*. Oscar wasn't a mindless loop. He was a thinking, feeling child. Time had matured him in some ways, and it had altered him in others, but I would have whipped out my checkbook if someone promised they could animate Maud, or Mom. For either of them to haunt Woolworth House... That would be a true blessing.

"I don't like hiding," he pouted. "I want to play."

"How about we play"—I took the opportunity to pat myself on the back—"hide-and-seek?"

"You're it." He shoved off me and zoomed away. "Count to one hundred really loud, or I won't hear you."

"Got it." I watched him go. "I'll give you a head start."

Happy for the extra minutes, he didn't question the fact I wasn't keeping time.

"*Donuts,*" Lethe squealed and steamrolled her packmates to reach me.

"I haven't changed my name." I held the box over her head. "It's still Grier."

"Donuts," she growled, claws poking through her fingertips. "*Now.*"

The weepy-gooeys must have passed. These must be the scratchy-maimies.

"Don't bite." I popped her hand. "Lethe, no. Bad girl."

Masculine laughter rolled over her shoulder, and Hood made a gimme motion behind her back.

Nostrils flaring, she narrowed her eyes to slits. "Do *not* let him have them."

"Okay, okay." As the tension drained from her shoulders, I feinted left then passed the boxes off to Hood on my right. *"Run."*

He sprinted off into the night, his mate hot on his heels, and I doubled over laughing.

Beside me, Linus shook his head. "I thought you needed to talk to her."

"*Fiddlesticks.*" I straightened then anchored my hands on my hips. "The temptation was too strong."

And I was a total wimp who didn't want to break the news of her brother's promotion to her.

A call distracted Linus from outing me while I scanned the tables looking for the check-in point.

"I'll ask," he said to the caller then brushed his fingers over mine. "Do you have a sample of Dame Marchand's handwriting?"

As much as I wanted to tell him I had torn her letter into pieces then set them on fire, I had it tucked in my pocket like a sap. "I have the note Johan delivered."

Hand covering the receiver, he held the phone away from him. "Would you mind if I scanned it?"

"Why?" I retrieved it, embarrassed that while I might not have tossed it, I had rumpled it within an inch of its miserable life. "Who's asking?"

"Bishop." He studied me and then the paper. "Anca says a new collection has been logged into the Athenaeum."

The Society's Athenaeum once contained original tomes on all subjects necromantic, but the grand building housing the collection was devoured by fire back in the 1300s. The loss hit the community hard, and several High Society families had dedicated their lineage to restoring the collection they now called the Athenaeum.

Contents of the Athenaeum might be owned by the Lyceum, but it was guarded by the Elite. An index of currently available titles was accessible to all Society members, but its location was a closely guarded secret. You could request a book, and an Elite would bring it to you. Then he or she would breathe down your neck while you spent your four allotted hours with it before personally returning it to the collection.

But while the index might be easy to access, we didn't have time to check them out one at a time when we had no clue what information each book contained. That meant we had to go to the source. Somehow, we had to get our hands on the whole collection.

An emotion I hesitated to label as hope swept through me. "Do you think she would be that obvious?"

"Her signature is almost illegible, but her name was typed on the intake forms. The bulk of the collection is logged in as journals written by Marchands. The Athenaeum curates the rarest and most valuable tomes, and generational diaries don't fit the bill."

"Unless the journals are actually instruction manuals on goddess-touched necromancers," I mused.

"Anca wants to check the signature against an authenticated source before she pursues this lead further."

"Here." I passed over the letter. "I'm happy to help in any way I can."

Linus took the paper, and his fingers trembled with the same urge to crush the hateful words as mine.

"I don't mind if Bishop sees it," I reassured him. "Flush it, burn it, feed it to the paper shredder when you're done. I don't care. I shouldn't have kept it. It's toxic, and I'm trying to purge my life of negativity."

"She was your grandmother," he said gently. "It's natural that you'd want to hold on to her last words."

"They're acidic." I raked my hands through my hair to keep from reaching for it anyway. "It's a miracle they didn't burn through the paper."

They sure scorched themselves into my brain. I would never forget them.

"Are you sure you want it destroyed? I could scan it and file it in the basement."

"I wanted to meet her." A lump made swallowing hard. "I didn't expect a miracle. I didn't even expect to like her. I just...wanted to meet the woman who raised Mom. I wanted to see where Mom grew up. I wanted to be able to picture it in my head."

"We can petition the new Dame Marchand after a respectable mourning period."

"Looking back stops us from moving forward." I shook my head. "I have to let it go. There's nothing in Raleigh for me." I gazed up at the old house where I had spent most of my life, the only home I had ever known. "Woolly, Oscar, Lethe, Hood, Marit, Neely, even Cruz." Linus arched an imperious eyebrow. "And you." I banished the sadness thinking of stolen futures always brought me. "You're my chosen family. You're the people I love and who love me back. You're all I need."

Lips cool on mine, he kissed me gently before heading into the house.

HOW TO WAKE AN UNDEAD CITY   111

I was still tingling in all the right places, tempted to follow his lead, when I spotted Neely.

"You look fantastic." He bumped me with his hip. "What did you think of your goodies?"

"They were great." I dredged up a smile, a real one, for him. "I didn't realize you were on the clock."

"I'm used to holding down two jobs and moonlighting on the side. Sitting around the house, even though it's a great old house and you've been a terrific hostess, I'm going nuts. It was a relief to have a purpose." He hesitated. "I didn't get *too* purposeful, did I?"

"Ignorance is bliss." I patted his shoulder. "You exceeded my expectations, and I don't mind if you exceeded the budget while you were at it."

"Oh good." He flashed a brilliant smile. "I didn't see any luggage. What happened to the clothes? The toiletries? The flash?"

Wincing, I admitted, "We had to leave them in the van. We'll have to retrieve them later."

"And the makeup?" He clutched at his heart. "Did you leave that too?"

"Yes?"

"It'll melt." He shut his eyes. "Rest in peace, you beautiful darlings."

Fighting the smile that kept tickling the edge of my mouth, I maintained a solemn mien. "I'm sorry."

"You should be," he chastised. "What a waste of quality product."

"She had larger concerns than skincare." Cruz wrapped his palm around the base of Neely's neck in a claiming gesture that made me question if he worried I might turn Neely into a vampire if left unsupervised with him. "Look on the bright side. This means you'll get to order replacements for what she ruined."

"You're right." Neely glowed with purpose. "There's this red lipstick I wanted to try on her, but I told myself it was too much for meeting her granny. I didn't want to give the old biddy a heart attack."

Using his gentle grip, Cruz steered Neely back to their table while his husband prattled on about carmines, crimsons, and corals.

Watching them go, I spotted Marit making eyes at a gwyllgi twice her height and three times her width. She was arranging canned food as the foundation in a box before passing it on to the next table for their contribution. That's where the gwyllgi came in. He lent his considerable muscles to the task of delivering each completed one to the next table.

I was on top of her before she noticed me, and when she did, her face went all dreamy.

"He's so handsome." She started filling her next box. "And so tall. And so muscly."

"Have you spoken to him at all?" They had been working in companionable silence when I noticed them.

"Oh, not much." She frowned at me. "Why?"

"No reason." I held up my hands. "I'm sure it's only what's on the outside that counts."

Marit touched the bright-red birthmark covering the lower half of her face, and I tasted foot. I hadn't meant it as a dig at her looks, just her tendency to choose guys based on theirs. Pretty was nice and all, but substance was required for a relationship to last past hormones.

"Okay, you win." She rubbed her chin like the birthmark might scrub off with enough pressure. "I'll talk to him."

Catching her hand, I dragged it away from her face. "You got this."

The better we got to know each other, the more I suspected she judged people based on their physical appearance rather than their personality to beat them to the punch, and I hated how the world taught women to tie their worth to their looks.

Marit was beautiful inside and out, and I would keep chipping away all her preconceptions until she saw it too.

"With any luck"—she recovered her bravado—"I will be getting that."

The lumbering giant of a man with gentle eyes offered me a shy grin that made Marit whimper.

"I'm Jack." He stuck out his hand, which engulfed mine. "You must be Grier."

"I am Grier." I gestured toward Marit. "Have you been properly introduced to my friend?"

"Marit," he whispered, staring at the ground rather than her. "I overheard Neely call her that."

"I'm pleased to meet you, Jack." Marit beamed at him. "A girl should know the name of the guy she's been rubbing elbows with for the last four hours."

"Yeah." He shifted on his feet. "I should have mentioned it earlier."

"You're entitled to a little mystery." She placed her hand on his forearm and wet her lips as she tested the muscle beneath her palm. "Nothing piques a girl's interest quite like a brooder."

"I'm a pianist," he confessed. "I zone out sometimes." He rolled his massive shoulders. "The music..."

"A musician." Face lit up like Christmas, Marit leaned in closer. "Would you play for me sometime?"

Leaving her to reel in her catch, I found an unmanned station and fell into a mindless rhythm. I couldn't spare long, an hour or two tops, but I needed this. Both the mental break and the physical exertion of doing something to help Savannahians.

Coming home minus Plan A and Plan B goaded me to put in sweat equity to pay off the guilt of leaving in the first place.

All too soon I ran out of time. Three hours. More than I had meant to give, but nowhere near enough.

Crossing the yard to Woolly, I rested a hand on the nearest column, the paint faded, flaking in places.

"I'm so glad to be home." I rested my forehead against the aged wood and smiled as her warmth flooded me, better than a hug. "Linus still in the office?"

Woolly grew distant, checking on his location, but indicated the kitchen.

"Lethe and Hood aren't back yet." I scanned the yard, thankful for the extra security to keep an eye on them. "Let me know when they show?"

A faint strain of music, her wards recalibrating, filled my head that I took for her agreement.

I found Linus at the stove, humming softly while he stirred a pot that smelled faintly of cinnamon.

"I baked blueberry muffins, though *blueberry* is a generous descriptor considering the mix came from your pantry, and they're blue pellets instead of anything found in nature."

"You're such a food snob."

"There are also steel-cut oats with dried cranberries, pecans, and golden raisins mixed in." He handed me a tall glass with frosty sides. "Your smoothie, with an extra shot of Vitamin L to make up for the stress put on your body during the trip."

Relief hit my gut like a fist on the first sip, untangling the knots lodged there since yesterday. "Are you eating?"

"I ate earlier." He popped a raisin from a small dish into his mouth. "I couldn't hold another bite."

"Mmm-hmm." I took another sip or five. "Would you like some milk to wash it down?"

He wasn't the only one capable of embracing the role of caretaker. I just had to be sneakier about it.

From the way he explained his bond with Cletus and the other wraiths, I wondered if his ability to draw on their power had struck him as a more economical food source. Hardly a surprise, but he had admitted to running a few experiments on himself during his adjustment period. Such as skimping on food and water in order to determine how long he could survive on his new powers alone and then how little he could ingest to remain at peak efficiency.

Since he was a man who enjoyed cooking, and was good at it, I had a working theory of my own.

Linus didn't take care of himself. That wasn't theory, that was fact. So if he discovered he could cut more corners in his self-care routine by not cooking healthy meals for himself, or even ordering them in, he would in a heartbeat. What likely started as an experiment had become routine, and I aimed to break him out of his rut.

This might all blow up in my face. It wouldn't be the first or last time I was wrong about him. Linus may not need sustenance taken in through traditional means, but I couldn't help wondering.

Lately, he was eating more. At first it was to fool me into believing his appetite was normal, then it was sampling while he worked in the kitchen.

After our confinement at Woolly, where we took all our meals together, I had caught him stealing single grapes from the fridge or biting into a strawberry here or there. Now he had a second raisin in his hand, and I pretended not to notice him pop it into his mouth while I poured him a glass of two percent.

To placate me, he took a few sips, but I caught him drinking from the corner of my eye while I mixed extra toppings into my bowl of oatmeal. While he was in no danger of polishing off the full eight ounces, he had managed two or three. A couple more pulls, and he just might set a record.

A balanced diet was the first step, and then who knows? Maybe he could be eased into REM too.

Pleased with the progress of my own experiments, I hummed as I claimed my seat at the counter.

"I need to make a few calls." He topped off his glass for me. "I'll be in the office when you're done."

I took my time eating, and I cleaned my plate. It was weird not having Lethe breathing down my neck or stealing food. Maybe that's why I chewed thoughtfully, enjoying the novelty of cleaning a plate without help. When I was done, I washed the dishes I'd dirtied then meandered to check in with Linus.

The office wasn't an actual office. Well, it *was* an actual office, but it was also a façade. Maud had done all her work in the basement, in her sanctuary. The room where I found Linus had a desk, chair, laptop, and the other amenities you would expect. Including the printer/scanner/fax machine flashing as it awaited further instruction from him.

Amelie had worked out of that room, and I had updated the antiquated equipment as needed. I hadn't expected to get much use out of it, seeing as how I didn't need to entertain clients the way Maud had on occasion, but it looked like the investment was paying off.

"Well?" I leaned against the doorframe. "Any news?"

When Linus turned, he held a bronze bowl no larger than his cupped palm. A tight ball of paper filled the center, and he palmed a box of matches off the desk then offered them to me. "Not yet."

The matchbox weighed fifty tons in my hand. "You scanned and sent it?"

"I forwarded a copy to your email," he said, understanding my hesitation. "You can access it any time you want, or never again. It's your decision."

Filing emails wasn't so different from filing away memories. The information was there, on your computer (or in your head), when you wanted to access it. But clearing your inbox erased it from the forefront of your mind, giving you an excuse to forget, for a little while.

"Let's do this." I struck the match and dropped it before I changed my mind. The hateful words blackened and curled, and Linus used the eraser on a pencil to mash them into fine ash. "I do feel better." I took the whole thing from him and tossed it in the trash. "I should set fire to more of my problems."

The old house creaked around me, nervous about me getting any ideas.

"I was joking about the fire." I patted the nearest wall. "Sadly, if you go around setting fire to every person who annoys you, you get labeled a murderer for some reason. I've done my time. I'm not going back in the clink."

Even if the mental picture of the Grande Dame running circles while swatting at her hair as it haloed her in a plume of flame did amuse me.

And then there was what I would do to Boaz...

"I don't entirely trust that smile." Linus reclaimed the matches and tucked them into his pocket. "What were you imagining just now?"

"I don't want to lie to you." It set a bad precedent. "I also don't want to tell you the truth."

Head angled to one side, he pursed his lips. "Did it involve my mother?"

Dang it. How did he always know? "When did you say Bishop would get back with us?"

Willing to let it go, he pretended I hadn't invited his mother to a mental BBQ. "The comparison shouldn't take more than a few hours."

Nodding to myself, I murmured, "So anytime now."

That was great and all, but confirmation might still come too late. We had to act, and soon, if we wanted to prevent the media from discovering the truth, that an *unnatural* disaster had hit Savannah.

As much as it pained me to accept defeat, it had to be asked, "When do we start talking next steps?"

"I'll speak with Commander Roark and request a meeting. We can coordinate with the sentinels, combine our efforts."

"That works." The bustling lawn scene drew my eye. "We can't keep going like this. We're already pushing the limits. If the Society didn't have the mayor and the governor in its pockets..." I rubbed my arms, but I couldn't banish the chill. "We have to drive Lacroix out of the Lyceum, even if that means we smoke him out."

"Corbin's intel makes it impossible to guess how many of Lacroix's followers are loyal by choice and how many are acting under compulsion. We need to minimize casualties for the sake of the innocents, but you're right. We have to take action before our situation draws national attention. We have to end this, and we can't afford to wait any longer."

A chime rang out from Linus's phone, and he checked his messages.

"Bishop confirmed the note matches the signature." A frown cut his mouth as he read. "However, Anca crosschecked those against historical data she compiled while performing the initial search you requested. Neither sample matches letters of record on file for Severine Marchand."

Foolish hope kindled in my heart. "Does that mean she didn't write the note?"

Confirmation she didn't hate me wasn't the same as her loving me, or liking me, but it was something.

"He'll touch base when he can confirm an ID." He put away his phone. "Perhaps I was too hasty in urging you to burn her note. It might have come in handy."

"Do you think the new Dame Marchand might have taken steps her mother wouldn't to punish me?"

"I'm not sure." Linus rubbed his jaw. "From what we've heard, she appears to be the quiet sort. Her lack of ambition is evident in the fact Severine kept her granddaughters, and not her daughter, close. Heloise was driven to impress her grandmother, and Eloise has proven she was paying attention to all the lessons her grandmother taught them, but there's no evidence their mother has shown any initiative."

"Assuming the new Dame Marchand is as delicate as we've been led to believe, I would put money on the note being Eloise's doing." I fisted my hands on my hips. "But how did she talk her mother into handing over the collection? It's a Marchand family heirloom, and our bloodline is a closely guarded secret, or it was." I dropped my arms. "Severine's heart must be turning in its box."

"The new Dame Marchand might not be aware of what her daughter has done." Linus picked up his phone. "With Severine and Heloise gone, Eloise may be assuming that role as her mother is assuming the title. I'll tell Bishop to check Eloise's handwriting against the note and the signature."

"Family drama makes me tired." I sank into the chair behind the desk. "I never thought I would say this, but I was better off before I learned Dad's name, and I was definitely better off before I met Mom's side of the family."

"This was bound to happen." Linus crossed to me. "Severine kept an eye on you all these years, and her granddaughters did too. They would have reached out at some point. The same is true for Lacroix. You didn't bring this on yourself. They were always waiting in the wings, hoping for an opening to walk through."

"*Grier.*"

"Did you hear that?" I spun in the chair toward the window. "It sounded like..."

A furious zing rippled through the wards, and yep. Woolly expelled Boaz with enough force to send him flying.

"Crap." I leapt to my feet and ran, skidding onto the porch just as he tried to bull his way in a second time. "Woolly, no." I took the stairs two at a time and demanded of him, "What's gotten into you?"

"Lacroix made his move." Anguish cut lines into his cheeks. "All the sentinels we thought he killed..." He rubbed his hands over his face, leaving crimson streaks behind. "He compelled them, Grier. He held them prisoner until he rounded up a dozen or so then gave them orders to return to their units and open fire."

"Goddess," I whispered and went to him. "How bad is it?"

"We lost thirty-two men and women." His shoulders hunched. "Becky..." He wet his lips. "Lacroix discovered she was a sentinel and compelled her to take down Commander Roark. That was his special assignment for her. I was in a meeting with him and a few others when she walked in, drew her weapon, and..."

"I'm sorry." I eased forward, about to yank him into the hug he needed, when a commotion near the property line I shared with the Pritchards distracted me. "Who is...?"

Blonde hair flying loose around her shoulders, eyes bright with panic, Adelaide ran across the yard and threw her arms around Boaz.

"You didn't call." Her grip on him tightened until he returned the embrace. "You jackass. You knew I would hear about the massacre from the sentinels you posted outside the house, and you didn't call."

"I didn't think." He bowed to the need for comfort and buried his face in her neck. "Becky's gone." The blood on his hands streaked the ends of Adelaide's hair when he clenched his fists in the pale length. "I was on duty, and I couldn't... It all happened so fast. I had to..." His shoulders juddered. "I killed her, Addie."

Grateful when Linus came to stand with me, I folded myself against his chest as Amelie skidded onto the scene.

Bad enough that Boaz had to watch his partner fall, but to be the one who pulled the trigger...

Adelaide eased him onto Woolly's lowest step, and Amelie settled in beside him, leaning against him.

I doubt any of them were thinking what a colossally bad idea it was to risk Woolly's wrath. Lucky for them, the old girl had a good heart, and she had loved Boaz for a long time. She might be mad at him, she might never get over his betrayal, but she would always have a soft spot for the boy he had been.

As much as I hated to interrupt them, I had no other choice. "Did the commander make it?"

Head in his hands, Boaz stared at the blood flecking his boots while Adelaide and Amelie hovered over him.

"No." He raised his chin, and I could tell the effort cost him. "I couldn't process what was happening. We hadn't heard the other reports of sentinels turning on their own yet. We had no reason to distrust her." His gaze slid back to the ground. "She walked right in and killed him, and I..."

"Shhh." Adelaide raked her fingers through the longer hair on top of his head. "You don't have to talk about it. You're okay. That's the important thing."

"Yeah." A hard laugh punched out of him. "I wouldn't want to miss the wedding."

"Boaz," Amelie snapped, climbing to her feet. "That was uncalled for."

"It's fine." The concern wetting Adelaide's lashes and streaking her cheeks dried as if the tears had never fallen. "I should go."

When he didn't call her back, I went after her since Amelie couldn't. "He shouldn't have said that."

"Hey." She slowed, allowing me to fall into step with her. "That's my line."

The smile creeped up on me, reminding me why I liked her. "How are you holding up?"

"We have food, water, and gas for the generator." She laced her fingers at her navel. "It's a big ask, I know, but can you talk to him? He'll accept comfort from you better than he does from me."

"I'm not going to pat his head or rub his belly, but I'll kick him in the ass to get him moving in the right direction." I met her stare head-on. "That's the best I can do."

"Thanks." She made a vague gesture toward the Pritchard house. "I should be getting back."

As I watched her go, I resisted the urge to grab her by the shoulders and shake sense into her.

Marrying Boaz was one thing. Both their families would benefit from the union. I could see that in hindsight, even accept it. But she had rushed over wearing her heart on her sleeve, and he dusted it off like lint.

As usual.

"You can't fix this." Linus came up behind me and wrapped his arms around me, propping his chin on top of my head. "They have to figure it out on their own."

"I can't help it." I leaned back against him. "I like Adelaide. I want better for her than she's getting."

"She chose him," he reminded me. "There's no going back, for either of them."

"I'm warning Cletus. He can get word to Clem for us."

The wraith materialized in seconds and spread his hands in a show of them being empty.

No news, in this case, was good news.

"Lacroix made his play," I told Cletus. "Don't let Corbin out of your sight for a blink, okay?"

Cletus bobbed his head then disappeared back to stand guard over my progeny.

Heaving a sigh, I forced myself to step out of Linus's comforting embrace. "Do you have a tattoo gun here?"

"Yes."

"Can you give the remaining sentinels the same tattoo you gave me? It holds against Lacroix's compulsions. I've tested it time and time again." I faced him. "We can't turn a blind eye when we can help protect the sentinels who are putting their lives on the line for the rest of us."

"I can bring in help, other artists, and more equipment." Wisps of black flickered in his eyes. "The problem is the ink."

The blend contained Volkov's blood to boost the wearer's immunity from Last Seeds.

There had once been an arrangement between the two of them that resulted in Linus having the blood, and test subject, he required to experiment on himself until hitting the perfect ratio for use in his design.

For the sentinels' sake, I hoped we could stretch what remained of his supply thin enough to cover everyone. "How much do you have left?"

"Not enough." He shook his head. "Not nearly enough."

I swallowed hard. "Then I guess we go get more."

SEVEN

"**N**o."

That was Linus's entire argument against me going with him to see Volkov. Hard to counter when his succinct reply left me no wiggle room, but that had never stopped me. This needed doing, and I wasn't letting him go alone.

Bold as brass, I hurled my suspicion. "He's in the city."

The cool assessment in his eyes skated dangerously close to a mask. "You're fishing."

Fiddlesticks. He knew me too well, which meant he ought to know I wasn't giving up or giving in.

"You visited him several times," I reminded him, "but you couldn't have gone far. You were always home to fix me breakfast, and most mornings I saw you before I went to bed."

"Volkov is dangerous."

"Weird." I arranged my features into oblivious puzzlement. "I didn't get that vibe from him. I'm sure he didn't mean to kidnap me, hold me prisoner, or force me to marry him. It was all a big misunderstanding."

Linus pinched the bridge of his nose. "He's been asking for you."

A cold lump formed in my gut. "That's good then. He gets what he wants, and we get what we need."

Black filled his eyes from edge to edge when he dropped his hand, and eternity stared back at me.

"I can't promise to honor your decisions then break my word when it's tested." Mist rose from his skin, and I was glad. It meant he wasn't hiding his quirks, any of them, from me. "I'll make the visitation arrangements."

Uncertain how victorious I felt, considering winning meant spending quality time with Volkov, I found myself in need of a distraction. "How can I help?"

"Call the Mad Tatter." He prowled the room, the promise of violence simmering beneath his skin. "Ask Mary Alice to send six of her best."

We couldn't very well invite humans into the city at the moment, let alone allow them to work on the sentinels and the Elite without raising questions. There was also the small concern they might go back out into the world and replicate the design without understanding what it meant. He knew that but...

Phone in hand, I searched for her number. "I shouldn't specify necromancer or...?"

"She'll know who I mean," he reassured me, giving away nothing.

With no one to blame but myself for pulling the assignment I was about to take on, I dialed up the Tatter and asked to speak to the boss.

"You destroyed my guest suite," Mary Alice said in place of *hello*.

"See, there were these vampire assassins," I began. "And then—"

"Who do you think you're talking to?"

Information broker. Right. "Linus told me to call you."

That cut her off mid-rant. "He did?"

"He said tell you to send six of your best to Savannah."

"Six? *Six?* That's half my stable. I can't short my clients."

"All right." I cast around for Linus, but he was already gone, making his own calls. "I understand."

"It will take a few hours."

Thinking I must have misheard, I pressed the phone tighter to my ear. "What?"

"You heard me. Give them six hours. They'll be there." She huffed. "Tell him he owes me a mural in the guest suite once repairs are complete. I'm talking full color, full wall, full everything."

Giddy with success, I closed the deal. "I'll let him know."

"And *you* will be receiving the bill."

The eye twitch developing on my right side made me glad she couldn't see me. "I'm happy to pay it."

"Take care of my people, Grier." A cold edge cut through her voice, slicing through the crotchety-grandma routine. "You won't like what happens if you don't."

The call ended, and I stood there absorbing the threat from a woman I now had much less trouble imagining as a ruthless maven of Atlanta's underground.

Woolly rustled a nearby curtain with the patience of someone tapping their foot.

"Linus trusts her." I pocketed my phone. "She can't be all bad."

The curtains parted until they framed Boaz, who hadn't moved from his spot or lifted his head from his hands since he ran off Adelaide. And Amelie, who didn't appear to be making any headway soothing him.

"Point taken." I jerked them closed again. "We can't always trust our judgment where our hearts are concerned." I strained my ears, but I was alone. "Where is everyone?"

The temperature in the room lowered as her presence retracted to take a look around but shot back to me in a snap.

The jumble of images dumped in my head left me scrambling. "Oh no. *Oscar.*"

Between checking in, Boaz delivering his brutal news, and Linus and I planning next steps, I had totally forgotten him. For hours. Only the request for a headcount had turned up his absence.

"You want me to have fifty billion kids when I can barely keep track of a single ghost boy?"

The old house huffed air through the floor registers in a sigh that told me I was wasting my breath. Apparently, she felt that nine months was plenty of time for me to mature into a mother-type person.

"Cover for me." I shot out the back door and jogged for the woods, where two familiar gwyllgi, both romping on four legs, met me. "Don't mind me. I'm just winning the mother-of-the-year award for shooing Oscar off to play hide-and-seek then forgetting I was supposed to do the seeking."

Hood whined in sympathy, but Lethe chuffed with amusement.

"Laugh while you can, *Mom*." I breezed past them. "Your day is coming."

Thank the goddess, my adoptive son was super low-maintenance. Being dead meant he didn't eat, sleep, or drink. As long as I kept him entertained so he didn't relapse into poltergeistism out of boredom, I was set. Except when, like now, I totally and completely failed at ghost motherhood.

With any luck, I would cut my teeth on Lethe's and Hood's brood —or they would cut their teeth on me—before I was expected to figure out how to rear my own offspring.

Woolly.

Enough with the kid thoughts already.

Irked, I shot her a mental picture of my own—me lounging on an operating table, waiting for a tubal.

For a second, I wondered if houses could faint. Her presence retreated from my head, and I took full advantage of the quiet to focus on locating Oscar.

Once I got far enough into the woods, I chose a tree to hide behind then gave Woolly the signal to send Oscar back out. I waited until he zoomed past, clearly hunting me, before I tapped his shoulder.

"Tag." I spun and ran, calling over my shoulder. "You're it."

"We were playing hide-and-seek," he protested. "You didn't find me."

"I know." I slowed. "I suck."

"You mean *sucker*. You fell for it. Woolly told me guilt trips work every time." Laughing, he tapped my shoulder. "Now you're it."

"Hey." I snatched him out of the air. "Woolly better not be giving you pointers."

"No." He wriggled in my grip, but it was too late, and he knew it. "Please."

"Show no mercy." Familiar with his ticklish spots, I homed in on them until he was gasping and laughing, black tears painting his cheeks. "That's rule number one."

Only when I was certain he was worn out did I sling him onto my hip for the trip home.

Exhausted, he leaned his cheek on my shoulder. "That was fun."

"I'm glad you think so." I kissed the top of his head. "And I'm sorry I forgot to come get you."

Chubby fingers twining in my hair, he nestled closer. "Why did you?"

Oscar's tendency to wink out when he got tired meant he had a poor grasp on the passage of time. He might not realize how long I stood him up, or even been present from the time I should have started counting until he showed up looking for me at Woolly, but that only made it worse, not better. I was supposed to be his keeper, not the other way around.

"Boaz came by with some bad news. One of his friends died, and he's upset about it. We all are. She was a sentinel, and she helped a lot of people. She even helped me out once."

"I'm sorry she's dead." He grew quiet. "Will she become a ghost? Like me?"

"No." Her family would be performing the culmination soon, if they hadn't already. "She won't be a ghost."

"Oh." His voice grew small. "That's good."

Drawing back to look at him, I wondered, "Why?"

"I didn't like being a ghost. Nobody could see me or talk to me. It made me so mad, I hurt people. I was lonely and sad all the time, and I just wanted to go home."

Only his use of the past tense kept me from cringing. "Are you happy now?"

"Yep." He planted a smacking kiss on my cheek. "You're not my real mom. She was older." His cool fingers traced where faint crow's-feet had started gathering beside my eyes. "You're still kind of a kid. I like that. It means you remember all the best games."

"You're family, Oscar. You're welcome at Woolworth House for as long as she's standing."

Since the old girl would outlive me, that seemed like the most binding promise to make. Assuming she got her wish and I did have fifty billion children, I would ensure they grew up right alongside Oscar, treated him like a big brother, and always made him welcome in our home. Because they would grow up and move out, but he...wouldn't. Unless he trusted one of them to wear his button and take him with them, and I had trouble imagining I would ever trust my offspring that much. They would have me for a mother, after all.

And sure enough, the thought of kids had popped right back into my head the second Woolly's traitorous roofline came into view.

Grumbling under my breath, I narrowed my eyes at her. "Your day is coming, missy."

Oscar sat up and looked around. "Who's Missy?"

"Someone who is going to be in a lot of trouble when I have a spare minute." I lifted Oscar and set him on his feet. "Here's the deal. You can't let the sentinels know you're here. Some of them can see you, and some of them can't. Let's just assume they all can and not let them spot you, okay?"

Oscar drifted up to my eye level. "Boaz and his friends might take me if they find me?"

Leave it to a kid to see right through adult BS. "Yeah." I tugged on his collar. "They might try."

"I'm not worried." He jutted out his chin. "You won't let them."

"No, I won't." I ruffled his hair. "But I hope it won't come to that."

"I'll be good," he promised. "I'll go play in the basement."

"Not the..." I blinked, and he was gone, "...basement."

Linus and I had made the space as ghost boy friendly as possible, but I didn't want him treating downstairs like a playground. As much as I hated the role of disciplinarian, I might not have a choice but to reinstate his ban.

With Oscar sorted, at least for now, I went in search of Linus. I found him standing on the porch, deep in conversation with Woolly. A noise that I swear resembled a baby rattle shook nearby. I decided to pretend it was bags of rice shifting on the sorting tables and not yet another hint dropped with the force of an anvil.

"I've made the arrangements," he greeted me, smile seesawing on his lips. "Change, and we'll go."

The battle between grim acceptance of our destination and Woolly's total and complete lack of subtlety had him close to caving into a full-on grin, and I found that impossibly adorable.

"What's the dress code?" I took the steps and kissed the corner of his mouth twitching the most. "You're dressed to the nines as usual. What should I wear?"

Puzzled by the kiss, he didn't hesitate to return it. "A burlap sack?"

"Shoot." I snapped my fingers. "Neely threw out my very last one when he purged my closet of clothes that no longer fit."

"What you have on is fine." He tugged the hem of my shirt, his fingers sliding underneath to touch skin. "You are, however, covered in mud. I would appreciate it if you changed your shoes before we get in the van."

"We're taking the van?" I couldn't stop my gaze from skating across the yard in search of Hood. "Is this not a solo mission?" I popped his hand when he tickled my ribs. "And by solo, I mean other people will be joining *us*."

"You have made your stance on solo ops quite clear."

"Good." I reared back. "Give me ten."

As I hit the stairs on the way up to my room, I heard Linus on the phone with Bishop. I was tempted to loiter and see what I could overhear, but we had a car ride ahead of us. I could quiz him then.

Woolly stuck with me while I pulled on jeans, a soft tee, and clean sneakers. I wasn't sure what one ought to wear to face one's kidnapper, but the fact I was walking into a prison of my own free will meant I had earned the right to be comfortable while I was doing it.

A rustling noise drew my attention to the podium where Eileen resided when not in use.

"I would forget my head tonight if it wasn't sewn on." I lifted the fabric covering her, and she blinked up at me. "I'll be back in a bit."

The grimoire basked in a moonbeam, her pages fluttering in what passed for a contented sigh.

On my way back to Linus, I considered the ramifications of the times when I used my own blood as ink on her pages. Maybe she was just shy, and she was finally opening up to me. Or maybe I had somehow given her already impressive reanimation a boost.

Mulling that over, I posed a theoretical to Linus. "You know how Boaz sprouted a new leg when I used that healing sigil on him?"

"Yes."

"Do you think Eileen could sprout—and I'm just spitballing here —arms or legs if she really put her mind to it?"

For a moment, he only stared at me. "You wrote the healing sigil on her pages in your own blood."

"I did." I chewed my bottom lip. "As a book, she's never had arms or legs to regrow but..."

"...the leather used for the cover belongs to several different fae." He rubbed his jaw. "Why do you ask?"

"She's always blinked at me, but now she's rustling pages to get my attention, that kind of thing."

"You are the most fascinating woman I have ever met."

Flushing beneath the undeserved praise, I passed the credit. "The book is the one doing all the tricks."

"We'll put it on our to-do list." He checked the time on his phone. "We don't have long."

"Visitation hours about to end?"

"There are no visitation hours where I put Volkov."

Until this exact minute, I hadn't realized he had put Volkov anywhere. "But you can get in."

"I can." He ducked his head. "Are you sure you want to do this?"

"Linus..."

"You're healing," he said softly. "Bit by bit, day by day. You're mending what Atramentous broke."

"I'll always have moments where I hear water dripping or smell mold that isn't there. Small, dark spaces will probably always make me hesitate." I shrugged like it cost me nothing. "I'll never be the person I was before Maud died, and I'll never be the person I'm becoming if I shy away from the hard stuff."

"As I said, you are the most fascinating woman I have ever met."

Footsteps on the stairs kept my center from fully liquefying in a rush of lovey-doveyness.

"Ready?" Hood, back on two legs, jingled keys in his palm. "The van's at the gate."

"Where's Lethe?"

"Napping." His eyes softened. "She ate all twenty-four of her donuts, then shifted and chased me until she passed out. I had to carry her from the den up to our room."

Awed by her stomach capacity, and grateful for yet another excuse not to tell her about Midas, I took the stairs first, which is why I was the one who bumped into Boaz, who still hadn't budged from where Adelaide left him. Though Amelie appeared to have given up on him and gone back to work.

Head down, he didn't waste energy lifting it. "Where are you off to?"

"We have some business to handle." Figuring he could use it, I squeezed his shoulder on my way past. "We'll be back."

The procession caught his attention, and his eyes cleared a bit. "Do you need another set of hands?"

A distraction might be just what he needed, but we couldn't afford one where we were going. "We got it, but thanks."

"Hood won't be allowed past the front gate," Linus said. "We could use a third man on the inside."

Until he mentioned it, I hadn't considered the ramifications of bringing Hood along. But he had a point. Lethe, Hood, and Midas had worked for my grandfather at one point, on the estate where I was held after Volkov kidnapped me. The magically enforced NDA they signed might cover Volkov to some extent. It was hard to know, and we couldn't afford to guess when we only had one shot at getting this right.

Despite the valid reasons, I was still shocked he had extended an invitation to Boaz.

Granted, he was the only non-human, non-gwyllgi in sight, but I figured he would need to be the last man on Earth to earn a hand up from Linus. Maybe I was projecting, and I was the petty one.

"Okay." Purpose shoved Boaz to his feet. "Where's our ride?"

"This way." Shaking his head, Hood started toward the gate. "You got shotgun."

Mild surprise that Hood offered made me wonder if I had missed a memo somewhere.

They were both being *nice*. To Boaz. Without me begging, threatening, or bribing them first.

The thought crossed my mind that Adelaide had spoken to them too, hoping they could help pull Boaz out of his tailspin, but I didn't think she'd had the time. With gwyllgi hearing being what it was, Hood might have overheard what she told me and relayed it. Though that sounded like a more Lethe thing to do.

Whatever brought about this stroke of good luck, I wasn't going to question it. I was too glad to share the burden of Boaz to needle

Linus and Hood to death over their motives. The bottom line was they were both good men, and while they might not respect Boaz, they respected his grief over the decision he'd had no choice but to make.

Hood led the way, and Boaz followed him. Linus and I fell in behind them, and I couldn't resist sneaking a peek at his face to see if I could divine what he was thinking. He caught me at it and dared me to ask with a look, but Boaz was too close for me to pose the question without him overhearing and me coming off as an ass, and Linus knew it.

With no other recourse available, I was forced to elbow him.

He laughed under his breath, his eyes crinkling at their corners.

Annoyance fluttered away, as it always did when he let me see him, the real him.

To ensure his passengers kept to their assigned seats, Hood held the door for Boaz to make certain he sat shotgun. As a nod to his doorman days at the Faraday, he bowed to Linus and me while he opened the side passenger door for us. We climbed in, and I happily claimed my usual seat while Linus sat across from me. Our knees bumped, and I didn't think it was an accident. I also didn't think I minded.

Flirty Linus was irresistible, and that's exactly what he was being by nudging my foot with his.

Leaning forward, I whispered, "What has gotten into you?"

PDA wasn't his style when Boaz was around. Usually, he kept his hands to himself to avoid sparking yet another confrontation.

"Am I not allowed to play footsy with my fiancée?"

"The timing, not the activity, is what I find questionable."

"We need to light his fuse and see if he explodes. This ought to do the trick."

"Ah." I saw the logic at once. "You want to see if he's steady enough to be our wingman."

"We need Volkov to cooperate." Linus scooted to the edge of his seat. "More, we need his consent. He isn't required by law to share his blood, and we can't take it without sparking a fresh conflict between what remains of the Undead Coalition and the Society."

"I'm willing to take it for the sake of protecting our remaining sentinels."

"I hope it won't come to that. He's been reasonable thus far."

"He's slick as spit, all right."

"He'll strike a bargain with the proper motivation." Linus tapped my knee with his fingers. "He claims he wants to apologize to you, to start making amends."

"I can fake amends-making if it gets us a pint or two of contrition out of him." Just the thought of playing nice with Volkov twisted my gut into knots, but I could do it for the sentinels. "I assume there is a medical wing in this facility?"

"Yes." Linus kept inching closer, and I mirrored him. "They'll provide all the supplies we need to draw his blood and transport it back to Woolworth House."

Lips brushing his, I murmured, "Good."

"Stop making out back there," Hood yelled too loudly. "Strap on your seat belts."

Muscles clenched in Boaz's nape, and his shoulders flexed, but he didn't turn.

"How much farther?" I kept my nose touching Linus's. "And who else knows where to find him?"

"About five minutes, and only the sentinels on staff and my mother." He reclined as my question hit its mark. "Do you think Lacroix will come for him?"

"I doubt he's a priority." I bit down on my next thought. "Corbin was primed to be his heritor-in-waiting. Lacroix had started grooming him for the position. Now that's blown up in his face." I leaned back too. "I don't know if he's holding on to Corbin in the hope he can be indoctrinated over time, or if Lacroix plans on using him as leverage when or if the right opportunity arises."

"It depends on how desperate he is to sire his own vampire bloodline."

"The former means he won't need Volkov. The latter makes a rescue attempt a possibility."

"We're here." Hood rolled to a stop and popped the locks. "See you in thirty."

"What's the plan?" Boaz twisted in his seat. Relief that he hadn't caught us necking was plain on his face, but he kept a civil tone. "You want me to play guard dog?"

Hood cut him a look at that, but he rolled his eyes rather than take offense.

"Volkov wants to see Grier. I'm going to offer him the chance if he cooperates. The visit will be supervised, by the two of us, while he gives his donation. I won't keep her in his presence a second longer than is required. Your job is to keep your eyes on Grier at all times. My attention will be divided. I need someone focused on keeping her safe."

"I can do that." A ghost of his old smile flickered. "If it's okay with Grier."

"What we're here for will help protect the sentinels from another massacre like the one that happened today." I wanted him to understand there was no room here for personal grudges. If I could set mine aside, then he had to do the same. "For Becky, I trust you to watch my back."

With a nod, he shut his eyes. "I deserve that."

Trust was a tender subject between us. That couldn't be helped. And after the stunt he pulled with Adelaide, I wasn't in the mood to be generous. But I also wasn't willing to lose more people when between Linus and me, we had the means to protect them.

"We should go." Linus reached for the door then stepped out before helping me onto the sidewalk. "We'll get the time promised to us, but not a second longer."

On the ride over, I let myself be distracted by Linus. Now that we had arrived, I had no choice but to soak up our surroundings. The faded Victorian with the small side garden was tidy, but the fence surrounding the yard was high and set my back teeth vibrating. I would bet the first bite out of my next donut that meant high-powered wards.

"This is it?"

At first, I thought I had spoken the thought out loud, but Boaz had beat me to it. "What he said."

"I had no idea this was in the city." He studied the street sign, which told me there would be questions raised to his superiors later. "How many inmates?"

"Six is the max allowed," Linus informed us, "and they're at full capacity."

Behind us, Hood pulled out onto the empty road while we approached the front door. Here, the pretense vanished. The woman who answered wore her hair shorn on one side with braids tickling her breastbone on the other. Her skin was dark, her hair black, but contacts gave her a yellow iris in one eye and a yellow pupil with a smiley face in the other.

"Hey," she greeted Linus. "Didn't expect to see you back so soon."

"We're cleared for a visit with one of your residents," he replied smoothly. "Can we come in?"

"I can't very well stop you." She stepped back and allowed us to enter, but she paid me particular attention. "You must be Grier Woolworth. I've heard a lot about you. This place must be nicer than your old digs, huh?"

Impact slammed the woman against the wall, and the porcelain figures on the shelf above her head rattled. Forearm braced across her windpipe, Linus let her scratch at him and gasp without blinking.

Boaz looked to me for instruction, but I had nothing.

I eased a step forward. "Linus?"

"I endure your sly remarks, Rue, because I don't care what you have to say about my mother or me." He gave her just enough leeway to lift her head, then he cracked it against the wall a second time. "Grier has endured enough. Play your games with me if you must, but you will leave her out of them."

"Sorry, but that doesn't work for me." I closed the gap, anger fueling me. "Rue, is it?" I tapped his wrist, and he lowered his arm. "You're going to keep your mouth shut and your opinions to yourself. He has never said or done anything to earn the types of remarks I have no trouble imagining you making."

Rubbing her throat, she rasped, "You can't know that."

"Yes, I can." I rested a hand on his shoulder and guided him out of her space. "Linus is a gentleman. The only people who imply otherwise have left him no choice but to repay their behavior in kind." Her mouth opened, but I cut her off quick. "I saw what you did, baiting him. It had nothing to do with me. You were targeting him through me, and I won't be used to hurt him." I folded my arms across my chest. "Now apologize."

Her lips flattened into a mulish line. "Sorry."

"Great." I clasped my hands together. "Now we can all be friends."

Rue eyed me like I was a few seeds short of a strawberry, but she accepted the temporary truce for what it was and led us past the formal living room you would expect to find in such a home, through a door reinforced with steel backing, and into a narrow hall painted a dull, institution-beige color. Holes had been patched, badly, on the walls. The floor was scarred linoleum, and some squares were missing entire corners.

This wasn't the cushy pen I had imagined for Volkov, but it was a long way from Atramentous.

Three identical doors spanned the left side of the hall, the pattern repeated on the right. Those must lead to the cells, or what passed for them around here. But we didn't stop there. We kept going, straight for the larger entrance right in front of us.

"He's already in medical." Rue didn't turn her back on us as she used her master keycard to swipe open the lock. "You have thirty minutes starting from the time I shut this."

The door clanging behind us caused me a moment of blind panic that turned my hands into claws, ready to rake my nails against the metal and scream until Rue released me, but I gritted my teeth and took in our surroundings. This room was more hospital than prison. Stark, bright, and gleaming with stainless surfaces. I was relieved to find that Volkov had been strapped to an exam table facing away from us.

"This is unexpected," he rumbled, a thick Russian accent rounding his voice. "You came just last month. Are you so eager for more of our conversation? Perhaps tonight you can tell me what purpose my blood serves you." He settled into the cracked plastic. "Otherwise, I might not be so eager to…" He whipped his head to the side, nostrils flaring, but he couldn't see me trembling. "You smell like her."

Ignoring the implied question, Linus strolled closer. "I have a proposition for you."

"It is maddening." Volkov sucked in oxygen until his nostrils whistled. "Did you bring me a piece of her clothing? Have I finally bartered enough to earn that small token?"

"There is no price you could pay high enough to deserve that."

"A shirt is not so much to someone who has the woman herself." His voice turned sly. "I could ask for something more…intimate. She and I were almost betrothed. One might argue I even have a right to it."

The mask of potentate was sealed so flush to Linus's skin, Volkov had no hope of getting a rise out of him. I hadn't noticed Linus slipping it on, but he was a master at showing the face required to get the job done.

"Give me two pints of blood, and I will give you the time it takes to collect them with Grier."

The plastic creaked once before Volkov bared his fangs and started thrashing. "She is here. In this room. That is what I smell."

Unmoved by the display, Linus watched his tantrum with a bored expression. "Do we have a bargain?"

"Yes," Volkov hissed. "Bring her to me. Let me see her. The smell is driving me mad."

Boaz tensed when Linus waved me closer, but he didn't attempt to restrain me, and he didn't say a word about what I was about to do.

Maybe he was capable of learning after all.

Black edged my vision, thicker with every step closer to Volkov. I steadied my pulse as much as I was able before circling in front of him.

"Grier," he breathed. "You came."

"You agreed to cooperate," I reminded him, and he went still. "Why did you want to see me?"

"I should have refused your grandfather when he confessed his plans for you."

"You made your choice." I managed a politer tone than he deserved. "You can't unmake it."

Shifting to stand near his feet, I swapped sides with Linus to give him better access to the equipment.

"I did care for you." He ignored the prick of the needle. "Surely you must know that."

"You used your lure on me." The spot between my shoulders twitched with the memory. "You took away my free will whenever it suited you."

"I made mistakes." He began to grow agitated. "I am admitting to them now."

Linus raised his hand just enough to catch my eye to signal he needed more time.

The opening gave me an excuse to ask a question I had been wondering for a while now. "Did you know Odette Lecomte was Lacroix's lover?"

"I did," he admitted after a considering pause. "However, I was ignorant of her connection to you."

"Mmm-hmm." As a key player, he would have known it all in case he required the ammunition.

"You were promised to me," he reminded me softly. "When I am free of this place, I will claim what is mine."

"Lacroix has named a new heritor," I fibbed. "He doesn't need you."

"Lies," he hissed. "Lacroix promised…"

"Lacroix talks out of his ass. A lot." I shrugged. "He's not going to hand his granddaughter over to a prisoner. He's not much for jail-house weddings. We never discussed it, but he doesn't seem the type. He's big into pomp and circumstance. Probably expects a lot of lace and silk at my wedding, and that's just what he'll be wearing."

"You will wait for me," Volkov ordered, hurling his compulsion at me. "I will get free, and I will be rewarded, as promised."

The urge to bend to his desires rolled over me like water off a duck's back.

Having pitted myself against Lacroix so often lately, I could appreciate the nuances of Volkov's power. He was nowhere near as strong as my grandfather, but he was young. Give him a few lifetimes, and he would mature. So would his lure, until he could have anyone he wanted with the crook of his finger. Unless they had protection against him. Protection Linus would soon make available to the public.

A nod from Linus told me he had what we came for, so I no longer felt obligated to play nice.

"I'm engaged," I announced with no small amount of glee. "That's why Lacroix can't hand me over to you, or anyone else. I don't belong to him. I never did. I wasn't his to give."

Volkov loosed a bestial roar and thrashed against his restraints.

"You are *mine*." He gnashed his teeth. "I smell my blood on your skin. It intoxicates, *solnishko*."

Tension shot down my spine, but I kept putting one foot in front of the other as I walked away.

Rue waited until all three of us clustered in front of the door before releasing the lock and letting us out.

When Linus excused himself to the kitchen, I stood in the hallway with Boaz.

"You're Boaz Pritchard." Rue looked him up and down. "I didn't put it together at first, seeing as how you're here with Linus." A nasty smile cut her mouth. "I should have known where Grier goes, you follow like a dog on a leash."

Leave it to her to zero in on the one member of our party neither of us had warned her away from.

"You've got some chip on your shoulder," I said casually. The contact lenses made it so that's all you focused on when you first looked at her, but I was paying closer attention now. "How did it get there?"

"I don't have to explain myself to you." Pivoting on her heel, she walked off and left us alone.

"I recognize her." He kept his voice low. "She went to school with us."

"Your year or mine?" Public schools hustled a lot of kids through their doors, but I felt confident I had never met her. "I'm drawing a blank."

"She was younger than me, older than you. There's no reason why you would remember her, but I can tell she remembers you."

I watched her go, annoyed I couldn't pin down the memory. "Why's that?"

"She came on to me. I politely declined. She wouldn't take no for an answer. It got ugly. I was forced to break it down for her how I didn't date girls younger than me. I was into age and experience." He grimaced. "She left me alone after that, until I hit Cass Manfred's graduation party. Rue crashed it, and so did you and Amelie. Rue caught me walking your troublemaking ass out the door with my arm around your shoulders so you couldn't escape. She misunderstood and started screaming at me when I came back in to find my drink."

"You do tend to have that effect on women." I shrugged. "Why take it out on Linus?"

"He's engaged to you?" He shrugged back. "Maybe she wanted to hurt you the way you hurt her."

Without a scrap of doubt, I could tell him, "Linus would never cheat on me."

"No, he wouldn't," he said with equal certainty, "and that leaves antagonizing him."

"What you're saying is, she's got poor taste in men and a death wish."

Laughter huffed out of him. "Yeah."

"You have to apologize to Adelaide." I bit my tongue, but it was too late. The damage was done. "Sorry, I have no right to stick my nose in your business if I ask you to keep yours out of mine."

"I don't know what to do with her," he admitted, growing somber. "She cares about me. It's not love, nothing like that, but she could squeeze out tears if I was found in a ditch one night."

More than a few, if her earlier display was any indication of how deep her feelings had grown.

"That's setting a high bar." I snorted. "Do you feel anything for her?"

"I don't want to keep hurting her." His worried eyes found mine. "But I don't know how to stop."

That wasn't an answer, but maybe he didn't have one, and maybe not blurting out a meaningless *sure* or *of course* was a step in the right direction.

"You can learn." I passed on the best advice I had to offer, given how new I was to being half of a whole. "Take notes from successful couples. Think Neely and Cruz or Lethe and Hood. Watch how they make it work, how they treat each other. Modify their formula to suit your needs. Go from there."

Linus rejoined us with a cooler in hand, and Boaz tensed his fists at his sides but deflated in the next heartbeat. "I'll work on it."

Eager to get while the getting was good, I started toward the exit.

We found Rue propped against the reinforced door, playing an app on her phone. "You've got three minutes left."

"I'm afraid a new clock is ticking." Linus hefted the cooler. "We need to go."

"You never leave early." She kept pressing buttons, but the jaunty music had died. "Why break tradition?"

"Open the door." Mist swirled across the surface of his skin. "Or I will open it for you."

Panic thrust its balled fist down my throat, cutting off my air, and I sucked in a whistling breath between my teeth.

I was back in prison.

The way out was blocked.

The guard had the key in her pocket.

We were stuck in here, with the inmates, with Volkov.

Trapped, trapped, trapped.

A sour taste coated the back of my throat, but the convulsive swallowing wasn't helping.

Linus brushed his fingers across my cheek, his fingers icy, his nails gone black as midnight.

The cold shocked me back to my senses, and I rallied as Rue glanced up at us.

"Give me a minute." She took her time turning off her phone and situating it just so in her pocket. The keycard she pretended to have misplaced until Linus bared his teeth. "Found it." She swiped it through the lock, but he was done waiting and yanked the door open. "Hey, you need to step off me. This is my job."

"What was so important about those three minutes?" He swept past her, into the living room, searching for danger. "Rue?"

"I have my orders." She thrust her shoulders back. "You ask for a slot, you use it."

"Wrong answer." Boaz captured her wrist and twisted her arm expertly behind her back where he secured her with a zip tie. "Looks like you're headed for a time-out."

Outside, Hood laid on the horn in one long bleat, a signal it was time for us to go.

"Have a seat." Boaz shoved Rue down into a wingback chair and secured her ankles to its legs. "Comfy?"

Dread pooled in my stomach, but there was no time for an interrogation. "What will you do with her?"

"I'll call this in." Boaz stood and dusted his hands before pulling out his phone. "Let someone else get to the bottom of it."

Across the room, Linus stood looking out onto the street, his expression tight.

Windows down, Hood yelled, "Move your asses."

A prickling sensation stung like bees across my nape. "Vampires."

"Get to the van." Linus thrust the cooler into my arms then nudged me out the door. "I'll be right behind you."

The tattered wraith's coat unfurled across his shoulders, and midnight pooled at his feet.

"I'm not leaving you." I regained my balance, handed the cooler to Boaz, then shoved him toward the van. "Go."

Planting his feet, Boaz refused to budge. "I'm not leaving either."

And neither, it seemed, was Rue. Calling for a sentinel to escort her to their base would have to wait.

The moonlit scythe glinted in Linus's fist, and I couldn't see his face beneath his cowl as I cut my palm.

"Hand," I demanded, and he offered me the one not holding an instrument of death. "Don't give me the look just because you know I wouldn't be able to see you giving me the look. Two sigils never hurt anyone."

"Grier." He caught my fingers in his. "I love you."

"I love you too." I wriggled free. "You're still getting another sigil." I drew it on his wrist, where his wraith's cloak might offer some protection. "Boaz, you're next."

While Linus watched our backs, I drew several on Boaz in the hopes at least one wouldn't smudge.

Outside forces might not budge the design, but even an impervious sigil could fall victim to the wearer's sweat or a careless itch that got scratched all the same.

"You really do love him," Boaz murmured. "You're not afraid of him."

"I really do, and I'm really not." I finished with him then started on myself. "Did you think he was using his scythe on me behind closed doors?"

"Pretty sure he does, yeah." He scrubbed his palm over his hair, awkward in a way he never used to be with me. "You were running around in a sheet after spending the night with him."

The joke came too soon, but it still forced a mortified laugh out of me. "Do *not* say that where Lethe can overhear."

Is that a scythe in your pocket, or are you just happy to see Grier?

Did Grier help you sharpen your scythe last night?

Did you scythe Grier last night?

And so on.

I would never hear the end of it. Ever. And forever was a long time for folks like us.

Cursing the three of us soundly, Hood let up on the horn and exited the van while cracking his knuckles.

The wash of red magic as he assumed his gwyllgi form reminded me to close my own ward. A quick swipe of my wrist sent magic humming as a wall of compressed air formed a hard shell around me.

No sooner had my ears popped than a group of six vampires rounded the corner with crowbars, sledgehammers, and bats in hand. They looked ready to smash the heck out of something, but that something wouldn't be us.

"Good evening, gentlemen." Linus strolled toward the vampires. "Can I be of assistance?"

"Ain't you heard?" the one on the far right drawled. "Savannah belongs to the vampires now."

"I'm afraid we'll have to agree to disagree." Linus swept the scythe in a warning arc in front of him. "Savannah is under Society protection."

"Hey." The third one wedged in between the others. "That's her."

"Grier something," the fourth one agreed. "Lacroix's grand-daughter. He said you might come after Volkov. Guess he was right."

He smiled, fangs on display, and ran his tongue along one point. "This night just keeps getting better and—"

A dull thud preceded his head hitting the pavement and rolling into the street.

"You might not be scared of him," Boaz muttered next to me, "but I might need fresh boxers after this."

Ignoring the carnage, Linus kept his tone polite. "Leave, and the rest of you will be spared."

"You killed Dan," Number Two bellowed. "What the actual fuck?"

With Two's eloquent battle cry ringing in our ears, Number One charged us. He must have been an older vamp. The way he swung his sledgehammer reminded me of a Viking wielding an ax. He used the shaft to absorb the scythe's blows, his movements practiced and brutal.

That left Boaz and me with Two, Three, Five, and Six.

"I can already smell the vampire BBQ," I taunted. "I hope someone brought sides."

Squeezing my hand, I coaxed fresh blood into my palm that I used to draw sigils on my ward. I lined up a row of four and slammed my palm against the wall of air. Magic blasted out in a wave, striking two out of the four before they could dodge.

Unlike last time, when I was protecting my friends, these vampires didn't crisp on the spot. They hit the pavement and rolled, the wind knocked out of them.

Well, that was embarrassing.

"Make up your mind," I grumbled at the seeping cut. "I can't invite them to a vampire BBQ if I can't ignite the grill."

Two shots fired behind me, the proximity causing my ears to ring. Boaz had winged one of the remaining vampires, but the other was bulling straight for us, and the two I had knocked down were getting to their feet.

More blood, more focus. Less fear, less doubt.

Teeth gritted, I slammed my bloody palms against my ward and sent a blast of energy hurtling toward my targets.

Impact stunned them, and panic tightened their eyes. Then it was over. They turned to ash and swirled away on the breeze.

A shocked gasp punched out of Boaz, and when I turned, the gun wilted in his hand. "How did...?"

There was no time to fill him in, and I preferred to keep the scope of my emerging powers to myself and Linus, who remained locked in combat with Number One.

I couldn't blast the vampire without risking Linus, and I couldn't join the fight either. Not only did I not have a weapon, but getting too close to Linus while he did his thing was a recipe for decapitation. All I could safely do was stand there and feel like a total—

A deafening shot rang out, and Number One hit the ground with a clatter of his hammer.

Linus whirled toward us, scythe raised, but I didn't have to turn to know Boaz had taken the shot.

"Thanks," Linus panted.

A shrug rolled through Boaz's shoulders. "Don't mention it."

Before I finished marveling over their cordiality, I realized we were a man down. "Where's Hood?"

But neither Linus nor Boaz had an answer for me.

EIGHT

About the time my heart lodged in my throat, Hood trotted around the corner of the neighboring house with an arm dangling from his mouth. He wagged his tail at me and kept going, finding a comfy spot on the lawn to dig into his treat.

A necromancer I might be, but blood magic was the extent of my experience with corpses. Once you got into chewing, gnawing, or otherwise munching on the dead, I was out of my comfort zone.

Skirting the snackish gwyllgi, I hit the sidewalk. "Let's go, uh, see where he got that."

The cloak vanished from Linus's shoulders, and I heard Boaz exhale with what I suspected was relief.

"We should return to Woolly." Linus fell in step with me. "It's dangerous for you to be on the street."

I pinned the back of my wrist to my forehead. "Good thing I have a big, strong potentate to protect little ol' me."

A smile wanted to curl his lips, but he forced them into a flat line. "You can take care of yourself. You've more than proved that." He skated his fingers down my arm. "But there's a difference in you looking for trouble and it finding you."

"Make you a deal. We figure out where the rest of Hood's snack came from, and then we'll go home."

"I'll take that deal."

"Goddess," Boaz breathed from behind us. "Hood did all that?"

A blocky SUV sat with all four doors standing open. The back tires had been gnawed until they flattened into rubber puddles on the asphalt, and teeth marks punctured what remained of the rear bumper. The vehicle's occupants, who lay in pieces strewn across the sidewalk and onto the lawns of nearby houses, appeared to be vampires.

Thank the goddess for the evacuation order. Otherwise, we would have had some explaining to do.

"This was a nice ride for the goon squad." I stepped over random appendages to reach the driver's side with its buttery-leather seats stained crimson. "They could have stolen it. Plenty of empty vehicles to choose from." On car lots and in driveways. "But why split into two teams? It's a minimum-security facility, but still." I rifled through the contents of the dash and searched the floorboards. "And why leave their transportation a street away when every second counts?"

Boaz rubbed his jaw. "Looks like these guys sent the muscle ahead then played lookout."

"Grier." Linus crouched over a body missing everything south of its rib cage. "This complicates matters."

One of its severed arms crooked on the asphalt, still gripping a crossbow.

"They found us." I looked at him. "Again."

Understanding dawned, and Boaz paid closer attention. "These are the archers who hit the *Cora Ann*."

"Yeah." Among their many and growing accomplishments. "Looks that way."

"This doesn't fit," Linus murmured as a second crossbow was discovered beneath a dismembered torso.

"I don't see assassins caring about Volkov one way or another," I agreed. "Two teams?"

"One dispatched after we left the safety of Woolworth House and the other..." Cold, hard onyx filled his eyes. "A source tipped them off where and when to be in order to confront us and protect Volkov."

"Why can't just one villain be after us? Or even multiple villains united under one banner? It would be so much easier to keep track of them." Volkov. Lacroix. Odette. Eloise. "What if we offered them matching T-shirts with a catchy slogan so identifying them was easier?"

The maniacal laughter is free, but the hits cost extra.

Come for the vengeance, stay for the finger sandwiches.

I make evil look good.

The edge of exhaustion creeping into my voice must have tipped Linus off, because he bundled me in his arms before it hit me how tired all this made me. After Atlanta, I was still running on fumes.

"I'm okay," I breathed against his chest, my fingers tightening in the fabric at his spine.

"No, you're not." He kissed my temple, as if sensing the headache waiting to pounce. "But that is okay."

Laughing softly, I nudged him back before I decided to burrow in and never leave. "Let's finish this."

"We need to test their weapons." Linus bent and started gathering samples. "The previous assassins always used poison. If these vampires were part of that unit, their knives would have been treated."

"I wish we had thought to test—" Geez, I really was slow on the uptake. I never thought to wonder what else might be stuffed in that duffle bag along with our would-be assassin. "You brought the Atlanta vampire's crossbow with us to Base Four."

"I did," he confirmed. "The initial tests confirm the presence of wraith's bane on the arrowheads."

An uneasy feeling tingled through my limbs. Archers firing on the *Cora Ann* with brass-tipped arrows. Vampires chasing us through

City Market, their arrowheads dipped in wraith's bane, a poison designed to take down Linus. Daredevils rappelling down buildings and busting through windows. And now this.

The former Grande Dame, Abayomi Balewa, had admitted to hiring the assassin in the Lyceum, but she hadn't taken credit for the archers.

Eloise had teamed up with Balewa under the guise of Angie Dearborn, but hiring assassins, archers in particular, made no sense when they had wanted to sacrifice me for my blood.

There was only one other possibility, but I couldn't believe she hated me that much. After what she did to Linus, I had been made brutally aware Odette was ruthless, but the child in me who had loved her struggled to believe, even after everything she had done, that she would put a price on my head.

"We'll figure it out," Linus promised, reclaiming the cooler. "Are you done here?"

I scanned the area one last time, then we returned to the street outside the facility housing Volkov.

"What do we do about our friend Rue?" I stared at the frilly curtain in the window. "Her bad attitude paved the way for this delightful interlude. Coincidence?"

"No such thing," Boaz drawled, reaching for his phone. "Give me a sec, and I'll arrange transport for her."

"No, I'll put in a call to Mother." Linus cut his eyes toward Boaz, expecting a one-liner no doubt, a jab below the belt, but none came. "Volkov will be secured and then relocated, and Rue will be detained in a cell at the barracks until we can spare someone to interrogate her."

Hood lounged on the sidewalk, gnawing on a femur in plain sight, which told me he had cased the neighborhood while he waited on us to finish with Volkov and determined it was free of humans who might raise an alarm. When he spotted us, he spat out his chew toy, trotted over, and shifted before sliding behind the wheel.

I caught him digging between his teeth with a fingernail. "Need a toothpick?"

"I can manage." He finished the task then cranked the van and pointed us toward home.

"You keep interesting company these days." From this angle, Boaz wore a pinched expression. "I don't think I realized just how interesting until this little ride along."

A text notification pinged Linus's phone and saved me from defending my choice in friends to him of all people.

"Bishop matched the signature to Eloise," Linus informed me, but he didn't look happy about it.

That ought to be good news. "What's wrong?"

"The form was filed months ago."

"Severine was alive and well then. So was Heloise for that matter."

Unless they held breathing against me, the Marchands had no right to a grudge at that point.

"The authentication process takes time, weeks depending on the Athenaeum's backlog, but it doesn't explain why Severine would allow Eloise to act on her behalf. She was being tutored by her grandmother, which would have granted her certain liberties, but Severine was willing to disinherit your mother, knowing she had born a goddess-touched granddaughter, to preserve the family name. If Severine decided to let lifetimes of accumulated Marchand knowledge go, even out of spite, I believe she would have overseen the transaction personally." He lowered his phone. "The collection is an heirloom. Marchands have bled for that knowledge, bred for that knowledge. It's as good as blood to her, or it was."

Rays of hope speared through me before I could pinpoint their origin, and I reached for him.

"The letter. The one Johan delivered. It matched the signature, remember? That means Severine didn't write it." The bright spot was lost to an eclipse when the larger implications hit me. "Eloise must have written it." I ran calculations in my head. "The date on the slip.

Check it." I wet my lips. "I bet it was around the same time as my release from Atramentous."

Linus bent his head and started typing. "I've sent him the date."

"You knew it off the top of your head?" Granted, I had tried to put as much of that dark period in my life behind me as possible, but I couldn't have given you an exact day I walked out of there. Detox from the drugs had left me shaky and my brain a foggy mess. "How do you remember this stuff?"

"The woman I had loved for half my life was being released, so yes. I committed the date to memory."

"Well, when you put it like that." I invited myself into his lap and wrapped my arms around his neck. "You're adorable, you know that?"

"I am the night," he said with a straight face. "Fear me."

Clearly, I wasn't the only meme addict in this relationship.

"Nah." I nestled against him, feeling my first laugh break free. "I'd rather cuddle you."

"You're murder on a reputation," he chided, voice thick with amusement. "Potentates aren't cuddly."

"I beg to differ. You're a potentate, and you're quite cuddly. Why, I could probably—"

"Please stop." Hood turned on the radio. "I have a full stomach, and it's turning."

"You and Lethe are just as bad." I harrumphed. "You're worse now that she's pregnant."

Hood narrowed his eyes at me in the rearview mirror, but he didn't contradict me.

A call had Linus shifting my weight to one side so he could lift the phone to his ear. This close I heard both sides of the conversation, but I tuned out Mary Alice and Linus while they discussed the terms and conditions for borrowing the artists.

Nestling back against him, I let my hormones cool while I turned this new information over in my head.

Linus finalized his arrangements just as things were starting to gel for me.

"Whoever took the initiative," I said, "it looks like the Marchand collection is now part of the Athenaeum. How do we find it? And how do we gain access?"

Two things the Grande Dame hinted were impossible feats.

"You want access?" Boaz twisted in his seat, his face gone pale. "Grier, no."

"Boaz," I sighed his name. "You can't keep trying to protect me from everything."

"You don't understand. I'm an Elite. I've transported books for the Athenaeum, and I've done my time guarding its doors."

The reminder drew me upright. "You know where it is."

"Yeah." He scrubbed his palms over his scalp. "You can't go there, Grier."

A creeping sense of dread crawled over me. "Where is it?"

Battling loyalties played across his face, but he exhaled, "Atramentous."

"Atramentous." I heard my voice as if from across a great distance. "I have to go back."

Back to the damp, the mildew, the quiet sobs, and the smell. *Goddess*, the smell. Unwashed bodies, urine, feces. Death.

A whimper lodged in my throat where I could almost taste the dank atmosphere. No matter how hard I swallowed, I couldn't clear my airway. I couldn't breathe. I couldn't...

The world dropped out from under me, and even with me in his arms, Linus couldn't catch me.

THE SCENTS of fresh dough and sugar set my stomach rumbling, and I cracked open my eyes to find Lethe holding a donut an inch from the end of my nose.

"I told you this would work better than smelling salts." She cast a smug grin over her shoulder. "Since I'm an excellent best friend, I'll even let her eat it." She looked back at me and mouthed, *"No, I won't."*

Rolling my eyes at her wasn't happening just yet. I was still too woozy for that. "Help me up."

Clamping the donut between her teeth, Lethe clasped hands with me and tugged until I was vertical on what I realized was the couch in the living room at Woolworth House. "Where's Linus?"

"He was interrogating Boaz, but that was a while ago. You've been out for a couple of hours." She took another bite. "He told me to let him know the second you woke." Tilting her head back, she yelled, *"Linus.* She's awake."

The boards groaned beneath the couch, and Woolly's presence bumped me in gentle inquiry.

"I'm embarrassed," I told the old house. "Otherwise, I'm fine."

The instant my brain put two and two together, that to view the whole collection rather than check out one title at a time I would have to visit the remnants of the Great Library, shelved in the basement at Atramentous, it got four, and it was lights out.

"Do you want a donut?" Crumbs flew when Lethe spoke. "I can grab you one."

"Where did you get them?"

"An angel of mercy set them on a sorting table." She licked her fingers. "I was told they were for whoever wanted them, and I'm a whoever, and I wanted them."

"They were for the sentinels working the barricade, and the volunteers helping out here."

"I'm a volunteer." She attempted to look affronted. "I'm helping out."

"You've also eaten three dozen already."

Pulling on a frown, she cocked her head at me. "What's your point?"

"Lethe," I began, hoping to win her sympathy. "There's something I have to tell you, about Midas."

"You mean that he grew balls and claimed second in the Atlanta pack?

"Yes?"

"He texted me about it as soon as you left."

Annoyed with them both, I thunked my head against the cushion. "You mean I was ravaged with guilt for nothing?"

"Not for nothing." Her shoulders drooped when she thought about it. "He didn't want it—*doesn't* want it. But he did it. For me, and for you."

"Where does that leave you?"

"I'm not sure." Her eyes met mine, a curious light in them. "I'll let you know when I decide."

"You've always got a home here." I patted her shoulder. "Both of you. All of you."

"Thanks."

Footsteps on the front porch caught my attention long enough for Lethe to escape into the kitchen where I had no doubt she murdered the remaining donuts before I took her up on her offer.

"I should have been here." Linus hurried over and claimed Lethe's spot. "I'm sorry."

"You're fine. You didn't miss much." I wiped the back of my hand across my mouth. "I'm not sure if I was drooling, or if it was Lethe. She was holding a donut to my nose, so it's possible this is her saliva."

A throat cleared behind me, and I whipped my head toward the sound. "Hood."

"Here." He passed me a paper towel with two donuts stacked on top. "I saved these for you."

A blur streaked across the living room, and he grunted as impact drove him into the nearest wall.

Alarm spiked Woolly's wards, the music in them a sudden crescendo that pushed me to my feet.

"You stole my donuts." Lethe knocked him down flat then straddled his throat. Her thighs squeezed, and her rounded belly covered the lower part of his face when she leaned forward to apply pressure. "My. Donuts. *Mine.*"

Dreads fanned across the planks, expression dreamy, he rasped, "Damn, you're hot when you..."

His voice petered out, and his eyes rolled back in his head. The hand cradling the donuts hit the floor, sending them tumbling under the couch for the dust bunnies to feast on. Not that it would stop Lethe from picking off the lint and eating them. She'd done it before and would again.

"*Grier.*" Lethe clutched her stomach, but she couldn't see all the way over it these days. "I killed him. My mate. The father of my child. And I murdered him over two donuts. They weren't even cream filled. They were glazed. *Glazed.*"

Linus took one side of the distraught gwyllgi, and I took the other. We hooked our hands around her upper arms and lifted her off Hood, removing the obstruction from his airway. We sat her on the couch, where she covered her face and started weeping in great, ugly waves of misery.

Linus knelt beside Hood and checked his vitals. "He's unconscious, but his pulse is steady."

"Hear that?" I called over her caterwauling. "He's alive. Linus says he's okay."

"He's alive?" Eyes red, nose dripping, she sniffled. "I didn't k-k-kill him?"

"I'll see if I can bring him around." Linus pulled out his modified pen. "You go calm down Lethe," he murmured to me. "Stress isn't good for her in her condition."

Shoving off the planks, I crossed to her, plopped down on the couch, and hauled her against me.

"Hush." I grimaced when she wiped globs of snot on my shirt. "He's okay, you're okay. The donuts are okay. Everyone is okay."

"I attacked my mate over an inferior pastry," she sobbed. "That's *not* okay."

Don't blame hormones. Don't blame hormones. Don't blame hormones. "It must be a pregnancy thing."

"I'm not hormonal," she growled. "I'm just hungry."

Few things had ever terrified me as much as realizing I cradled a pissed-off lizard-dog thing against me. Gwyllgi tended to eat people who annoyed them, and I didn't want her primal brain deciding I was some kind of delicacy she had been fattening up for the kill through the course of our friendship.

"I bet we can find more donuts if we split up and check the packing stations." Risking my hand and possibly my life, I stroked her hair. "We bought dozens upon dozens. They can't have eaten them all yet."

The reason for the leftover donuts hit me in the gut, and I sucked in a sharp breath.

Thanks to Lacroix, many of the sentinels I had intended to treat hadn't survived to indulge.

"You okay?" Lethe straightened. "You're not going to faint again, are you?"

"No." I took the opportunity to put a foot of space between us. "I was thinking about the sentinels."

"I shouldn't have eaten their donuts." Tears pooled in her eyes. "I'm a monster."

This time, she lifted the hem of her shirt to blow her nose, and I scrambled away from her bulge.

"You don't have to sit so far away." She wiped her cheeks. "I'm not going to eat you."

"Your stomach." Her belly was taut like she had swallowed a basketball. "How much did you eat?"

"Oh, that." She glanced down. "She grows a little more every day. That's how this works."

"Linus." I heard the shrill note in my voice, and so did Hood, who shot upright. "You need to get over here."

"I'm coming," Hood rasped. "Move aside, Lawson." On hands

and knees, he crawled the six feet between them and plunked down on the floor at her feet, looking puzzled. "What's wrong?"

"That." I pointed at her navel. "That's what's wrong."

"You're freaking me out." Crimson washed over Lethe's eyes. "Start making sense. Right now."

"May I?" Linus indicated her baby bump. "Fair warning, my hands are cold."

Lethe stared at her lap. "If it will wipe that look off her face, go ahead."

Linus almost succeeded in hiding his reaction when she recoiled from his icy touch, but not from me.

"That's actually kind of nice." Lethe relaxed beneath his hands. "I bet you come in really handy during the summer."

Willing to play along, he found a smile for her. "I have my uses."

"The baby?" Hood prompted. "What's wrong with my girls?"

"Nothing as far as I can tell." Linus covered Lethe's stomach with her shirt then stood. "I felt the baby kick, which is a good—if puzzling —sign." At Hood's look, he clarified. "Spontaneous fetal movement begins at eight weeks, but the fetus is too small for it to be noticeable. Most first-time mothers experience the sensation eighteen to twenty-two weeks into their pregnancy. I'm not sure if that timetable holds true for gwyllgi, but wargs and humans have the same gestation period."

"Eighteen to twenty-two weeks?" Hood choked on his tongue. "Are you telling me she's five months pregnant?"

"Developmentally, as near as I can tell, yes."

"We'll be parents in four months." The color drained from his face. "Sooner, at this rate."

"We'll still get to be parents." Lethe leaned down and kissed his pale cheek. "That's what matters."

"We need to get a healer or a physician in-house to monitor you." I cupped her knee and jiggled her leg to get her attention. "Do you have any other contacts in the area?" I hated to ask, but it was careless not to take advantage of the resources at her disposal. "Can your mom send someone?"

"I'll make the call." Lethe glowered at me. "But I won't be happy about it." She tapped a finger against her chin. "I have to think how to phrase this just right. Otherwise, she'll pop up on your doorstep, and nobody—and by nobody, I mean *me*—wants that to happen."

"I'll leave you to it." I rose and cut a line straight for the back porch where I dropped onto the swing. Eager for a distraction, I checked my messages and found one waiting from a jeweler in Atlanta. About to read his reply, I noticed I wasn't alone. "Hey."

"You can't blame yourself." Linus stood in the doorway. "You saved the child, and Lethe."

"I mashed fast-forward on her pregnancy. At this rate, she'll be in labor in two months."

"You performed a miracle, not cast a curse."

"Miracle is a loaded word." I didn't fuss when he sat next to me. "Don't put the weapon in my hand. The first time it misfires, the villagers come after you with torches and pitchforks."

"You have a fixation with torches and pitchforks."

"I watched a lot of classic monster movies with Amelie when we were kids. Those mob scenes set unrealistic expectations. Like those eighties flicks that led an entire generation to believe quicksand would be the greatest danger they faced as adults." I held up my phone. "I've seen the memes. I know what I'm talking about here."

"Do you think it's possible you're fixating on Lethe to avoid thinking about what Boaz told us?"

"The thought crossed my mind. I squished it like a bug."

Silent laughter twitched his shoulders, but his expression held worry. "You don't have to go."

"You're not going alone." No matter what, that remained true.

"Grier..."

"Linus..."

He gathered my hands and brought them into his lap. "You need to take this seriously."

"I have to laugh or I'll cry, and I don't want to fall apart." I let the chill of his skin numb my rising terror. "We don't have the time to glue me back together again. Neither does Savannah."

"I don't want you to go back there." He tightened his grip. "I have an excellent memory. I could—"

"I want to see the collection for myself." I wished I could wipe the cold sweat off my palms, but Linus was holding on too tight. "We can't guess what books we'll need. There are too many, and one person can't skim them all in time." I wet my lips. "With Savannah under siege and Lacroix poised to breach the Lyceum, we might go down in history as the first special exceptions awarded for civilian visitation to the Athenaeum."

"All right." He bobbed his head once. "All right."

The porch light dimmed, and Woolly's wards thrummed with staccato annoyance.

"I wanted to check on Grier," Boaz called. "Everything okay in there?"

"I'm good." I got to my feet and went to greet him, me on the stairs, him safe on the lawn. "I had an involuntary response to our upcoming trip, that's all."

"*Our* trip?" Muscle bulged in his jaw as he grinded what he really wanted to say to dust. "Our trip. Yeah. Okay." He wiped a hand over his mouth. "Okay."

Color me surprised that he handled the news so well. Sure, he was turning a shade of rage-fueled purple that made me worry for his blood pressure, but he kept swallowing every no-doubt-belligerent comment balanced on his tongue until he got them all down.

"I'll put in the request," Boaz decided. "I'm familiar with the location, the staff, and the procedures. I can ask if the interim commander has any objections to my acting as escort since it's my job to keep tabs on you."

The reminder set my own molars scraping, but there was no point in arguing for his reassignment when the sentinels' ranks had been so heavily depleted. After this, he would have no time to act as my shadow. "How soon can we leave?"

The truth was, I was putting on a brave face, but I worried it might crumble if we waited too long.

The rumble of engines and snap of doors slamming caught my attention.

"Linus." Hood stuck his head out, spotted us. "You have guests."

"The artists." Linus drew me to my feet using our joined hands. "Come meet them?"

Boaz noticed my hesitation and volunteered. "I'll come around front."

We passed through Woolly, whose lights burned brighter with her curiosity, and met four women and two men on the lawn. Their styles ranged from jeans and tees to pink tutus over orange fishnets to a button-down shirt with a black satin vest. The art adorning their bodies was just as varied and vibrant as the people wearing them.

"Tatters." Linus projected his voice from the top step. "I'd like to introduce you to Grier Woolworth, my fiancée."

A round of cheers and applause moved through the small gathering.

"Grier, this is Bo, Jean, Jean Too, Lao, DeShawn, and Ringo."

These people had come a long way to do us a favor, so I focused on that spark of gratefulness to find a genuine smile for them.

"Welcome to Savannah, and to Woolworth House." I met them on the grass. "It's great to meet you all." I set out down the stone path leading to the carriage house and waved for them to follow. "I'll show you to your rooms, and your temporary shop."

The fit was tight for six people plus their customers, but I had overheard Linus and Mary Alice breaking them into shifts of three prior to their arrival. That would help cut down on the crush of bodies. Any spillover would have to end up at Woolworth House, which I wanted to avoid if at all possible, and so did Woolly.

"If there's a piece of equipment you need but can't find, or if you run low on supplies, just come to the main house. Someone is there at all times. Ask for Amelie, and she'll get in touch with us."

"I should supervise the initial stages." Linus brushed his lips over mine. "I'll also be instructing the artists on how to safely modify the insomnia tattoos. That might take some time."

Unable to help myself, I ran my fingers through his hair. "Becky would appreciate you looking out for the other sentinels."

"Coordinate with Hood and Boaz," he said, never one to accept praise easily. "Once you decide on a plan of action, I'll be ready to go."

Breaking away from him, I located Boaz near the front gate. On my way, I chose the first two sentinels I came in contact with and handed them over to him. "Here you go."

"Thanks." He glanced between them and me. "What am I supposed to do with them?"

"You're out of your mind if you think you're helping with the Lacroix situation without a tattoo." I shoved him toward the carriage house. "Trust me. It's saved my life, or at least my freedom, more times than I can count."

Mouth tight, he led the others to get their tattoos, leaving me to respond to the jeweler in peace.

The attached image blurred until I had to blink my vision clear and focus on the details.

"Mom is sending her healer." Lethe took the phone out of my hand. "What's got you sniffly?"

"Give me that." I grabbed for her, but she was gwyllgi-fast. "You can't just butt into my texts."

"Oh, wow." Her eyes went glassy with emotion. "He doesn't know?"

"He doesn't know." Using her distraction, I snatched it back. "Don't tell him."

"My lips are sealed."

While I appreciated the sentiment, I highly doubted that was physically possible for Lethe's food portal.

"Keep them that way." I pointed a warning finger at her. "I'm going upstairs. I need to get started on a new sigil design."

The spot between my shoulders itched as she watched me go. She wasn't buying that was the reason, and she was right, but it was one of them.

Once I was alone, I shut the door and used privacy sigils to make sure no one disturbed me.

I had a plan, and claiming Eileen from her perch, I set about hammering out the details.

NINE

Linus found me an hour and a half later. Dawn was behind us, and I was fading. From the patient expression on his face, I suspected he had come to me much sooner, but if he knocked, I hadn't heard. That was the point of the wards. But through them, there was a...I'm not sure how to describe it. I sensed him in the hall, like an invisible string wrapped around my heart had received a firm tug.

He noticed the grimoire first, smelled the blood ink in the air second. "You've been busy."

"Just because you stopped giving me lessons doesn't mean I've become a total slouch."

Eileen kept drawing his interest, but he didn't press me for details. "Did you speak to Boaz?"

"I got sidetracked." I tucked my pen into my pocket. "Did you tattoo Boaz?"

"I did."

"You're really not going to ask?" I grasped his wrist, checking his pulse. "It's killing you. I can tell."

"You locked yourself away for a reason. I assumed if you wanted to share that reason, you would, when you were ready."

"I wasn't hiding from you." It needed saying. "Anything you want to know, all you have to do is ask. I'm an open book for you." I pressed my hand against his chest. "I hope you can tell me anything too."

"Since you feel that way..." He eyed the grimoire. "What were you doing up here?"

"Putting all those hours of tutelage to good use." I patted Eileen's cover. "I've cobbled together a few sigils from my genetic memory to create a mental vault."

The interest vanished, replaced by wariness. "Playing with minds is dangerous."

"The idea is to form a temporary short-term memory pocket where I can store things until I can write them down."

Understanding struck him, but he couldn't erase the proud glint in his eyes. "Clever."

"Necessity being the mother of all invention and whatnot." I shrugged. "We get one shot at the Marchand collection. One shot before Savannah runs out of time. If I can do this, if it works, it's the best chance we're going to get to nail Lacroix."

For Lacroix to wear a medallion as protection, I must be able to take him down with my magic just as easily as I killed other vampires. Or maybe I could break his compulsion over his minions. *But*, and it was a big but, we had to get past its magic before I could work my own.

There was no time to read and absorb every word on every page in every book.

This one time, hopefully with Linus's blessing, I was going to cheat on my homework.

But for now, I was ready to trade sigils for snuggles and get some shut-eye.

THAT NIGHT we received our special dispensation via Boaz, who had been approved to act as our guide through the bowels of Atramentous, and while I was grateful for a friendly face to show us the way, I couldn't deny part of me was hurt he had been stationed there and never told me. I'm not sure why when he had kept so many secrets.

Adelaide, for instance.

On our way out the front door, I noticed the carriage house was full to bursting with sentinels wearing Saniderm patches over their fresh tattoos to quicken the healing process. I was sure, in a day or two, a sigil would finish the process, but for now the clear material kept out dirt, germs, and pretty much everything else.

The usual joking was absent. So was the horseplay I expected to see when so many of them gathered. A tension thrummed through the crowd, and more than one face wore an expression that made it clear they considered the tattoos as memorials.

Given the fact our all-access pass only covered three, I expected Hood to stay behind.

I really should have known better.

"Boaz, you're with me," Hood called, jangling the van keys. "We're all playing so nice together, I don't want to jinx it."

Woolly flapped her shutters before I climbed off the porch, a summoning I couldn't ignore.

The others went ahead while I lingered with an arm wrapped around the nearest column. "What's up?"

A stack of photos flipped through my mind: a starless night, a dripping sink, mold on the caulk in the shower.

"Trust me, if there was another way, I would take it. I don't want to go back, but I have to do this."

"I'm with Woolly," Amelie said softly from behind me. "Are you sure this is a good idea?"

"It's the only one we've got that stands any chance of working." I shifted to face her. "Linus will be there. Boaz too. They'll get me out again, and all in one piece."

Twisting the fabric of her tee, she asked, "Is there anything I can do to help?"

"You're already doing it. You're keeping an eye on Woolly, and you're working your butt off to make sure supplies get where they're needed most."

"It doesn't feel big enough." She smoothed her hands down the wrinkled material, shut her eyes. "Big is what gets me in trouble." She squared her shoulders. "I can do small."

Proud she was learning to rein in her ambition, I clamped a hand on her shoulder. "Thank you."

"I owe you." Her smile was fleeting. "I'm still paying that debt."

Aware the others were waiting, I had to let it go. "Call if anything happens."

Woolly's senses trailed over me as I took the stairs, and she waved her door as I climbed in the van.

Despite the years I had spent in Atramentous, I had no clue where it was located. Grief had blinded me after my sentencing. I had gone numb, unable to believe I was alone again, and unable to fathom what awaited me. The exit hadn't gone any better. The lingering drugs in my system kept the edges too hazy for me to recall much of anything. In some ways, it was like I stepped out of the medical ward and onto my lawn. But there was a flight in there somewhere, and a taxi home.

"I handled all the arrangements." Linus studied my face. "We'll be there and back within nine hours."

"Four hours with the collection?" Through the buzzing in my skull, I thought I remembered hearing that number somewhere. "Any idea how many titles?"

"Forty-eight individual volumes, plus thirty-two journals and assorted notes indexed for reference."

"We're going to need more than one extra vault to hold that." I couldn't imagine it all fitting in my head. "I wonder if one person can wear more than one sigil. Compartmentalize, I mean."

"Using the sigil once is dangerous enough." Linus gave me his best professorial look. "It's untested, and its origins are a genetic database of memory we have no means of validating except as you rediscover each design. There's so much we don't know about the goddess-touched condition." A smile got the best of him, and he indulged. "The sigils in your head connect and reconnect in organic ways as unique as your individual thought process, and you have proven time and time again your instincts are solid."

"Trusting my gut where magic is concerned has worked out so far." I fidgeted in my seat, wishing it was as accurate in other areas of my life. "However, I will allow that I haven't warped anyone's brain." I frowned, considering. "That I'm aware of."

"You're going to experiment on yourself."

"Yes."

"Then you're going to experiment on me too."

"Linus, no."

"Grier, yes."

"You wrote the book on self-inflicted mad scientisting."

"And you showed me the error of my ways."

"I don't want to scramble your brain." I reached out, raking my fingers through his dark hair. "I like your brain."

"I like your brain too." He pressed a kiss to my wrist. "That's why I wish you would apply the sigil to me first, in case there are any immediate side effects."

"You wish, hmm?" I pretended to consider him. "Too bad I'm no genie."

No, really. Just think of all the *rub my lamp jokes* going untold.

THE FLIGHT WAS OKAY. I had no complaints about our accommodations. Linus had booked us first-class seats, and we received preferential treatment because he was the Grande Dame's son and a regular customer of this particular necromancer-owned airline. No, it was the destination that kept me fidgety.

The drive to Atramentous was just as okay as the flight. Linus arranged for a van, same make and model as the one at home, and that gave us plenty of room and separation from the front to allow me time to mentally prepare for what awaited us.

No sooner had I settled my nerves than we slowed next to a guard shack. I couldn't hear the exchange over the roaring in my ears, but Hood must have said the right thing. The red-and-white-striped gate arm rose, and we drove under it without a hitch. Except for the one in my chest.

Chain link fence gleamed in the van lights, the rows upon rows of razor wire glistening like wet teeth.

The final gate required us to exit the vehicle while it was searched, and then we were each patted down. They found my knife, as expected, and tossed it on the backseat. Everything in our pockets, down to the lint, they forced us to leave in the van.

I had never been more jealous of laundry fuzz in all my life.

"You will walk out of there again." Hood clamped his wide palms on my shoulders. "Even if I have to tear this hellhole down brick by brick, or watch Lethe do it, you will return home. This place can't hold you, and these people have no power over you."

"Thanks." I gave him a brief hug. "I needed to hear that."

"Take care of her," he ordered Linus. "You're the next best thing to pack, and that means our oaths are yours."

"This particular oath is no trouble to uphold at all," Linus assured him. "Atramentous won't keep her. It won't touch her. If it tries, you won't have to bother with Lethe or with bricks. I'll level this accursed place myself."

Three guards marched to the checkpoint from the other side, ready to escort us the rest of the way on foot.

I almost jumped out of my skin when the gate clanged shut behind us, and one of the guards chortled.

"Elite Pritchard has been cleared to act as your escort. Do not leave his sight. He is personally responsible for your safety and your conduct." The guard flanking Linus droned on, clearly used to the drill but oblivious to our ultimate destination. "Do not speak to the prisoners unless you have the authorization to do so. Do not attempt to pass them contraband. You will be punished to the fullest extent of the law if you're caught in collusion with an inmate."

"Grier remembers the rules." The chortler held the clipboard with our names. "You spent what? Four years here? Five? I read about it in the paper."

"You must be new," Boaz said, smiling brightly. "Why the hell else would you open your mouth in front of him?"

"Who?" The chortler checked his clipboard, frowned. "Linus...Lawson."

The click in his head as the last name registered was as audible as his gulp.

Moonlight glinted off the blade of the scythe that appeared in Linus's hand, made all the more terrifying by the fact his tattered cloak hadn't manifested along with it. The expensive suit clashed with the weapon dangling casually at his side, and the guards scattered when they spotted the threat.

"I'm a potentate," he informed them. "I have a right to carry a weapon on my person at all times and dispensation to use it whenever I feel threatened, even by a small-minded toad in uniform."

"Understood," the chortler croaked. "Sir."

"Now that we've got that settled," Boaz said, smoothly cutting in front of us, "we'll be on our way."

The guards didn't protest, and Linus didn't let go of his scythe, but they did follow at a respectful distance.

Their fear bolstered my resolve, and when Linus offered me his hand, I balled my fists to keep from taking it, from clinging to him, from letting him protect me from the past. "I can do this."

"Yes, you can." He brushed a lock of hair behind my shoulder, and his fingers tangled in the strands. "Just remember, you don't have to do it alone."

"I'll keep that in mind."

We took a short walk up a paved road lined with pines slowly being devoured by moss and rot. Each step brought us closer to Atramentous, and as it came into view, I was stunned by its ordinariness.

The exterior resembled any number of human prisons. There were guard towers, another fence, more razor wire. The facility itself was small, so small, considering how large it loomed in my nightmares.

"This is it?" The question tumbled out before I could catch it, and I hoped the guards tailing us hadn't overheard.

"This is the surface." Boaz cast me an unreadable look. "This is how they hide it from humans in plain sight. It's registered as a private prison, and its official line is it incarcerates inmates based on contracts landed from some nebulous government agency."

We were greeted at the door by a woman in uniform who smiled when she recognized Boaz. No surprise there.

"It's been a while." She raked hungry eyes over him. "How've you been, sugar?"

"Busy." His aw-shucks routine deepened as they chatted. "You know how it is."

"Heard a rumor you're engaged." She chuckled like it was the greatest joke of all time.

"It's no rumor, Barfoot." He eased past her to punch a code she handed him into a keypad. "I'm off the market."

"Pity." She trailed her fingers across his back as he held the door for us. "When you get bored playing house, you know where to find me."

A hard glint darkened his eyes, surprising me, but he kept his voice playful, and she didn't catch his temper igniting.

"Yeah." He couldn't, or wouldn't, look at me. "I do."

Determined to stay out of his relationship with Adelaide, for real this time, I kept my mouth shut.

The sterile space we entered reminded me of the waiting room in an ER, and I shuddered. Even here, the damp smell of mold permeated the air. Or maybe that was my imagination.

"Stairs to the left." Boaz pointed to a corner. "Elevator to the right."

"The elevator." I wiped my palms on my jeans. "I want this done as fast as possible."

Boaz inputted a second code in the access panel that had the doors sliding open.

What I would have given for those digits during my stay.

The slow creak and hard bumps of the car were the only sounds as it lowered us down the shaft.

We bottomed out with a soft thud that jarred my knees and made me grateful I had no memory of ever using it prior to now.

"We have to walk the length of Row A to reach the next elevator." Boaz hesitated, but he didn't ask me if I was sure I wanted this. We had come too far to go back. "Keep your head down, eyes forward, and put one foot in front of the other."

Six feet past the elevator, I stepped onto a grate slicked with algae, and a sob lodged in my throat.

Here the sterile veneer had cracked and peeled away to reveal the true face of Atramentous.

Here the smooth walls gave way to craggy rock and iron bars flecked with rust the color of dried blood.

Here the moans of the incarcerated beat against my ears like fists the inmates were too weak to raise.

Tendrils of midnight caressed me, but Linus kept his distance. Only his allowing me that tenuous moment to acclimate, without the sensory overload of physical contact, kept me from bolting back the way we'd come.

Make no apologies for surviving.

I had withstood Atramentous for five years.

I could endure it for less than five hours.

If I could just take another step. Just one more step.

There—

No.

Okay.

Try again.

The next time, I made it. And bit by bit, I conquered the long hall, blinding myself to the pitiful souls shoved into the small cubbies bored out on either side of us.

The Society sentenced the worst of their worst criminals to life down here. But I was living proof that the justice system didn't always get it right. How many other innocents had the system failed to vindicate? How many humans had been caged and forgotten, along with the secrets they carried about our existence? How many of these people would make it out of here alive? The answer to that was easy at least. None. Atramentous was where the convicted were tossed to die.

Old Grier had, alone in her cell, with her mouth and her eyes dry.

Another elevator down, another walk through my past, another brick with which to build fresh nightmares.

We repeated the process three more times, for a total of five levels, the lower floors as quiet as tombs.

The air grew ranker as we descended, until my eyes watered, throat burned, and nose grew stuffy. The cells shrunk, and the lights dimmed until even my necromancer vision struggled against the endless blackness.

Filthy inmates lay in heaps on the floor, their eyes blank and their chapped lips slack.

That had been me. For years. A grungy, mindless heap of skin and bones waiting to rot.

The *drip, drip, drip* of water dried the spit from my mouth until I wanted to clamp my hands over my ears and hum over it.

The staircase leading up into my head loomed, pristine and warm, a safe place for me to hide. But I was done with taking the easy way out. I would stay present, I would do my job, and then I would go home.

"This is it." Boaz plugged in his code then waited for the green light before pushing open a reinforced steel door. "Go on in."

Golden light spilled across my face, blinding me, and the

familiar smell of old books overrode the stench polluting the corridor. Boaz didn't have to tell me twice. I couldn't scurry through fast enough.

The jolt of stark white paint, untouched by the ugliness above and around it, and the gleaming tile hurt my eyes after having spent so long in the dark. As my vision adjusted, I distinguished the shape of a guard bent over the thick spine of a hardback thriller. Not exactly Athenaeum material.

"Pritchard," he grunted.

"Marx," Boaz grunted back.

Muscles tight enough to snap, I held my ground, expecting Marx to pat us down, quiz us, something.

"Civilians in the stacks." Licking his thumb, Marx turned the page. "Guess there's a first time for everything."

"Guess so," Boaz replied.

That was apparently that.

Whooshing out the breath I hadn't realized I had been holding, I felt sensation returning to my limbs.

Without setting down his book, Marx rose and used an old-fashioned iron key to twist open a locked door behind him. "You know the rules. Make sure your friends here follow them. You know how pissy Baker gets when protocol is broken."

The scraping of metal on metal left me shivering like the first chemical rush after a plunger depressed.

Don't think about it, don't think about it, don't think about it.

Anyone looking to drug me and fling me into a cell would have to go through Linus first.

Boaz strode into an antechamber and entered a third code to access the Athenaeum.

Breathe in. Breathe out. In. Out. Innn. Ouuut.

I crossed that final threshold, heart knocking against my ribs, and gaped at the books filling floor-to-ceiling shelves.

"Gloves." Boaz offered me a white cotton pair. "There are no guards in this chamber, but it is monitored remotely. They'll kick you out in a heartbeat if you break the rules. They weren't kidding about that."

Given that the sum of all surviving necromantic knowledge resided here, I couldn't blame them. A glance at Linus confirmed he was almost drooling over the vastness of the information here for him to absorb.

"Why store it here?" More books than I had ever seen in my life surrounded us, and given what a packrat Maud was, that was saying something. "The damp is bad for them, and I can't imagine the location makes it easy on its keepers to conceal their comings and goings."

"This area is climate controlled." Boaz pointed out carvings on the shelves. "There are sigils to prevent moisture damage, tearing, flaking, spine cracking." He crossed to a monitor and woke it with a touch. "As to the why, Atramentous is a fortress in the middle of nowhere. It's the last place any sane person wants to go or would ever expect to find a library. As to the rest—" He shrugged. "Prisons require guards. Prisons like Atramentous require Elite guards. No one looks twice at an Elite reporting for duty here. Everyone is aware of Atramentous's reputation, and they want the best-trained soldiers the Society has to police the worst criminals the Society has produced."

"Enlightenment found in the dark," Linus paraphrased the line from Severine's forged last words to me. "The Society does enjoy its cruel irony."

"This is an impressive setup," I admitted. "What I don't get is why you wanted to come here."

"Isn't it obvious?" Boaz made quick selections on a touchscreen, proving his familiarity with the indexing system.

"Yes, that's why I asked. I already know, but I wanted to hear you say it."

"I had to see it for myself." He kept going, digging through the archive to locate what we sought. "I had to know if it was how I imagined." He mashed a final button and collected a printout. "It was worse." He passed it to me. "I wish I had never requested library detail. Whatever answers I hoped to find, they weren't in this place." He exhaled in a rush. "But I can't help wondering if maybe it was all part of the goddess's plan."

The strained quality of his voice caught my attention. "What do you mean?"

"I might not have been telling the whole truth about receiving special dispensation."

"What?"

"There was no time. It can take months for a book petition to be granted." He looked to Linus for backup. "The Lyceum has fallen, Savannah is in chaos, and the Grande Dame is too busy playing general to hold the formal hearing required. The odds of her gathering enough dames and matrons to cast the votes required are nil. So, I had a friend on the inside give me her code."

That explained the handsy greeting he received upon arrival and why the woman had taken liberties. Boaz only had one kind of female *friend*, and they tended to be *very* friendly toward him.

"Commander Roark had the right to override the Grande Dame. He was the ultimate authority when it came to the Athenaeum." Boaz rubbed a hand over his buzzed hair. "So I forged the paperwork to give us immediate access and then backdated it. That got us down here. But without him to issue a password override, I had to borrow one."

"You're an idiot." I gave him a quick hug before I changed my mind. "A total moron."

And we were all going to get in *so* much trouble when this was over.

"Yeah." His arms came up and held on for the briefest moment before releasing me. "That's what the women in my life keep telling me."

"Maybe you should listen to them once in a while?" Fresh urgency to get this done and get gone before Boaz's deceit was discovered kindled in me, and I led the way to the section where the Marchand collection was being stored. "Hard to believe everything known about the goddess-touched condition is right here at our fingertips." I almost caressed the first spine before I caught myself. "Here goes nothing."

As we rehearsed in the van, I reached for Linus's hand, playing damsel overcome by memories for the cameras, and he removed his twist-tie ring and pressed it into my palm. Curling against his chest, I pricked my fingertip and drew the sigil first on myself and then, when I didn't turn into a mindless zombie, I gave him a matching one.

The fit of smugness that had me glancing up at him died a swift death when I saw his eyes had bled black from corner to corner.

Thumb poised to smudge the sigil, for all the good it might do, I shook him. "Linus?"

Jaw tight, he blasted out a sigh. "That was harder to watch than I anticipated."

"Remember this the next time you're tempted to play guinea pig for yourself."

"Time's wasting." Boaz tapped the face of his tactical watch. "You two need to get reading."

"We'll discuss the dangers of field-testing original sigils later," Linus assured me, forever unfurling in his eyes.

"Sure thing." I patted his cheek, which caused Boaz to tense on my periphery. "He would never hurt me, Boaz. Not in a million years."

"Never," Linus agreed, and blue sliced through the black. "That doesn't mean I won't lecture her on sigil theory until her ears bleed."

The great thing about having sex with your former tutor is boobs are really distracting. I've gotten out of a lot of not-quite-homework by flashing them, and he never seems to catch on. Or if he does, he doesn't seem to mind. They were my *get out of lecture free* cards, and I played them every chance I got.

"I'll take the left." I kissed his frosty lips. "You take the right."

Power tingled in my palm when I lifted the first book. The thin barrier of the cotton glove I pulled on was no match for it. Like called to like, and its energies prickled over my skin. A glance over at Linus's studious expression convinced me he wasn't experiencing the same sensations. Otherwise, he would have been examining me out of the corner of his eye to see if it affected us both.

Shoving that aside for later reflection, I turned to the first page and began reading.

An audible click filled my head, and I wobbled beneath the tangible weight of...I don't really know what. But when I picked up where I had left off, I couldn't read enough.

A fierce hunger burned in my gut, igniting a longing for an unnamed craving, but I couldn't be sated. The more I read, the more I wanted to read. The quicker I read, the more the words blurred. I couldn't have stuck a straw in the spine and slurped it up faster than I was devouring it with my eyes.

More, more, more was all I could think as my brain began sizzling with information overload.

The jolt of a cool hand on my nape snapped my head up, and I gulped like I had been drowning without realizing how far I had drifted.

"Our time is up," Linus told me. "We have to go."

Sinking back into my skin, I pulled my thoughts back in order. "How did I do?"

"You cataloged the entire collection," he marveled. "I finished my half, but it's superfluous."

The instant he set down a book on his end, I had snatched it up and gulped down its information. I remembered that, the agony of waiting, the thirst for the next long drink at what had seemed like an endless fount of knowledge. But to hear it had run dry after all...

Suddenly parched, my tongue darted out to wet my lips and found them cracked.

"Did you retain it?" Bracing his hands on my shoulders, Linus stared into my face. "All of it?"

"Yes." I rubbed the heels of my palms over my face, but it did nothing to erase the lines of text burned into the backs of my eyelids. "I have the worst headache."

Boaz peered over Linus's shoulder. "You've got what you need?"

"Yeah." I swayed when I attempted to step around Linus. "It feels like you stacked all those books on top of my head, and if I don't balance them, they'll fall."

"Let's get her out of here." Boaz crossed to the panel and entered the code. Throwing his weight into it, he swung open the massive door and led us back into the antechamber. "I need a second to lock this."

Sweat poured down my spine, and the room began to spin. The edges stretched and twisted until they resembled the cramped handwriting I had spent the past four hours reading, but I couldn't make out the words. They were gibberish no matter how I squinted.

"Hush," Linus whispered in my ear. "You're reciting from the books."

Mashing my lips together got us past Marx, but I was babbling again by the time we reached the first elevator. All we could do was hope a verbal purging wouldn't erase my temporary memory bank.

Linus held me and stroked my back, guided me and shielded me, as Boaz led us to the surface.

"Hey, handsome." The female guard sashayed over to Boaz and all but climbed up him as she wrapped her arms around his neck. "Miss me?"

"Actually, no." He clasped her wrists and peeled her off him. "I didn't." He strapped on a stern expression. "I already told you. I'm engaged. That means I'm off the market. I appreciate your help, but I'm not pulling down my pants—or yours—to pay for it."

What a fine time for him to sprout a conscience. Goddess preserve us.

Fury turned the scorned woman incandescent. "You'll regret this."

Uncertain if she meant to bash his head in with the radio she snapped off her belt or commit career suicide by admitting to her peers she had let Boaz in without authorization, I couldn't take the chance.

Using the twist tie I hadn't returned to Linus, I pricked my finger again and wrote a sigil on her forehead that caused the harsh lines to soften and her lips to go slack.

"This is front gate," a man barked. "Visitation, do you copy?"

Boaz took the radio from her limp fingers and held it to her mouth.

"Ten-four," she said dreamily. "Have a nice day."

Boaz caught her when her knees buckled and laid her out on the floor. "What was that?"

"I don't know." I massaged my temples. "I reached for a solution, and that sigil presented itself."

"The information is fighting to get out." Linus hooked an arm around my waist. "I feel it too, pushing at the edges of my brain. Just hold on a little longer, and try not to use what you've learned until we can examine the sigils outside of our heads."

"Sure thing." I slumped against him. "Can I nap now?"

Without hesitation, Linus scooped me up in a bridal carry. "Of course."

Given my history with the prison, the guards didn't ask too many questions about why Linus had to carry me out. The chuckler, having recovered his bravado, made a snide comment about me being too weak to make it in Atramentous, like I hadn't already done my time. I squeezed Linus's arm, but I could tell it cost him to do nothing.

Just when I thought we were in the clear, a high-pitched shriek raised the hairs down my arms.

Sirens.

Ten times louder and harsher than the severe weather sirens in town, these screamed warning. Danger. *Escape.*

"That's the emergency siren." The chuckler glanced around before zeroing in on us. "You'll have to come with me."

Panic unfurled wings in my chest and took flight, and I wriggled against Linus until he hushed me.

"Sorry, man." Boaz knocked him out cold with a single uppercut. "But you had that coming."

Another guard swung his gaze to Linus then backed away slowly before breaking into a run.

"You won't make it." The remaining guard, just as wary of Linus, raised his hands. "No one does."

Boaz took the guard's weapons then ordered him back to visitation.

"How do we get out?" Linus asked Boaz when we were alone again.

"People don't *get out* of Atramentous." He worked his jaw. "I thought we had time."

"We're not *in* Atramentous." Linus maintained his cool. "We're in a yard surrounded by a fence."

"You're splitting hairs, Lawson, and you know it."

"Grier, you're going to have to wake up now." Linus bit the cap off his pen then swiped a sigil across my forehead. "How do you feel?"

The fog swirling through my head began to lift, and clarity seeped in. "Like I should have whammied that guard harder."

"Your brain is working overtime. The sigil boosted its capacity, but it's depending on your body to fuel it. Holding on to all the information you crammed into it is exhausting." Linus lowered me down until I bore my own weight. "The sigil I used on you won't last long against the strain, but it should keep your head clear until we get out of here."

Nodding that I understood, I searched his pinched expression. "How are you holding up?"

"I'm hypothesizing on your condition based on mine." A tiny smile flirted with his mouth. "We're both going to crash, and hard. Soon."

"Then we better get out of here fast." I picked the scab on my palm until fresh blood welled. Using my finger, I drew fresh impervious sigils on Boaz, Linus, and then myself. "We're walking out of here."

Any larger, and Boaz's eyes would swallow him whole. "We can't just—"

"I'm not going back." I'm not proud of how my voice broke. "I am *not* going back." Linus massaged my nape. "We go through. Together. All of us. We're walking out of here."

"We go through," he agreed. "Together."

A switch flipped, and a calm, cool, and collected soldier stood in Boaz's place. "We go through."

All the fear and concern twisting him up vanished. I wondered at that, and then I got it.

Boaz had cut the last tie between us. He was forcing himself to stop looking at me as his sister's best friend, as the girl who had crushed on him for years, as the woman whose heart he had broken, and see me for who and what I had become. Really see me, all of me.

Thanks to his injury, he had missed out on the miracle of his healing. But he would be wide awake for this. There would be no going back, no pretty little lies he could tell himself. For better or for worse, the whole truth of my potential would be laid bare to him.

I was no longer helpless Old Grier. I was New Grier, and she was fierce.

As much as I once craved validation from him, I almost regretted the loss of the last shred of innocence between us. He would never look at me the same way again, and there was a sadness in shedding the last vestiges of our childhood.

The guard took aim, at me. He must have thought I was the weakest link, or he hoped Linus's and Boaz's chivalrous streak ran deep enough that it would stop them in their tracks.

"I'll handle this." I dipped into the knowledge filling my head to bursting and isolated the perfect sigil.

"No." Boaz stepped in front of me. "I got you into this mess. Let me get you out of it." He rolled his shoulders. "I want the fault for this to land squarely where it belongs—on me."

The light trot he started off in kicked up to a punishing jog after the first bullets pinged off his ward without inflicting any damage. He reached the first man and disarmed him. Using the butt of the rifle, Boaz knocked the guard out cold then made the rounds to the others who were too stunned to stop firing and run. He disabled them, but he didn't kill them. Maybe that would win us points when this went to trial.

Goddess.

A trial.

I didn't have to try hard to imagine sentinels cinching their hands around my upper arms then hauling me out of Woolworth House while I kicked and screamed for Maud.

Yanking myself out of that emotional tailspin was hard, maybe the hardest thing I've ever done, but I got my head back on straight. Thanks to Amelie, I had money tucked away where no one would find it. I had resources, though I hesitated to use them. The pack had hidden Taz, they would do the same for me, but it would bring down a lot of heat on their heads. And that didn't take into account Linus or his duties or the repercussions for shirking them if this all went south.

But what alternative did we have? Lacroix had Savannah by the short hairs. We needed help, or the city was going to fall, and the rest of the country would hear when she hit her knees. The existence of supernaturals would be out in the open, and hysteria would sweep across the world. True witch hunts would begin, and I would get my chance to see if torches and pitchforks were as passé as Linus believed.

Boaz waved us on, and we ran through the checkpoint to the other side.

"Ever consider marketing this?" Boaz indicated the sigil. "The Elite would pay an arm and a leg for one."

"This magic, my magic, isn't for public consumption." The vague dream of becoming a practitioner, an innovator, like Maud, had died somewhere between Volkov kidnapping me and Odette's betrayal. I had no idea what I wanted to do, aside from embrace Linus's dream for me of running my own ghost tour company, but it wasn't designing weapons for the Society to use against its enemies, and it wasn't adding to the number of vampires walking the earth. "I outed myself, and I can't change that, but I won't sell, trade, or license this sigil or any others."

After careful consideration, he said, "Okay."

I could tell he didn't get why I wouldn't want to share this knowledge, but it was enough that he respected my decision.

"That can't be good," Boaz breathed. "Your friend shifted."

Sure enough, Hood paced the length of the last gate between us and freedom on all fours.

"I hope he didn't eat the guard," I panted. "That's not going to look great for any of us."

By the time we reached the gate, Hood had resumed his human shape. He swiped a keycard he must have lifted off the guard I hoped he hadn't picked out of his teeth, and let us through.

We didn't waste time with questions, just sprinted for the van. And almost tripped over the prone guard, who was crumpled on the asphalt with blood matting his hair. I leapt over him, not my finest moment, and dove for the backseat.

Once Hood cranked the engine and peeled out of the drive, he singled me out. "I didn't kill him."

"Are you sure?"

"I've killed enough people to know." The patronizing tone didn't help with my nerves. "After the alarm was raised, he tried ordering me out of the van. I declined. He insisted. I was forced to convince him to see my point of view."

"I hope he doesn't suffocate," I muttered.

"I turned his head to one side," Hood said smugly then sobered. "Did you get it?"

"Yep." I tapped the side of my head. "Now to see what it is I got."

Linus hauled Eileen, who I should have packed, out of his bag. "I brought her along, just in case."

The grimoire blinked up at me, her many eyes scanning the darkened interior in every direction, and she flipped open on my lap.

"See?" I pointed to her blank pages. "That's what I'm talking about."

"Here." He passed me a modified pen with a fresh ink cartridge. "Purge."

My hand didn't wait for the order before it started moving across the page. "What about you?"

"I came prepared." The heavy tome he lifted glittered when we passed beneath a streetlight, its scales the size of my thumbnail and shaped like acorns, if acorns ended in razor tips. "We can compare notes when we're done, determine how accurate the information is we gathered. If we produce two identical duplicates of an original, we can verify not only that your mind expansion design works, but that the information we gathered is correct."

I bumped his knee with mine. "Not so superfluous after all, huh?"

Heads bent over our grimoires, we spent the drive to the airport and the flight home absorbed by transcribing all we had read. We took a break in the SUV on the way to Savannah, wary that our misfortune might have spilled out into the neighboring towns, but the Society had done an admirable job of locking down the surrounding area.

The barricade was laughable. There weren't enough sentinels left, even with aid coming in from other cities, to prevent any real trouble. Still, their presence was a comfort, and I was grateful for every woman and man who risked their lives in the wake of such tragedy to protect the city.

Boaz elected to stay with the sentinels. He wanted to argue his case with the new interim commander before Atramentous sent a team to retrieve us. Linus was thinking along the same lines, attempting to contact his mother and give his report before she heard the news elsewhere.

That left me to sit and reflect over Eileen, who I barely remembered filling with pages and pages of knowledge it would take a lifetime to fully absorb and learn to apply. Information I once felt ought to be put into the hands of all goddess-touched necromancers, until the scope of my power, and the potential for its abuse, made me grateful the Marchands had hoarded their knowledge.

"We're here."

I opened my eyes, not sure when I closed them. I hadn't had much of a nap, but it had refreshed me better than the sigil Linus used on me earlier. That, or the plan blooming in my mind's eye had erased my exhaustion. "I have an idea of how we can take down Lacroix."

Linus awarded me his full attention. "Purging jogged something loose?"

"Lacroix's amulet contains a lock of Mom's hair. She wasn't goddess-touched, but she must have carried the gene." I scratched my hairline, wishing I could reach my brain, where I itched even worse. "Hair is good for a century, depending on the strength of the practitioner, but its power fades over time. For him to be so cocky, so certain it will protect him from my magic, he must have a fresh sample. While it's possible he sourced it elsewhere, I don't see why he would bother when he had Mom under his roof for a time."

"A servant could have taken a sample from her hairbrush, or Odette might have collected it later."

I read the question in his eyes and answered, "He can't use my own hair against me."

Surprise creased his forehead. "This is new information?"

"Yes." Though I might have figured it out if I had thought about it. "Trusting my hair, blood, or anything else, means trusting my magic to always work against me when it doesn't always behave the way it should when applied to me."

"A goddess-touched artifact, made by another goddess-touched necromancer, can negate your power." He organized my rambling with his usual eloquence. "Your magic acts and reacts in unpredictable ways when you use it on yourself. He would be gambling with his life at every encounter, and he's too canny for that."

"A talisman containing the same essence as his medallion would nullify his protections." I winced as my nails drew blood and forced my hand into my lap. "There's only one source we can be certain is undiluted and hers."

Her heart.

As much as I wanted to do this on my own, I wasn't certain I could open the box that had haunted a shelf in Maud's office since Mom died. Maud kept it just high enough I couldn't reach it when I was a kid, and by the time I was tall enough to take it down, I couldn't bear to look at it, let alone touch it. And if I couldn't hold the box, how could I collect a sliver of its contents?

Linus gathered my twitching hands in his lap, and his were rock steady. "Let me do this for you."

"Okay," I said weakly, hating that I didn't put up a fight, that I was too grateful when he let me off the hook.

But that's how relationships worked. You leaned on each other when you couldn't stand on your own.

"Atramentous will dispatch sentinels to bring us in soon if they haven't already." I linked our fingers and walked with him up the front porch steps. "Lacroix struck first and hard. We need to make sure he doesn't get a chance to show us what else he's got up his sleeves."

TEN

Purging hadn't fixed the massive headache throbbing in my temples, but it had eased off some. There must be more to dump out of my brain, but I'm not sure where I would put it. Eileen was... Huh. Actually, Eileen was holding every drop of information I had poured onto her pages so far. Either she had an infinite number of them, or I had discovered another quirk brought on by combining goddess-touched blood and sigils with a fae skin-bound book. Though, I suppose it was called *magic* for a reason.

Without another trip to Atramentous, to the Athenaeum, we had no way to be one hundred percent certain I had retained all the information. Likewise, we couldn't be certain without a page by page comparison that I had transcribed all I had retained. But I had gotten this far using my gut as the gauge for my goddess-touched powers, and it said the sigil had done the job.

The lock on the basement door was thirsty, so I fed it a few drops of blood to ease the way.

As we descended into the black void cloaking the stairs meant to deter uninvited guests, Woolly nudged me with her consciousness, the planks popping with a demand we stop and explain what had us so grim-faced.

When I hit the bottom and Maud's personal library came into view, Woolly killed the lights and pitched us back into darkness.

"We found a way to make Lacroix vulnerable." I hooked my hands on my hips. "We need Mom's heart."

A spark lit in the vicinity of Maud's office, her real one, not the dummy office upstairs.

"Yeah." As much as the light beckoned, I couldn't get my feet to budge. "Linus?"

"I'll be right back."

He strode right to the office without stumbling or tripping a million times like I would have if I had tried to navigate the clutter, and he went straight where the golden box holding Mom's heart had rested in a place of honor, on a shelf that had been eye-level with Maud when she sat at her desk.

Wrapping my arms around myself, I waited with Woolly as precious metal scraped when he cracked the hinged lid. I shut my eyes, pretending this wasn't happening, that we weren't desecrating my mother's remains because my psycho grandfather refused to allow her peace, even in death.

Linus's utter stillness jerked me to attention, and I craned my neck to see better. "What is it?"

"Woolly, enough with the theatrics." The bite in his voice gave me shivers. "Turn on the lights."

A haunting moan drifted down from the ceiling where the old floorboards buckled and warped.

"Now," he ordered, and she obeyed without another peep.

Light flooded the space, but I wish she had kept me in the dark. Whatever put that ravaged look on his face guaranteed I would be wearing a matching expression soon. I hurt, and I didn't even know why yet.

Try as I might, I couldn't unstick my feet. They were glued in place.

For that reason, Linus brought the box to me. He hadn't shut it, which saved me from fumbling it open, but I found the paralysis had traveled up my legs into the rest of my body.

"Grier." He gentled his voice. "There's nothing to see. You can look."

"No." Shock ricocheted through me, and I snatched the box out his hands. "It can't be."

This was Maud all over again.

No heart, no heart, no heart.

Knees buckling, I crumpled before Linus could scoop me against him.

"I don't understand." I looked up at him. "Linus? I...I...don't understand."

Slowly, he joined me on the floor and reached for the box, which I hadn't wanted to touch but couldn't seem to let go of now that I held it. "Check the lid."

Expecting an inscription, I almost recoiled from the note pinned there. "Read it to me."

With gentle fingers, he pulled it free. "Are you sure?"

"Yes." I cradled the box to my chest. "Please."

The care he showed as he unfolded the message both moved me and tempted me to snatch it from his hand and devour it with my eyes the way I had the books in the Athenaeum.

All this time, the box had been a decoy, a trick the Grande Dame must have learned from Maud.

Goddess, I was tired of no one ever telling me the truth. All these empty gestures were just that—empty.

"*My darling girl,*" he began. "*I never wanted a child.*"

A knife to the heart would have hurt less than hearing him read those words, Maud's words, to me.

About to let the paper collapse into its creases, Linus asked, "Should I keep going?"

Unable to find my voice, I nodded then wrapped my arms around me as tight as they could go.

"*I didn't understand why your mother pined for one. I had never been around them, and I had no wish to surround myself with miniature people who had yet to learn the art of conversation or personal hygiene.*"

A broken laugh escaped me, and it felt better than the hurt.

"*I can't say I would have stepped in when your mother passed had you been anywhere other than here when it happened. I could dismiss the charm of a smiling photo tucked into an envelope, or the drawing of a young hand that already showed promise, but I couldn't shore up my heart against you from the moment you walked into my home, looking every bit like your mother, and offered me a yellow dandelion with a milky stem.*"

The memory, so hazy around the edges, drifted on the edge of recollection.

"*I was tempted to send you away after Evie died. You were her spitting image, and I saw her looking out at me from your face. That is perhaps why, in the end, I couldn't bear to part with you. You were all that remained of my dearest friend, and I told myself I could let her go if I kept you, that she would live on through you.*"

Tears ran hot and slick down my cheeks, but there was no point wiping them away when there was no end to them.

"*But I fooled myself, darling. And I fooled you too. Until you opened this box, which means I am dead and you are looking for answers to questions you never knew to ask. I am sorry for how I raised you. I did my best, but I am no Evangeline. That is why I preserved her, as much as possible, for the both of us.*"

Dread pooled in my gut. "Preserved her?"

Linus skimmed the page again. "Do you want me to keep reading?"

"No." But I gestured him on.

"*I wanted you to grow up in a house filled with love, and I feared I wouldn't be equal to the task. To ensure you never felt the lack of your mother, I surrounded you with her. Four walls, a floor, and a ceiling make a house, but her spirit made this our home.*"

The room began spinning, slowly at first, then gathering more speed.

"*I was never prouder than the day you took my last name. I never wanted a child, but I wanted you.*" Linus tore his gaze from the paper. "*Love eternal, Maud.*"

"I don't understand." I rested the back of my head against the wall. "I don't understand anything anymore."

Woolly cocooned me in her presence while the pages of books on the shelves rustled a hushing sound.

Then I understood.

And what Atramentous had failed to do, Maud's letter accomplished.

It broke me. Shattered me. Smashed my sense of self to dust and scattered it to the four corners.

Mom was...

Mom was...

Woolly.

"How could she?" I sobbed against Linus when he pulled me onto his lap. "*How could she?*"

There wasn't so much difference between what I suspected Maud had done to Mom and what I had done to Maud. Both of us had damned someone we loved to a half-life.

"She should have told me." I pounded on his shoulder. "Why didn't Maud tell me?"

Rather than answer my question, Linus addressed the house herself. "Evangeline?"

The whirl of cool air from the vents overhead sounded like a sigh held too long gusting free.

"This is too much." Tired of taking it out on him, I curled in a ball against his chest. "I just—I can't, Linus."

Woolly slid into my head with ease and began flipping through the pages of a photo album that existed nowhere except in her memories. Snippets of video interspersed the stills, all viewed from Evangeline's perspective. A lifetime cobbled together in fits and starts, stops and pauses, and that was her proof and her confession.

Maud, impossibly young, dancing the tango with Clarice while Mom cackled in the background.

A dark-haired man with eyes the exact shade of mine smiling down at her. When his rich voice promised, "I will love you always," I could tell she had believed him.

Grief, as vast and endless as the ocean swallowing her when those same eyes closed for the last time.

Maud opening the front door of Woolworth House, taking one look at her best friend, and wrapping her arms around her while Mom sobbed her heart out against Maud's bony shoulder.

Maud staring down at me with hard eyes that softened when I passed her a weed I picked from the lawn because I thought it was pretty and she thought it indicated gardening potential.

Mom's hands covered in blood where she gripped the wheel of her car, the sound of tires pealing on asphalt.

The next clip showed Maud's face, red and splotchy and slick with tears, screaming at her.

"Live, damn it." She shook Mom. "Evie. Think of your little girl. Think of Grier." Her voice broke. "Think of me." The scene went dim. "What will we do without you?"

Finally, Woolly showed me the moment she awakened, not as a person but as a place.

"Forgive me, old friend." Maud stood in her library. "I couldn't let you go."

The spirit of Evangeline Marchand stretched out her senses, testing the boundaries of her new body.

"I don't know what the hell I'm doing. Why did I think I could raise your child? She needs you, not me."

Evangeline went to comfort her friend but found only the rustle of curtains and creaking of floorboards for a voice.

"You warned me." Maud leaned her forehead against the wall. "I didn't listen. I never do. Not even to you. You told me one day I would go too far, and you were right."

The rest were snapshots of my life, as seen through Woolly's eyes, proof she had watched over me every single day, until Atramentous, and after. And then she withdrew, giving me space to think without the past clogging my mind.

"I don't remember a time when Woolly wasn't Woolly," I said softly. "I assumed she had always been...herself."

Since Mom died the day after we arrived in Savannah, she always had been this way for me.

"The first time Amelie stayed over, she asked me why our house was haunted," I told him. "Until she mentioned it, I figured all necromancers lived in haunted houses. I didn't realize Woolly was special."

"You were young, and you moved around a lot." Linus stroked my back. "You had no reason to know any different."

"It made me curious." And a little bit scared, if I was being honest. "I asked Maud the next night."

"What did she tell you?"

"That Woolly wasn't a ghost, that our house wasn't haunted. That Woolly was a gentle spirit who looked over us, like a domovoy. And when I asked what that was, she gave me a book on Slavic folklore and told me to read up on them." I slanted him a look. "Maud named her Lady Woolworth. Do you remember that? But *never* Lady for short. The title was a mouthful for a kid. Over time, I started calling her Woolly, and it stuck."

"A benevolent household spirit guarding its descendants sounds closer to the truth than the version she told me." Linus grew pensive. "She claimed she once had a lab assistant who asked too many questions. One night, he showed up for work, pulled a book down off a shelf without permission, and it hit him in the head, killing him instantly. That it was his spirit haunting the house."

I fought off the laugh that wanted to surface. "How old were you?"

"This was right after you arrived, so ten or eleven. Old enough to not quite believe her, but young enough to acquire manners overnight. I never asked her about Woolly or took a book without asking from that day on."

"She was a good mom." I pressed my face against his chest. "She wasn't a mom-mom, but she was good to me. I always felt loved. I never felt unwanted or like a burden. She was the best not-mom a kid could ask for."

"Maud loved you, very much. Anyone could see it. Even Lacroix gave her a wide berth."

"Imagining him scared of her does make me feel better," I admitted, gathering my resolve around me. "She raised me. He's going to learn to fear me too."

"We'll figure another way to take out Lacroix."

"This can work," I insisted. "We still have a chance."

The old house lingered on the edge of my perception, giving me space as a withered shadow cloaked in tattered fabric appeared before me.

Cletus reached for me, stroking my cheek with cold fingers, and I took his bony hand.

The violent spike in my emotions had summoned him to me sure as the goddess made green apples, and his presence scraped my already frayed nerves raw.

Maud and Mom.

Mom and Maud.

Best friends trapped in separate eternities neither ever imagined nor wanted for each other.

"Maud..." I swallowed once, tried again. "Do you remember where you put Mom's heart?"

The wraith tilted his head, thinking on the location or questioning what I meant, I couldn't tell. But when he continued to drift, offering no insight, I accepted what I had known all along.

Maud wasn't in there. Not really. Her memories and thoughts had been erased, leaving vague emotions, faint instincts, an echo of who and what she had been in life.

"It's okay if you don't know." I squeezed his fingers. "You can go back to Corbin now."

Cletus lingered seconds longer, staring at me from beneath his cowl, but whatever he wanted to convey, he lacked the faculties to communicate.

All I could do as he vanished was hope one day that might not be the case, that I might recover more of Maud during my life, or, failing the discovery of a miraculous cure to wraithism, learn how to lay her to rest when Linus and I ran out of days to walk the earth. She deserved that peace, and I would see she had it before I had mine.

Once I was certain my voice wouldn't wobble, I screwed up the nerve to ask Woolly, "Where did Maud put your heart?"

Woolly showed me a picture of herself, as viewed from the driveway. That was it. Just...the house.

"Your essence was absorbed by Woolworth House," I realized. "Maud must have made a paste with your heart instead of using your blood for ink in the binding."

"The severity of the accident, and its public nature, must have limited what Maud could collect without human interference." Linus considered me. "That, or at the time of the accident, she hadn't yet decided to take such drastic measures. She might not have gotten the idea until she brought the heart home with her after it was presented to you. With Evangeline's blood unavailable, it would have been Maud's only source for a tissue sample at that point."

"And if Maud used the heart for ink, the mixture would have dried on the wood." I drummed my fingers on the wall. "Can you show me where the sigil was drawn?"

A warped bookcase groaned, and several leather-bound journals toppled onto the floor.

I got to my feet and gave an experimental tug then glanced back at Linus. "Help me move it?"

Together we lifted the sagging wood and hauled it into the middle of the room. Behind it, painted on the wall, in ink too viscous to ever fade, throbbed a dark crimson sigil that beat...like a heart.

"Mom," I whispered, still unable to believe, and the sigil thumped harder in recognition.

Maud truly had made Mom the heart of our home, and I wasn't sure if I hated her or loved her for it.

All those times I let humans pay to spend the night in a haunted house, I had been pimping out my own mother to the supernaturally devout. I had gotten money in exchange for giving them a chance to gawk at her.

Make no apologies for surviving.

Those visitors might have gawked, but they also coughed up money that kept her lights on and ramen in my pantry.

Warmth curled around me, air blowing from a vent clear across the room, and Woolly offered one last image: a wooden stake.

"I won't disrupt the sigil," I told her, and Linus frowned as he pieced together what I meant.

"Your mother is the house. This is her heart, but she is present everywhere."

Relief shuddered through me. "Do you think a piece of trim would work just as well?"

"Yes." He studied the rhythmic pulsing a moment longer. "We need to conceal this first to protect her." He gripped the bookcase. "One smudge could break the sigil."

And Mom would die, for real this time.

Maud hadn't asked her permission, and Mom hadn't given her consent. Mom might not want—

The question hadn't fully formed before Woolly plucked it out of my head and tossed it aside to make room for all the nursery ideas I suspected she had been collecting from the home improvement shows Lethe had been bingeing lately.

"All you have to do is ask," I forced out, hoping I never had to make good on the offer.

"You offered to set her soul free," Linus surmised. "She declined."

"I think...maybe I'm the only one who can." I studied the sigil one last time, its design echoing through me, resonating with a half-forgotten sketch drawn on a paper in red crayon. "This design..." I had to fight through the guilt threatening to sink me. "It's familiar."

"Do you think Maud asked for your help?"

"Yes." The harder I concentrated, the brighter the memory shone. "I'm not sure, but...I think she asked me to imagine Mom hadn't died, that we were bringing her home, where she would be safe always. I..." I shook my head. "Maud wanted a sigil that would prevent Mom from leaving the house ever again, and I gave her enough, even then, to do this." Another thought occurred to me. "What are the odds she used my blood to create the ink? It would explain why Woolly and I are tied so closely to one another."

Maud had treated Woolly with such respect, like she was a person, a member of our family. I had grown up doing the same, taking for granted that she had always been how I remembered her from the start.

"I assumed your bond was stronger because Woolly helped raise you, but it's possible the connection goes deeper. She's always viewed you as her child, and she always welcomed your friends. She's a significant figure in your life."

"I'm not sure if I can forgive Maud for this," I admitted. "But if I don't—if I can't—there's no hope she can ever forgive me either."

"Love drives us all to make mistakes in the name of protecting those we cherish." He lifted his end of the bookcase, and I did the same, helping him set it back in place. "The ends don't always justify the means, and the reverse is also true, but I think, in this case, Woolly is cognizant enough of her past, her history, and her present circumstances to make a sound decision for herself."

Linus jolted, and then he laughed outright.

"Babies again," I muttered. "She hit you with the nursery ideas, didn't she?"

"She's got a detailed list of how she wants each nursery to look."

"Each nursery?" I felt faint. "How many kids does she think I'm having?"

"From my count?" Linus pursed his lips. "Twenty-four. There was also a puppy this time, so that's new."

Eyeing the ceiling, I huffed, "You're choosing pets for them too?"

Woolly zapped me with the image of a small puppy with russet fur and only a hint of scales covering her forehead zooming through the house while a boy with Linus's hair and my eyes toddled after her, clapping his hands with delight.

"Not a puppy." I heard the wonder in my voice, the acceptance that Lethe's baby bump was an actual child, not just a persistent food belly. "Lethe and Hood's daughter."

"Only one?" Linus chuckled. "No litters in her future?"

The old house appeared to consider that, but she had her priorities in order.

Priorities that made a lot more sense considering they would be her grandchildren. No wonder she wanted a house full of them.

Unsure, I asked the old house, "Do you want me to call you Mom?"

Woolly shared the same image as before—the house as viewed from the driveway.

"Okay." I lingered a moment longer. "If you change your mind..."

The floor beneath us rolled in a gentle wave, Woolly urging us along.

Obviously, she had absorbed the chaos of my day while sharing her vision for the future with me.

"She's right." I nudged Linus toward the stairs. "We have to go."

"Where will you get your sample?"

"There are a few warped planks I've been meaning to replace near the back stairs. I can shave a slice off one of the raised ends without doing much damage."

"All right."

We bumped into Amelie on the porch, who was sitting on the swing with a box of toiletries at her feet.

"You guys look like you're in a hurry." She glanced up, checklist in hand. "Am I in the way?"

"This won't take but a minute." I chose the board with the worst damage, knelt beside it, and pulled out my pocketknife. "Brace yourself, Woolly." Tension strummed through our connection as I cut a sliver as big as my thumb. "Done." I checked with her, but she pushed assurance she was fine back at me, so I turned to Linus. "Your room or mine?"

Amelie cleared her throat and got busy sorting and resorting her piles.

"Yours," he decided. "You don't have anywhere to spread out in mine."

"True." Holding the sliver in hand, I led the way up to my room. Linus cleaned off the desk while I gathered my supplies and pulled up my chair. "Please let this work."

"It will." Linus sat on my bed to give me room. "What kind of charm do you have in mind?"

Lacroix wore his as a quarter-sized medallion around his neck, but I had other plans.

"Not a charm." I opened the locked desk drawer and produced the goddess-touched artifact. "A weapon."

Afraid to read his expression, worried his concerns might spill onto me, I blocked him out and took my trusty knife in hand. I used the tip to hollow out the rounded end of the stake enough for me to press the sliver from Woolworth House into the hole. The next part was tricky, so I closed my eyes and reached deeper into that well of knowledge, both what I had been born knowing and what I had learned from the Marchand collection, and selected the right tools to create the perfect instrument to bring down Lacroix.

Slicing open my thumb, I smeared the length of ancient ash wood with sigils whose purpose I twisted to suit my needs then pressed the wound onto the end like a cap.

Magic punched out of me, hit the stake, and rebounded as the artifact fought back.

One final push drained me, and I slumped over the desk as exhaustion swirled around me.

"TELL me I didn't impale myself." Eyes shut, I patted my chest and abdomen. "It would be super embarrassing to forge my first weapon and then kill myself with it."

"You didn't impale yourself." Linus sounded amused, so that was good. "You're not dead, either."

Hands falling to my sides, I exhaled with relief. "The stake?"

"See for yourself."

Cracking open my eyes, I noted Linus had carried me to my bed and dropped me on top of the covers. The stake rested on its side on my desk, and it glowed red with power, pulsing almost like...a heart.

"It worked." I pushed upright to lean closer. "It actually worked."

"Now that you have your weapon, how do you propose we get close enough to Lacroix to use it?"

"I'm thinking your mother can help with that detail."

Furrows pleated his brow. "Mother has no means of accessing city hall."

"Good thing we don't need city hall."

"You want her to let us into the Lyceum." He considered me, and then the stake. "If she revokes her protections, and we fail, the Lyceum will fall."

Us.

We.

That Linus viewed me as his partner, in all things, made my heart swell until I worried it might burst.

"If we fail, we'll be dead," I pointed out, "and the fall of the Lyceum will be someone else's problem."

"I'll call Mother's temporary aid. Henrik will know where to find her. We can meet in the barracks on Habersham Street."

"I need to see Amelie before we go."

"All right." He must have read my desire for a private chat. "I'll be at the gate with Hood."

Unsure how to dim the stake's glow, I stuck it in the front of my bra while I sifted through my drawers. To mute its light, I ended up pulling on a black tank top I covered with a matching turtleneck I already regretted in this heat. On my way downstairs, I rolled up the long sleeves. Marginally cooler, I made a pit stop in an unoccupied guestroom then sought out Amelie and found her unmoved.

"Back again?" She set aside her clipboard. "Did you need something?"

"Yeah." I claimed the spot next to her on the swing. "You have all the passwords for my bank accounts, right? The hidden ones?"

"I set them up, so yeah." She frowned. "I sent you hard copies so you could go in and change them."

"I never got around to it." I shrugged when she rolled her eyes, unsurprised I had dragged my feet. "I'm glad, all things considered." I reached over and took her hand. "I have to go do a thing, and if I don't make it back from that thing, I need you to do a few things for me."

Amelie tightened her fingers around mine. "That's an awful lot of things."

"First, I want to bequeath Adelaide enough money to pay off her family's debts so she doesn't have to marry Boaz if she doesn't want to go down that road." Though I was starting to worry she was too set on her path. "Second, I want the deed to Woolworth House signed over to Lethe and Hood." They were the only ones I would trust to protect Woolly, Oscar, and Keet for me. "Third, I want you to take what's left and start a new life for yourself. You won't have to have the new identity Adelaide promised you. You can buy your own. You won't have to live on an allowance from Boaz, you'll have plenty of money. You can have the fresh start you wanted, without any strings attached."

"That's..." She sniffled, her eyes glittering. "That's an amazing offer, but you're going to do the thing, and you're going to make it back from that thing." A single tear rolled down her cheek. "Atonement can't be bought, it must be earned. I'm learning that." She brought me in for a hug that reminded me of my childhood, or maybe it was the way Woolly lingered nearby. "If the worst happens, and it won't, I'll coordinate with Mr. Hacohen to make certain your other bequeaths are awarded."

"There's a fourth thing," I said, untangling from her before I lost my nerve. "Tell Boaz to find a woman he can love and dedicate his life to making happy. Tell him not to settle and not to let her settle either. Tell him...I forgive him, for everything, and I wish him every joy."

Wiping her nose with a crumpled invoice, she laughed. "Assuming Adelaide takes the money and runs."

"Assuming," I agreed. "But my possible untimely death might come too late to save her. I think she might actually care about the oaf."

"No accounting for taste." She attempted a smile that slid off her mouth. "Grier, don't go."

"I have to." I gazed off my porch, across my yard, to what I could see of the city. "There's too much at stake." Thinking of the literal stake in my bra, I barked out a laugh. "Remember what I said."

"I'll remember."

As I took the steps into the yard, I pretended not to hear her weeping.

Saying goodbye to Lethe would gut me, and I figured I needed all the guts I could muster for what we were about to do, so I took the coward's way out and met Linus at the fence without looking back.

Hood stood at the gate, his mouth tight. "You're ready to go?"

"Yeah." I tugged on the collar of my turtleneck. "I'm ready."

He narrowed his eyes on me. "You're sure?"

Of course, he knew what I was doing. I probably smelled like the big chicken I was. "I can't face her."

"Too bad," Lethe snarled and launched herself at me, wrapping me up in a combination of hug and chokehold. "You don't get to leave without me. Screw telling me goodbye, I'm going with you. We're doing this together."

"You're pregnant," I wheezed. "You can't risk your daughter."

Drawing back, she punched my shoulder. "Then I guess you'll have to babysit me for a change."

"You're impossible." I rubbed my throat. "Hood, I can't believe you're okay with this."

"You're pack" was all he said, all he had to say, and I fought tears all the way to the van.

ELEVEN

We found the Grande Dame watching a screen with three Elite who appeared to be tracking movement; theirs or Lacroix's, I wasn't sure. She wore black cotton slacks paired with a ruby blouse and tennis shoes that matched her top and reminded me a bit of Dorothy's slippers from *The Wizard of Oz*. Her hair was pulled up in a militant bun on top her head, and fine tendrils had escaped to frame her face.

This was as casual as Clarice Lawson got, and that was before you noticed the pearl studs in her ears or the cosmetics that almost succeeded in hiding her exhaustion.

"Mother," Linus said when we entered what passed for Savannah's Society headquarters these days.

Monitor forgotten, she rushed to Linus and pressed a kiss to each of his cheeks. "It's good to see you."

"It's been a busy few days for us all." He glanced around, and I did too. We noted how the men and women no longer stood apart from the Grande Dame but with her. Days spent in the tight confines of the barracks, paired with their horrendous loss, had demystified her in their eyes. "Grier and I need a moment of your time."

"Of course." She turned back to the small gathering. "Keep an eye on them. I won't be but a minute."

The others nodded, first to her and then to us, before returning to their stations.

"Come this way." She led us to a single room that must have been meant for an officer. "This is as private as it gets here, I'm afraid."

There was nowhere to sit except on the bed, so we all elected to stand.

"I'll ward the room," I offered and set about getting it done.

After our ears popped, she studied Linus. "I heard an interesting rumor."

His calm left me in awe of his acting skills. "Oh?"

A bad feeling coiled in my gut. Had he not told her what happened?

"I was contacted by the unit commander at Atramentous of all places. Apparently there was a bit of a dustup when three unauthorized persons used a stolen code to gain access to the Athenaeum." Keen eyes spearing him, she continued. "They assaulted an officer on their way out, the same officer whose code had been used, then cut a path of destruction right through the front gate." She let that settle between us. "This is, to my knowledge, the first time a prison break has occurred in Atramentous's history. It is also, as far as I know, the first time non-Elite personnel have viewed the Athenaeum in its entirety."

Lips curving, Linus slid a glance my way. "That is an interesting rumor."

"What were you thinking?" Gone was the cool, the calm, the collected. Her fury crackled in the air around us. "You helped Grier break back in after I finally got her out? Why on earth? And with Boaz Pritchard of all people? He was appointed to her for a reason, to keep an eye on her, not let her run wild."

The amusement fell away, and Linus turned serious. "Boaz was our way in."

"Goddess," she exhaled. "That explains the female guard's code being the one compromised."

The urge to defend him after he had finally, *finally* stood up for himself kicked my pulse up a notch, but I held myself in check. We were here to ask for her help, on multiple fronts, so I let the insult slide.

"Tell me the rest." She snapped her fingers. "And tell me the truth, all of it. Or else I can't help you fix this mess."

Linus shared a lingering glance with me, asking for permission. He would tell the story to prevent me from ratting out Boaz, but I was in this up to my neck too. I wasn't going to let him drown alone.

"Boaz told us special dispensation had been granted for us to visit the Athenaeum and that his request to escort us was approved." I wet my lips. "We didn't realize until after we had gained access that he hadn't been completely honest with us."

Awarding me her full attention, she glowered with abandon. "What would possess you to return there?"

"We planned a trip to Raleigh to visit Dame Marchand. We intended to barter with her for access to the Marchand's collection on the goddess-touched condition. We needed those books in order to find a way to void Lacroix's resistance to my magic. With him out of power, and his compulsions broken, his army would fall apart. We could reclaim the city with minimal casualties." I fidgeted where I stood, recalling how many lives had already been lost. "On our way, we stopped in Atlanta to meet with Tisdale Kinase, to ask for aid she ultimately denied, and Johan Marchand—Severine's husband—paid us a visit. He informed us his wife was dead and presented me with a letter from her."

Curiosity overcame her, and she shifted closer to me. "What did it say?"

"A lot of things. Private things." Hurtful words I hoped I wouldn't have to relay in their entirety, even if they came from a cousin and not her. "What matters is the Marchands donated their entire collection to the Athenaeum to prevent me from gaining access."

"And Boaz, being an Elite," she finished, "knew where to find the Athenaeum."

"He helped us for the sake of the fallen."

The slight purse of her lips hinted she hadn't bought the line, not in its entirety, but she let it go. "After all you've suffered, you returned to Atramentous."

"Yes."

"You didn't hesitate." A note of reluctant pride entered her voice. "You went back there for the good of the Society."

More like the good of Savannah and all her inhabitants, but I took the out I was given. "Yes."

The Grande Dame worried one of her earrings. "How did Boaz get you as far as visitation?"

"He forged paperwork that indicated Commander Roark had granted our petition."

"He was there when Commander Roark died," she murmured. "There were no survivors to contradict him."

"That's my understanding, yes."

"The paperwork would have held," Linus continued the story, "except he wasn't given an access code. He was forced to borrow one from the guard working visitation. She was a willing participant until we prepared to leave, when Boaz made it clear in no uncertain terms that he wasn't interested in her sexually now or ever."

"Foolish boy."

For once, we were in total agreement, though I couldn't bring myself to admit it out loud.

"This is what happened." She massaged her temples. "Linus, you and Grier were granted permission from Commander Roark to visit the Athenaeum. Boaz met with Roark to collect the clearance papers, and that's when Elite Heath entered the room and opened fire." Her arms lowered as she reimagined those events, twisting them to suit her. "That's why Boaz accompanied you to Atramentous, to arrange for the use of Elite Barfoot's code since no new ones could be issued until an interim commander could be appointed."

"The video won't corroborate your version of events," Linus said gently. "Elite Barfoot and Elite Marx won't either."

Not to mention the guards we took out at the gates, some with more force than others.

"I'll handle it." She pushed hairs away from her face. "I'm the Grande Dame, and you were acting in the best interests of the Society."

"Protecting us might cost you your title." Linus measured her with a frown. "Are you prepared for that?"

"You're my son." She frowned back at him. "Do you honestly think I wouldn't give it up to keep you safe?"

Rather than answer, Linus embraced her. "Thank you, Mother."

"I assume there's more to this visit than a confession?" She pulled back and straightened her clothes then fixed me with a stare. "I hope, given the trouble your shenanigans have caused, you accomplished what you set out to do?"

"I did."

"Then all that's left is gaining access to Lacroix in order to implement your plan." The Grande Dame wasted no time getting to the point. "You want me to lower the protections on the Lyceum so you can enter beneath city hall."

"I do."

"You understand that if you fail, the Lyceum will fall."

Like mother, like son. "This is our best chance of regaining control of the city."

With a dramatic sigh, she flicked a wrist. "I suppose we can always burn it to the ground if that fails."

"I would prefer not to set Savannah on fire, but yeah. That's always an option."

Older vampires, ancients in particular, being flammable and all.

"Oh." Cruel interest sparked in her eyes. "I do have one spot of bright news."

Linus inclined his head in an invitation to share.

"Sentinel Rue has been relieved of duty. She was interrogated on the Volkov situation, and she is now being held pending a formal hearing. She admitted to acting on Lacroix's orders, which she received through her vampire boyfriend." She gave her son a resigned look. "I believe he was killed during the altercation outside the facility."

Linus gave nothing away with his placid expression.

"This incident highlights the need for the sentinels' handbook, particularly the chapters on fraternization, to be revised."

Vampires are not our enemies.

Necromancer children learned that at their mothers' knees. But Lacroix's actions would condemn his species to censure and distrust. It wasn't right, and the Grande Dame would see that when this standoff ended. She was too politically savvy to wallow in ignorance for long, but any condemnation on her part would send ripples throughout the Society. For everyone's sake, I hoped her temper cooled sooner rather than later.

"Lacroix must not be done with Volkov." I got queasy just thinking about it. "Why else protect him?"

Our old pals, the vampire assassins, must have showed up late to the party. We had already gone in, so they got stuck waiting. Hood found them before they got a chance to take aim at me. But the brawlers? Gramps must have worried the Society would transfer its inmates out of the city until we restored order, and he didn't want to lose track of him. They must have been positioned in the yard, behind the wards, or they would have been Hood's meal instead of the assassins.

"I'll have Sentinel Rue questioned again," the Grande Dame decided. "If Lacroix wants Volkov, we must ensure he doesn't get him." Her focus homed in on Linus. "Will you two go alone?"

"Lethe and Hood will be accompanying us." He stuck his hands into his pockets. "Boaz will, I'm certain, attempt to come as well."

"Good." The Grande Dame tapped a finger against her lower lip.

"Muzzle him until I can speak with him. Don't allow his sudden plague of conscience to ruin us." Satisfied that was one more loose end snipped, she gestured toward the sigils on the door. "Smudge those, please. Let's find paper and a pen." She shot Linus a look over her shoulder. "I can show you how to bring down the wards surrounding the Lyceum. How you get from there into city hall is up to you."

There was only one way—up. The elevator shaft was the sole connection between the two.

As I was preparing to remove the wards, the Grande Dame hugged me from behind.

"You and I have never seen eye to eye, but you are family." She released me. "I do love you."

Shock zapped my brain like a lightning bolt. She had spoken the words to me many times over the years, with varying degrees of affection, but just now, she appeared to mean them.

"Take care of each other" was the last thing she said before smudging the sigil and striding into the control room like she owned it.

The sentinels relaxed with her back among them, when they once would have snapped to attention.

Lacroix might be the worst disaster to strike Savannah, but he was doing wonders for the Grande Dame. She had the sentinels eating out of the palm of her hand. One even handed her the notebook and pen she sought before she could ask for them.

"Here is the list of streets waiting on their supply delivery," she said, loud enough for her voice to carry. Her hand, however, drew sigils followed by careful instructions in the margin. "There you go." She passed it to Linus with reluctance. "Be careful out there." She glanced at me. "Both of you."

Linus kissed her cheek. "We'll be in contact soon."

A sentinel waited behind her, a printout in hand. Dismissing us, she turned to hear his report.

We left the barracks and rejoined the Kinases in the van.

"We good?" Lethe gnawed on a round jerky stick that almost brushed the ceiling. "Did she have an alternate way in?"

"We're good," I confirmed. "We can access the Lyceum and bring down the wards."

Hood met my eyes in the rearview mirror. "What did she say about the rest?"

"She told us she would handle it." I gusted out an exhale. "Now we wait and see if she can."

Thanks to her championing my release, from Atramentous no less, her reign as Grande Dame had begun in controversy. Clarice hadn't held the title for long, and she had crossed Abayomi Balewa to get there. There were those, both High Society and Low, who believed she had freed me because of our familial connection. Soon those same grumblers would have fresh ammunition.

Clarice had freed me *after* discovering I was goddess-touched. She had extended to me the first pardon in the history of Atramentous. The fact my grandfather was holding the city and the American seat of the Society hostage on her watch painted an ugly picture of gross incompetence at best and rampant corruption at worst.

"We will if she can't," Hood promised. "We have the resources to make you vanish, both of you."

Gwyllgi had kept Taz a step ahead of the Marchands. They could do the same for us. I believed that. But it would cost me Woolly and Keet and all my non-gwyllgi friends. I hoped it wouldn't come to that.

"What about Boaz?" Massaging my temples, I was reminded of Clarice's favor. "We have to bring him with us, by the way. The Grande Dame wants him isolated until she wraps up damage control."

Assuming they didn't clamp her in irons and then come straight for Linus, Boaz, and me.

"We can always use the cannon fodder," Lethe said as she bit off a mouthful. "We'll let him go first."

Linus attempted to hide his smile, but honestly? He didn't try all that hard.

BOAZ WAS easy to spot when we rolled up to the barricade. The other sentinels gravitated toward him. His larger-than-life personality had that effect on people. He made friends easily. Keeping them was the problem. And right now, he was shaking hands and checking in with each individual so they felt valued and their sacrifice respected. They were looking to him as a figurehead, and he was stepping into the role with both feet.

The others waited in the van while I went to collect him, and when I got close enough to overhear their conversations, I realized these were sentinels and Elite from neighboring cities, volunteers who came to offer aid when they heard what happened to Commander Roark and so many of Savannah's finest.

And it hit me then, not all of it was bluster. Some of it—no, most of it—were condolences for Becky.

"Boaz," I called when I grew tired of fighting against the current. *"Boaz."*

"Grier?" He spotted me and waded in, and the others got out of his way. "What's up?"

"The Grande Dame requested you accompany us to..." I hesitated, given the number of ears perked around us, "...escort her...to the—"

"Got it." He patted my shoulder, letting me off the hook, then waved to the new guys. "I'll be back."

With Lethe riding shotgun, he was forced into the back with Linus and me. I climbed in first next to Linus, leaving Boaz to take my preferred seat across from us. Once he got in, he couldn't stop laughing.

"It wasn't that funny," I grumbled. "I didn't expect you to be shaking hands and kissing babies when I arrived."

"You're a crap liar," he countered, ignoring the dig. "That's why you always let Amelie do the heavy lifting when we were kids."

Annoyed he was right, I glowered at him. "Aren't you the least bit curious why we circled back for you?"

"We're breaking into the Lyceum." He shrugged. "What else could it be?" He pointed to the gwyllgi in the front seats. "You've got your crack team, and me. I'm guessing this must have something to do with our earlier adventure. Otherwise, I wouldn't have made the cut."

"Huh." I pretended to consider him. "You're smarter than you look."

The flat look he shot me was ruined by the way the corner of his mouth twitched.

"This is where the joyride ends," Hood announced. "We go in on foot from here."

He parked in front of a pet store promising freshly baked dog treats and slung on a backpack that caused me to quirk an eyebrow at him that he ignored.

"The tunnel starts beneath a restaurant off Bay Street." Linus held the paper in front of him like he was reading a treasure map, and it struck me how much Oscar would have loved to be a part of this. Too bad it wasn't a kid-friendly adventure. "There's a cellar with access."

The gwyllgi ranged ahead and behind, making certain we didn't have any company. Given how easy we had been to find lately, I wasn't holding my breath. There was a tracking sigil fixed on Linus or me, or both of us. What else could it be?

The shops were closed because of the "storm." There was no one to let us in, so we had to do the honors ourselves. About to use a sigil to pop the lock, Boaz stepped up and pulled a few pieces of metal from his pocket.

"I got this." He knelt and started to work. "Elite know all the fun tricks."

The ones who didn't would have to learn them. Most had no magic. A few, like Boaz, had a little juice. Or so I had heard from one of his fellow sentinels. Other than his ability to perceive Cletus, he had never shown the slightest indication of having more power than the average Low Society necromancer.

A few clicks later, and he pushed open the door to let us pass.

We flowed in, and he locked up behind us, pausing to check out the window.

"The cellar is in the back." Linus indicated the kitchen. "The entry point is a metal panel inset into the floor."

Sure enough, a large and ancient-looking square of metal sat in the center of the room like a drain minus the slats. The kitchen staff had arranged a few prep stations over the top, so we put our backs into moving them aside.

"I don't see a handle." I walked the edges, about four feet down either side, and kicked at it. "How does it open?"

"There's a ward protecting it." Linus crouched with a brush and a pot of ink, a must for uneven surfaces, and painted on a few sigils that dissolved into a flaky mess upon completion. The edge opposite him shimmered, and I crossed to it in time to watch as a large ring of hinged metal appeared. "Good thing there are five of us."

"Look." Lethe pointed to the far wall. "It's a pulley system."

Behind Linus, on a wall that had been bare when we arrived, now hung a massive hook of the right scale to fit the ring. A wench the size of a beer keg had been mounted at waist height, its handle rusted and pitted with age.

"Okay then." I did the honors of dragging the hook on its hefty chain, threading it through the ring and securing it back onto itself. "Let 'er rip."

Lethe started cranking the handle while Linus checked the mechanism to ensure it was sound. Boaz and Hood stood at the opening, primed to act if this entrance had been compromised, and I stood there with my pocketknife in hand, ready for whatever came next.

A shimmer down the chain caught my eye. "Linus, did you see that?"

"The sigil must be time-delayed. We disrupted it, not disabled it." He peered into the opening. "Mother must not have known. Otherwise, she would have warned us we were on the clock." He squatted to get a better look. "I can see the stairs. They're clear. Hood?"

"Mold and water. There's nothing alive down there."

Mold and water. Two of my least favorite things.

"Good." Linus straightened. "We should go now before the sigil times out."

Hood and Lethe bumped him aside and descended together. Linus and I did the same. No sooner had Boaz cleared the steps, than the door slammed shut over our heads with a reverberation that jarred my back teeth.

The dank smells, the absolute darkness, conspired to fling me back into my nightmares, but I had faced Atramentous, and this was nothing compared to that. The water here smelled stagnant, not fouled. The mold struck me as richer, more verdant, but there might just be more of it since there were no inmates to lick it clean.

I can do this.

Piece of cake.

Thank the goddess I didn't say cake out loud…

With Lethe, I might as well yell *stampede.* Except, of course, we would be the ones getting trampled. By her. And when she found out there was no cake? Pfft. Fake cake got people killed.

"I hope your mother wasn't misinformed about anything else." I allowed myself a moment to rearrange my features, to steady my pulse. We had bigger worries than burgeoning panic attacks. We had to stay alert. "It would suck to die in a tunnel the city filled in a few years ago without the Society noticing."

"We need light." Lethe rested her hand on my shoulder. "Our night vision is excellent, but we still need a light source."

"She's right." I was losing the shape of things as my eyes adjusted to the complete darkness. "Hang on."

I tugged the turtleneck over my head and then cursed. The glow from the stake had subsided to a faint shine.

"I'm glad you're cooler," Lethe said dryly, "but that didn't help with the whole seeing-where-we're-going thing."

I growled at her softly, but she just laughed. Even Linus, who knew the reason for the long-sleeve top, smiled. I might not have seen it, but I *felt* it.

"Here." Boaz pressed a pencil-length piece of metal into my hand then guided my thumb to press the button on top. "And here." He did the same for Lethe. "And here." Hood grunted a thanks. "I only have one more." He addressed Linus when he said, "You'll have to share with Grier."

There was a time when he would have tossed Linus the penlight and claimed his spot next to me. He would have seen it as his right, and he would have known it not-so-secretly delighted me. But those days were gone for both of us, and that was a good, if melancholy, thing.

With our four thin beams of light, we had no trouble navigating the tunnel using the map the Grande Dame had drawn for Linus.

The slightly uneven shapes of handmade bricks fanned out around us. They were beautiful, a throwback to the birth of Savannah.

Lethe turned a slow circle. "How has no one noticed there are tunnels crisscrossing the entire city?"

"Oh, they've noticed." I shared a look with Boaz, the only other product of a public-school education present. "They blame pirate captains who ordered their crews to round up drunk bar patrons and dump them on their ships to save time on recruitment speeches, runaway slaves waiting to punch their ticket for the Underground Railroad, burial grounds for Yellow Fever patients, cisterns for drinking water, cisterns for sewage, storm drains." I shrugged. "I'm probably forgetting a few."

Clicking her tongue, she started down the tunnel. "How have humans survived for so long?"

"There are a lot more of them than there are of us," Linus said, "and they breed faster."

"Like rabbits," Hood agreed.

"Don't talk about rabbits." Lethe rubbed her stomach. "I'm hungry."

"I brought trail mix." Hood trotted to her side and pulled a sandwich baggie out of his backpack. "That ought to tide you over."

All at once his decision to bring a backpack made sense. "You packed nothing but snacks, didn't you?"

"I don't ask you about the contents of your bag," he said primly. "Don't ask about the contents of mine."

"That's right, baby." Lethe made crunching noises. "You tell her."

"Good grief." I kept pace with Linus. "We came down here willingly with these two?"

"No." Lethe twisted, tossing a peanut at my head. "I didn't give you a choice."

Only training with her gave me reflexes quick enough to avoid taking it in the eye.

"You didn't catch it!"

"You mean with my pupil?"

"What a waste." She stood over it like a mourner at a funeral. "Food, Grier. That was food."

"Here." Hood passed her a stick of jerky. "Will this make it better?"

"Depends." She sniffled. "Do you have more than one?"

"How long have we been mated?" He held out three more. "Better?"

"Much." She ripped into the first one. "Now hush. I like to pretend I can hear the jerky begging for mercy as I chomp it to pulp."

A red sheen covered Hood's eyes. "That's my girl."

"So," I said too loudly, and my voice echoed back to me. "Should we have brought a ball of yarn to unroll as we go? Breadcrumbs to scatter? Or is this a straight shot?"

"Mother's notation calls this the catacombs. I assume that means it's a network that fans out from a central hub somewhere within the city."

I whipped my head toward him. "You didn't know it existed?"

"Oh, I knew there were tunnels that led to the sea, to the Lyceum, and several other critical points, but I didn't realize they all connected, or used to, or that they had a name. I assumed they were each separate to lower the risk of ambush."

As much as I wanted to tease him about there being something he actually didn't know, it was a sore spot for him. I might have done it anyway if we had been alone, but we weren't, and I wasn't going to give Boaz an opening to walk through. Though he had been downright decent toward Linus on this trip.

"The first turn is coming up on our right." He lifted my hand, holding the penlight, and identified the tunnel. Several yards later, we turned right again. And on it went, twisting and turning until we were lost beneath the city with only a scrap of paper for guidance. "We're almost there."

"Good thing too." Hood shrugged out of his backpack, dumped it upside down, and shook it. "She's out of snacks."

Lethe growled at him, but she didn't disagree that tight quarters and an empty stomach, when hers was a bottomless pit *before* the baby, might not end well for some of us.

"Do you hear that?"

The sound of Boaz behind me caused me to jump after his quiet. "What?"

"Voices."

The gwyllgi cocked their heads, and we fell silent while they listened then confirmed.

"How did you hear that before we picked up on it?" Brow pinched tight, Hood swept his gaze up and down Boaz. "Are you magically augmented?"

"No." He tapped his right ear. "I stuck a pencil in my ear as part of a dare in elementary school. The kid who instigated it shoved me out of my chair when I pulled off the trick. The side of my head hit the desk next to me, and the point burst my eardrum."

Linus frowned at him. "A sigil could have repaired the damage."

"You're right." He laughed. "If I had told my parents, they would have gotten it healed, but I kept it to myself. I'd gotten in trouble for jumping off an old barn roof into a pond and impaling my leg on a discarded Christmas tree the week before. I had just gotten off punishment, and I didn't want to get in trouble again."

"You figured permanent hearing loss was the lesser of two evils?" I gaped at him. "Really?"

"I told them, eventually, but it had been months at that point. There was only so much a sigil could do since it had healed on its own, more or less. Teachers thought I was blowing them off or acting out when I didn't respond, but I couldn't hear them. Over time, I started living down to their expectations of me." He wiped a hand over his mouth before he said more. "Anyway, after you healed me..."

"First you sprout a new leg, and now you're telling me you have super hearing." I leaned against the nearest wall, not caring if it got me slimy. "Anything else?"

Lines zigzagged across his forehead. "I regrew a toenail I lost when I was sixteen?"

"Just a new nail, right? It's not glowing or radioactive or anything?"

"Not that I've noticed." Boaz laughed under his breath. "I can show you sometime if you're interested."

Again, I waited.

Again, I was in for a shock.

Boaz didn't hint at what else he might show me or anything else inappropriate.

With a flick of my wrist, I cut my light across his scalp. "Did you suffer brain damage that maybe caused the sigil to reset your entire personality too?"

"Can we focus on the voices?" He tugged on his ear. "Please?"

Embarrassment was new for him too, but I wasn't sure if I had stepped in it by calling him out on his self-improvements or if there was more to it. Determined to make up for it, I followed his suggestion.

"Does this mean the Lyceum has been breached?" No matter how hard I strained, all I heard was dripping water. "We ought to be directly below it, or we should be soon."

Even if the vampires stuck their heads in the elevator shaft and yelled down it, we shouldn't be able to hear them as long as the wards held.

"It means we've got company." Lethe bounced on the balls of her feet. "Lacroix must have had the same idea, sending his people down to find a way up into the Lyceum. Our secret tunnel must intersect a not-so-secret tunnel somewhere along the line."

"You're all getting sigils." I sliced open my palm. "Who wants to go first?"

No one volunteered, but they didn't argue against the precaution. Having experienced the impervious sigil, they would be stupid to pass up the offer, and even Boaz was proving he could learn.

I started with Lethe and added an extra sigil over her navel, then I moved on to Hood and then to Boaz. Linus waited until last, but I had already put one sigil on him tonight. A second wouldn't hurt.

"Okay." I brought up the ward around myself and kept my knife at the ready. "Let's go introduce ourselves."

TWELVE

L ucky for us, Lacroix had only spared two vampires for this particular expedition. That, or they were traveling in pairs, and we had come across the frontrunners. The necromancers in the group didn't have to lift a finger. The gwyllgi shifted and did all the dirty work. And if Lethe got a little carried away, I didn't judge. Much. I mean, it's not like she had just eaten an entire backpack's worth of snacks. Did she really need to rip off that guy's arm to carry around with her for later?

To ease around the feasting gwyllgi and the corpses, we walked in single file. We found the entrance right where the Grande Dame said it would be, and there were indications the vampires had found it too, but they hadn't had any luck accessing the Lyceum.

"Stand back." Linus studied the paper. "We can't be sure how this door will open."

Tracing the thin beam of light along the wall, I came up empty. "I don't see any hinges."

"There may not be any." He nudged me behind him. "I have to stand under it to draw the sigils."

"Guess that math holds," Lethe said, wiping her mouth as she strolled up to us. "We'll still have two necromancers left if it squishes Linus flat as a pancake." She scrunched up her face. "Oh, no. Wait. Boaz shoots blanks. That means you can't hog all the glory, Linus."

Boaz offered her a smile as sweet as he liked his iced tea but didn't say a word, just took up position to guard the tunnel in case there were more vampires on the way.

"Give us an estimate of where the opening begins and ends. Lethe and I will brace it so that it won't swing open until we're ready." Hood waved me over. "You can hold the light. I'm sure he planned to grip it between his teeth, but that's what friends are for."

A blank mask slid over Linus's features, obscuring them. Not Scion Lawson. Not Professor Lawson. Not the potentate either. This was...not a mask at all. It was shock leaching all expression off his face. The easy inclusion in the group had stunned him.

Oh, Linus.

Crossing to him, I captured his face between my palms and stared at him until he thawed, and then I pulled him down to me and wrapped my arms around his waist.

"You are valued," I whispered in his ear. "You are trusted." I nipped his earlobe. "You are loved."

Lethe clamped a hand on his shoulder. "You're also pack."

"Thank you." His lips brushed my cheek, spreading chills. "For seeing me."

The days of him walking into danger alone were past. The days of him taking the hit to spare me, to spare us, were gone. The days of him experimenting on himself without supervision? Yep. Also done.

It would take him some time, but he would learn to accept being family in a way he never had been. The family I had collected over the years might not make sense to most High Society necromancers, but they had my back. Always. We shared no DNA, but we had shared tears, hurts, and grief. That bonded us thicker than blood.

"Get into position." Hood braced his palms against the low ceiling where Linus indicated, and Lethe mirrored him. Smiling at his mate, whose mouth was smeared with blood, he told Linus, "Do your worst."

"Or your best." I stood at his shoulder, angling the light to supplement his night vision. "I would like us to all walk away from this. Maybe even limp. I could deal with limping."

Linus painted on the sigil, and the ceiling began to ripple and then warp. Above us, a narrow hole opened that stretched farther than we could see, and a ladder mounted to the brick was revealed an arm's length away.

The gwyllgi were left holding up air and lowered their arms once the illusion fully dispersed.

"That was anticlimactic." Lethe fisted her hands on her hips. "What a waste of a motivational speech."

Hood slung an arm around her shoulders. "You can go first, if it makes you feel better."

Lethe shrugged him off her. "Like I was giving you an option."

No boost required, she leapt the short distance to the ladder and started hauling herself up and out of sight. Hood followed close behind, both of them gone silent.

"You're next." Linus tucked the map into his back pocket then bent to offer me the boost Lethe hadn't needed to reach the lowest rung. "I'm right behind you."

I started climbing, but I hung back until Linus joined me, and, okay, I might have waited for Boaz too.

I'm not sure how long it took to reach the top, but my legs wobbled like a newborn colt's when Hood pulled me into an alcove before yet another tunnel mouth. We shuffled together to make room for the stragglers, and then we fell in behind Linus.

Not too long after, he turned and addressed the group in a whisper. "Almost there."

A golden hatch about four feet around capped the end of the passage. There was nowhere to go but up, and I had no doubt, given the twenty-four-karat entrance, we had reached the underbelly of the Lyceum.

This time, Linus didn't use a sigil. He threw his back into twisting a dial marked with sigils into the correct position. Each time he paused, I heard a click. The ornate hub made for one heck of a combination lock.

The shriek of metal hinges made me cringe as Linus eased the hatch open, and I almost laughed when I saw where it spat us out. "This really is your mother's private exit."

The en suite restroom attached to her office spread out before us, and when I stepped onto the tile floor and turned, I saw the tunnel mouth was disguised as a circular mirror on this side.

"Anyone need a potty break?" Lethe joked. "I bet there's gold-plated tissue in this joint."

The others joined me, and we began the slow process of clearing the Lyceum. So far, so good.

When we reached the gleaming silver doors, Hood pried them apart to reveal the elevator car.

"That'll be fun to shimmy through." Lethe rubbed her belly. "I hope I can suck in enough."

Mentally, I hoped she couldn't, but I was smart enough to keep my mouth shut.

Hood took point, strolling in and locating the top hatch then coaxing it open with practiced ease. When he walked out, he smiled at my surprise. "I worked at the Faraday, remember? I covered Midas's shifts on his off days. Spend enough time in an elevator pushing buttons so residents don't have to, you start amusing yourself with running escape scenarios for the day when you've officially had enough of being stuck in a box with strong perfumes, strong opinions, and strong prejudices."

"There are also entitled idiots who go elevator surfing," Lethe informed me.

That sounded all kinds of dangerous. "How is that a thing?"

"Social media." She made a face. "Our kids aren't getting internet access until they're fifty."

Hood nodded agreement, and I wished them both luck with that.

We lived in a digital age, and kids were plugged in from the cradle, it seemed. Even Oscar had his own cell. Granted, he was slightly older than fifty. Maybe I wasn't such a bad parent after all.

"I'll go up first." Linus rolled his shoulders, and his tattered cloak unfurled. "Are you ready?"

To face my grandfather? To face Odette? To witness the consequences of their actions?

"No." I touched my fingertips to the center of my chest, where the stake was concealed. "Let's go."

Linus gripped the edge of the opening then pulled himself through the gap on top of the car in a feat of strength that *almost* made me regret whining all those times Lethe made me lift weights in addition to running and defense training. He got to his feet and tested the ladder for signs of tampering then gave us a thumbs-up before starting to climb. He was several feet in the air when Boaz sidled up next to me and put his hand on my shoulder.

"Let one of us take the shot, if it comes down to it." He squeezed. "You don't want Odette on your conscience."

"Thanks." I patted his hand. "But we might not get the chance to draw straws."

Dropping his arm, he stepped back to wait his turn. Hood lifted me through the opening, clucking his tongue the whole time. Fine. *Maybe* I would make more of an effort to develop upper-body strength.

Lethe came up after me, and then Hood, with Boaz bringing up the rear yet again.

Sweat popped on my forehead, and my palms grew slick. This was more exercise than I had expected, and the vertical climbs were turning my muscles to taffy.

Exactly five eternities later, Linus slowed to examine a door. Without looking back, he made a universal hand signal for up then a number one.

One more floor. I could swing that. Sure, I could. Yep. No problem. *I got this.*

Lethe caught up to me and half covered my back to keep me from splatting from exhaustion.

All right, so I didn't got this.

Safe within the cage of her arms, I finished the climb otherwise unassisted. And when Linus pried open the next set of doors and gave the all-clear, I shoved him in with a hand on his butt so I could collapse in a heap on the tile beside him. Lethe climbed over me, and I let her. Hood too. But Boaz was on a tear about propriety apparently and waited on me to get out of his way. Since that wasn't happening without help, Linus hooked his hands under my arms and dragged me, flipping me over in the process to give me a view of the ceiling and his quiet amusement. He held a finger to his lips before I could release the groan moving through my sternum.

"Go on without me," I mouthed.

"Okay," he mouthed back.

"I was joking." I shoved up onto my elbows to better glare at him.

"Me too." Gently, he pressed his lips to mine. *"Do you need to rest?"*

"Just let me catch my breath."

Lethe and Hood worked alongside Boaz to ensure there were no surprises waiting for us while I caught my fourth or fifth wind. I was losing count. Linus stayed with me, his cloak growing darker and more substantial than ever.

I was sitting upright by the time they circled back, and their somber expressions did nothing for my confidence. I pulled the modified pen from my pocket and drew a sigil for privacy on the nearest doorframe.

"We count thirty vampires on this floor," Lethe said. "Most are in the next room playing cards between us and the stairs. No sign of Lacroix or Odette."

"We can't get past them without alerting the others." I capped then recapped my pen. "We'll have to use obfuscation sigils and hope for the best."

"That won't mask our sounds or scents." Linus stared at the pen, and I felt like an idiot. The ink was blood, and I had perfumed the air with the one thing guaranteed to send vampires running—straight for us. "We'll have to go down one at a time to minimize the noise."

And the scent of spiced blood ripe for drinking.

"I'll go first," Boaz volunteered. "I've been bringing up the rear all night. It's time for a change of pace."

The others shrugged off his request, but it struck me as too calculated, too casual for such a hothead.

"You go down there hunting Lacroix without backup," I said, "and you'll end up dead."

"He forced me to kill my partner, Grier." He wiped a hand down his face. "He turned all those sentinels against the people they were sworn to protect, against each other."

"He's going to die," Linus told him without looking at me. "I have no objection to you being the one who kills him, but Grier is right. He's an ancient. He's clever, has no regard for lives other than his own, and you would be throwing away your life if you make an end run for him."

"I can be a team player," Boaz said at last, voice tight. "I'll wait."

Figuring that was as close to a promise as I was going to finesse out of him, I drew an obfuscation sigil on his throat and braced myself when he disappeared. As I worked my way around the room, they talked strategy for how to locate and subdue Lacroix and Odette. *Subdue* was the word they used for my benefit, but I was the one carrying a stake with his name on it. I had no illusions about how this would end.

"Fiddlesticks," I muttered, tapping the pen across my open palm. "Lacroix's charm protects him from my magic. We don't know if that extends to defensive sigils or only voids offensive sigils." I extended the pen in Linus's general direction. "You draw on the sigils." After he smudged the one I had drawn on him and reappeared, I shrugged. "Better safe than sorry."

Before I passed it over, I drew on my own obfuscation sigil and vanished from his sight.

"Grier." The way he said my name gave me chills. "What are you doing?"

"Lacroix won't hurt me if he finds me." I rose and sneaked a few paces away in case Linus attempted to grab me. As long as I kept moving, he would have trouble spotting me. It wouldn't stop the gwyllgi from tattling, but they were supposed to be on my side. "He needs me for his precious heirs, and I need answers." As a concession, I added, "You'll be invisible to him, all of you, until he clues in that I'm not alone." That particular sigil worked best on the unwary. "I'll have plenty of backup, more than ever. The risk to me is minimal." I screwed up my pride then swallowed it. "Please, Linus. I need closure."

"All right," he said softly. "We'll do this your way, but if he harms you, I will kill him. Answers or not."

Aware nothing I said would change his mind, I nodded before remembering he couldn't see. "Okay."

Odette's sentence would be life, given her advanced age, and Lacroix would never see the moon rise again if the Grande Dame got ahold of him. This was my one chance to ask them the questions that had plagued me my entire life and get answers straight from the source.

Once Linus finished his work, I smudged the ward protecting us from being overheard.

We had agreed Boaz would leave first, but we had no way of tracking his progress. Thirty seconds after he should have been clear, Linus exited the room. Half a minute after that, it was my turn. I discarded my shoes for fear the damp sneakers would squeak on the tile, and I padded into the hall with my heart drumming in my ears.

A prickling sensation crept down my spine, and I didn't have to look to know the doorway I was passing opened into the room full of card-playing vampires. Their conversation was low, their focus on the game absolute. At least until the simple action of me walking, covered in sigils, stirred the faintest breeze.

"Do you smell that?"

"Blood."

Four vampires shoved from the table to crowd the door less than a yard away from me.

"Herbs."

"*Necromancer.*"

There was no time to check with the others, no way to discuss how best to handle this. I had to eliminate the threat before they raised the alarm and we all paid the price.

Careful not to cut too deep, I nicked the tip of my pointer and drew sigils on the wall of compressed air insulating me. I let my focus narrow to the vampires, to the danger they posed me and my friends, and I slammed my palm against the sigils, sending a wave of energy through the room.

The blast killed them all, turned them to ash that floated down in blackened flakes.

"Pick up the pace," Lethe whispered directly into my ear. "We just started the countdown."

Sooner or later, these vampires would be discovered. Sooner rather than later if we didn't hurry up and begin neutralizing the rest. *Neutralizing.* Such a sanitary word for murder. But what bothered me more than the scene before us was the fact I couldn't decide if what I felt was relief over having mastered the sigil or horror over such power residing in me.

These vampires had killed humans and necromancers alike. Not all of them had made that choice of their own free will, but some of them had, and we had no way to tell the difference. With Lacroix alive, there was no difference. He was in total control of them, one way or the other, and all we could do was hold tight to the belief that what we did was for the greater good.

We reached the main floor and found more vampires posted at all the windows and doors.

Unable to coordinate with the others, I stuck to the plan and began sweeping my quadrant for signs of Lacroix and Odette. I didn't have to go far before I heard her laughter bouncing off the walls as she told stories of her daring youth—her words, not mine—that proved she had edited her life story for my ears.

Creeping forward, I reached a doorway and peered around its molding to spy on a queen addressing her loyal subjects.

Odette lounged in a chair, elevating her, while more than a dozen female vampires simpered at her from their places on the floor. Most appeared so enrapt by her tales, I had to wonder if Lacroix hadn't ordered them to pay her their undivided attention. Perhaps to free him up for his own pursuits.

Now that I had her in my sights, I blanked. I had so many questions, but it's not like I could ask them over the heads of her undead ladies-in-waiting. Lacroix was absent from the court, but I bet engaging with her would bring him running.

As the thought occurred to me, an unforgiving hand closed over the back of my neck, its cruel fingers digging into my flesh, and Odette tossed a loving smile toward me but not at me.

Lacroix.

"Even blinded from seeing your future," she said smugly, "I knew you would come straight to me."

"What brings you for a visit?" Lacroix marched me forward, ruining the sigil so Odette could see me too. "Have you come to relay your terms for surrender?"

"The Society will not surrender, and neither will Savannah." A growl tickled the back of my throat. "Neither will I."

The sound made him pause. "You've been spending too much time around gwyllgi."

"Nasty beasts." Odette fluffed her layered skirt then clucked her tongue at Lacroix. "I don't see why you ever employed them."

"They came highly recommended," he said shortly, "and they did their jobs well. I had no quarrel with the pack." He mashed his lips together. "Until Evangeline."

"That woman," Odette seethed, "did this world a favor when she passed into the next."

Odette couldn't be more wrong. Mom was alive and well, in Woolworth House.

"Did you know?" I doubt Maud told Odette about how she preserved Mom, for her sake as well as mine, but Odette was a seer. She might have figured it out on her own. "About Mom? Did you know?"

"How could I not?" Her face settled into familiar lines as she frowned. "I was there when she died."

She had misunderstood me, answered the question she thought I was asking, and it had me tasting bile.

Woolly's memories—*Mom's* memories—of the accident included the squeal of tires as she bled out.

"You drove her off the road," I said aloud, and it sounded just as crazy as it did in my head.

"I despise motorized transportation." She shuddered. "I much prefer to walk, but sacrifices must be made."

That exact preference would have immediately eliminated her from a suspect pool, had there been one. But Mom's death had been treated as a hit-and-run, not a murder. And Odette didn't have a license. I hadn't even known she could drive. We walked everywhere when I visited her on Tybee. I saw now there was a reason for that, another careful layer applied to her alibi.

"Don't cry, *bébé*."

Tears raced, hot and fast, down my cheeks. "She was my *mother*."

"She was an insolent young woman who betrayed her husband's memory by fleeing with his child after his death." Lacroix shook me like a dog. "She had no right. *None*. You are my blood. To do with as I see fit."

"They were planning on moving away." I glared at him through watery eyes. "I read her letters to Maud."

"Your mother—" He snapped his teeth together. "George fell in love with her. That was not our plan. He was set in her path to make her fall for him, to birth a child of my line in the hopes our calculations were correct, that breeding him to a Marchand would produce a goddess-touched child."

The news my father had been hand-picked for my mother sucker-punched me. But Lacroix's fury was a balm all its own. Dad had loved Mom. I might have been engineered, but I had also been conceived in love, and when Lacroix caused a rift, Dad sided with her. He would have walked away from Lacroix, from his title as heritor, and... "How did my father die? The truth."

"A clan member challenged his right to inherit. They fought. My son was slain. That is the truth."

But not the whole truth. A clan member, not a cousin, as he had confided to me at the ball.

No doubt there were other inconsistencies in his version of events, but I could never spot them all.

"You're the clan master. You choose your own heritor. That means you decided to replace George before he defected with Mom and took me with him. You set his death in motion." The tears staining my cheeks dried. "Who killed him?"

Lacroix didn't condescend to answer, but then, I should have known.

Danill Volkov had been Lacroix's heritor when he kidnapped me, but Volkov spun me a tale about how he was only thirty-five, and I had believed him. Thinking back on it, he might have wedged that tiny fact in my brain long before Linus had protected me with a tattoo and given me a nudge not to question it. Otherwise, I was just that stupid that it had never occurred to me he was older. *Much* older.

"Volkov killed my father." I couldn't feel my lips. They had gone numb. "For the title and...for me."

Suddenly, Volkov's rabid insistence I belonged to him made a lot more sense. As did the avowal he gifted me. His blood in my tattoo might have provoked his possessive instincts, but the reaction had seemed extreme from someone I hadn't known all that long. But if he had killed my father, and I was part of the prize package, he had been waiting twenty years for me.

That was a long time for a vampire to fixate only to be thwarted. Not so long for a Last Seed, in the grand scheme of forever, but maybe Volkov wasn't so old after all. Just enough to best my father, just enough to be hungry for more status, just enough to be willing to accept betrothal to an infant.

Lacroix's old-fashioned sensibilities would have demanded legitimate heirs, which meant his plan had been to discard Volkov, who was sterile, in favor of another human Lacroix relative who could impregnate me after his transformation. But Volkov must not have known that.

And just when the murky waters of my life ran clear, Odette waded in to muddy them again.

"George was a lovely man, but he was weak." She tsked. "He fell prey to your mother. She, more than anyone, killed him with her selfishness."

Blocking out the cruel taunt, I sifted through all she had said and done and found no real truths. I wanted more than evidence of her envy, her pettiness. I wanted the reason why she hated my mom.

"Fame has made you vain," I told her, jabbing her in a tender spot, "but no so vain you would kill my mother out of envy."

"You give me too much credit." She rose to her feet. "Do you know what Maud was working on when Evie died?"

"No." I recoiled when she laid her hand on my cheek. "She didn't talk much about her projects."

Many of them were NDA protected or too dangerous to share the details with a teenager. Particularly one she was training as an assistant versus a practitioner.

"An elixir that granted eternal youth."

Necromancers turned humans into vampires at whatever age they signed on the dotted line and made the wire transfer. The potential market for such an elixir was there in humans who wanted to spend eternity in their prime, sans fangs, but Maud had never been one to waste her time on vanity.

"Why would she...?" I shut my eyes to stem the tide of grief. "She wanted to give Mom forever with Dad."

Necromancers enjoyed extended lifespans, but Last Seeds lived forever unless they were killed.

This was more proof that what my parents had was real. They loved one another, so much that even Maud had been moved to take strides toward ensuring their bond endured beyond a single lifetime.

"After George died, Maud stopped the experiment." Odette lowered her hand, her fingers curling into a fist at her side. "I appealed to her vanity, to her pride, but she would not be coerced. Without George, there was no point. Evie wouldn't want eternity without him." Her eyes, small behind her thick lenses, crackled with fury. "Maud gave no thought to others in similar circumstances. She doomed more love than existed between those two by quitting her study. She was selfish, and so I decided to be selfish too. She took from me the best chance I had of spending eternity with my Gaspard, and so I took Evangeline, the person she loved best, from her."

"Bold enough to commit murder," I said coldly, "but not brave enough to take the credit."

Odette slapped me so hard my head jerked to one side, and I tasted copper. "You are your mother made over."

"Thank you." I nailed Lacroix with as much loathing as I could muster. "You let Odette have her way. You figured with Dad gone, if Mom was out of the way, I would have no one. You expected to waltz in and claim guardianship as my paternal grandfather, but Maud wouldn't give me up. She must have suspected you were involved in my parents' deaths." I laughed softly at Odette. "Maud had no idea you were hooking up with Lacroix. She would have ruined you, both of you, if she had known."

"Maud trusted me." She tapped her forehead to indicate her third eye. "I would have seen if she had an inkling what I had done and decided to move against me."

"You couldn't see me." The story I had been told, that Odette was blinded to my future so that I could make my own decisions, was a lie. Just like everything else she had ever told me. But I wasn't certain if this meant she could see my future, or if she had merely invented fake reasons to flatter her blind spot. "Why didn't Maud take the same precautions?"

"Your mother was responsible for masking your future, and at great cost to her health. The instant those treacherous gwyllgi helped Evie escape, she branded you with a sigil used on all goddess-touched necromancers in the Marchand line to hide them from discovery. She carved years off her life to protect yours, and we might never have located you had she not returned to Savannah."

"She placed her faith in Maud," Lacroix intoned, "and Maud failed her."

"Maud had no idea she was luring Mom into a trap." I struggled against Lacroix and was rewarded with a biting reminder of his nails that I couldn't get free unless I started a fight I couldn't yet win. "That's why you hung around, isn't it, Odette? You stayed in Savannah, near Maud, hoping Mom would reach out one day and you would be there to intercept her."

"Beach living suited me." She touched the shells braided in her hair. "That part was no hardship."

There was just one more thing I had to know, already knew, but had to hear from her lips. "Did you kill Maud too?"

"You were withering away beneath her tutelage." Odette softened her voice. "You wanted to be a practitioner. It's all you ever talked about. Your power would have outstripped hers, and so she placated you with warding." She laughed, amused. "A goddess-touched necromancer ignorant of her birthright, left as a custodian for an old house and traded off to marry her sister's son like chattel." Her eyes glittered. "Clarice would have figured it out after you wed Linus, and she would have clapped her hands with glee to have bought such a fine mare to breed into her line."

Teeth bared, I channeled Lethe to full effect. "Did. You. Kill. Maud?"

"Who else could have slipped past her wards?" Odette twisted one of her thin braids, admiring the athame in her hand. Its slender blade reminded me of the Grand Dame's admission that such a weapon had been used to kill Maud. Perhaps even that very one. "You must have asked yourself a thousand times. The old house too, yes? Maud trusted me, *bébé*. Her home, it trusted me too. The poor thing had no idea. None. I made sure of it. Even while you were in prison, I visited Woolworth House to reinforce the sigils I placed that night to erase Maud's death from its memory. I had to be certain, you see, that I would remain above reproach."

The stairway leading up into my head loomed, but taking that path was too easy, and I had taken it too often. There was no point in asking why she had stolen Maud's heart. She took it out of spite, I believed, to punish Maud for perceived sins against her.

Dragging Lacroix back into the conversation to distract him from the hand I slid into my pocket, I challenged him. "You let me go to prison for her murder."

"Scion Lawson was staying with his aunt that weekend. He was meant to take the blame. You beat Linus to the scene, and there was nothing we could do. Given the status of all those involved, and the severity of the crime, the Elite acted too quickly for either of us to intervene. The best we could do was make arrangements to ensure you received the blood to which you had become accustomed." He clucked his tongue at Odette. "I was quite displeased by how things resolved, but that was then. Here we are, all together, as we always should have been. You will wed my heritor and give me immortal children with my blood in their veins. That is your purpose in life, your reason for existing."

"I'm engaged."

"Phillip," he called, ignoring me, "heat the brand." Using one of his nails, he sliced through the collar and back of my shirt to expose my spine. "This is a beautiful piece. Your lover is a talented artist."

He touched the design and hissed. "You've been branding the sentinels with these as well." He heard my sharp intake of breath and laughed. "At first, we assumed it was a memorial design, but its true purpose became clear soon enough. We have discovered if you burn through the topmost layers of skin, cauterizing the lines, it nulls the sigil."

Meaning his people had captured and killed more sentinels. "You're a monster."

"I am a man with a vision. You will come to share my perspective in time."

"I'm done with this conversation." I pulled out my hand, flicked open the knife. "I've gotten all the answers I need from you both."

"Petulance is an unattractive quality in a woman." He tapped my spine. "I will soon remedy that."

Phillip arrived with an electric cattle brand one of Lacroix's people must have smuggled in. The tip of the wand glowed red and distorted the air around it with heat.

"Any time now," I muttered.

"I do applaud your spirit." Lacroix accepted the brand, twisted it this way and that, admiring its glow. "This will hurt, quite a bit. I will do my best to dull the pain, after."

Seconds before the metal pressed into my skin, a bullet pierced Lacroix's hand. His fingers seized, and he dropped the brand with a clang, cursing in his native language. Before he could recover, a brutal impact drove him to the ground and brought me down with him. Vicious snarls revved beside me, music to my ears, and blood flew as a gwyllgi gnawed on the hand digging into my nape. Lacroix released me with a shout.

"You guys didn't waste any time." I scurried back and fished the stake out of the front of my bra, grateful he had checked my spine and not my chest for the protective tattoo. "I was starting to think Lethe talked you into making a burger run."

"We just wanted you to get your answers," Boaz drawled from

somewhere to my left. "Goddess knows you've waited long enough to hear them."

"Kill them," Lacroix ordered, his fangs lengthening to wicked points. "Take the scion as leverage, and bring my granddaughter to me."

Snapping his hips to one side, Lacroix flung off his gwyllgi attacker—Lethe judging by the yelp of pain. I got confirmation when her blood broke the line of the sigil, and I spotted her on her side, chest heaving.

Not good. That meant the impervious sigil wasn't sticking as well to her as it was to the others.

Her distant fae heritage might be responsible for how my magic interacted with hers, but since Hood appeared unaffected, I was betting the issue was the amount of healing I had pumped into her not that long ago. Magic, my specific type, was hit-or-miss when I used it on myself, and it might be acting wonky on her because of that surplus. But the whys hardly mattered now. We could worry about those later.

A throaty bay rang out behind me, and Lacroix went down again, his skull cracking on the tile.

There was no time to gloat as Hood savaged him, the vampires were upon us.

Midnight unspooled from the center of the room, its tendrils unfurling across the floor as Linus materialized within arm's reach of Odette. The sigil on his arm was smudged, and so were his fingertips.

"He's acting as bait," I whispered, furious. "Oh no you don't."

Using the tip of the stake, I sliced open my palm and raised a fresh ward around myself. I drew sigils on the wall of compressed air in front of me and slammed my palm against them. Power swept the vampires off their feet, but there was no ash. No death. The sigil hadn't incinerated a single one.

So much for cracking the code on how to modulate that particular design.

Alone in a sea of temporarily disabled vampires, Odette clutched the arms of her chair, but I could see the blade of the familiar athame she kept tucked under her hand, glinting metallic against the wood.

Scythe in hand, Linus stalked her. There was no bargaining with him when he was on the hunt, so I didn't waste my breath. But I remembered the feel of his blood slicking my palms too well.

Odette couldn't see my future, so she never saw her death coming.

The stake was in my hand, my fingers gripping it the way Taz, Midas, and Lethe had taught me, and I hurled it with every ounce of strength I had left. The wooden tip pierced her heart, a perfect shot, and despite it all, it broke mine.

I had loved her. So much. So very, very much. But death stripped away all masks, and her true face was one I didn't recognize. That didn't stop the tears from pricking the backs of my eyes.

Clutching the shaft with both hands, she slid from the chair onto her wobbling knees. Bright crimson poured through her fingers, seeping down her blouse onto her skirt, drawing the eye of every vampire in the room. Understanding filled her glazed eyes when they shot to Lacroix, and she crumpled onto the floor.

"Gaspard," she rasped, bloody hand reaching for him. "My...love..."

Across the room, I watched the light go out of her eyes and felt nothing. This woman had run Mom off the road, murdered Maud in her own home, and sent me to prison. She had slit Linus's throat to buy herself time to haul Lacroix to safety, and she had condoned all the deaths his reign of terror had brought to Savannah. She was a heartless monster, the same as him. In that respect, they had been a perfect match.

And yet, the child in me who remembered all those lazy summers collecting shells and eating ice cream on the beach with her could no longer stem the tears, even if the Odette I had known only existed in my memories.

"No." Lacroix roared like a lion and flung Hood off him. "Odette."

He crawled to her on his hands and knees, scooped her limp body into his arms, and sobbed against her throat. With a wail of animalistic misery, he ripped the stake from her heart and flung it across the room. Rocking with her corpse, he murmured in her ear, pressed kisses to her neck, and shook with the force of his grief.

Dread blossomed in my gut when Boaz appeared behind Lacroix, having wiped off his sigil, wanting Lacroix to know who had come for him, and pressed his gun to the base of the ancient's skull.

"This is for Rebecca Heath, and her family." He got off one shot, and Lacroix jerked on impact, but he didn't seem bothered much as he lay Odette down with infinite care. "Surrender, Lacroix. You're not walking out of here."

Lightning fast, Lacroix struck Boaz, knocking him against the far wall where he landed in a heap.

A cold knot cinched my chest tight, but he shook it off and began to push into a seated position.

"I loved her." Lacroix gazed out the nearest window. "I loved her as I have loved no other."

"Stop him." I fumbled through the sigils in my head before I remembered my magic was useless against him until *after* I staked him. "He's going to rabbit."

Hood lunged for Lacroix, teeth bared, but the vampire hit the window, and glass shattered outward.

Landing in a crouch on the sidewalk, he dusted himself off, and strolled in the direction of the empty shops and hotels lining River Street like a man without a care in the world...or a man without anything left to lose.

The few vampires remaining stirred, as if woken from a spell. They blinked at their surroundings, clearly puzzled to find themselves in city hall, but a few appeared more lucid than the others.

"Do not leave this building," I ordered them. "If you go out there, there's a chance he'll sink his hooks in you again. And if you come after us, or the sentinels, you will be incapacitated, and you might be killed."

A haggard man looked to his comrades. "We will do as you ask, Dame Woolworth."

"Thank you."

Padding up to me, Hood nosed my hand then tossed his head, waiting for me to climb on his back.

The second I gained my seat, he bolted for the window, forcing me to hold on for dear life. All I could do was press my face into the fur at his nape and crush my eyes shut as he made the leap.

The impact when his paws hit the sidewalk rattled my teeth, and I hadn't recovered when Lethe appeared at his side, stake in mouth. She spat it at me, and when I caught it, it was covered in crimson drool.

Her chuffed laughter as I slid it between my boobs almost covered my steady mantra of *eww, eww, eww.*

Almost.

THIRTEEN

The gwyllgi used their superior noses to track Lacroix to Jackson Square, but soon I didn't require help to find him. Plumes of smoke choked the sky, blacker than the night, and bright embers danced on the breeze, sparking new fires where they landed until an entire block roared, an inferno that promised to devour the city whole.

"He's put his vampires to work." I swore as we passed several carrying lighters and whatever accelerant they could set hands on. "And fast. *Too* fast. This must have been his contingency plan all along."

No wonder the vampires had been looting. They weren't causing general mayhem, they were gathering supplies.

"Where is Lacroix?" I twisted but couldn't spot him. "We have to take him down before he puts torches into the hands of every vampire in the city."

As much as I wanted to point out that this validated every fear I had of torches, if not pitchforks, I recognized it for panic spinning my thoughts in wild directions to distract me from the horrors unfolding around us.

A sharp bark brought Hood to a skittering halt, and he spun on a dime, unseating me. I hit the asphalt on my tailbone and growled through my teeth at the shooting pain, but Linus was scooping me up and setting me on my feet before I could attempt to dust off my palms.

"He's there." Linus rushed toward a square filled with ancient oaks that hissed and crackled as they burned. "Come on."

We ran for him, and the gwyllgi fell in beside us.

"What are we going to do?" I kept pace with Linus through sheer grit. "There's no one to man the fire station. Most of the city is empty. *We* emptied it. Now there's no one to help us get this blaze under control."

"Focus on Lacroix." Linus only had eyes for my grandfather. "We can't help anyone until we take him down."

Knowing he was right, I shoved down the grief over so much history being lost and zeroed in on the cause of all this. As we neared the ancient, I drew the stake from my décolletage and prepared to attack.

"The Lyceum will burn for what you have done," he said, but there was no heat in his voice. "I will make a funeral pyre of this city for my love, to send her spirit to her goddess."

I jerked to a stop, torn between finishing this confrontation and saving the Lyceum. It was an instinctive reaction, and I pushed through it. We could repair and rebuild, but not if Lacroix wasn't stopped before there was nothing left but ash.

Moonlight glinted off Linus's scythe as he held it aloft, and its wicked edge, wet with blood, comforted.

Lacroix appeared oblivious to the threat Linus posed, unable to tear his gaze away from the stake in my hand, crusted in Odette's still-wet blood. His nostrils flared as he scented it, and his eyes bled full black. The emotion absent in him only moments ago roared to life, spilling over his lips in grief-filled rage as he charged me with his mouth open, fangs on full display.

The gwyllgi closed in on him from behind, but not just the

Kinases. More than a dozen lizard-dog things converged on Lacroix, the whole Savannah pack, but they didn't beat him to me.

Gone rabid, Lacroix snapped his teeth at my throat and slashed at my abdomen with his claws. So much for birthing his dynasty. I avoided a killing blow thanks to months of intense training, but I wasn't his match in experience or strength. His quick jabs kept me too busy blocking to extend my arm and stake him.

Already tired from what it took to get here, I was flagging. I wasn't going to last much longer.

Linus materialized behind Lacroix, the dark maw of his tattered cloak gaping, and hooked his arm around the ancient's throat, maneuvering him into a headlock while he writhed and scratched him, shredding his forearm and voiding his impervious sigil, presenting me with a clear target.

"Prove you're my granddaughter." Lacroix hissed through clenched teeth. "Prove you're just like me."

Just like me.

No, no, no.

I was nothing like him.

Nothing.

Palming the stake, fingers matched in the imprints left by Odette's blood, I raised it for the kill shot.

Then the choice was taken out of my hands, literally. Boaz plucked the stake from my fingers and rammed it into Lacroix's heart. He held it there, twisted it, while the ancient scrabbled to rip it out, but the pulsing glow from before kindled in his chest and exploded outward in a blast of light that turned night into day.

The nearby vampires cringed and hid as their flesh sizzled and popped, screeching curses and sobbing.

Lacroix's arms drooped, and he sought me out one last time. "I..."

Black crept over his skin as it burned until Linus hissed and leapt back, dropping the body.

Lacroix collapsed into a pile of ash, and flame engulfed his clothing.

Whatever last words he had for me, they went unspoken. I couldn't say I mourned the loss.

The artifact I'd altered had consumed him from the inside out, and the stake was all that remained.

All except for the swath of destruction he left in his wake.

Fire devoured building after building, and its hunger only grew as it consumed more of the old houses.

"How do we stop this?" River Street wasn't far, but it's not like we could dip our buckets in the Savannah River and douse this blaze one gallon at a time. For one thing, we didn't have buckets. *Hold it together, Grier.* The warning didn't help. I laughed, giggled really, a hysterical sound that ended on a sob. "We have to stop this."

The vampires had straightened, a few regaining their senses while others stared dazedly as the city burned. There was no help to be found there.

"We need to evacuate." Linus grabbed my arm. "We can't save this block. We have to get ahead of the fire if we want to save the next."

"No." I tucked the stake back into my bra and drew my pocketknife. "He doesn't get to take this from me too."

Dad. Mom. Maud.

Five years of my life.

Lacroix had done his best to take everyone and everything away from me, and I was done letting him win.

The Marchand collection throbbed like a headache at the base of my skull, the knowledge not yet spent, and I shut my eyes to mentally flip the pages that hadn't eroded until I found the only solution available to me.

Blade slicing to the bone, blood dripping from my hand onto the thirsty earth in an offering, a plea.

"Grier," Linus whispered, broken. "No."

Unable to look at him, I started walking, creating a sigil that spanned from dirt to pavement. "I don't have a choice."

He didn't argue against it again, but he couldn't look at me either.

What I was doing...if it worked...meant we would belong to, belong *in*, two different cities.

As surely as the vampires had set fire to this square, I was sending our future together up in smoke.

But the fire was catching too fast, and Woolly wasn't so far away. I couldn't lose her. I *wouldn't* lose her.

The sigil pulsed once as it closed around me, a shock wave that rumbled beneath my feet. A jolt of pure energy raced up my calves and electrified my nerves on its way to tingle in my scalp.

Alongside the presence of Woolworth House, which had been a part of me for as long as I could remember, a second identity nestled in, rooting itself in the fertile soil of my soul, claiming acreage in my mind as its own.

Savannah.

The city hurt, a physical ache, and it leaned on me, asking for solace, seeking comfort.

Words burbled up the back of my throat, cutting my reply to him off cold. I had to let them out or choke.

"I, Grier Woolworth, claim this city." The nearby cobbles rattled with the force of my voice. "She is mine to protect, to cherish, to nurture. Our bond is unbreakable. I am...the Potentate of Savannah."

More power than I had ever imagined welled up in me as the city claimed me back, and through that fledgling connection, I saw how to save her.

"I have to set a ward." I erased the sigil then grasped Linus's cold, limp fingers in mine. "Watch my back?"

"Always," he promised, love and sadness mingling in eyes gone black.

"Evacuate the square," I called to Lethe and Hood. "Keep the street clear."

Teeth gritted, I cut a fresh line across my palm and made a fist to squeeze it like I was juicing an orange. Blood dribbled onto the pavement, and I started to walk, careful to mark off the burning area.

Under my breath, I prayed to the goddess I wasn't draining myself dry for nothing.

The world fuzzed around the edges by the time I finished lining the square, and I had to sit down or risk falling down to do the rest.

"Stay behind me," I rasped to Linus. "Don't interfere, no matter what happens."

Moving into position, he stood at my shoulder. "I won't make that promise."

Tugging on the new bond I shared with the city, I channeled her energy through me and into the ward. I felt it set and reached out to test it. A hard wall of compressed air met my fingertips, and I almost cried with relief. That would prevent the fire from spreading. It wasn't enough, but it was a start.

Pushing out a hard breath, I thumbed through the information crowding my brain until the right sigil combination struck me. I drew it on the exterior of the ward, coated both my hands with blood, and slammed them as hard as I could against the barrier.

A low hiss, similar to a balloon deflating, buzzed in my ears.

Head cocked, Linus dangled his scythe from his fingertips. "What is that?"

"Air," I panted. "Funneling it through the top of the ward."

"Removing the oxygen to suffocate the fire," he realized. "That's brilliant."

A weak smile wobbled on my mouth as the whistling stopped and the blaze coughed and spluttered before extinguishing. Through the exhaustion, I held on until the glow of embers died and the ward began trembling. And then I realized the barrier wasn't shaking, it was me.

The power slipped through my fingers, and the ward collapsed in a deafening blast of energy that threw me back against Linus's legs, knocking him onto the pavement beneath me. Head pillowed on his thigh, I closed my eyes and let go.

FOURTEEN

Warm and safe, I snuggled into my covers and breathed in the scent of detergent. I was halfway to sleep when a cool hand brushed my forehead and the words making me feel protected solidified in my head.

"The night birds are calling, calling, calling," Linus sang in a voice gone raw from overuse. *"The princess she's falling, falling, falling."*

"Come to bed." I reached for him. "I'm tired."

"You're awake." He cupped my face, ran his thumbs across my cheekbones. "Thank the goddess."

Woolly nudged me, and when I didn't budge, tried again.

"Hmm?" I struggled to prop open my eyes. "I'm so tired."

"Then rest." He pressed kisses in a row across my forehead. "I'll stay right here."

"Mmm-kay."

The old house wrapped me in her presence and lulled me back to sleep.

"ARE you ever going to wake up?" A small finger poked my side. "*Grier.*"

"Go away." I turned to face the wall. "I'm sleeping."

"You've been asleep for *days*." Straddling my side, Oscar dug his heels into my rib cage. "Get up, get up, get up."

"*Oomph.*"

"Play with me." He bounced up and down. "Hey, this is kind of fun. Like riding a horse. Yee-haw!"

"Oscar," Linus called from the doorway. "Let Grier rest."

"All she ever does is sleep." The weight vanished. "What's wrong with her?"

The thought occurred to me that something must be the matter, but I was too tired to care.

THE RUMBLE of my stomach woke me, and I groaned into my pillow. "Food."

Bacon. That's what I smelled. Lots of it.

"You're so predictable." A crunch sounded above me. "I don't know why no one tried food until now."

Unwilling to lift my head, I flung out an arm. "Gimme."

"Open your eyes," Lethe bargained, "and you can have a whole slice."

With supreme effort, I got one lid raised. "Gimme."

"I said *eyes*, not *eye*." She bit a strip in half and handed me the rest. "Eat that and then try again."

I found my mouth by trial and error then chewed and swallowed.

"Hey." She jabbed my shoulder with her finger. "You can't fall asleep again. Bacon is here. No one says no to bacon."

"Not hungry," I grumbled as I nestled back into the mattress. "Go 'way."

"Linus," she screamed. "She's not hungry. We have to get her to a hospital. Stat."

A laugh stuck in my throat, but it turned into a snore.

"I DON'T KNOW if I should be in here."

Amelie's voice drifted to me from a great distance, but I couldn't surface to reassure her.

"I'm not sure you'd want my company if you had a choice."

I shifted on the mattress, turning toward her, but I was so very tired, and sleep was so very nice.

"Lethe is in the hall. She wouldn't leave me unsupervised with you." She laughed, a huff of sound. "I deserve that, and you do too. She's great. Terrifying. But great. I'm glad you found each other." She covered my hand with hers. "I might not be your bestie anymore, and that's on me, but I still love you. I don't want to lose you before I get a chance to make things right between us."

The mumbled assurances that wanted past my lips turned into a yawn.

"Wake up soon." She kissed my cheek. "We miss you."

A TICKLING sensation brought me awake, and I swatted at the annoyance.

"Look, Sleeping Beauty, I've been working on your makeup for hours. Don't touch your face."

"Neely?" I peeked through my lashes at him. "Makeup?"

"He was practicing for your funeral," Cruz said from the corner where he read a paper.

"Necromancers don't..." I spotted Marit on a chair in the corner, texting away with a dopey smile and a hickey the size of Maryland on her neck. "What's going on?"

"Wait." Neely dropped his brush. "Are you actually awake?"

"Yes?" I stretched, and it felt divine. "Why are you guys in my room?"

"*Linus,*" he yelled. "Get your mighty fine behind in here."

Cruz peered at Neely over the fold, but his husband only fluttered his lashes innocently.

"You know who has a nice ass?" Marit set her phone on her lap and mimed squeezing the air. "Jack."

"Am I still dreaming?" I pinched myself and yelped. "No such luck."

Footsteps pounded on the stairs, and Linus appeared in the doorway. He lingered on the threshold, staring like he worried one wrong move might send me under again.

"You guys are freaking me out." I shoved upright. "What gives?"

A presence far vaster than Woolly reached out to me, its energy familiar and...content.

Savannah.

Pulse jumping, I recalled everything. Every blood-drenched moment. Including joining Linus's ranks.

Lethe, pissed off and snarly, tackled me in a hug guaranteed to leave bruises and knocked me back onto the bed, but I held on just as tight.

"What is that?" I tried to glance down, but she was stuck to me. "Did you swallow a watermelon?"

"You dumbass." Ignoring the question, she kicked me in the shin, and sheets tangled around our legs. "You stupid, stupid— Great. Now I'm crying." She paused her rant to wipe her face. "You could have died. You almost did. Now you've tied yourself to the freaking city. I hate to tell you this, but that was the most idiotic—if mildly heroic—move I've witnessed in my whole entire life."

Tension in the air raised hairs down my arms, and I checked on that new, foreign presence. "I don't think Savannah likes you referring to her as *the freaking city.*"

"What the actual hell, Grier?" Lethe gaped at me. "Why does Savannah have an opinion? *How* does she have an opinion?"

Hoping to be saved, I spun the question to the one person who might know. "Linus?"

"Cities aren't, as a rule, sentient in any recognizable way. But there are energies flowing through them at all times. Humans, vampires, necromancers." He included Lethe. "Gwyllgi."

All those lives, all that activity, leaching into the soil, wafting on the air, swirling through the water.

Bits of life that nourished until Savannah almost, *almost* attained what I hesitated to label as awareness.

"There's also the nature of your blood and its tendency to...*awaken* its recipients." He gestured toward Woolly. "You've also been bonded to a house for the better part of your life. For that alone, you would be more sensitive to the city's presence, better able to interpret its moods and needs."

I scooched to the edge of the mattress, kicking at the cover twisted around my ankle. "Is Atlanta so vibrant?"

"Yes." His glance slid away. "She's very much alive."

"And she misses you?" I had seen for myself how much he missed...her.

"Cities are entities so vast and old, they don't recognize individual people. Atlanta misses her conduit, a living connection to the world around her."

"So, any conduit would do?"

We all turned to the doorway to find Amelie with her fingers laced at her navel and a determined set to her jaw.

"There are certain requirements but..." Linus hesitated before allowing, "...more or less."

"Your bond to the city—" She drifted nearer. "Can it be revoked?"

"There's a loophole in the binding so that if I ever abused my position or became unable to perform my duties, I could be released from them." His attention zeroed in on her. "Why do you ask?"

"Grier was always going to be emotionally tied to Savannah. I was never sure how you two were going to make the long-distance thing work." She picked at her nails. "Now Grier is physically tied to Savannah, and the city appears to have an opinion on the matter. I'm guessing Savannah won't like it if her new BFF ditches her to follow her heart."

"Amelie..." I began, sick with certainty I knew where this was heading.

"I've been trying to figure out a way for you to be together, and I've been trying to figure out what to do with the new life I'm about to be given." She laughed softly then looked to me. "I've had a lot of time on my hands lately, and it was easier thinking about your problems than mine. At first, anyway. And then it hit me that I'm about to be free, and I'm about to be a whole new person, and I want that person to be a good one. Decent. I want her to be better than I was—am. I want to atone for my crimes in a meaningful way." She dropped her hands to her sides and kicked up her chin. "I want to be the next Potentate of Atlanta."

A profound hush spread over the room as we absorbed the magnitude of her offer.

"Amelie." Linus pinched the bridge of his nose, lowered his hand, touched it again. "That's generous of you, but I can't turn you loose on my city, given your history. Ambrose is still bonded to you. He will be for the rest of your life. I can help you learn to control his urges, but what you're asking..."

"The position might help her hide her condition," I said pointedly to him, knowing he would catch my meaning. "Potentates employ wraiths for backup. Who's to say she can't use Ambrose the same way? Who, aside from you, would have to know? He's bound to her now, that gives her control over him."

A spark I hesitated to label as hope brightened his navy eyes. "It's possible."

"You've got a crack team in place," I reminded him. "They could monitor her, help keep her in line."

"The process for assuming a mantle already in use requires twelve months of on-the-job training as well as another twelve months of probationary work done with minimal oversight." He slid his hands into his pockets, thinking. "At the end of those two years, you would have to convince the Society, as well as the other powers in the city, that you could continue on alone. They would put your nomination to a vote." He exhaled slowly. "Assuming you claimed the title, it would be yours until you named a successor and began training them to replace you. Otherwise, the Society and all other factions must agree that no Society oversight is required in that place, at that time."

A snort escaped me. "And that will never happen."

Atlanta was home to the busiest airport in the world in addition to multinational corporations. The revenue it generated, and the global access it offered, made its health too vital for the Society to let it go unchecked.

"Are you sure this is what you want, Amelie?" As much as I wanted to grab her offer with both hands, I had to consider more than my own future. I had to factor in Linus's, and Atlanta's. I cut him a look. "Are you sure it's what *you* want?"

"You understand you've volunteered for two years of extensive training as well," he said dryly.

"Um." No, I hadn't realized that. *Fiddlesticks.* "Yes?"

"As the nearest potentate in good standing, your education will fall"—he smiled a little smile—"to me."

"Oh?" That perked me up nicely. "Do tell."

"I'll be forced to divide my attention between Atlanta and Savannah during the initial twelve months, but I see no reason not to reside in Savannah during Amelie's probationary period." He pretended to consider me. "However, that might be construed as granting you an unfair advantage."

All innocence, I stole a move from Neely's playbook and fluttered my lashes at him. "Does that mean you'll stay with your mom until I'm official?"

"Ah, no." He was quick to decline, too quick, and he flushed. "The carriage house ought to do."

Disappointment washed through me until I considered it would be a return to the routine that had made me fall in love with him in the first place. A two-year engagement made sense if we wanted to keep our professional and personal lives above reproach. Claims of favoritism would still be made once Society tongues started wagging. How could they not? But there was nothing we could do about that.

While I *might* consent to my fiancé moving across the yard from me, I wasn't swearing Linus off romantically for two years to fully level the playing field. And it's not like Amelie and I would be in direct competition. Our territories were hundreds of miles apart. Our appointments would be earned based on merit. Or, in my case, kept. Since I jumped the gun a wee bit.

Hmm. I wonder how Linus felt about co-potentating with his future wife?

Not that I wanted to discourage Amelie, but I had to be certain this wouldn't blow up in all our faces. "Have you spoken to your brother about this?"

"No." She kept her head high. "It's time I started taking responsibility for myself, and that begins with making my own decisions."

"All right." I could respect that. "When do we start?"

"As soon as these come off." Linus lifted the hem of his pants to reveal an ankle monitor. "You and I got six months' probation to be served at Woolworth House for accessing the Athenaeum without proper authorization." He flicked a glance at my ankle, but what I thought was an offending sheet was, in fact, a fabric strap with a flashing tracker identical to his. "Boaz received a twelve-month sentence to be served at the Lyceum."

"Your mom wants to keep an eye on him." I huffed out a laugh. "Where will he sleep?"

"He'll be escorted to and from the Lyceum by sentinels. When he's not there, he's expected to remain at the Pritchard family home." The corners of his eyes crinkled. "He's also no longer your shadow."

"That's it?" I drew my leg onto the mattress to poke at the device.

"Atramentous is only giving us a slap on the wrist?" I tapped the blinking light. "Or ankle, as it were."

"Our combined efforts freed Savannah from Lacroix's influence, saving countless lives, vampire, human, and necromancer alike, and preserved the Lyceum. You also avenged the fallen." The edges of his lips curled. "And while the Grande Dame can't publicly condone your actions, you saved the city from burning. That's fact. There were too many witnesses to discount your willingness to sacrifice yourself. That's why your claim to the city won't, at present, be revoked."

"And," Lethe interjected, "since you had to go and bind yourself to this hunk of dirt, I had to do the same."

Stunned, I shot to my feet again. *"What?"*

"Oh, don't act so surprised. You know your man bought me a house. It's not a donut, but it's a start."

"What about the Atlanta pack?" Her mother would kill me. "What about your position as second?"

"The Atlanta pack has Midas." She pointed to Hood. "Drumroll please..."

Grinning from ear to ear, he obliged.

"I'm the brand-spankin'-new alpha of the brand-spankin'-new Savannah gwyllgi pack." She extended her arm and wiggled her fingers. "You may kiss my hand, supplicant."

"You're staying?" I launched myself at her. "Are you sure?"

"You're pack." Hood patted the top of my head. "We have to stick together."

"Plus, I've already hired a chef for the *massive* kitchen in our new digs." She kissed my cheek. "Thanks for that, by the way. Jaquez is the best housewarming gift I've ever received."

Given the small fortune I had paid in takeout since she came to Savannah, I had to believe Jaquez couldn't be that much worse. "I'm so glad you like him."

"And," she said, pulling back, "Hood and I would rest easier knowing you were just one yard over." She rubbed her belly under her loose tee. "We don't know what to expect with this little one. Her prenatal development is off the charts. Her postnatal may be too, so it makes sense to stick close."

"Atlanta isn't that far," I pointed out. "I could be there in a few hours if you needed me."

"You heard me about Jaquez and my ginormous kitchen, right?" She gave me a gentle shove. "Linus put the nails in your coffin, sweet cheeks. Free house, free chef. Why would we ever want to leave?"

"Free...?" I mentally wrote a check to Linus to cover the expense. "Doesn't get better than free."

"Right?" She danced into Hood's arms. "Have I told you how much I love you today?"

"You can stop buttering me up. I ordered second lunch before we came upstairs." He kissed her tenderly then wrapped his arm around her shoulders. "Stop teasing Grier." He focused on me. "We're paying fair market value for the house, so you can pop your eyeballs back into your skull. They'll get fuzzy if you let them roll around on the floor too long."

"Now who's teasing Grier?" She elbowed him, but he gave her a look. "Oh, fine. Jaquez was retained for three months. Let's call it a probationary period. That really is your housewarming gift, but as long as he works out, we'll hire him full-time."

Though it made my wallet cringe, I didn't want her to think I was cheap. "I don't mind—"

"Don't give her an opening," Hood warned. "This one will run— not walk—straight through it."

"More like waddle." She pulled her shirt taut over her stomach and turned to the side. "Check this out."

The curve of her belly was almost twice as pronounced as when I inked the impervious sigil on her navel, and dread twined through me, twisting my gut into hard knots. "How long was I out?"

No one answered.

"How long?" I shot to my feet. "Linus?"

"Twenty-six days, five hours, and thirty-seven minutes," he said softly. "Give or take a few seconds."

"Goddess," I breathed. "What happened?" I patted across my chest, over my stomach, and down my hips but found no scars or tender wounds, nothing to account for the missing time. "I don't remember getting hurt."

"You lost a lot of blood," Lethe volunteered. "Linus had to transfuse you to keep you alive."

Knees wobbly, I sank back onto the bed. "Why do I have a feeling there's more?"

"You tapped into the latent consciousness of an entire city." Linus raked a hand through his hair, tugging on the ends like he might pull out a clump. "Grier, if you hadn't still been feeling the effects of the sigil you designed to expand your mental capacity, your head might have literally exploded by flinging open the gates of your mind and inviting an entity that size to join with you."

"Oh," I whispered, grateful to still be around to receive the dressing-down I deserved.

"Part one of your training will include memorizing passages from the Marchand collection, and I mean the old-fashioned way, not through magical means. You must learn to control your powers, to understand them, in much the same way as Amelie."

"How is the city?" I fisted my hands in the cover. "The people?"

"Recovering. Rebuilding." He shifted closer. "The barricade was taken down three weeks ago."

Thinking of the sentinels who once manned it pushed my thoughts in another direction. "Your mother?"

"She remains in power." He chuckled at that. "With the sentinels on her side, her platform is stronger than ever."

"I'm glad." As much as it would have once galled me to admit it, "She's good for the Society."

"I think so too," he said after a considerate pause before turning a probing stare on me. "Do you still have a headache?"

"Not exactly." The ache from the extra memory was gone, as was most of the content I had absorbed. "There's one passage from the Marchand collection that keeps circling in my head, though."

"Oh?"

"Goddess-touched necromancers are anathema to their brethren," I recited. "They are healers, not reanimators. Their progeny are the only true and perfect immortals. The Deathless are the product of a healing so deep their cells continue to repair any and all damage for as long as they exist."

"Corbin will be interested to hear that," Linus mused. "Perhaps that explains your effect on..." noticing Amelie was still in the room, he rephrased, "...other spiritual matter."

And why Corbin didn't smell like a vampire or require much blood to survive.

Cletus's sentience, Oscar's awareness, the city's awakening...

Those weren't healings, exactly, but they were unprecedented events linking my blood to their greater cognizance. Perhaps the answers were all there, in Eileen or in my head.

Thanks to our walk down memory lane—or the corridors of Atramentous, as it were—I had the next five months of uninterrupted time to sift through what I had learned and had yet to learn.

"How is Corbin?" I glanced around. "Where is he?"

"He's malnourished and was injured badly during his captivity. Caring for a Deathless vampire has had its learning curves, but he's on the mend. Woolly offered him a room. I imagine he's there now, resting."

"And Clem?"

"Boaz secured him a position within the sentinels. He'll want to see you now that you're awake. I'll send him a text to let him know."

A massive yawn stretched my jaw, and all the various side conversations died a sudden death.

"Chill." I stood and stretched. "I'm not going to pass out again."

A ghostly blue head topped with a sailor hat popped through the wall as Oscar noticed the commotion.

"Maybe you should rest," Lethe suggested. "I can bring you a tablet so you can catch up on the news."

"Actually, a walk sounds good." I shooed Oscar away, trusting him to find me downstairs where we could have a more private reunion. "Linus? Care to stroll with the invalid?"

Having noticed Oscar, Linus hooked his elbow, and I took his arm. "One lap around the yard, then back to bed."

"The yard?" I startled. "I thought we were under house arrest?"

"You're bonded to Savannah." Careful with me, he guided me downstairs and onto the porch. "We couldn't be certain you could commune with her through Woolly and her wards, so I suggested an expanded house arrest. Allowing you access to the earth seemed prudent. However, we will be in breach of our parole if we cross any property lines."

"I can live with that." I brightened at the prospect. "This is sounding more and more like a vacation."

I would be able to visit with Lethe easier and play with Oscar, who had yet to appear, more.

Linus pulled me closer. "Five months together with nothing to do but read and—"

"Read?" I threw on the brakes. "Be very careful what follows that *and*, mister."

"—and make love to my fiancée followed by cuddling and snacks?"

Nodding my approval, I rested my head on his shoulder. "Those are acceptable pastimes."

We walked a bit, edging toward the woods, before Linus asked, "Can you sense the city stronger now?"

"Yes." I felt her in every step. "You were right to worry. The wards dampened the connection, but I don't think that's a bad thing. A layer of separation when I need one, while I'm adjusting, is probably a good thing."

As we waited on Oscar, an elegant woman with silver hair at her temples stepped onto the path, cutting off our route. Perhaps going for stealth, she wore a black pantsuit that flattered her trim figure with matching ballet flats, but I could tell at a glance she wasn't the hired-thug type, so this must be personal for her.

The scythe appeared in Linus's hand, pure reflex, and it earned him an indulgent smile.

I leaned against Linus to cover my hand as I reached for...the knife that wasn't in my pajamas.

Just as I was starting to worry about the kid, Cletus appeared at my shoulder, bony fingers clacking.

"Get the others," I urged him. "Hurry."

Now all Linus and I had to do was buy ourselves time for backup to arrive, and we'd need it for anyone with enough juice to waltz right onto my property without my knowledge.

"You do your blood proud, Grier." The shape of her face rang a distant bell. Dare I say, an alarm bell. "Your momma would have been dancing on the ceiling when you claimed the city for your own."

"I'm sorry." I cocked my head at her. "You look familiar. Do I know you?"

"We've never met." Her smile was amused. "I'm Rhiannon Marchand, your aunt."

"The new Dame Marchand." I tightened my grip on Linus. "I was sorry to hear about your mother."

"I doubt that very much." She kept her smile pinned in place. "How far are we from where my daughter was killed?"

Despite her amiable expression and tone, I noted the hard emphasis on the *k* in killed.

"She was taken down on the front lawn by a sentinel before she could abduct me."

"Hmm." The new Dame Marchand stared through the trees, but we had wandered too far from the house for her to see the exact spot. "I heard you gained access to the Marchand collection." She focused on me. "There was no other explanation for Lacroix's death, but I had to be certain. How much did you take?"

"Not a single book," I said truthfully.

"You got what you came for, though. I didn't anticipate your willingness to return to Atramentous."

"Eloise told you what she did," Linus surmised. "That she forged Severine's signature on the acquisitions paper."

"Dear boy, who do you think guided her hand? She never would have thought of it herself. I had to nudge her along." She toyed with a button on her suit jacket. "Eloise is my heir. I would have chosen her regardless. Heloise was a hammer, like her grandmother. Ellie requires more training before she fully steps into the role of Dame Marchand, but she's got a knack for subtlety."

"Like her mother," I finished for her, uncertain where this was headed. "Why are you here?"

"I'm certain you can imagine myriad reasons for this visit."

"How did you know where to find me?" Her expensive clothes were pressed, unlined. Her flats showed little dirt. She hadn't been squatting in bushes while she waited for me to wake up and decide to go for a walk. And even if she had, the pack regularly patrolled the property. "How did you get past the gwyllgi?"

"A summoning I painted on the ground, baited with a fresh kill and a time-delayed sigil to lull them to sleep once their bellies were full." She shrugged. "I'm familiar with the species. Their stomachs do most of the thinking for them."

"You didn't answer the whole question." Linus stared at her. "How did you know where, specifically, to find her?"

The reason for the pointed question caught up to me a second later. "Well?"

"You must have noticed you're easy to find these days, but I see you haven't yet figured out why." Her smile chilled my blood, but it wasn't mean or unkind, and that made it worse. "You would have put it together if you'd had more time." She checked the gold watch on her wrist. "As it is, I have a flight leaving in a few hours, and it required longer to wake you than I expected."

A chill swept down my spine at the casual power she wielded over me.

That explained how she knew *when*, but not how she knew *where*.

"Goddess-touched necromancers are marked at birth with a sigil whose pigments fade but protections remain. It shields them from detection, allowing us to hide the young and vulnerable from threats." She fingered the hem of her cuff. "You were older when your mother imprinted you, but it worked just as well. While it hid you from your grandfather, which was her only concern, it can't shield you from someone who knows how to look."

Relief over finally identifying the culprit swept through me. "You hired the vampire assassins."

And this meant I owed Mary Alice a mental apology for thinking she would ever betray Linus.

"I was assured they were the best." She touched her bun to check its neatness. "I do apologize for their ineptitude. Their contract stipulated that your death be fast and painless. I regret they were unable to deliver on their end of the bargain."

"I'm surprisingly good with them not murdering me," I said, "but thanks."

"Why target Grier?" Linus meshed our fingers in a show of support that ended with a cool weight filling my palm. The pocketknife he bought to replace the one I never returned to him. "Her mother was disowned. She has no ties to the Marchand family."

Using our hands for cover, I finessed the blade open and pricked my skin. Blood pooled between our palms, and I very slowly, very carefully, began drawing protective sigils on us both.

"Mother took care to ensure Grier could reclaim her birthright if she chose. Grier would have robbed my girls of their rightful inheritance and the title of Dame Marchand." A kernel of remorse filled her eyes. "It's not your fault your mother carried the right genes, or that I might have murmured a few words in the ear of an old friend who had taken up with Gaspard Lacroix. It's not your fault Gaspard used that information to select an heritor who would most appeal to Evie, or that he planned on breeding you to reestablish his line." She rolled her eyes. "Don't you find it always comes down to blood with vampires?"

"Yes," I whispered, struggling to absorb the larger implications. "You wanted Mom out of the way."

"I was born first. *I* was the eldest daughter. I should have inherited the title, but Marchands ignore age in favor of genes when it suits them, and it's laughably easy when dealing with twins. Mother miscarried six times with six different Last Seeds before her mother married her off in the hopes she could at least produce necromantic offspring to carry on the family legacy.

"After it was confirmed I couldn't give Mother a goddess-touched grandchild," Dame Marchand continued, "she had no use for me. Evie was her shining star, and Mother thrust me into the shadows to hide her failure. The only way I could inherit was if Evie was no longer an option." Her calm expression never wavered. "A nudge here or there, whenever she hinted she might return home to provide a safe and stable upbringing for you, pushed Gaspard, and by extension my old friend, to extreme measures."

"Extreme measures? You mean murder." Rage kindled in my veins. "How can you be so cold? She was your sister."

"Every day of my life, I was told I was nothing." A thread of heat simmered in her tone. "Evie's death made me something." Her hands tightened at her sides. "Mother picked a husband for me who gave me twin daughters. Neither carried the gene, so neither received preferential treatment. But with two girls, she had twice the hope for the next generation. She even named them, stole that small joy from me, not that I ever told them as much. She hoped it would bind them tighter than I had been with my sister, never realizing *she* was the reason I despised Evie."

"You set the assassins on me and got rid of the Marchand collection the second you heard I was being released from Atramentous." Thinking of Eloise, I recalled her telling me she had been in a meeting with Severine when Odette called to quiz Dame Marchand about my father's identity. Eloise claimed not to have overheard their conversation, but she used that call to explain away her appearing on my doorstep. "Odette told you. All of it. You were still in touch."

The entire time Odette "helped" me find my father, she had known his name—known *him*—all along.

All my request to Odette had accomplished was giving her an excuse to openly contact the Marchands.

"I sent Eloise to determine how best to...manage the situation." Dame Marchand's mouth tugged down at the corners. "But Mother learned of her trip and dispatched Heloise to bring you into the fold before you could be eliminated. That assignment cost one of my daughters her life, and it caused Mother untold grief." She smiled a little at that. "Once again, she bet on the wrong daughter and lost."

"Did you kill Severine after she informed you Grier had obtained permission to visit, or did you wait until she discovered you had disposed of the Marchand collection?" Linus posed the question with utter calm at odds with the black seeping into his eyes. "Johan claimed he was not his wife's confidant, but his decision to leave Raleigh within hours of Severine's death paints a different picture. He carried the note for you to buy safe passage."

"Interesting theory." She blinked once before shaking off her surprise. "You will, of course, never be able to prove any of it. Johan suffered a massive stroke just yesterday. Died alone in his bed. Romantics will say a broken heart was to blame."

With Odette and Lacroix out of the picture, and Johan conveniently dead, she was close to getting away with a series of perfect crimes that had been playing out since before I was born.

"You've confessed to a lifetime of sins," Linus said, voice colder than I had ever heard it. "Sins against Grier, which I tend to take personally."

"You're not going to take my head, young man."

She dipped a hand in her pocket in the split second it took him to shield me from the perceived threat.

His shoulders blocked my view, but he jerked hard, and then he crumpled at my feet.

Dropping to my knees, I rolled him onto his back and spotted the opalescent knife blooming crimson on the left side of his chest.

It felt like my heart had been the one struck.

A goddess-touched artifact. It must be. Otherwise, the impervious sigil would have held.

"Wraith's bane, a lethal dose by my calculations." She watched while he gasped for breath then appeared to lose interest in his decline. "I altered the formula to compensate for his ready access to a healer capable of purging him."

Of course, she had supplied the vampire archers. I should have done that math when she admitted to hiring them. The poison was too rare, and too specific, for even assassins to have on hand. That left the bronze arrowheads, but Odette could have easily tipped Rhiannon off to the gwyllgi's lethal allergy.

"They say if you want something done, it's best to do it yourself." She withdrew a sleek knife that gleamed like onyx. "I regret the necessity, but there was one vital element of your creation over which I had no control. Lacroix fed George himself after his transition. The blood of an ancient flowed through George's veins when he and your mother created you, and that same magic flows through you. You are too powerful to go unchecked."

Activating the sigils I had inked on earlier, I snapped the ward into place around us.

"You learned nothing from Lacroix." She hurled the knife, and it pierced the barrier then lodged in my shoulder. "You can't protect against weapons forged by your own kind." She pulled an amulet from the neck of her shirt. "Did you really think I would come here alone *and* unprotected?"

At the rate these charms were popping up, I had to wonder if Mom had died with a bald spot.

A third blade filled her hand, this one the mottled blue of turquoise, her grip sure. She had used the knives often to own such confidence.

I touched the smooth handle protruding from my shoulder, and pain radiated through me in agonizing waves. Gritting my teeth, I yanked out the blade with a throttled scream.

Linus gazed up at me, breath hitching, unable to speak or do more than tremble.

All my sigils and wards and healing were useless against her. The blood she so despised—rendered null.

She could do it. Kill us both. Leave our bodies for our friends to find. Hop a plane and fly back to Raleigh. She would have accomplished all she set out to do. Eliminating Mom and me, cementing her status and her favorite daughter's inheritance.

Blood from my wound smeared the grass, and the earth trembled beneath my palm.

A chorus of howls lifted the hair down my nape, even as relief coasted through me as Cletus rejoined us.

I didn't have to do this alone. I wasn't alone. Not anymore. Not ever again.

Dame Marchand cocked her arm, poised to land her second strike, but she missed her mark by a mile when what resembled an ant bed punched through the grass beneath her feet, pitching her off-center. She drew a fourth blade, wary now, but nothing else happened.

"Tell your mother hello for me," she said, tearing her gaze from the lawn.

Twin mounds of fresh earth erupted where she stood, and she leapt aside, but each time one dropped in a puff of dirt, another peaked, forcing her to dance out of their path. She couldn't hold still long enough to aim.

"*Fiddlesticks,*" I whisper-screamed at Linus. "You're missing it." I swallowed hard at the puddle of my blood seeping into the ground. "Savannah is..." I wet my lips. "She's protecting me."

The anthill-sized mounds kept my aunt on her toes long enough for backup to arrive.

Lethe hit Dame Marchand in the small of her back with her massive paws and knocked her on her face.

Quick as whips, thick kudzu vines burst from the ground, wrapping Dame Marchand in a green cocoon.

Lethe jumped back, padding out of range, but the vines ignored her, continuing to tighten their grip on my aunt until she was pressed face-first into the ground with grass stuffing her cheeks. Gentle ripples of earth boiled around her, kicking dirt on her back, and the vines kept cinching like the ground might swallow her whole.

Circling me and Linus protectively, Hood kept an eye on his mate out of the corner of his eye.

Wary of the writhing vines, Clem disarmed Rhiannon then secured her wrists at her spine with a zip tie. Beneath her, the grass swayed and pitched in gentle waves that reminded me of how Woolly manipulated her floorboards.

From the direction of the house, Corbin limped toward us with a baseball bat in hand and Oscar propping up his bad side just in time to watch the vines form a noose around Rhiannon's throat that squeezed until she blacked out before patting her on the head with a leafy tendril.

But I had no time for reunions. I checked Linus's vitals, praying the goddess granted me one last miracle.

"Hood," I yelled. "Bring me a splinter from Woolly's porch."

The gwyllgi tore off for the house while I stripped Linus down to his waist.

"We've got to stop meeting like this." Hands shaking, I smeared my palms with fresh blood and used them to ink sigils over every inch of his exposed skin. "This is going to work, and then you and I are going to have a long talk about making your impervious sigil permanent," I rambled as I inked him, fingers made clumsy with fear. "Just hold on."

"Here." Hood leaned over me, placing the sliver of wood on my palm. "Is that enough?"

"We'll have to hope so." There was nothing else I knew to do. Dame Marchand had worn a charm I bet matched Lacroix's down to the number of Mom's hairs used. Given their connections, I would wager she made both herself. "I'm sorry for this in advance."

I drove the splinter, a good two inches of it, into Linus's upper arm, praying it would be enough to void the power of the goddess-touched artifact used to injure him.

He didn't even flinch.

Leaning over him, I pressed my hands against his chest and shoved magic into the sigils until it filled him, overflowed him, and leaked from his pores in a soft glow that dissipated on the air.

"Wake up, wake up, wake up," I chanted, blocking out everything but him. "Come on, Linus."

A chilly hand closed over my wrist. "I'm...tired of...always being the...damsel."

Tears flooded my eyes and dripped off my chin to where the healing sigils had already begun flaking, their magic spent. Sniffling, I wiped my cheeks dry on the backs of my hands. "Do you think your mother will let you wear a hennin to the wedding?"

A laugh, hardly more than an exhale, parted his lips. "You remembered."

"Yes, well, I tucked it away in the event I got quizzed on the material later."

Though I had trouble imagining the proper name of a pointy princess hat coming up in casual conversation—except with him.

"Grier." Proving he understood me better than anyone, he took one of the hands I had curled into his shirt and lifted it to the side of his throat. The scar Odette had given him bumped under my fingers, a reminder he had survived. "I'm still here."

"How do you feel about us investing in a literal ball and chain? Or just the chain?" Stupid tears made his outline wobble. "That's what they call marriage, right?"

"No chains." He tunneled his fingers into my hair, the cool tips pressing against my scalp. "I promised I would never cage you, and I won't start now."

"You're not caging me," I protested, sniffling. "*I'm* caging *you*."

"The fear that haunts you haunts me too, every time you take a risk, every time you embrace your gift. It terrifies me, what you're capable of, because others will see only ways to exploit your talent and not what it costs you. But I stand by you, I support you, and I always will."

"Just not from an arm's length away." Hopeful, I made him a better offer. "Six feet?"

"No."

"What if I let you wear the key as a necklace?"

Had he attempted to shackle me to him, I would be insulted. No, I would be furious. I would hiss and scratch and claw my way free and never look back.

Thankfully, Linus was less feral than I on that account. But then again, he hadn't learned to fear the dark, the press of algae-coated walls, the dank flavor of air shared by a thousand souls trapped in the same...

Gritting my teeth, I yanked myself back from those grim memories and breathed in the comforting scent of my future to clear away the past.

Brushing long strands of hair away from his face, I couldn't stop touching him. "Is it safe to move you?"

"I think so." He pushed up onto his elbows. "I'm dizzy but..." His eyes spun in their sockets before he shut them. "I should lie down."

"Yes, you should." I caught him by the shoulders and eased him back. "We'll get you upstairs and put to bed." I kissed his forehead, his cheeks, his eyes, his chin, and then his mouth. "Maybe if you're a good boy, I'll even join you."

A smile crinkled his cheeks, but he was already fading.

"What do we do with her?" Lethe stood over an unconscious Dame Marchand. "You've got plenty of acreage. I could make her disappear."

"I can make her disappear too." I gestured Hood over to help with Linus. "Clem, round up a few sentinels to help you take her to the

Lyceum. Put her in a cell. I'll be in touch with the Grande Dame shortly to explain the situation."

And why the prisoner arrived resembling a leafy green burrito.

"That's it?" Lethe snarled. "You're letting her off that easy?"

"I'm not a Marchand, or a Lacroix. I'm not going to kill people to achieve my own ends. I'm a Woolworth, and that means we do this by the book. She goes to the Lyceum, she gets a trial, and—goddess willing—she'll be sentenced to Atramentous."

Hello, Marchand-Woolworth blood feud.

Eloise, who had gotten off scot-free for her crimes thus far, would be livid after this.

"I still say it's not enough," she grumped.

"Trust me." A shiver coasted down my spine at the memory of how I had been treated. "It's enough."

FIFTEEN

Linus slept in my bed, tucked under three blankets, for hours. I sat in the chair I pulled from my desk and watched over him until my eyes burned with dryness. Only a solemn promise from Woolly to ping me if he woke convinced me to go downstairs with Lethe for a snack break in the kitchen.

"Linus didn't come back without freckles or laugh lines," Lethe observed as she served me French toast from a takeout box. "You didn't reset him the way you did with Boaz and me."

"I didn't mean to reset either of you." I took a banana from the bowl on the counter and sliced it thin over my stack. "Maybe it's because he wasn't as near death as you two?"

"He almost died." She watched me with interest then gave me a banana for hers while she hit the fridge. "This time and last time."

"He's bonded to a wraith." I accepted the bottle of caramel she passed me and squirted it over the top to make us bananas Foster French toast. "Maybe that's the difference."

Lethe knew about Cletus, that *he* was actually a *she*, and that she was Maud. But with so many guests in the house, it was too dangerous to touch on those subjects.

"Maybe." Holding up a finger, she located the powdered sugar then dusted our plates. "Guess you'll find out when you start your lessons."

"Guess so." I cut a bite and savored the fruits of our labors.

"Your lessons with your old tutor."

"Mmm-hmm."

"The tutor you're now boinking."

A piece of fruit went down the wrong pipe, and I coughed until my chest hurt.

Stroking a banana suggestively, she unpeeled it. "Gives new meaning to the phrase *pop* quiz, eh?"

"Stop tormenting Grier." Corbin limped into the kitchen and claimed the spot beside me since Lethe was too busy molesting fruit to sit still. He had showered and changed into clothes Hood loaned him, and all but the shadows in his eyes had improved. "Got any of that left?"

"Take mine." I pushed the half-eaten plate over to him and glowered at Lethe. "I've lost my appetite."

"Crybaby," she accused. "Want a bandage for your emotional boo-boo?"

"You heard the news about your new vocation?" Ignoring her, I nudged my untouched glass of orange juice toward him as well. "Sorry I had to bargain on your behalf. The deal I cut was the best I could do."

When I brought Corbin's intel on Lacroix before the Grande Dame, she offered amnesty for his crimes on the condition he served one hundred years as a sentinel with the option for promotion to Elite status.

"Being a sentinel won't be so different from being a hunter. I'll live in the barracks, take orders, go on missions." He dug into my leftovers. "I'll take that over prison any day." He tapped his fork on the plate. "Besides, after what happened, Savannah needs all the help she can get. I'm happy to pitch in."

"When do you report for training?"

"Next Friday." He squished a banana slice into mash. "Mind if I stay until then?"

"Not at all." I touched his arm. "You're my progeny. You're always welcome here."

"Thanks." He ducked his head. "Do you think I'll get any siblings?"

"You're worried about the whole eternity thing?"

"Yeah. A little." He set down his fork. "I don't want to be alone."

"Stick with the sentinels. Work your way up to Elite. You'll always have a family at your back that way." I hated to encourage Woolly, but this needed saying. "Pretty sure I'll be procreating in the future. You can be Uncle Corbin. And then Great Uncle Corbin, so forth and so on." I gave him a pat. "You'll never have to be alone unless you decide that's what you want."

"Thanks." He laughed. "Again."

Oscar drifted through the ceiling to hover at Corbin's shoulder. "You promised."

"I did, didn't I?" He scraped his plate clean over the trash can then loaded it in the dishwasher. "I'll set up the targets and show you how it's done."

"Target?" Alarm zinged through me. "What are you two doing?"

"Oscar asked me to show him how to fire a gun." Corbin looked at me, all solemnity. "After everything that's happened, he wants to learn how to protect his family and his home."

"And you thought it was a good idea to teach a poltergeist to fire a weapon, why?"

"Oscar," Corbin said calmly, "can you wait for me at the range?"

"The range?" I squeaked. "When did we get one of those?"

Clearly, I needed to spend less time unconscious. These people required constant adult supervision.

After the ghost boy blasted off, Corbin waved me over to a cardboard box hidden behind the couch.

"I asked Clem to source these for me." He parted the flaps to reveal two clunky orange and blue plastic guns that shot foam darts.

"Oscar felt helpless when Dame Marchand attacked you, and he hates that. He wants to stop bad people from hurting good people. This will empower him." He shrugged. "Safely."

"Poor kid." As I inspected the darts, I noticed targets folded in the bottom of the box. "I appreciate you doing this for him."

"I don't mind." He rolled a foam cylinder between his fingers. "He's always going to be around too. One day, we might be all we have left." He cast off that bleak thought and smiled. "I figure I ought to get on his good side."

I hadn't thought of it quite like that, but he had a point. Unless Oscar crossed over, he would be here to watch over future generations of Woolworths and pal around with Corbin. I liked the idea of that. Very much.

"I better go." He lifted the box onto his hip. "I promise I won't let him shoot an eye out."

"I appreciate that. Undead optometrists are harder to come by than you might think."

I watched him go then caught myself staring up the stairs. Woolly's presence remained with Linus, so he must not have woken yet. But there was something I had been meaning to ask, so I hunted down Lethe, who was polishing off a stack of sausage she hadn't offered to share.

Picking at my nails, I hovered in the doorway. "Did a package arrive for me from Atlanta while I was sleeping?"

"Yep."

A flutter of nerves made me regret what little I had eaten. "No one opened it, did they?"

"No." She licked her fingers clean. "I intercepted it myself. I thought it was my Vietnamese delivery, but no. The box was too small, and it smelled like *twu wuv* and not coconut rotisserie chicken with rice."

"Linus doesn't know, does he?"

Casually, she kept on stuffing her face. "He was with you, so no."

Relief coasted through me. "Where is it?"

"In a hole I dug." She relished my shock. "What? It seemed like a good idea at the time. I had no idea how long you would be out. Actually, you should be thanking me. Nowhere is safer than a good hole."

Unwilling to wander so far from Linus, I gave her a nudge. "Can you please go get it for me?"

"Oh, sure. Send the pregnant lady out into the murder woods."

"You like both murdering and woods."

"I can't argue with that logic." She pushed away from the counter. "Give me ten."

I followed her onto the back porch and sat on the lowest step, sliding my feet through the cool grass.

"You saved my bacon today," I said, and hoped Savannah heard and understood.

A single dandelion pushed through the dirt to blossom between my toes.

I was taking that as a yes.

Though I would have to chat with her about inviting weeds onto the lawn.

Then again, maybe schooling an entity as large as an entire city wasn't the brightest idea. I had been meaning to hire a gardener anyway.

"Here you go." Lethe tossed the box to me. "Original tape and everything. I buried it in a sandwich bag."

"I'm impressed." I turned it over in my hands. "You didn't even peek."

"I can be good, it's just not as much fun as the alternative." She admired the tips of her fingers as they lengthened into claws. "Well? I can only be so good for so long."

"Pushy." I held out the box and let her swipe through the packing tape. "I want your honest opinion."

She snorted. "Like I ever give you anything else."

"Good point." I opened the flaps and lifted out a ball of bubble wrap I carefully unwound to reveal a ring box nestled like the peanut center of an M&M. Cracking open the lid, I peered inside and didn't feel the slightest twinge over how much its contents had cost me. "What do you think?"

"Other than you could have bought me another house for that?" She whistled. "He's going to love it." She leaned closer. "What's with that groove in the center?"

Snapping the box shut, I winked at her. "You'll see."

"Tease."

"Can I talk you into helping me make this a night he won't forget?"

"As long as it doesn't involve the limbo, the mambo, or any other bos that require me to bend, shake, or lift my leg higher than my waist, sure."

After disposing of the shipping box in the trash can outside, I pocketed the ring and ran it upstairs. I ducked my head into my room to check on Linus, but he was sleeping peacefully, and Woolly chided me for bothering him. Taking her scolding on the chin, I scooted down the hall to the same unoccupied guestroom and reached under the bed to locate the last and most precious item.

Legs crossed, I set to work on my project while keeping an ear out for Linus.

SIX HOURS LATER, Linus was stirring, and I was as ready as I would ever be. I had resumed my vigil at his bedside, certain all my preparations were in order.

"You didn't have to sit with me." He extended an arm, and I took his hand. "How long was I out?"

"Thirteen hours, give or take."

"What did I miss?" He brought my hand to his chest and placed it over his heart. "Anything interesting?"

"No."

"You're...quiet." The way his lips pursed made me think *quiet* was a copout. "Are you all right?"

"I'm so nervous I could puke." A smile seesawed on my mouth, and I reclaimed my hand before I got him all sweaty. "Are you hungry?" Hearing I was about to barf was sure to spark his appetite. Goddess, I was a hot mess. "Good." I didn't wait for him to demure. "I made food."

Startled pleasure brightened his eyes. "You cooked?"

"Don't get too excited. It's just the house specialty. Grilled cheese."

A childhood favorite Volkov had ruined for me, but I was reclaiming.

"I'm sure I'll love it."

"Be right back." I dashed downstairs and shoved the sandwiches I made earlier into the toaster oven to reheat them. Then I cut them into small wedges and stacked them on a plate I garnished with parsley. It was tradition to eat them with milk when we were kids, so I poured us each a glass and arranged everything on an old silver serving tray I unearthed from the attic. Careful not to spill all my hard work, I padded up the stairs. "Here we go."

"This looks delicious." He pushed upright and swung his legs over the side of the bed. "Do you want me to eat at the desk?"

"You're not the kind of guy a girl kicks out of her bed over crumbs." I set the food on my dresser since the plates had started rattling with my jitters. "But there's something I need to do first." I snapped my fingers, and nothing happened. "I said, *there's something I need to do first.*"

Head cocked, he arched an eyebrow. "I heard you the first time."

"Um, hold that thought." I ducked into the hall. *"Lethe."*

"What?" The door to the hall bathroom swung open on her adjusting her elastic top pants. "I had to pee."

"Lethe."

"I'm ready, I'm ready." She whipped out her cell. "Last time was practice. This time's for real."

Inhaling until my lungs protested, I waltzed back into the room. "Where were we?"

Uncertain, he guessed, "Cheese toast?"

"Yes, that." I raised my voice. "But *there's something I need to do first.*"

Nothing happened.

Absolutely nothing.

Hours of prep work and sneaking around and...nada.

Linus waited a moment, reading into my expectation, before admitting, "I don't understand."

"Neither do I." I stormed out into the hall and caught Lethe cramming the cheese toast into her mouth when I had no idea how she had sneaked it out of the room without us noticing. "You're fired. Go sit in your room and think about what you've done."

"I'm pregnant," she mumbled, crumbs flying. "I have needs."

"Go." I pointed, snatching her phone from her back pocket. "You'll get this back later *if* you're a good girl."

Glaring at me over the rim of the first glass of milk as she chugged it, she pivoted on her heel and left.

"Sorry about that." I locked the door behind me. "It's hard to find good help these days." Modified pen in hand, I drew sigils on the doorframe to give us privacy for when Lethe inevitably slinked back to eavesdrop. "Did you happen to notice our food's disappearing act?"

"I did," he admitted, "but I've found it's best not to take food from a gwyllgi, particularly a pregnant one, even if it's mine."

"You're not wrong."

Polite to a fault, Linus smoothed a hand over the sheet. "What am I missing here, Grier?"

Waiting until the ward popped our ears, I pushed the first button Lethe had queued on her home screen. "Let there be light."

The yards and yards of twinkling fairy lights I spent hours taping all the way around the room where the wall met the ceiling emitted a romantic glow on cue.

A smile poised on his mouth. "What is all this?"

"I'm not finished yet." I pressed the second button. "Let there be music."

The first notes of a smoky love song poured from the Bluetooth speakers hidden around the room.

A flush spread over his cheeks, his freckles standing out in sharp contrast. Fidgeting with his sheet until it covered his bare legs, he cast around the room for his clothes, but I liked him in boxers and a tee just fine.

"This is the part where I would have offered you grilled cheese, but we'll skip that." I crossed to him and went down on one knee between his thighs. "I picked a bouquet of roses from the garden for you, a mix of reds and yellows, but I asked Hood to carry them because my hands were full, and—"

"Lethe," he said softly.

"Yeah." I laughed under my breath. "Lethe."

She had mistaken the romantic gesture as his, and I was too good a friend to deny him the brownie points.

"I don't need the flowers, or the grilled cheese. You put in the effort, and I appreciate the thought."

"Before we write the whole evening off as a loss, I did manage to hold on to one thing."

"Oh?"

"The first time I asked you to spend the rest of your life with me, your mother had just tried to engage you to another woman." Sweat broke across my forehead when I reached in my back pocket. "I announced my intentions to marry you without asking you first, without talking to you about plans for your—and our— future at all."

"Grier—"

"We've discussed it since," I talked over him before he derailed me. "I just wish I could go back and do it right. Since that can't happen, I can at least give you this."

"I would be just as happy with a trip down to the kitchen." He rubbed his thumb where his bread tie ought to be, and a pang of guilt for not returning it to him after Atramentous struck me. "There's a loaf of white bread on the counter."

"Just open the box." I shoved it at him. "Please."

Without taking it from me, he cracked open the lid and unerringly spotted the surprise first. "My ring."

"Here." I pulled the heavy platinum band he had otherwise ignored from its velvet resting place and held it out to him. "Give this a spin."

Per the jeweler's report, the band was four millimeters thick and twelve point five millimeters wide. But it didn't glint silver. It had been hand-antiqued with the careful application of black rhodium to make the four princess-cut diamonds that alternated between four round brilliant cut diamonds pop even more. The comfort fit edge promised Linus could do his work without fear of getting poked by the metal end of his original engagement ring. But what first drew Linus's eye was perhaps my favorite feature. The jeweler had left a thin groove woven around the ornate scrolls and beneath the stones to wind the stripped metal bread tie. Thanks to the largest princess-cut diamond sitting a smidgen higher, I had room to tuck the twisted ends underneath the stone, just as the jeweler instructed.

"I don't know what to say." He smoothed his thumb over the band, smiling when the pad didn't catch on errant metal. "It's perfect." He leaned down and kissed me gently. "Thank you."

"There's one tiny thing I have left to do." I took the ring from him, still impressed by the weight, and cleared my throat. "Linus Andreas Lawson—"

"Yes."

Laughing with delight, I slid the ring on his left hand's ring finger and pressed a kiss to that knuckle.

Holding out his hand, he admired the band. "Am I correct in assuming you won't let me out of bed?"

"You would be correct, yes."

"There's a metal box under the bed in my room. Will you bring it to me?"

Thrown by the change in subject, I braced on his knees and stood. "Sure."

I smudged the privacy sigil then padded to his room, amazed Lethe hadn't set up camp outside the door after she finished her snack. The box was right where he'd told me it would be, but it weighed a ton. I yanked on the handle until it toppled onto its side, its contents spilling across the floorboards.

Aside from an alarming number of teeth from extinct animals— all packaged and labeled like collector's coins—which I scooped up and dumped back in, there was one other item.

The hand-sized jewelry box and red bow gave it away as a gift he meant for me.

I really hoped he hadn't spent as much on this as I had on him, but tonight was not for counting pennies.

Back in my room, I held up my find. "Unless you've developed a sudden desire to play dentist with me, which is where I draw the line, and it's a hard line, no pun intended, I believe this is the prize at the bottom of the cereal box."

"Open it."

Resolved to put all thoughts of money out of my head, I gaped at the platinum necklace on its bed of crimson velvet. The thin chain and lariat style made it casual enough to pair with jeans and a tee, but the three karat diamonds capping each dangling strand sent my jaw crashing to the floor.

"I..." Despite my best intentions, I folded like a house of cards. "I can't accept this. It's too much."

"The first stone," he said, ignoring my protest, "the bluer one, is the memorial diamond Maud had made with Evangeline's ashes. I found it while we were sorting correspondence in the basement. The package from the lab that grew the diamond was never opened."

"Mom," I whispered, rolling the stone between my fingers, wishing I hadn't blocked out Woolly so she could share in this moment.

"The second stone, the whiter one, is the memorial diamond I had made from Maud's ashes. I used the same company so that they would be as near to identical as possible." He traced the longer chain. "I had always suspected, but Mother confirmed that she had kept Maud's ashes. I can guess why, but she would deny suffering the human mentality of wanting a token of a lost loved one."

Considering Maud's heart had never been found, and it was the keepsake we passed down through generations, I could understand the Grande Dame wanting to hold on to some tangible piece of Maud.

Tempted as I was to share the gift with Cletus, I had to accept it meant nothing more or less to him than a pretty bauble from Linus to me. His lack of recognition would only hurt Woolly, who was all too aware now of what we had all lost when I brought Maud back as a shadow of her former self. And the absence of sentiment might hurt me even more.

"Growing a diamond from ash costs marginally less than buying a mined one," he assured me, misreading my discomfort, "and while I could have purchased a sterling lariat, I decided you would rather I invest in a setting that would protect the diamonds than skimp in this instance."

Vision wavering, I couldn't look away from the magnitude of the gift he had given me.

And I couldn't seem to find my voice to protest again.

"I intended to give this to you on our wedding night so the two most important women in your life could be present, but given all you've been through, I thought you might take comfort from receiving it early."

"I've got your number, mister." I blinked away tears before they fell. "You can't receive a gift without giving a bigger one."

The blush from earlier returned, turning his pale cheeks rosy, but I didn't poke fun at him again.

The truth—that Linus received so little in return for what he gave others—was no joke.

Lifting the necklace from its case, I slipped the long chain over my head. The precious stones nestled between my breasts, and I covered them with my palm, pressing them into the skin over my heart in an almost-prayer.

"As much as I love this and never want to take it off, I have more plans in store." I flexed my toes against the floorboards. "Maybe trying to get in your pants while wearing Mom and Maud is a bit..."

"Yes," he agreed and had the box ready and waiting by the time I reached him.

"The way I see it, we have three options. We move this party to another room, move the necklace to another room, or move past sex to parent-approved cuddling with you beneath the sheets and me on top of them."

Clearing his throat, he shared a look with me. "I would prefer option two."

"Me too." Cradling the gift against my chest, I returned to his room where I put the necklace back in the box under his bed. "Much better."

"What are you doing under there?"

I jerked upright so fast I banged the top of my head on the underside of his bed. *"Fiddle-freaking-sticks."*

"Yeesh." Lethe rushed over to help guide me out without denting my skull again. "Don't kill yourself."

"Nothing about tonight is going according to plan." I sucked air between my teeth while I explored the tender spot on my crown. "I give up. I'm done. Naked gymnastics will have to wait."

"I tried telling you the place on Abercorn should be your love shack, but you wouldn't—" Her hands shot to her stomach. "Ouch." She rubbed her belly, which was shockingly large this close. "I should have stopped after that third triple pepperoni pizza."

"Come on." I stood and hooked an arm through hers. "I'll walk you down to the kitchen and get you something for heartburn." I pulled, but she didn't budge. "Lethe?"

"I think I just peed myself."

"No." I checked her over, and my stomach dropped into my toes. "Your water broke."

"No, no, no, no, no." She staggered back. "It's too soon. She won't survive being born this early."

"Sit on the bed." I herded her toward the mattress then shoved her down. "I'll get Hood."

On the way past my room, I popped my head in and called, "Lethe's in labor."

Eyes going wide, Linus threw aside the sheet covering his lap. "I'll be right there."

"Lethe," I yelled down the hall, "cross your legs until I get back."

After I ran downstairs, I sprinted across the porch then down into the yard.

"*Hood.*"

Gwyllgi hearing being what it was, I wouldn't have to scream long for one of them to hear and find him.

"*Hood.*"

A single voice bayed a response, and I could have wept with relief as it drew closer.

"It's Lethe," I called. "She's having the baby."

"Baby?" Hood stumbled out of the trees. "Lethe...? She...? A baby?"

"That does tend to be the end result of a pregnancy, yes." I threw an arm around his waist to support and guide him. "She was with me when she started complaining about stomach pains, and I tried to walk her downstairs for some antacids, but then her water broke, and I set her on the bed while I came to find you."

Okay, so maybe he wasn't the only frazzled one. "What about the healer?"

"He won't arrive until next month." Hood's eyes sparked with crimson flecks. "There should have been more time."

Neither soon-to-be parent had pointed the finger of blame at me yet, but I worried that would change if this delivery didn't go off without a hitch.

The racket must have attracted Clem's attention. Corbin's too. They waited in the front yard with Oscar.

"Lethe's having a baby," I blurted on our way past them onto the porch. Clem and Corbin both took a healthy step back like childbirth was a virus they might catch if they stood too close, and Oscar mimicked them.

Chickens.

The crystals in Woolly's chandelier quivered with excitement when we raced beneath them.

"Did we miss anything?" I shouted up at her as we hit the stairs.

Scattered images popped into my head: Lethe snarling at Linus, Linus working on a sigil over her navel, Lethe kicking Linus in the chest, Linus hitting the opposite wall.

"Goddess," I breathed. "Can't leave them alone five minutes."

Dazedly, Hood asked, "What is it?"

"Nothing." I patted him. "We're almost there."

We tumbled into the room on top of each other, both of us eager to check on our other halves.

Linus sat at the base of the wall where Lethe had kicked him, clutching his ribs on the right side.

I crouched in front of him. "Did she break anything?"

"Just winded me," he panted through his teeth. "Bruised, not fractured."

"How is she?" I hiked up his shirt and used the modified pen in his hand to draw a healing sigil over the injury. "Better?"

"Much." Still a smidgen weak from the poison, though the sigil ought to help with that, he let me help him to his feet. "Any word on the healer?"

"He'll be here." I sighed. "In about four more weeks."

"We might not have four more hours." He stopped a healthy distance from her legs. "I timed the contractions. She's progressing quickly."

Chewing my bottom lip, I wrung my hands as my friend thrashed. "Can we get a healer here from the Lyceum in time?"

"No," Lethe snarled. "No necromancers."

Afraid she would say that, I growled back, "Then who's going to deliver this baby?"

"You do it."

I looked over my shoulder at Linus. "Can you?"

"Not him." Lethe curled on her side to face me, eyes pleading. "You."

"What do I know about babies?" I stumbled back. "Are you nuts?"

"I'll walk you through it." Linus caught me before I could escape. "If she'll let you touch her, you can use a sigil to help with the pain."

A raw moan parted Lethe's lips, and her toes curled with the agony before relaxing again.

"Oh." I fumbled his pen. "Um." I almost popped out the cartridge. "Okay?"

"You've got this, Grier." He supervised from his position at the foot of the bed. "Once she's calm, I'll explain how to check for dilation."

"You can stand at the head of the bed," Hood said, catching his drift, "or you can get out."

Avoiding Hood's glare, Linus circled behind me then went to stand beside Hood, just out of his reach.

The next few hours passed in a group effort that might postpone Woolly's grandchild expectations indefinitely after I witnessed an actual child birth.

Hood comforted Lethe, who calmed after I numbed her below the waist, though the newly minted alpha in her was still pissed to take orders like *push* or *don't push* from Linus since he was both a man and not technically pack yet.

Linus, goddess bless him, instructed me on how to coax a new life into this world. He didn't even mind when Hood snarled at him or Lethe snapped her teeth, tiny speckles of foam flying in his direction.

And I...I saw real estate I'm not sure a best friend should view without a medical degree of some kind. As much as I wanted to be traumatized by the hands-on education in gwyllgi anatomy, I had to admit it was pretty cool witnessing the moment when a couple became a family.

WITH THE HAPPY parents busy cooing at Baby Kinase, and half the Atlanta gwyllgi pack, including its alpha and beta, on the way for a visit, I was happy to escape onto the back-porch swing for a breather.

"I get why they call it the miracle of birth." I patted the spot next to me after realizing Linus had followed me. "I just hope Lethe doesn't feel miraculous again any time soon."

"Heir and a spare," he said, smiling.

"Ugh." I leaned my head on his shoulder. "Don't remind me."

"Next time, she'll give birth in her own room, in her own house."

"The house next door."

A chuckle jostled me where I rested against him, and the happy sound warmed me.

"You're still in your underwear." I traced the hem of his boxers where they rested against his thigh. "How scandalous, Professor Lawson. What would the other faculty members think?"

"I'm resigning from Strophalos," he said casually. "It's a small thing to give them notice I don't plan on returning from my sabbatical."

"Are you sure you want to cut ties so soon? You've got two years left you could be teaching."

"I want to spend as much time in Savannah as possible." He covered my hand with his. "And it's not like I couldn't teach here. Strophalos was never about the prestige for me, it was about occupying my time."

A man who didn't sleep had plenty of it on his hands.

"*Or*"—I meshed our fingers—"you could remodel the upstairs apartment on Abercorn into a one-man tattoo parlor where you can practice your art. There's room enough for two chairs if you want to take on an apprentice."

"Hmm." He stared off into the night. "I never considered branching out on my own."

"Neither did I." I jostled him with my elbow. "I needed a nudge. Maybe you do too."

For the span of a few sways, we sat there together, in the quiet, thinking on what could be.

"We have guests arriving soon," he reminded me. "We should go make ourselves presentable."

"*Or*, and I'm just spitballing here, we could barricade ourselves in my room, use a sigil to block out Lethe when she swears revenge for us not running interference between her and her mom, and pick up where we left off earlier."

"How much does her forgiveness cost?"

"About three dozen donuts." I shrugged and took his hand. "I can afford it."

We stood together and traded the balmy night for Woolly's cooler interior.

A line of pack members come to pay their respects snaked down the stairs, and we jostled our way past them onto the crowded landing. With Lethe and Hood busy holding court, we slipped into my bedroom without incident. But before I finished drawing the privacy sigil, cool hands bracketed my hips, and I glanced over my shoulder to find lean muscle covered in ink on display for my ogling pleasure.

Given permission, I looked my fill. "You seem to have lost your shirt."

"Fiancée or not," he said seriously, "boxers seemed too presumptuous."

Amused that he thought it was possible I didn't want him, I replied just as solemnly, "You deemed the shirt the lesser of two evils?"

"The tattoos have an effect on you." His expression wasn't confidence, but calculation. "It seemed the safer bet."

"I can see how you might think that." Turning in his arms, I brushed my fingertips over the intricate designs marking his skin. "You could always say you tripped and your shirt fell off, but bare legs are much harder to explain."

"You see my point."

"No," I said, tongue in cheek, "but I feel it."

"Hmm."

"That sounds ominous." And yet I couldn't find it in myself to mind as he began easing me out of my clothes, even when mischievous black wisps curled off his fingertips everywhere they touched me. "What are you—?"

The cool mist built until it blanketed the room in absolute darkness. I froze, unable to see through the gloom, and my heart started pounding. I wet my lips, anticipation raising gooseflesh as much as the lower temperature.

"You're not playing fair," I complained into the abyss. "How am I supposed to ravish you when I can't see you?"

"I'll be doing the ravishing this evening." His voice came from behind me, and I spun. "You give so much of yourself, let me give this back to you."

Pretending to agree, I waited until he put his hands on me, slid his fingers into the elastic band of my panties, the only clothing he'd left me, and slid them down my thighs. With him bent over, it was laughably easy to tip him off balance.

Air whooshed from his lungs when he hit the floor, not in pain but surprise. "Grier?"

"That's my name. Don't wear it out." Kneeling, I groped my way up his thighs to his hips. An accidental side trip along the way caused him to suck in the breath he had lost, and I smiled as I reached for his waistband. "Oops."

"*Grier.*"

"Hey, I apologized." I tugged his underwear down in a smooth glide. "You didn't fall that hard."

"You said *oops*," he hissed as my lips followed the trail made by my eager fingers.

"Haven't you heard?" I climbed over him, settling my weight on his upper thighs and leaning forward to nibble his hipbone. "It's the thought that counts."

When I took him in my mouth, he speared his fingers through my hair and groaned. Fascinated by the sting in my scalp, the slight loss in his flawless control, I took him deeper, coaxed him higher.

And then I was the one flying, lost in the dark as his cool hands lifted me over him. I braced my palms on the floor to either side of his head then moaned when he gripped my thighs and sank into me. I leaned down so our chests brushed with each of his thrusts, and I turned my face into the column of his throat. I worried the tender skin there with my teeth, and when he slid a hand between us, I bit down too hard and drew blood. More potent than champagne, the heady punch of his flavor went straight to my head.

The feel of him in my body, the taste of him on my tongue, was too much. I crushed my eyes shut as first one and then a second orgasm rippled through me. Lips still on his neck, kissing away the small hurt, I whispered, "I love you, Linus."

The words caused his steady rhythm to falter, and he came sighing my name into my ear.

Tremors quivered through his arms when he locked them around me, holding me flush against him, accepting what he needed, what he wanted, what I was so happy to give now that he had embraced his right to take it from me.

An eternity later, after my eyes uncrossed and the darkness abated, I kissed the bruise rising on his neck. "I didn't mean to break the skin."

His hands traveled up and down my back, exploring the less visible knobs of my spine. "I don't mind."

"I'll use a sigil to heal it," I offered. "I just have to get feeling back in my...everything."

"I don't mind," he said again, his voice warmer and more relaxed.

Unsticking my damp chest from his, I narrowed my eyes on him. "You *liked* it."

"It wasn't altogether unpleasant." His lips tweaked in the promise of a smile. "You would be cutting out the middleman."

"I can't believe what I'm hearing." I tried for scandalized but probably failed. "You want me to feed from you." I tapped my nails on his chest, over the tattooed city seal of Atlanta. "You have a secret vampire kink."

"Vampires hold no appeal." He stared at my mouth. "You, however..."

"Mmm-hmm." I twisted his nipple and relished his yelp. "You're not fooling me. You've got your science face on."

"I might be curious about the long-term effects of a goddess-touched necromancer feeding on a fellow necromancer. Both on the subject and the donor." Rubbing his abused chest, he shrugged. "I can't turn off my brain."

"There is that whole dying thing," I said dryly. "I'm not saying you should flip the switch, just maybe dial it down, especially when we're supposed to be basking in the afterglow." Dragging my fingers through his hair, I smiled down at him. "I like you like this."

"At your mercy?"

"All that veneer cracked, the layers peeled away. You look... rumpled. With a side order of smug." I shifted my hips and pretended not to notice his rising interest before he distracted me. "You should look smug more often."

"I promise to be smug as often as you're willing to rumple me."

"It's a deal."

Searching my face, he murmured, "I'm sorry your romantic evening didn't go entirely as planned."

"Things might have gone a tad off script." I pressed a kiss over his heart. "But you did agree to marry me while not under duress, so that was nice. You got bling, I got bling, and we helped Lethe give birth to the cutest baby girl I've ever delivered. I don't know about you, but I'm impressed with us."

"Come on." He helped me up, led me to the bed, thick with extra blankets on his side, and lifted the covers. "Climb in."

I did, happily, and he crawled in after me. Once he settled on his pillow, I draped myself across his chest. His arms came around me, and I pressed a smile into his skin when his breathing changed. I fell asleep to the steady beat of his heart, content with our off-script night —our off-script life—and ready to embrace whatever the goddess had in store for us next.

ALREADY MISSING LIER?

While *How to Wake an Undead City* wraps up Linus and Grier's main story arc, we'll be seeing them again in a series of novellas that kicks off with *How to Kiss an Undead Bride* and ties up a few loose ends.

Join my newsletter or my Facebook group to keep an eye out for your invitation to the wedding!

I also hope you'll join me for *Shadow of Doubt*, the first book in TBGTN spinoff, The Potentate of Atlanta.

Sure Linus is hot and all, but could you survive having him for a boss? Amelie—make that *Hadley*—is about to find out.

Turn the page to read the first chapter of *Shadow of Doubt*!

SHADOW OF DOUBT

THE POTENTATE OF ATLANTA, BOOK ONE

CHAPTER ONE

Regret tasted like a discount food truck taco. *Frak.* I might still be new to the city, but Sal swore on his mother's grave he used real chicken this time, and I bought it. Literally. Goddess only knows what he fed his regular customers until the health department caught up with him. Hence tonight's discount. He was trying to lure in a fresh crop of suckers, and my forehead must have looked freshly stamped.

Rinsing my mouth out with a gulp of flat soda of undetermined flavor, I was tempted to chase this bad idea with another one. The Italian ice stand the next block down made for a good palate cleanser, but they served at a glacial pace worthy of their product, and I wanted to finish watching *Robot Space Tentacles Attack Earth* before I called it a day.

The shadow pretending to be mine unspooled its grasping fingers across the sidewalk in front of me and made a *gimme* motion.

"Fine." I tossed my half-eaten meal, wrapper and all, into the darkness where it vanished. "Don't come whining to me if it makes you sick."

The fingers shifted into a hand and formed the letter C. No. Wait. It mimed holding a drink.

"Are you serious?" I lifted my cup and got a thumbs-up in response. "Hope you like backwash."

The void swallowed my offering and snapped back into shape, mimicking me once again.

This is what I got for feeding it Tootsie Rolls for good behavior. Now it wanted a taste of everything.

Halfway down Peachtree Street NW, I got a text from Bishop, who might as well have been my parole officer given how often he required check-ins when the boss was out of town. Rumor had it he had been a desk jockey prior to my arrival. Lucky me, he had decided —or the potentate had decided for him—to hit the streets to keep a particular eye on the newest member of Team Atlanta.

>>We got trouble.

Nice and vague, just the way I like it.

>>Details to follow.

An address popped onscreen that forced me to pull up the GPS app.

I had been a resident of Atlanta for a year and two days, but Peachtree Streets still looked the same to me.

On my way.

Using a rideshare app exclusive to the city's paranormal population, I arranged for transportation. I didn't have to wait long for a sporty two-seater painted lime green with black racing stripes to squeal up to the curb. The driver honked twice, and when I didn't break my neck sprinting around the car, she lowered her window.

Skin so pale it was translucent, I figured her for a vampire, but she hadn't sent a warning tingle up my spine. Her wide blue eyes, the color of her pronounced veins, locked on me like a tractor beam, like her will alone could haul me into the passenger seat. Her spiked pixie cut highlighted the roundness in her cheeks, and the elastics on her braces matched her hair and her wheels.

Open palm smacking her door, she called out, "Are you coming or what?"

Looking her over, I felt my eyebrows climb. "Are you old enough to drive?"

Returning the favor, she leaned out farther. "Do you see a student driver sticker, lady?"

Another texted nudge from Bishop forced me to take my chances. "Let's go."

I climbed in beside her, noted the aftermarket stereo system that belonged on a spaceship, and exhaled through my teeth.

"I'm an ace driver," the girl snarled. "Stop huffing and puffing over there."

"Does your attitude get you many tips?" I strapped in. "How about positive reviews?"

In another life, I had taken pride in the number of glowing reviews I collected on the job. Those were the days. I didn't get thanked for the one I did now, and I sure didn't earn any tips. Heck, I considered it a good night if I made it home without blood on my clothes or spit in my hair, and those were the more sanitary bodily fluids that got splashed on me.

"I have to make rent." She stomped on the accelerator but mercifully left the radio off. "To do that, I zip as many slow pokes across town as I can in a night. Gas don't pay for itself. Neither do groceries. Maybe keep that in mind when you're typing up the review I can hear you mentally composing over there."

That stupid taco came back to haunt me as she cut lanes, slashed through an exit, then slammed on her brakes.

I swallowed it back down, hit release on my seat belt, then reached for the handle. "Thanks for the lift."

"What's he doing here?" the girl mumbled. "Hey." She locked the doors. "What's he doing here?"

"You've got to be more specific." A manned barricade blocked the sidewalk. "Who?"

"Midas Kinase."

The sound of his name broke cold sweat across my forehead. "I don't know."

But I could guess, and I would need only one. The Atlanta gwyllgi pack wouldn't trot out its heir and chief enforcer for anything less than a capital crime involving a pack member in good standing. And the last thing I needed was to cross paths with him—or his keen nose.

Gwyllgi scent memories filed away all sorts of information, meaning my identity was only a sniff away. I had taken precautions, magical ones, but this wasn't how I wanted to learn if I had bought the promised charm or just an old silver band that sometimes turned my finger green.

"You're Hadley Whitaker." Her eyes rounded until they swallowed her face. "*The* Hadley Whitaker. I saw your name pop up on the app, but...geez. You're really her?"

"Yep." I tapped on the window so she would take the hint. "I'm really me."

"No shit?" She all but bounced in her seat. "You know the Potentate of Atlanta?"

Linus Andreas Lawson II.

Appointed by the Society for Post-Life Management, the ruling body for necromancers, over which his mother presided, to protect and serve this city.

Chills broke over my arms thinking of him, and my heart kicked hard once. "He's my boss."

"You're like his heir, right? Scion? I forget what you corpse-raisers call it."

Corpse-raiser.

This kid could teach a master class on how not to get repeat business.

"Right now, I'm a lowly employee of the Office of the Potentate. One day, if I play my cards right, I might get promoted to upper management."

"Wow." She sank back against her seat. "He's pretty hot if you're into the grim reaper type."

Once upon a time, I might have agreed with her. But on bad nights, I still dreamed of him.

The moth-eaten black cloak that hung from his shoulders, the threadbare cowl that hid his pale face. All that, I could stomach, but his scythe...the way moonlight glinted off its blade when he raised it to strike a killing blow...

I stood on the right side of the law these days, but one look at him had me feeling cold steel parting the warm flesh at my throat.

"Is this like official business?" She scanned the scene. "Did someone bite it?"

While she gawked, I manually unlocked my door. "That's classified."

"That's a yes." She grinned at me, metal glinting over needle-sharp teeth that made me wonder if she wasn't as pixie as her hairstyle. "I'll be in the area if you want to call me up special." She passed me a crumpled piece of paper trimmed into a lopsided rectangle. On the front, she had painstakingly drawn a business card with colorful markers. On the back, she had crossed out the last four digits of her debit card number on a receipt for takeout. "The app won't let you pick who you get, but I'll charge their rates for a private ride."

"I appreciate it." I tucked the slip into my wallet so as not to ding her pride. "See you around."

As I stepped onto the curb, she peeled out, blasting rap music that rattled my bones from three feet away. She hadn't given me a chance to shut the door, so she yanked the wheel hard to one side and let momentum slam it for her.

"Goddess," I muttered, grateful to have survived the experience.

"Buy a car," Bishop advised, crossing the barricade to stand with me. "You won't suffer so many near-death experiences."

Adrenaline still pumping, I glanced over my shoulder. "Do you have one?"

"Hell no." A shudder rippled through his broad shoulders. "People drive like maniacs here."

Russet brown streaked the snow-white hair he kept trimmed short and styled neat. Not much. Just enough to tell me he had fallen off the wagon. His eyes, usually a brilliant titanium, were tinted the milky green of the corpse he had no doubt left in his wake.

"I heard Midas Kinase is here."

"Yeah. The victim is gwyllgi." Bishop studied me. "That a problem?"

"No," I lied, and he pretended to believe me.

"Come on." He led me to where sentinels, Low Society necromancers undercover with the Atlanta Police Department, held the line. "The pack reps are waiting for you."

"Goody." I had successfully avoided all remnants of my past life since arriving in Atlanta, but it looked like my number was up. "It just had to be a gwyllgi."

"You got this," Bishop murmured, misreading my hesitation.

Ahead, two men cut from the same cloth stood watch over their dead. Gwyllgi varied in height, but they ran toward beefy—in a sink-your-teeth-in kind of way—and these two were no exception. They lifted their heads in tandem upon scenting us and joined us at the barricade.

"Hadley," Ford said, his voice warm. "This your scene, darlin'?"

Ford Bentley, who had cracked a joke about his name the first time we met, wasn't laughing now. As the pack liaison with our office, he and I were on friendly-enough terms. Enough I recognized the endearment wasn't a come-on or condescension but simply polite habit.

Sorrow had turned his lively blue eyes dull, and his wild black hair showed tracks from where he had been pulling his fingers through its jagged length.

"Yeah." I locked my gaze on him to keep it from sliding to his left. "The POA is in Savannah."

That meant this was my case to solve, the first one I would tackle as lead.

And Midas was here to bear witness.

Perfect.

"Have you met Midas?" Ford twitched his head toward the slightly taller man. "He's our beta."

"We haven't been introduced." I dropped my gaze to the victim, using the gruesome tableau to help regulate my pulse. "I'm Hadley Whitaker."

"Midas Kinase," he said, his voice sandpaper rough, not with emotion, though I heard that too, but from an old injury no one so much as whispered about behind his very muscular back. "Are you sure we haven't met?"

Predator that he was, he scented my nerves and eased in front of me for a better look.

The predator in me unfurled in response, creeping across the asphalt beneath him, stretching shadowy fingers under his boots, tapping on individual treads, as if counting all the ways it could kill him.

"We both live in the city." I kept my voice bland and focused on the stag logo on his tee. Fine. I was ogling the way his biceps stretched the fabric to its limits. He had packed on serious muscle since the last time I saw him, but he hadn't been the heir then. His sister, Lethe, had held that title until deciding to break ties with Atlanta and start her own pack in Savannah. Guess her defection had landed him a promotion. "You must have seen me around."

The new haircut and style gave my blonde hair a fresh look with short layers and plenty of curls, and the hazel contacts, heavy on the green, plus a few magical augmentations, meant Midas would see only Hadley. Just the law-abiding citizen and enforcer of justice. Not the murdering, maiming, and marauding version of me that our mutual friends would have warned him about.

"Your scent..." Flaring his nostrils, he parted his lips. "It's familiar."

"I work a kiosk in the mall, and I run the Active Oval in Piedmont Park five days a week." I held my ground. "You could have picked up my scent anywhere."

Crowding me, he ducked his head, attempting to force eye contact, a dominance tactic that didn't work half as well on necromancers as it did on gwyllgi and did nothing for me. "What was your name again?"

"Hadley." I caved to the challenge, and my annoyance, which never failed to land me in hot water, and met his gaze. "Hadley Whitaker."

The full force of his shifter magic pooled in his eyes, turning the tranquil aquamarine to vibrant crimson. I should have been terrified. I *was* terrified. But goddess, I couldn't glance away after verifying he was every bit as gorgeous up close as I remembered from all the glimpses I had stolen of him through a curtained window.

Blond hair fell in waves to his broad shoulders and framed a face so beautiful I wanted to reach out and touch it, see if it was real. His jaw was hard, and muscle twitched in his cheek. His mouth was full, perfect. Soft, I bet. But his eyes. That's what captured and held my attention. The sorrow in them mirrored the remorse in mine, and I understood in that soul-bearing moment that he was dangerous to me on levels I hadn't conceived of before meeting him in the flesh.

The one thing I had been warned against doing—instigating a staring match—was exactly what I did while Bishop and Ford looked on in horror.

Clearly, they expected Midas to strike me down for the offense. I did too. And yet, I kept breathing.

"I have exceptional control," he rumbled, "but you're testing it."

Bishop stomped on my instep, and the jolt of pain yanked my attention to him and away from Midas.

"Fire ant." Bishop made a production of searching for more on the sidewalk. "Little bastards."

"Bastard is right," I groused at him before redirecting my attention to Midas's chest to avoid another standoff. "Mr. Kinase, I'm sorry for your loss. I respect your right to be present, but I have a job to do. I would appreciate it if you stepped aside and let me do it."

Midas yielded no ground but let me step around him. And if he figured my willingness to do so proved his dominance, well, bless his heart.

Ditching him and Ford at the barricade, I continued on with Bishop. "That went well."

"Yeah," he said, ignoring my sarcasm. "It did." He crouched over the body, what remained of it. "The pack isn't required to cooperate with us. Not when the victim is one of theirs. They could throw their weight around and block us from investigating. Their alpha prefers to handle these matters internally."

"There's no guarantee the person who did this is gwyllgi. That puts the ball back in our court."

Though I couldn't afford to let assumptions cloud my judgment this early in the investigation. I had to get this right, or I lost points with the POA, who would not want to cut his trip short to play pack politics.

"That's why I like you." Bishop chuckled under his breath. "You're so gosh darn optimistic."

"Har har." I snapped my fingers at the shadow nosing the corpse. "Make yourself useful."

The vague outline of me snapped out a salute then made a show of diving in headfirst.

"Showoff," I grumbled then caught Bishop staring. "What?"

"I'm never going to get used to that."

"All potentates have wraiths."

"That is *not* a wraith." His gimlet eyes dared me to lie to him. "It's so...*Peter Pan*. Do you remember the part in the cartoon where Wendy captures his shadow one night then sews it back on him the next?"

"No?"

"You never watched *Peter Pan*?" He clucked his tongue. "What kind of childhood did you have?"

A dull throb spread beneath my left eye, a distant memory of pain, and when I ran my tongue along my teeth, I almost tasted blood in my cheek. I would have spit to clear my mouth if it wouldn't have contaminated the scene.

Some girls learned makeup to entice, some learned to claim their spot in the girl hierarchy, but others learned it for more practical purposes. Makeup had never been armor for me, it had been camouflage. I learned how to apply concealer, how to set a proper foundation, so no one, not even my siblings, saw what happened to the family's spare when the heir misbehaved.

Goddess forbid we got a speck of dirt on the family name.

Thinking about how thoroughly I had raked that precious name through the mud before discarding it once and for all, I almost laughed, but freedom from that life had cost me everything.

Every-damn-thing.

"A long one," I rasped, drawing on the good times to erase the bad.

Motion caught my eye as darkness seeped from the body, giving no warning before it leapt into mine.

Cold plunged into my chest, wrapping my heart in an icy fist, squeezing a gasp out of me.

"Play nice, Ambrose," I snarled under my breath. "Or I'll put you in time-out."

Warmth returned to my torso in a petulant creep, but the biting chill speared my skull in the next second, giving me an epic brain freeze.

At least, once I thawed out, I had the information I'd requested from him. And since he had more or less behaved, I tossed a piece of candy into the darkness spilling from my soles across the concrete.

"You're training your shadow to do tricks." Bishop watched the candy vanish. "That can't be healthy."

"Nice streaks," I said sourly. "Who does your hair?"

"Point taken," he grumbled then gestured toward the body. "Walk me through it."

"The victim is a black female, early twenties." Squatting for a closer look, I started off easy, with the stats. "Five-nine or five-ten. Maybe one-sixty. Brown hair. Eye color is also brown." Next came the hard part. "The cause of death is…" I searched my memory for the technical term the POA would have used but came up empty. A gaping hole started below the victim's throat and ended at her hips. The soft parts had been devoured, the hard ones gnawed on. "She was eaten."

Bishop didn't dock me, just listened while I tried to keep the fumbling to a minimum.

"There are claw marks on the body as well as teeth marks." Bruising where the creature pinned down the victim while it ate made clear which was which. "There are defensive wounds on the forearms and hands." That stupid taco made its thoughts on the carnage evident, but I wasn't going to hurl in front of an audience. "She was alive when the creature started feasting."

The shadow I cast across her thighs turned its head, interested in something behind me.

"You keep saying *the creature*," Midas rumbled, a dangerous edge to his voice. "Are you implying the killer was one of us?"

"I'm not implying anything." I kept my back to him. "No gwyllgi did this."

He squatted next to me, our elbows almost brushing, close enough I smelled the soap and sweat on his skin. "How can you tell?"

"It's my job," I said flatly, but Ambrose shook a warning finger, chastising me for taking all the credit. "What I can't determine—yet— is the killer's species." There was no delicate way to ask, but I figured I might as well put him to work if he was going to hover. "Can you identify its scent?"

"No," Midas said after a pause that made plain he was deciding if the question insulted him.

I conducted the rest of my examination in silence, as much to keep my thoughts contained as to give the illusion I knew what the heck I was doing without the POA dictating my every move.

"I'm done here." I stood, ready to bluff my way through the pack reps, and Midas rose beside me. "Mr. Kinase, I will keep you and your alpha apprised of any further developments."

"No need."

"Are you...?" I squared my shoulders, cleared my throat. "Are you taking the case from me?"

"I thought about it," he admitted, and I had to swallow a plea to let me have this one chance. "I have a lot of respect for Linus, and he chose you as his potential successor. That means, if you ace your internship and trials, you and I will be crossing paths for the foreseeable future."

Relief fluttered through me on butterfly wings. "Thank—"

"But I can't allow this investigation to continue without pack oversight."

"—you," I finished dumbly.

"Ford." He gestured for him to join us. "You're with Ms. Whitaker."

Surprise flickered in Ford's eyes, but he smothered it quickly. "Happy to oblige."

Bishop, who filled the roll of aide to me when I wasn't doing the same for Linus, goggled.

"Looks like it's you and me against the world, darlin'." Ford grinned at me. "Let's give it a swift kick in its axis."

A soft laugh escaped me, totally inappropriate given the location, and I caught Midas staring at me, watching my mouth like he expected me to crack up again. Blanking my expression, I angled my chin higher. "Anything else?"

"Give me your number."

The moisture evaporated from my mouth when he captured me in his gaze, but I found enough spit to lubricate my tongue. "Ask me nicely, and I might."

"Please," he said flatly. "Give me your number."

Figuring that was as good as I was going to get, I rattled off my digits and waited, but Midas didn't offer his in return.

He didn't say goodbye, either. Just turned on his heel and left me wondering who had won our rematch. Bishop trotted after him, likely hoping to clarify our arrangements, and I left him to it.

"Women." Ford blasted out a sigh as I watched Midas go. "Y'all always want what you can't have."

"True." I reeled my attention back to him. "I want to be home watching TV with a bowl of extra buttery, extra salty popcorn on my lap while I marathon the *Robot Space Tentacles* trilogy, but it doesn't look like that's happening."

"You're a geek."

Steel injected my spine. "So?"

"A huge geek." He flared his nostrils. "That's probably what Midas smelled earlier."

"And?" Heat prickled my nape. "There's no law against being a geek."

As a matter of fact, Atlanta hosted one of the largest science-fiction and fantasy conventions in the world.

"You, being a geek, would know."

A flicker of shadow coiled near Ford's boots, but I stomped on it and sent it skittering.

"Fire ant," I mumbled when his brows winged higher. "Little bastards."

The rest of the on-site work fell to the cleaners who documented each paranormal crime scene in photos and video, collected blood and tissue samples, then made it all disappear before humans caught wind of a disturbance. There wasn't much I could do until they finished and uploaded their findings into the database, so I was done here.

"Come on, Lee." He reached in his pocket. "Can I call you Lee?"

"Sure." The almost familiar ring of the nickname made me smile. "Where are we going?"

"It's nearly dawn." He squinted at the sky. "I'm driving you home."

"Necromancers don't have sun allergies like vampires do."

"I know." He jingled his keys. "But if we hurry, you can still catch *Robot Space Tentacles Encircle the Earth.*"

"Ah." I nodded sagely. "I thought I caught a whiff, but I wasn't sure."

"This isn't the start of a wet-dog joke, is it?" He pointed out a jacked-up white pickup truck, a gleaming off-roader without a speck of dirt marring its glossy wheels, one I would need a boost or a ladder to climb in. "I'll warn you now, I've heard 'em all, and not a one made me laugh."

"No." I made a show of sniffing him. "Geek." I wiggled my nose. "You reek of it."

Grinning when he hooted with laughter, I headed for his truck, shadow—for now—obediently in tow.

ABOUT THE AUTHOR

USA Today best-selling author Hailey Edwards writes about questionable applications of otherwise perfectly good magic, the transformative power of love, the family you choose for yourself, and blowing stuff up. Not necessarily all at once. That could get messy.

www.HaileyEdwards.net

ALSO BY HAILEY EDWARDS

Made in the USA
Las Vegas, NV
23 October 2022